Praise for Gill McKnight

"A departure from the run-of-the-mill lesbian romance, *Goldenseal* is enjoyable for its uniqueness as well as for its plot. This is a story that will engage and characters you will find yourself growing fond of."—LambdaLiterary.org

"Gill McKnight has given her readers a delightful romp in *Green Eyed Monster*. The twists and turns of the plot leave the reader turning the pages to see who is the real victim and who is the villain. Along with the roller coaster ride comes plenty of hot sex to add to the tension. Spending an afternoon with *Green Eyed Monster* is great fun."—*Just About Write*

In *Green Eyed Monster*, "McKnight succeeds in tantalizing with explosive sex and a bit of bondage; tormenting with sexual frustration and intense longing; tickling your fancy and funny bone; and touching a place where good and evil battle it out... [T]he plot twists, winning dialogue laced with sarcasm, wit, and charm certainly add to the fun. I recommend this satisfying read for entertainment, fantasy, and sex that stimulate the brain like caffeine."— LambdaLiterary.org

"Angst, conflict, sex and humor. [*Falling Star*] has all of this and more packed into a tightly written and believable romance. McKnight has penned a sweet and tender romance, balancing the intimacy and sexual tension just right. The conflict is well drawn, and she adds a great dose of humor to make this novel a light and easy read."—*Curve*

By the Author

Falling Star

Green Eyed Monster

Erosistible

Goldenseal

Ambereye

Indigo Moon

Visit us at www.boldstrokesbooks.com

INDIGO MOON

by
Gill McKnight

2011

INDIGO MOON
© 2011 By Gill McKnight. All Rights Reserved.

ISBN 10: 1-60282-201-8
ISBN 13: 978-1-60282-201-6

This Trade Paperback Original Is Published By
Bold Strokes Books, Inc.
P.O. Box 249
Valley Falls, NY 12185

First Edition: February 2011

Credits
Editors: Cindy Cresap and Stacia Seaman
Production Design: Stacia Seaman
Cover Design by Sheri (graphicartist2020@hotmail.com)

Dedication

For B.
Love Mum.

CHAPTER ONE

The first one sprinted from her right-hand side and bolted before the car. Isabelle braked and watched it cross the road. It was a magnificent beast. She counted nine, maybe ten points on its antlers.

"Oh. So beautiful," she breathed, enchanted. Then she noticed its fear and alarm. Another whitetail, this one a doe, shot out of the tree line, eyes rolling with fright. They ran alongside the high banks of plowed snow at the roadside, confused by the man-made barrier. The larger animal lunged at the steep bank and began an ungainly scrabble over it. The doe followed, pushing and straining with powerful hind legs until it topped the bank and disappeared into the forest on the far side. Isabelle watched the snow fill their tracks long after they had gone. *Poor things were spooked by the car.*

"Damn" She scolded herself for not remembering to grab her camera. It was rare for a city dweller to get this close to such beautiful creatures. It would be some time before a photo opportunity like that came her way again. She tsked in self-reproach and put the Toyota into gear. The car rolled forward just as a third deer darted out of the trees. Isabelle slammed on the brakes, thrilled at her unbelievable luck. Three in a row! This time she reached for her camera, then hesitated. The buck was limping badly. It was smaller than the other two and even more frightened. It stumbled before her car looking lost and confused. It hobbled over to the snow bank, following its companions. Isabelle saw the dark patch on its flank drip scarlet onto the snow. It was bleeding. A gash ran across its rump deep into the hind leg. It limped to the escape route opened up by the others, and with an exhausted leap tried to climb. The incline was too steep and it slipped and slithered back onto the roadside. It had no strength left. It tried a second time and failed. Tired and defeated, it stood trembling, trapped by the wall of snow, unwilling to return the way it had come.

Isabelle grasped for the handle but didn't open the car door. What could she do? She was in the middle of nowhere with a wounded wild animal. Should she even approach it? What if it—

She jumped in her seat at the loud crash. Her car rocked violently from side to side and the roof crunched and buckled over her head. She cried out in fright, but the cry died in her throat as something springboarded from the roof of her car onto the injured deer, dragging it to the ground. It was a massive beast, red-furred and ferocious. It ripped into the deer's gaping wound with huge, curled claws. The whitetail exploded, shredded in seconds. Flayed limbs, strips of hide, a severed head, flew off in every direction. The snow became a churning cauldron of crimson. The beast reared upright onto its hind legs; squat and awkward, it flung back its heavy head and howled an unearthly, wavering cry. A howl filled with bloodcurdling triumph and defiance. Then it fell back on the deer's bloody carcass and gorged on the steaming entrails.

Isabelle was horrified. She gripped the door handle white-knuckled, her other hand squeezing the steering wheel, and sat frozen in disbelief. In less than a millisecond a…a…a rabid bear had just… had just wrecked her car and… *Oh God, that poor deer.*

A growl rumbled long, low, and very threatening beside her ear. Slowly, she turned her head to meet cold, yellow eyes, filled with sly intelligence. A second creature crouched by her car watching her. It pinned her with a look of calculated malice as it weighed up her strengths and many, many weaknesses. Isabelle's heart thumped in her throat until she almost choked. Ice water pumped through her veins and numbed her brain, her thoughts froze, her limbs turned into heavy, useless stumps. She couldn't move, couldn't think; she couldn't even blink. The twisted leathery face was inches from hers with only a sheet of glass between them. Thin black lips curled back in a leer, revealing rows of long, pointed teeth. For an elastic moment they regarded each other, unmoving, unblinking, frozen—then the moment snapped.

Fangs flashed against the window, saliva lathered the glass. Isabelle jerked out of her stupor and screamed. She slammed her foot on the accelerator. This was no bear. This was a monster. A monster from budget horror movies and mass-market paperbacks; a monster from her childhood nightmares. The Toyota lurched, tires spinning. The monster flung out a huge clawed hand and shattered the side window, showering her in shards of glass. Her cheek stung with a dozen little abrasions. The side-view mirror was ripped from the door. Isabelle screamed again, scrabbled to release her handbrake, and kept her foot pressed full on the gas. The tires bit and the car shot forward, its back end fishtailing wildly. She had no control over the steering and no care other than fleeing.

The Toyota flew forward in a clean line and rammed straight into the red-furred beast still crouched over its meal. With a sickening thud the beast bowled off the windshield and onto the roadside, a blur of wet, matted fur and blood. The impact slowed her and she nearly stalled. From the corner of her eye she saw the stricken beast writhing in agony. It bellowed with pain and the forest around her reverberated with a multitude of answering howls. Isabelle's ears burned with the eerie chorus. These two were not alone; there were more creatures out there. She gunned the Toyota harder as it zigzagged across the road.

A third creature hurtled from the tree line and flung itself onto the hood of her car. It crashed onto the windshield. The glass cracked but held. Her speed bounced the creature back off before it could gain any leverage. It fell back onto the road, only just missing her wheels. Through the crazed glass she saw another beast crouched farther along ready to spring at her car. Another crept out of the trees to join it. They were everywhere! Preparing to pounce. Everywhere!

Isabelle's mind blanked out with terror. She swung on the steering wheel, trying to swerve past the first ambush. A loud bang and her car rocked sideways. One of them was on the roof! Through her broken windshield she could see two more racing toward her. She was surrounded. Like lions hunting a wildebeest, they had surrounded her and were dragging her down by sheer numbers.

She spun the wheel hard right. The next one to reach her would break through the weakened windshield. She swerved to avoid the creatures coming straight for her, and swung the car from side to side hoping to dislodge the one on the roof. It clung on, roaring in anger. They kept coming until they were right on top of her. The first one leapt. She closed her eyes and hit the gas. There was a splintering crash. The windshield popped, showering her with cubes of glass. Isabelle opened her eyes. This one had hung on. It was less than two feet from her, huge and black, and its breath stank. It bared its teeth in a victorious leer. She was caught. The chase was over.

Isabelle screamed and jerked the wheel to the left. The Toyota cannoned onto the snowbank and rode up the incline at full speed. It flipped over the top and with a perfect pirouette landed upside down in a trench on the other side.

❖

She was curled in a tight ball, squashed in a corner of her mangled car. The air bag had deployed, but she had somehow slipped out from the seat belt that dangled above her. Had she lost consciousness? How much time passed? Snow and vegetation pushed through the shattered windshield, and she was covered in freezing muck. The air was heavy with the sickly odor of gasoline. She began to shake with pain and shock.

Isabelle twitched her fingers and toes; everything moved as it should. Her shoes were lost and her feet bare. Bizarrely, that upset her more than the possibility of broken bones. She stretched and straightened her limbs as far as the cramped space would allow. All movement was torturous and exhausted her. She was wet through and probably in the first stages of hypothermia. Blood was everywhere; its copper stickiness coated her face and clung to her clothes and hands. She didn't know where it was coming from. The car lay upside down and the world around her was broken and disoriented. It was quiet, very quiet, as if the crash had stunned the forest into silence.

Then they came.

Muted growls and snarls surrounded the car. The creatures had arrived at the crash site and prowled around the wreck looking for a way through the twisted metal. Isabelle pressed deeper into her corner and shook uncontrollably. Her nightmare was not over. A second later the car shuddered as they tried to shake it loose and flip it over. The Toyota groaned in protest but refused to move; it was firmly wedged roof down in the trench. The car creaked and cracked as broken pieces of plastic and metal rained down on her. After several minutes, the shaking stopped. Isabelle waited with bated breath. Would they give up and go? Did they know if she was alive, or even in the car? She squeezed as far back as she could, careful not to make a noise to give herself away.

There was a moment of silence, then a frustrated roar and the bodywork was pounded on, as if the car were being beaten into tiny pieces. Soon they would be able to reach in and simply pluck her out like a lump of crabmeat.

The vehicle jerked as the trunk lid ripped off with a loud snap. A fresh blast of cold air whistled through. Frantic scratching came from behind the rear seat. They were getting in through the trunk. She cowered in terror. The seat rattled and heaved, then began to disintegrate before her eyes. A whimper escaped her—and gave away her position. A clawed hand burst through the broken windshield and sank, deep as a butcher's hook, into her left shoulder. Isabelle screamed and writhed in agony. The claws bit into sinew and muscle, popping her shoulder socket. Everything faded. She could hear her voice cry out, high and thin, hear the air bag tear, or was that her flesh? From nearby came a triumphant roar, and in the distance, another cry, loud and fierce. It rang out clear and challenging, drawing ever closer. Then oily waves of black pain engulfed her, the air in her lungs thinned, and her chest heaved as she tried to suck more in. There were more howls that hung mournful and hollow in the frigid air. She was dragged inch by inch through the shattered windshield. Her skin was hot with blood; her heart beat sluggishly in her chest. She was sobbing; she was fading, the world around her became darker and darker. Then the chill receded, the glass and metal and brushwood no longer hurt, only the salty dampness of the pillow scratched her cheek. Isabelle opened her mouth, filled her lungs with rich, sweet air, and screamed and screamed and—

"Hey. Hey." Strong hands stilled hers as she clawed at air. "It's okay." The same hands caressed her face and pushed damp hair off her forehead. "Isabelle? Isabelle? It's okay. Can you hear me?" a voice whispered near her ear, smooth and deep and reassuring. "It's just a bad dream."

Tears blurred her vision. There was a soft glow from a nearby lamp. That voice? How did she know that voice? She blinked several times to clear her tears. They rolled round and plump down her temples and onto the cool cotton of her pillowcase. She lay on a soft, fluffy bed. Someone hovered over her, long black hair brushed against her cheek; dark eyes stared intently at her, filled with calm concern.

"Hush, Isabelle. It was just a dream."

"They hurt me," she whispered. She tried to move and winced as pain shot through her shoulder. Cool hands soothed her, held her, made her lie still.

"Shush. Keep still now. You'll pull your stitches. It was only a dream."

"A dream?" She blinked again and tried to punch through the haze of medication. Slowly, she returned to the real world, bringing all the fear from her dream with her.

"A dream? They hurt me." She gazed stupidly around the bedroom. She did not recognize it. A damp cloth was pressed against her brow. She looked up into the shadowed face. The lamplight played tricks with golden planes and dark angles. One moment she gazed on the face of an angel, the next a demon. She blinked hard and tried to focus. It was a handsome face…what she could make of it. A woman's face. She smacked her dry lips and swallowed. Her throat felt raw, as if she'd been screaming forever. She fixed on the face above; eyes as black as pitch stared back and noted her discomfort.

"Lie still. I'll get you some water." She moved to go, but Isabelle reached out and grabbed at her, her chilled fingers leaching heat from a warm forearm. The woman sat back down and waited. Isabelle licked her cracked lips and barked out a dry cough before finally asking, "Who are you?"

CHAPTER TWO

Hope heard Jolie's Jeep pull into the driveway. She made for the front door just in time to see Tadpole leap from the living room couch to join her for the welcome. The front windowpane was smeared with his damp nose. He'd had it pressed against the glass for ages, keeping lookout for Jolie's return. He flew past Hope and scratched at the door before she could scold him. He wasn't allowed on the furniture and he knew it, but lately he'd developed some pretty poor habits. Hope was too excited to lecture him this time. It was more important to tell Jolie the news.

She flung open the door and Tadpole raced out to greet Jolie. His manic barking drowned out every word Hope said.

"Quiet, the pair of you. It's like driving into a parakeet farm." Jolie reached for the grocery bags as Tadpole scrabbled at her legs for attention. "Can it, mutt. I can't hear Hope speak."

She caved in and ruffled his ears. It was all the reassurance he needed. He ignored her, his interest now centered on sniffing her tires and decorating them in his own special fashion.

"What's all the hollering about?" Jolie turned her attention on Hope.

Hope gave an exasperated tut. "Jori called from Little Dip. Elicia gave birth at three fifteen this afternoon." She was bursting with happiness at the news. "She had twins, a boy and a girl."

"Wow." Jolie was suitably impressed. "Andre owes me a fifty. He said it would be two girls." She snorted in smug amusement. "Thinks he can read a pregnant woman's bump. Idiot."

"You and your brother bet on the sex of Elicia's babies?" Hope tutted again and grabbed one of the grocery bags spilling from Jolie's arms. They walked up the path to the house. "Jori wants you to call him back as soon as you can."

"Oh." Jolie sounded perplexed. "I would have expected him to be sprinting through the woods, howling at trees and doing backflips, not waiting by the phone."

"Are you worried?"

Jolie shrugged. "Nah. Let's put this ice cream away before it puddles in my hands."

Hope began to put away the groceries while Jolie called Jori's cell. It was busy. Disgruntled, Jolie moved about the kitchen trying to help but generally getting in Hope's way. They began to prepare dinner and Jolie tried to reach Little Dip again. It was still busy. Hope watched her from the kitchen door.

"Are you worried? You look worried."

"Nope." Jolie redialed as if she could trick the phone into ringing at the other end. Busy. Hope watched her try her trick a second time with no luck.

"Why ask someone to call you and then be on the phone all the time so they can't get through?" Jolie muttered in disgust.

She tried again less than five minutes later.

"No luck?" Hope asked as Jolie's frustration built.

"Nah. He's probably bragging to half the world." Jolie flopped on the couch and reached for the TV remote.

"Excuse me, but didn't somebody say they were going to keep an eye on the rice?" Hope snatched the remote away.

"Rice cooks itself," Jolie said.

"Pudding rice does. Last time you ruined dinner with your laziness. Now get into that kitchen, Garoul, and do as you're told." At that moment the phone rang and Jolie sprang for it, saved from further scolding.

"Hello?" she said expectantly, only for her shoulders to slump. "Oh. It's you. I thought it was Jori. You owe me fifty…No! *I* said a boy and a girl. *You* said two girls…Don't you backtrack now, you cheating rat—"

"Oh, give it here." Hope pried the handset from Jolie. "Hi, Andre." She smiled into the phone. "Yes, great news…You can't reach him either?…Jolie's been trying for over half an hour now…Cajun chicken.

Okay. Bye." She hung up and turned to Jolie. "Go put on more rice. Godfrey and your brother are coming over for dinner."

❖

"We finally got him." Andre breezed through the front door. His partner, Godfrey, followed, pausing to tickle Tadpole, who had prostrated himself at their feet like a wriggling doormat.

"Is everything all right?" Hope emerged from the kitchen wiping her hands on a dish towel. "I know something's up. This one has the worst poker face imaginable." She nodded back at Jolie, who had appeared behind her.

"Who said she had to be playing poker?" Andre said.

"This is hardly the time or place for baiting your sister," Godfrey told him disapprovingly. He turned to Hope and Jolie, brimming with important news. "Jori's upset."

"What did he say?" Hope poured aperitifs and they settled down to talk.

"When we finally got through to Little Dip, Jori said Elicia had a hard time," Godfrey said.

"Oh no! Are the babies okay?" Hope asked. "Is she okay?"

Jolie sat beside her, grim-faced, and swapped a knowing look with her brother.

"They're all healthy, Hope. No worries there," Andre answered. "It means something different if a werewolf birth goes wrong."

"Wrong?" Hope was worried now. "What do you mean wrong?"

"You know that when both parents are werewolves they always have twins, right?" Jolie said. Hope nodded; she did know that. Andre and Jolie were twins because their father, Claude Garoul, was already a werewolf, and their mother, Patrice, had become wolven.

"Well, it also means the cubs' genetic makeup is much stronger, and the twins will be bigger and more robust than part-human cubs," Jolie continued.

"Yes. I suppose that makes sense," Hope said.

"It puts more stress on the mother during labor," Andre said. "Especially when she's a werewolf, because what can sometimes happen—"

"But not always," Jolie interrupted.

"No. Not always," Andre said patiently. "But what *can* sometimes happen is the mother loses it halfway through the birth and starts to transform into a Were."

Hope frowned. "And that means what?"

"The cubs are feral," Jolie stated flatly.

"No, not necessarily," Godfrey said. "Sometimes it can happen that way, but not always."

It surprised Hope that he knew about this, but then he had been with Andre longer than she had been with Jolie, so he knew more about the Garoul clan and its workings. Now he was anxious to reassure Hope that all was well with Elicia and the cubs.

"What Andre and Jolie mean is if the mother starts transmutation during birth, then her cubs are a little bit further...evolved...than their half-human, or even fully wolven counterparts." He spoke directly to Hope. "Their werewolf genes don't have to wait until puberty to be triggered. These cubs are fully active from birth."

"You mean werewolf babies? And toddlers? And preteens?" Hope blinked at the concept. "Oh, that's got to be hard. It's bad enough going through puberty as it is without becoming a werewolf, but at least the Garoul kids are prepped for it. But to be a werewolf from year zero? Oh, boy."

"It is hard. Like I said, that's why they always go feral," Jolie said with great certainty.

"Again, not necessarily." Godfrey was determined it was not all doom and gloom for Jori and Elicia's cubs. "Claude once told me that with special guidance, feral wolven could be taught to manage."

Hope turned to Jolie and Andre. "Did you two need special guidance? Both your parents are wolven."

Andre spluttered and Jolie just rolled her eyes.

"We are *not* feral," Andre said in mock indignation. "Well, at least I'm not. We've never been sure about Bigfoot here." He nodded at Jolie.

"Do you want dinner or not?" She scowled at him.

"Depends. Did you cook it?"

"You can go home hungry, you know."

"Stop squabbling and explain this to me." Hope interrupted their childish quarreling. "You have full werewolf parents. You're twins. Did you develop quicker than your cousins?"

"Mom never mutated when she was in labor with us. We developed more or less at the same rate as everyone else. The problem only occurs if the mother has a bad birth." Andre finger-quoted the "bad" bit.

"So this has happened before?" Hope said. She found it all fascinating. She knew so little about Garoul lore even though she had more or less married into this werewolf clan. She determined to pin Jolie down later and get a full history, complete with a family tree. Godfrey knew tons more than she did, but then Andre was the outgoing, nonstop talker type. Typical for Hope to fall for the reticent, emotionally challenged twin. She caught the look Jolie and Andre exchanged. It wasn't a good look.

She repeated her question. "Has it happened before?"

"Once. That we know of," Andre said.

"Yeah," Jolie said quietly. "Floriene and Luc."

"Floriene and Luc?" Hope said. She'd never heard of these particular Garouls. "Who are they? What about them?"

Even Godfrey looked mystified. "What happened?" he asked.

Jolie shrugged while Andre shifted in his seat. "Go on," Jolie told Andre. "I may be Bigfoot, but you're bigmouth. You tell them the story."

"Story?" Hope and Godfrey leaned in closer. This was something big.

Andre cleared his throat and began. "Floriene and Luc were our cousins—"

"*Were* your cousins?" Godfrey gasped. "They're dead?"

"How did they die?" Hope was agog.

"No. They're not dead!" Andre snapped, miffed at the interruption. "Stop interrupting and let me tell the story." He cleared his throat again with great deliberation. "Floriene and Luc were…are…our cousins." He gave Hope and Godfrey a glare, ensuring their silence. "They were born like *that*. I mean their mom transformed during labor—"

Jolie butted in. "And they were feral."

"*I'm* telling the story. You asked me to." Andre huffed at her.

"Well, I didn't realize you were going to be so goddamn slow…or awful. It's like pulling teeth," she said curtly. She turned to Hope and Godfrey and continued to steal Andre's thunder. "They grew up almost uncontrollable and eventually ate a guy and were sent away."

"They did not eat a guy," Andre said.

"Did so."

"Did not."

"Did s—"

"Will you two stop that and tell us what happened," Godfrey said, exasperated with them. Andre pushed ahead with his story, obviously intent on preventing Jolie from twisting any more facts.

"A hunter trespassed into the valley and shot this big bear he'd been tracking all day. Only the bear turned out to be Uncle Robért. He managed to wound Robért before the twins, who were with him, jumped the guy."

"And ate him," Jolie added with relish.

"They did not eat him. They mauled him pretty bad, though."

"And after they ate him they dumped him in the river and he floated down past where we were playing in the creek," Jolie said. "I saw it."

"When was this?" Hope asked, dismayed by the gruesome story.

Jolie shrugged. "About twenty-five years ago."

"They did *not* eat him." Andre glared at Jolie, who totally ignored him. He turned back to Hope and Godfrey. "We were only youngsters then, maybe nine or ten. We hadn't even begun to change—"

"And yet Floriene and Luc were out there eating people. See? That's the difference between a good birth and bad one." Jolie seemed incapable of shutting up now that she was competing with Andre for Hope and Geoffrey's attention. "A bad birth means out-of-control whelps. They grow too fast and become unmanageable and eventually dangerous. Feral, see! Like I said."

"Oh my God." Godfrey looked horrified. "What happened to the guy's body? What about the police?"

"Robért and Claude made it look like an accident. He was washed miles downstream," Andre said.

"I don't understand," Hope said after digesting this information. "These cubs with the bad births are almost uncontrollable? And yet they are out there running around not just Little Dip, but our city streets? How the hell do their parents cope? How can you take Junior to kindergarten if you can't guarantee he won't go all furry and bite someone in a squabble over the yellow crayon?" She was appalled at the ramifications of feral werecubs.

"They don't leave Little Dip," Andre said. "It's as simple as that.

They grow up there with Claude and Marie and the rest of the elders and learn everything they need to know about the outside world and controlling their wolven side. That's what Claude meant by special guidance. A feral is only a Were with no proper pack skills."

"They'll always be limited because their wolven side is so strong," Jolie added, tapping her temple. "It's easier to run wild and howl at the moon than buckle down and learn how to control your wolfskin and not eat humans."

"It must be hard on the parents if they have to give up everything and move to Little Dip to raise their kids," Godfrey said. "Poor Jori and Elicia. They must be worried sick."

"They can live in Little Dip if they want to, or go back to their city life and leave the cubs in the valley. I suppose it's sort of like boarding school." Andre tried to sound matter-of-fact, but there was a tinge of sadness in his voice.

"Even so. I can see why Jori's so upset. What a life-changing event." Hope sighed. "So where are these cousins of yours? This Luc and Floriene? You said they were sent away after they attacked that hunter?"

"They went north with their parents. Up into Canada. Grandma Sylvie sent them away. It was too dangerous. People can't go missing every time they wander into the valley. You can only have so many hunting accidents." Andre shrugged. "I don't know what happened to them after that. We were just cubs then. It wasn't a good time for the pack."

"No one knows where they went or what they're up to. We lost contact after their parents died." Jolie shook her head sagely. "It all smells very iffy."

Something did indeed smell iffy.

"Oh my God." Hope leapt to her feet, startling them all. "The rice. I can smell the rice singeing." She glared at Jolie. "You let it boil dry again, didn't you!"

Chapter Three

"Don't you remember me, Isabelle?"

"No." Isabelle stared hard, hoping for a memory to spark. The lamplight flickered across dark, wary eyes, and she thought she caught a glimmer of satisfaction. For a moment she thought she did know this woman, that the eyes seemed somehow familiar. The flash of a bronzed cheekbone, a strong jawline—this face was shadowy and elusive, curtained by a sway of hair as her caretaker ministered to her needs. The notion soon faded. "I'm sorry. I don't remember you at all."

"How do you feel? Does your shoulder hurt?"

Everything hurt. Talking hurt.

"Do you remember what you were dreaming about last night? Do you remember how you got here?" The questions were relentless and held a tinge of anxiety. Isabelle's mouth was dry. Her body ached and her head thumped. She was exhausted and didn't need this. Not now.

"There was a car crash. And a deer." She struggled to answer. The rim of a glass pressed against her cracked lips.

"Here, drink this. Sip slowly."

She took several small sips. It tasted oily and bitter, not water at all, but the coolness acted as an elixir on her parched throat.

"There were deer…and monsters. The monsters got me." Her voice rose in distress as she remembered this fragment of the dream. A hazy memory of waking as a child plagued with night terrors crept from the corner of her mind. This wasn't the first time she had cried out in the dark, or dreamt of being chased by monsters.

"Hush now. It was only a dream." She was soothed back to the present and enfolded in comfort. A comfort she somehow knew she'd gone without as a child. She drank more from the glass.

"Thank you," she whispered between sips.

"You need to rest." Her pillows were plumped and the smell of freshly washed cotton surrounded her.

"The drink will help with the pain." The voice ebbed and flowed. Close then far away. She shook her head to unclog her ears. The tension eased from her body as promised. Her pain melted away. Tired and torn muscles simply floated off her aching bones, and her roiling thoughts calmed to a simmer. Her gaze drifted around the room. It was plain and bare and nothing looked familiar.

"Where am I? And who are you?" she asked, forcing herself to focus. Her head was stuffed with the scents of lilac and lavender from the newly washed bed linen. Her sense of smell was overpowering. She struggled to sit up, refusing to fall back to sleep with so much left unanswered. "Where are my clothes? My bag? All of my things?"

"Gas leaked into your suitcase. Everything was ruined. Lie still." Hands held her in place against the pillows, and her last remnants of strength dissipated. Isabelle noticed the most important questions had been ignored. Where was she and who was this woman who seemed so determined to care? "You need to take your medicine, then rest."

"Can't," she mumbled, disappointed that she was, in fact, falling back to sleep. "Need to know…things." She couldn't stay awake any longer. Her eyelids flickered as she fought sleep. She focused on her benefactor, on her face, on her eyes. Black irises looked back at her. They shimmered with a dozen points of lamplight, like a starlit sky. Isabelle felt safe under that stare. And tired, so very tired. Her eyelids fluttered shut.

"Who are you?" she said.

"Isabelle. Isabelle." A deep, urgent voice called her back. She struggled to respond."Isabelle. You need to take all of this. Try to drink a little more." The glass returned to her lips.

"Who are you?" she asked, more determined, between sips of the bitter liquid. This was their trade-off. She would drink if the other would answer.

"I'm Ren."

"Ren," she whispered. The name sounded right. She savored it on her tongue. "Ren. Ren who?"

"Ren will do for now. Drink more."

"Ren," she said, and swallowed more medicine. She *did* know this woman…this Ren. A memory flitted by, shadowed and unsettling. It hovered on the edge of her consciousness, as ominous as a graveyard bird, its beady-eyed stare daring her to remember. All around her white sheets and eiderdown billowed up in warm, scented waves to drown her. The bird rose on its wing and disappeared, taking its cold warning with it. She knew she was sinking into a drugged sleep, that the bitter drink was taking her away to blissful nothingness. One last question surfaced before she slipped under its spell. "Who are you, Ren?"

"I'm your world, Isabelle." It was barely a whisper and she wondered at it, assuming she'd misheard. She let it go and slid away into sleep. The soft whisper followed her down, through tickling fronds of weed and beds of rippled sand, where it hooked her: its sharp barbs embedded in her dreams and reeled in her last thoughts. *Ren.*

❖

She was buried alive in ice. Clear, crystalline sheets of it covered her, a glazed lid to her coffin. This was an empty, lonely world. A place that existed inside her, far too close to her heart. Mighty forests stretched for miles. She could smell the sharp scent of pine sap and hear tree roots rumble in the frozen earth around her. She couldn't move, yet through the solid layer of ice above her she could see the sky, a featureless and arctic white dome. Against the endless space her black graveyard bird swooped in lazy circles with the lassitude of a vulture awaiting the feast. It gave a sudden shriek and fell out of the sky onto her, claws hooked, black beak clacking at her icy coffin. The lid cracked and the bird broke through. It ripped at her immobile face, bloodying her cheeks, tearing at the pink of her lips, then it pecked out her frozen eyes—Isabelle jerked upright in sweat-stained shock. She scrabbled at her face expecting to find empty, torn eye sockets. She could see! Her face and eyes were unharmed. It was just another nightmare.

She blinked several times to make sure. It had all seemed so real—the sharp wind and the bird's shrill clamor all around her.

The bedroom was dark and filled with eerie shadows, but at least it was solid and real. She trembled all over; her feet and hands were stone cold. Her teeth chattered even though her brow was beaded with perspiration and her heart thumped painfully in her chest.

"Here, drink this." A supporting arm held her shoulders and water trickled into her mouth. No oily aftertaste this time, just pure, cool water. She gulped it down.

"You're shivering like a leaf," Ren murmured and laid her back on the pillows. There was a rustle and then a cool draft as the bedclothes rose a little. Isabelle sighed as Ren slid in behind her and spooned around her. The heat that radiated off her was intense. Heavy-headed and sluggish, Isabelle melted back into the warm body and fell back to sleep.

It was pitch black when she opened her eyes again. She was blissfully warm, pushed up against a satin wall of muscle and heated skin. A forearm rested on her waist. Ren's other arm had slid in under Isabelle's neck and reached across her front to cup her injured shoulder. Ren's thighs were drawn up underneath hers. They were both naked.

Isabelle stiffened. She lay and listened to Ren's breathing. She was sleeping deeply. Her warm breath hummed against Isabelle's scalp. Her face was buried in Isabelle's hair, breathing her in, whispering her out. Lungful after lungful. Isabelle twitched. The sweat, blood, and tears of God knows how long were pungent on her body. She was embarrassed by her stale odor and by the intimate spooning, and yet she felt comforted by it, too. She took a deep breath, and at first faintly, then with certainty picked up another odor, a new smell, piquant and peppery. It was Ren's scent. Isabelle's mouth watered and her flesh tingled.

Afraid to move in case she woke her, Isabelle lay still and tried to orient herself with the darkened objects in the room. There was a straight-backed chair and a bedside table and lamp. To the left stood the blocky outline of a chest of drawers. She breathed in the comforting scent of Ren's nakedness.

How did she get here, and why was Ren nursing her with such care? Isabelle's thoughts were still a jumbled mass of jagged images, torn-up photographs of monsters and frozen wastes, of forests and blood. They all jostled in her head until it hurt. And with the images came whispers and warnings, half-formed thoughts and ideas that slithered away like snakes before she could grasp them. These were her memories, her life…all frustratingly out of reach. They danced around the edges of her mind and teased her inability to chase them all the way home.

If she could relax, perhaps they might creep closer? Her eyes grew heavy as the warmth of Ren's body lured her back into a healing sleep. The arms around her tightened and lips brushed her matted hair where it stuck to her sweat-soaked skin. Ren was surfacing from sleep; she murmured something indistinct against Isabelle's nape.

"Why are you doing this?" Isabelle asked quietly. "Are you my friend?"

Ren lay still for a moment, then moved her mouth away from Isabelle's neck to whisper, "Something like that."

The words breathed past Isabelle's ear, making her entire body erupt in goose bumps.

"Why are we naked?" Isabelle asked. Her voice trembled with an embarrassment impossible to conceal.

"I can heat you better skin to skin." Ren awkwardly pulled away. Isabelle felt the chill. Ren was a furnace, and she hadn't realized it until she'd lost contact with her.

"I didn't mean to…" Ren trailed off; her voice was brusque and unsure.

"It's okay," Isabelle mumbled. "I've got hang-ups." This little nugget stuck in her chest. She had inadvertently unearthed a bitter truth about herself. She had hang-ups. Well, so what? For the moment, she felt safe and warm, and she hurt less than before. Every time she awoke she felt stronger, more centered, more in control, and that had to be good.

❖

Ren lay awake and watched her patient for a long time. She breathed in tandem with her, monitoring Isabelle's sleep pattern, and watched as she slipped further into a dreamless sleep. Only then did she relax against her, allowing their skin to again touch. She lay and drank in Isabelle's raw scent, sour and unwashed, but it thrilled her. It filled her head with all manner of images. It was a complex scent.

Recent fear and old pain pulsed out of Isabelle, making Ren's chest ache with confusion. Her scent held stories and had a heart of honey underlaid with the solidity of oak moss, as ancient as the forest that surrounded them. Ren closed her eyes and held the scent, allowing it to burst upon her face like sunlight. Isabelle's tinkling laughter floated toward her through the trees. Lazy bees droned as Ren slipped through fir and alder, compelled to chase her and seek out the laughter.

She found her by a brook that gurgled over river stones and fallen branches. The silver waters cut through the rich, black earth. Isabelle stood by the riverbank, her camera focused on a fat toad.

Ren stood motionless and watched as Isabelle took her photos. She raised her head and sucked in the sweet forest air. It was laden with honey and oak moss—Isabelle's scent. A low growl rumbled in her chest. Ren knew these smells; they belonged to her forest, her home. And Isabelle belonged there, too.

"Take her." The urgent whisper came from right behind. She shook her head and scowled at the intrusion.

"Take her now. She's yours in every way. Even the forest knows it," the whisper continued.

Isabelle looked across; she raised her camera and laughed.

"Smile, you guys."

The camera flash in her memory made Ren blink. The moment was gone. All that was left was this injured woman in her arms, and her scent that told more than Scheherazade. For Ren, the belonging was doubtless and absolute. This woman was hers. They were life bonds. Now and for always. The taking, however, lacked honor. It made her want to snarl and bite and claw entire trees apart in anger. But right here and now, in this bed, all she needed to do was wrap herself around her mate and keep her safe.

The pull was strong. She settled in, and pushed her face into the nape of Isabelle's neck, and closed her eyes. Her ears twitched, straining for anything untoward, but all was as it should be. The wind blew down the mountainside and rattled the shingles and shutters. The old cabin complained as it always did on windy nights. The night sky was empty of forest calls. Satisfied all was well and they were secure, Ren finally allowed herself to sleep.

❖

"Listen up, mutt. This is your mission, and you'd better bite ass at it or you'll be nothing but a tail sticking out of my next burger bun. Get it?"

Hope backpedaled up the hall. Jolie's words snagged her attention from the full laundry basket in her arms. She peeped into the living room wondering what was going on.

Jolie sat stooped on the couch nose to nose with Tadpole. The little dog bristled with self-importance and excitement. He wasn't allowed on the furniture, but several times lately Hope had caught him on the couch, and here was clear evidence why. Jolie had sat him beside her for this important pack confab, and he loved it. He'd obviously received a big werewolf promotion somewhere along the way.

Hope frowned. What on earth was Jolie up to? By rights, she should be getting ready for her business trip. Both Jolie and Andre had been summoned to accompany Leone for the first meeting with the Lykous. The Greek werewolf clan had invited representatives from the ancient werewolf family of Garoul to visit their pack home in Zagoria, high in the mountains of northern Greece. Yet here was Jolie, spending her last few hours in deep conversation with Tadpole?

"Okay, it's like this," Jolie drilled him. "I'm the Alpha and you're the dog. When I'm away, your job is to protect Hope. You're my right paw, and between us we have to keep our den mother safe. She's the cornerstone of the pack, see?" Tadpole's tail thumped on the cushions. "Because if we don't have a den mother I'm gonna end up eating you. Understand?"

Tadpole didn't seem to understand. His tail thumped faster and more happily despite the dire warning. Jolie shook her head and straightened in her seat with a grunt of disgust.

"Stupid mutt."

"Den mother? Since when am I a den mother?" Hope stepped into the room and Jolie jumped guiltily.

"And you. Down. Now." Hope pointed at Tadpole. He skittered under the couch in a blink, leaving Jolie to take the flak. She glared at his disappearing hindquarters.

"Well, you are. Sort of," she said, defending her description. "We're a pack, Hope. A family unit, and he has to protect you when I'm not around. It's his pack job."

"He was already doing that before you came on the scene."

Jolie snorted rudely.

"He did so," Hope said. "So tell me, what does a den mother do, seeing as how I've apparently got the job without even applying for it." She sat on the couch in Tadpole's vacated spot.

"Oh. Mostly the laundry." Jolie eyed the overflowing basket at Hope's feet.

"The laundry?"

"Yeah, and the cooking. And gardening."

"I see. All the things you hate. How convenient. And what does the mighty Alpha bring to the pack?"

"The mighty Alpha brings home the meat."

"I can do that from the grocery run. You're beginning to sound mighty redundant, mighty Alpha."

"The mighty Alpha does all the mighty lovin'." Jolie slowly spilled Hope over onto her back.

"Oh?"

"Right word, wrong delivery." Jolie growled and began to nibble Hope's neck, lingering on her pulse point.

"Oooh," Hope moaned, then grabbed Jolie by the ears and pulled her back up off her. "No you don't. We have to get you packed."

She pushed them both into an upright position. "Seriously, I've never heard of a den mother. Marie isn't one. She's the Garoul Alpha."

"A den mother is more for the younger cubs. Like at the Little Dip summer camp when the young ones come to learn their wolven skills."

"Before they hit puberty and change?"

"Before and after they change. It's an ongoing education. In the wild a den mother would also look after the orphans. Or any feral cubs adopted by the pack. That sort of thing."

"You sound very vague about it."

Jolie shrugged. "I was brought up in a strong, well-organized pack. I had Aunt Marie as my Alpha and Dad as our trainer. I suppose in some ways he took over the role of den mother. After all, he's the one who taught us all how to lick our paws and clean behind our ears."

"I'd like to see you tell Claude he's a den mother. You'd be licking more than your paws," Hope said.

"Of course he's not *called* a den mother. But his role is more or less the same. He counsels the young ones."

"So the Garouls have all the pack components, but not necessarily assigned as gendered roles?"

"Yeah. We're a matriarchal clan, but after we have our Alpha in place, then the other ranks go to who's best suited for them. We do everything a wild pack does, only better," Jolie said with pride. "That's why other packs envy and respect us. We're the best."

"Well." Hope lifted the laundry basket. "As den mother of a mini Garoul pack, I think you should lick your paws and get ironing. You'll need these shirts for your Lykous meet and greet," she said as she unceremoniously dumped the basket on Jolie's lap.

Chapter Four

Isabelle awoke refreshed, with only the dullest of aches in her shoulder. The room was bathed in murky gray light, making her unsure if it was dawn or dusk. She was in bed alone.

She blushed furiously remembering the heat of Ren's bare body pressed against her. Who was Ren? Who was this woman who cradled her through nightmares and injury? Isabelle struggled to recall the shadowed features; all she could remember were midnight eyes that burned right through her. No amount of effort could bring Ren into clear focus.

Isabelle's head was heavy. Her sleep had been deep and drug-induced, laced with more bad dreams. But she had also slept through her earlier pain. How long had she been out for? How many hours, days? She flicked at the curtain and peered outside at the snow. Trees loomed in the descending shadow. The winter light had a gloomy quality, quiet and mournful.

Isabelle lay back and stared at the wood plank ceiling and made a quick assessment. She had no idea where she was. She had no idea who her host was, apart from the fact she called herself Ren. Her shoulder throbbed in its tight bandages but was less painful than before. The rest of her ached all over, and she had a thumping headache, but again, she felt better than she had earlier. All her belongings were apparently destroyed. Did that include her documents? She'd need those, especially her passport. She knew she had to cross the border into America... assuming she was still in Canada. Was she? Isabelle frowned. The longer she thought about it, the more complicated and insurmountable everything became. So what else did she know? Oh, yes, her bladder was full and she smelled rank.

She looked around the room and didn't recognize anything. She had no idea where she was. She concentrated, trying to pick out reality from tattered nightmare. Nothing concrete came to mind, nothing at all. She was Isabelle, and she'd maybe hit some deer and crashed her car. That was all she could remember at this point. Deer and blood and glass shattered all around her…and pure, unimaginable fear. Yes. Lots and lots of fear. It still lay coiled in her belly, tight and cold…right next to her full bladder.

She eased upright and propped herself against the headboard. The ache in her shoulder intensified with each movement but was bearable. She was in a small bedroom with plain wooden walls and simple furniture. The Spartan contents left her unsettled. There were no clues to where she was, no insight to who lived here. No books, clothes, or knickknacks whatsoever. Isabelle decided she liked clues. She liked to use her mind to work things out, to situate herself in the world. This room gave nothing away. The room was as minimalist as a convent cell.

She threw off the bed covers and cautiously rose to her feet. She was naked, but a blue cotton dressing gown hung behind the door. She wrapped herself in it and went exploring for the bathroom.

Barefoot, on shaky legs, she padded down a long, shadowy corridor lined with closed doors, except for one at the end. It lay ajar and she could see the lure of white porcelain bathroom fittings. She made straight for it.

So she was in a log cabin. How had she got here? She had no answers. She couldn't even recall her own name in full; her surname was still a mystery. Then again, she knew she was called Isabelle only because Ren used that name. Ren. Her rescuer? Her nurse? Who was she and why did she seem so strangely familiar? Was this cabin Ren's home? It was all crazy. She had to know something about herself. How else to prove she existed?

She tried not to panic and to stay objective. She'd been in a car crash and now she was here, somewhere, being looked after. Being well looked after, if the neat, clean bandage on her shoulder was anything to go by. She needed to use her wits, to think, to solve this puzzle, and concentrate on the immediate things…like the bathroom mirror.

Her bruised and battered face looked back in shock. She had a shiner of a black eye, almost cartoonish in appearance with its slit of bright blue iris shining through the puffy discoloration. Her nose had a small bump from an older injury.

So, she had blue eyes—well, black-and-blue eyes now—and a bumpy nose. Her hair was glued to her head, and there was a blood-encrusted cut running about three inches along her hairline. There was another older scar, thin and white, intersecting the corner of her mouth.

She was not looking at the face of a friend. This was a face she did not appreciate, or even like…perhaps had never liked? Dark rings circled her good eye; the other was a puffy mess. She was underweight, her face pale and peaky. Her cheekbones were too prominent, her nose too pinched despite its earlier break, and her mouth a tight, tired line. Dirty-blond hair hung in strings around scrawny shoulders. It was a bad haircut, much too long for her thin features. She had a lackluster, plain face with a dry, sallow complexion underneath all the bruising. Isabelle shivered. She was chilled, although her cheeks held two bright spots of color, round and red, like clown paint.

"Well, hello, Isabelle. Pleased to meet you, I think," she said to her reflection, then turned away abruptly. "Jesus, you're one ugly bitch."

No. No, that's negative thinking. I need to see something good. Something affirming. The thought came out of nowhere, but it was so strong it stopped her in her tracks. She turned back to the mirror and forced a smile. Deep inside she knew it was important to look for the good in her. As if she had spent too long hearing only the bad. The scar on the corner of her mouth creased into a lopsided grin that she sort of liked.

"And I have great teeth!" she proclaimed. Affirmation concluded and job done, another personality trait kicked in. Isabelle discovered she loved snooping.

Hungry for information, she explored everything around her. In contrast to the bedroom, the bathroom was bright and cheerful, with a wealth of personal items for examination. A faintly remembered scent lingered in the air, spicy and enticing. Homemade shampoos, soaps, and bath salts littered every ledge, but the alluring smell did not come from them. She snooped in the bathroom cabinet, rifling through razors, nail files, oils, creams. A linen hamper overflowed with fluffy, damp towels. Someone loved an indulgent bath time.

Glossy-leaved plants in brightly painted pots lined the windowsill.

A few cacti even managed to bloom in hot pinks and oranges. Isabelle picked up a small pot, hand-painted in a cheerful, childish daub. Little brown foxes, or maybe wolves, chased bright yellow chickens round and round the rim.

A stack of clean white towels lured her to the bathtub, and she checked the shower faucet for hot water. It ran full and scalding and she almost cried with relief. She shed her robe and stepped in, enraptured with the simple act of washing away the grime of God knew how long. Not caring her bandage would get wet, she let the hot water race over her. It took several shampoos before she was satisfied her hair was finally clean.

The bandage on her shoulder was soaked and she peeled it away, curious to see her wound. A row of stitches curved in a wide crescent across her shoulder. The blood-scabbed knots wavered irregularly across her skin like a sordid smile.

I've never had stitches before, not even for my lip, and that bled and bled. Curious how the oddest facts popped into her head while the important stuff eluded her. She could vividly remember a blood-soaked dishcloth wrapped around a bag of frozen peas pressed to her split lip. She remembered her fingers tingling from the frozen packaging and adrenaline pumping through her. And nearby, just out of her line of vision, someone was saying, "I didn't mean it, I didn't mean it," over and over again. "Sorry, sorry." She could recall his voice so clearly. She paused over this flashback. Who had hit her?

These were recalled emotions rather than actual fully fledged events, she reminded herself. It could be dangerous to accept such things at face value. She could inadvertently rewrite her own past to suit this blank of a present. She had facial wounds that were old; that did not mean she was a beaten wife, did it? She had to be careful.

The stitches felt alien to her tender flesh, and they nipped her skin in a burning itch. Some of the puncture marks did not need stitches at all and were healing quickly. Others went deeper into the muscle, causing her discomfort and stiffness. It looked like a painful injury, and Isabelle was glad she had slept through most of her recovery. She guessed she'd been heavily medicated, remembering the ill-tasting liquid she'd gulped down. What had caused the puncture wounds in the first place? Broken glass? Rent metal? Her dreams were littered with it.

A rosy rash peppered her chest and belly. Was she reacting to something? The rash looked harmless and did not irritate her. She rubbed at it briskly with the towel. Another thing to ponder. She needed to find Ren and discover what the hell had happened to her.

An unopened toothbrush packet lay by the sink. She hoped it was a guest one for her use, but was too shy to assume. She squeezed toothpaste onto a finger and scrubbed her teeth, and spat the bad taste out of her mouth. She finger-combed the damp tangles of hair and dispassionately examined her reflection again, looking past the obvious bruising for other signs of well-being, or not, as the case might be. The rash on her chest now decorated her throat. A glum sigh escaped her. She looked in her eyes and tried to peer deep within herself. Who the hell was she? She looked like someone who didn't care about herself. She looked ill and unhappy on a world-weary level that went so much deeper than the trouble she was in now. And she knew trouble. She could feel in her bones that she knew it well.

She gave her reflection a weary smile, really nothing more than a grim twitch of her lips and turned away. If she stood on tiptoe she could peep out the high, narrow window to see the view from this side of the cabin. She cracked the window open an inch. Outside, cedar trees swept down a steep incline, their heavy branches buried under a layer of thick, powdery snow. The crisp white ground and snow-laden trees glowed eerily under a rising moon, as atmospheric as a scene from her dreams.

It was dusk. Overhead, a cloudless, star-bright night was unfolding. The air smelled pure and frost sharp, and she wanted to be out in it, running and rolling in the snow, to lie in it and laugh up through the treetops to the stars beyond. She felt a delightful giddiness she associated with childhood, the high energy of not having a care in the world.

Isabelle pulled the window shut. She had drawn all the clues she could from this room and from the mirror before her. It was time to find her benefactress and thank her. It was time to ask all the questions she needed answers for.

She left the bathroom and returned down the hallway. A murmur of voices drew her to a closed door. A woman and a man were talking in the room beyond. She recognized the woman's voice. It was as mellow and dark as ruby wine, and had soothed her through numerous nightmares. One hand was on the door handle, the other raised to rap, when she realized the voices were hard edged with anger. Though she could barely distinguish the words, there was no doubt this was an argument. She hesitated to knock, unsure what to do.

"Burn it—" The abrupt cessation of Ren's sentence should have warned her. Too late she realized what it meant. The door flung open and Ren towered over her, her eyes narrowed to glittering slits. Isabelle stepped back, startled. This was her savior? This woman who pulsed with menace? For an instant they stood stiffly, then Ren's anger melted, the tightness in her face relaxed into gentler angles. Isabelle flushed with a mixture of embarrassment and relief. She'd have died if that anger had been aimed at her.

"Ren?" The name felt like a pure beam of light. But the person attached to it came as a surprise. Seeing her now face-to-face, Isabelle did not know this woman at all. Before, she had only been a lamplit shadow, a distant face distorted by fever and delirium. Now she finally stood before her outlined by the light, clear to her eye, and she was beautiful...but in a cruel, arrogant way, like the aquiline profile of emperors on ancient coins. Or the cold, impassive beauty of goddesses carved out of hard, unblemished marble.

"I thought I heard something." Ren's voice softened. No trace of her earlier anger remained. "You're awake." She sounded surprised and pleased. She stood back to allow Isabelle to enter the living room.

"Yes. I took a shower. I hope you don't mind," Isabelle murmured, still shy and overwhelmed.

"Not at all. Come on and sit by the fire."

Isabelle looked around her with interest. The living room was small and comfortable. Old, rust-spotted watercolors decorated the walls. A mahogany bureau sat by the far wall, conspicuous in that it was the only costly piece of furniture in the room. Beside it a tall, narrow bookcase stood in a corner stuffed to overflowing. Several more books were wedged under it, replacing a missing leg. Isabelle frowned in quiet disapproval; books should be better looked after than that.

Drawn up before the blazing fireplace sat a battered old couch, an open book and glass of wine perched on the armrest. It was a shabby and threadbare piece of furniture, but colorful throws and fat, bright cushions made her want to sink into it. The simple, homespun comfort of the room poured out warmth and drew her like a magnet. It was the perfect space to while away the long, dark winter nights. She took a step forward, then hesitated.

"How are you feeling? I'm not sure you're strong enough to be up and moving around just yet." Uncertainty undercut Ren's casual words. It was clear she was concerned and a little nonplussed at Isabelle being so well so soon.

"I'm feeling a lot better, thank you," Isabelle answered, aware of the young man who stood by the hearth. She drew her robe tighter around her thin body. He had just thrown a log into the fireplace and now straightened up to watch her enter. Isabelle watched the fire, fascinated. Thick wads of paper bloomed into flame sparking the log bark. He was burning a book. Behind her, Ren suppressed an angry hiss, and Isabelle bit her tongue to stop from tutting out loud. It was sacrilege to burn a book, she thought. No good could come of it. The burst of flame highlighted his thin, sharp face and pale gray eyes. He watched her coolly, with no sign of welcome.

"This is Patrick," Ren said, her tone hard. Their earlier argument had not been forgotten. "He's just leaving."

"Good evening," he said dully. Though he spoke to Isabelle, his gaze was glued on Ren. Before Isabelle could return the greeting, he turned away and headed for the door. "Will I see to it now?" He looked at Ren with doleful eyes.

She gave a sharp nod and dismissed him. Ren waited until the door clicked closed before giving Isabelle her undivided attention.

"Come and sit by the fire. Would you like something hot to drink? Tea? Cocoa?" She guided Isabelle over to the couch. "I make good cocoa."

"Cocoa would be lovely." Isabelle was hungry. The mention of a hot drink made her stomach grumble, but she was too embarrassed to ask about food.

"And perhaps some toast? How does that sound? I can't give you anything too heavy to eat just now."

"Oh. Yes, please. I woke up ravenous." She perched on a corner of the couch, holding her hands out to the fire, her toes wriggling in delight on the thick woolen rug. "It's wonderfully warm in here."

"Do you want a blanket for your knees? I don't want you chilled," Ren said.

"No. To be honest, my temperature is all over the place. One minute I'm shivery, the next I'm boiling up." She blushed as she recalled Ren's body blanketing hers last night, providing much-needed warmth. She felt the keen gaze scour her face. Isabelle drew her legs up under herself and curled into a snug ball among the plump cushions with their tired velvet covers.

"You've had a high fever. I'm relieved to see you up and about so soon." Ren's voice was relaxing to listen to, and Isabelle melted back into the couch. "You're a quick healer. I'm pleased."

She glanced up to see Ren smiling at her. A smile that played tricks with her temperature all over again. Waves of pleasure ran through her. It was luxury to be on the receiving end of that smile. No wonder she had a fever then the chills. She looked away and concentrated on the flames.

"I'll be back in a few minutes." Ren left for the kitchen, leaving Isabelle alone to contemplate the fire and her strange feelings. *Well, a fever would explain why my head's so fogged up.* She had a hundred questions to ask, but she needed Ren to return with the cocoa and hopefully all the answers.

Isabelle's gaze fell on the book lying open on the couch: Mary Shelley's *Frankenstein*. She felt a surge of excitement. She knew this book. Her mind conjured up a tooled red leather cover, with gorgeous etchings—a cherished gift given to her at some point in the past. This was a cheap, mass-market student edition, ragged and dog-eared. A section of text was underscored. Isabelle peered at the underlined paragraph: *"I am alone and miserable; man will not associate with me; but one as deformed and horrible as myself would not deny herself to me. My companion must be of the same species and have the same defects. This being you must create."*

"Try this." A steaming mug was thrust under her nose. Isabelle jumped, the book abandoned. She hadn't heard Ren reenter the room. The drink smelled rich and wholesome and her stomach gurgled in delight.

"And this." A plate with a toasted cheese sandwich also appeared. Isabelle nearly swooned with happiness; it was as if her mind had been read. Toasted cheese sandwiches were her comfort food, yet another recollection from out of the blue.

"Mmm." Her first sip from the mug was nectar. "This is gorgeous. It's the best cocoa I've ever tasted. Is there licorice in it? I can taste something bittersweet." She bit into her sandwich and gave another groan of appreciation.

Ren settled beside her, sitting a little too close considering it was such a roomy old couch. Her proximity made Isabelle nervous and she took another huge gulp from her mug, eyes wide over the rim.

"You've got the bluest eyes in the whole wide world." Ren smiled at her. It felt as if the sun had broken through a brooding storm cloud. Ren's smile lit up her entire face, the room, the cabin…the whole of Isabelle's wide, blue-eyed world, in fact.

"They're cornflower blue. Like summer," Isabelle said, uneasy that Ren studied her battered face so closely. She was the absolute opposite of Ren's dark, animalistic beauty. Ren's face was keen, her eyes hungry, and she moved with the grace and purpose of a predator. But when she smiled it felt like sunrise after a long, haunted night.

"I'm not sure who told me that. But they're cornflower blue," Isabelle babbled on, "when they're not all black and puffy, that is." Her answer surprised her. The memory had floated into her head and lingered, lost without context. She couldn't remember who had said this, or when it had been said, but she knew the memory was a true and happy one.

"They're my best feature," she said trying to spin out this little thread, see what it might weave. The memory made her feel good about herself and she instinctively felt this was a rare thing. Whoever had paid her this compliment had a fondness for her. Somewhere, someone once cared, perhaps still did. She was pleased at this little series of remembrances. Favorite food, the gift book, her eye color—she was beginning to fill out from the vaporous ghost she'd awoken as.

"They're *one* of your best features. You have many, many more." Ren reached over and casually adjusted the neck of Isabelle's robe where it gaped open a little. "I take it your memory's still a little vague? It will come back soon. I promise it will."

Her innocent gesture scraped the cotton across Isabelle's nipple. It hardened against the friction. Isabelle flinched, but Ren seemed unaware of her reaction. Ren held a sexual charisma that confused her. She was hypersensitized to her simplest words and gestures. Yet Ren seemed curiously casual, even relaxed around Isabelle's tense, scrawny body with its multitude of inhibitions and screaming defense mechanisms. Isabelle pulled away and curled up at her end of the couch tighter than a pink prawn.

"What happened to me?" She cleared her throat, clinging to her empty mug. It gave her something to do with her hands and placed a small physical barrier between them. Ren's nearness swamped her. A spicy heat rolled off her body, and Isabelle's senses sucked it all up greedily until her head swam. "I remember a car crash. Did I hit a deer? I remember a deer with an injured leg."

"Your car went into a ditch. You didn't hit a deer, but you may have swerved to avoid one."

"Where am I? How did I get here?"

"You're near the Bella Coola valley. I live in the Coast Mountains, and I found you on a branch road off Highway 20. I checked you over, and apart from your shoulder and this temporary memory loss thing, you seem fine. When the snow thaws I'll get you to a hospital for a proper checkup."

The names were familiar. She'd heard of Bella Coola and the Pacific Coast Mountains. Was she local to the area?

"So you're a medical person? A doctor or a nurse?" Her wound had been treated professionally.

"A veterinarian. But wounds are wounds, and stitches are stitches. I was more concerned with the bang you took to the head, but you seem to be mending well."

"It's only temporary. I'm already beginning to recall some things, as if my memory is on a sort of trickle drip. Things like my eye color, and toasted cheese sandwiches. And Bella Coola sounds very familiar…" She trailed off. There was such a long way to go in reclaiming her identity. She touched the small scar at the corner of her mouth. Not every memory would be a welcome one, but she would deal with that when it happened.

"You know my name." She looked up. "You called me Isabelle. But Isabelle who? Do we know each other?"

Ren nodded. "I know you, Isabelle Monk. I know you very well."

"Monk?" Her surname was Monk. Isabelle frowned. It didn't

sound right; it didn't fit. "So we're friends?" she asked, then blushed, recalling she'd asked this before when they were curled up in bed together.

"Yes. I think of you as a friend."

"How do we know each other?" It bothered her that she had to drag these answers out of Ren. A real friend would tell her all she needed to know; instead, Ren was holding back. Isabelle's anxiety levels began to rise.

"Do I live near here? Near you?" She pushed on. "Are we neighbors?"

Ren shifted slightly at this last question. It was the first sign of discomfort Isabelle had seen in her. She waited for an answer, watching every flicker on Ren's closed face.

"No." The answer was snapped. "You live somewhere else." This was added almost grudgingly. Isabelle frowned at this sudden mood swing. She realized that up until now this had been some sort of game to Ren. Now she was truculent when the questions weren't so easily answered, or rather, answered to her liking.

"Well, where then?" Isabelle pressed, aware of the change in atmosphere, as if the temperature had dropped imperceptibly by degrees as her panic rose. "Where do I live?" Ren had to tell her. Then the thunderous thought struck—what if Ren was not a friend after all?

There was a moment of silence as Ren contemplated her answer.

"I don't want to tell you," she finally said.

"What? Why?" Isabelle was shocked.

"Because I don't want you to go back there."

"What?" Isabelle turned to fully face Ren. She was confused and angry at this response. This was no time for games. She needed to know these things. Ren reached out and held her chin in a firm grip.

"I don't want you to go home," Ren repeated slowly. "You're not safe there. You're safe here, with me. You have to stay with me." She leaned in and her mouth covered Isabelle's in a hard kiss. Isabelle jerked as a tingling rush thrummed across her lips. Her heart hammered. Scalding heat rolled through her veins. Ren kissed her thoroughly and with lazy authority until Isabelle's entire being lurched, fluttered, and disintegrated like a cherry blossom. She was captured inside this sweet, blossom-scented, and dangerous kiss. Warnings howled inside her head. She'd heard these cries before—She twisted away, breaking the kiss, and pulled her face free. She had to save herself. Isabelle didn't need anymore fog-fueled moments. She was fractured enough.

"Don't," she gasped in dismay. She did *not* kiss women. This she knew for certain. And not like that! "You can't kiss me like that."

Ren leaned back. The muscles of her face were hard as flint, her eyes drilled into Isabelle's until she shrank back against the couch. She felt woozy and hot and glanced at her empty cup with suspicion. Ren reached toward her and she flinched, but Ren merely tucked a damp curl behind her ear. "When your memory returns I think you'll find I can," she said.

Chapter Five

W hat do you mean you can? What does that mean? Because let me tell you right here and now, you damn well can't." Isabelle's explosion had them both blinking in surprise.

Ren moved back, irritated. She gave Isabelle a sweeping, calculated look. Her cheeks bloomed under her tan and her eyes sparked dangerously, but she said nothing.

"What's going on here that you think you can just lean in and kiss me?" Isabelle said. "Are you trying to tell me we're lesbians, because let me tell you right here and now that I am *not* a lesbian!" She was very firm about that. Definitely not. Ren gave her a big, black-eyed blink and her knees liquefied. *Okay then...*

"What I mean is..." Isabelle blustered on, ideas and theories and guesswork bursting out of her. "What I mean is, well, I may not be *totally* into men..." That felt true. "But that doesn't make me a lesbian either. In fact, I suspect I'm not very sexual at all. Why, I could be a nun!" She was grasping at straws and she knew it. Ren narrowed her eyes at this hypothesis, and Isabelle shut up. She was being ridiculous.

A huge yawn caught her unawares. For the second time, she eyed her empty mug, sure it contained more than just cocoa.

"No. You are not, and have never been, a nun." Ren rose and held out her hand. "It's time for bed."

"I am *not* going to bed with you."

"I'm putting you to bed, not taking you," Ren thundered in exasperation.

"Oh." Isabelle accepted the offered hand and was pulled to her feet, a little embarrassed at her assumption.

Ren led her back to the bedroom. Her head swam and her legs felt leaden. The sleeping drug in the cocoa had kicked in. She was spilling toward sleep and it annoyed her. She wanted answers for her millions of questions, but her head was so fuzzy she was unsure what mattered more, her questions or Ren's bizarre behavior.

"You never answered me," she said, remembering the thread of their earlier conversation.

"I did. You're not a nun."

Moonlight spilled through the windows and illuminated the room in irregular blocks of soft light.

"That's not what I meant and you know it. You avoided my questions."

They stood by the bed, Isabelle unwilling to get back in it. She'd spent eons in that bed. It was the last place she wanted to be. She fought down another yawn. Ren reached over and casually tugged her closer by the sash of her robe.

"I—" Isabelle clasped Ren's muscular forearms, as if that would stop her if she chose to kiss her again. Ren lowered her head. Isabelle held her breath and closed her eyes in anticipation, her fingernails dug into Ren's skin. Ren's breath brushed across her cheek, and then her lips grazed her ear, so delicately every hair on the nape of her neck rose.

"I want you to remember us," Ren whispered. "Not be told how it was."

Isabelle gave a delicious shiver. She tilted her chin. Her lips were so close to Ren's jawline that the merest pucker would—The room spun as she was lifted and laid down on the bed. Ren chastely drew the blankets up to her chin and withdrew, leaving a chasm of chilled air and confusion between them.

A knowing smile played on Ren's lips.

"I have to go out tonight, and *you* need to sleep. It will help you heal," she said. "You shouldn't be running around so soon after your accident. You need rest."

"I don't want to sleep. I want to talk." Isabelle wriggled upright. She was embarrassed at her urge to kiss Ren, and relieved she'd not given in to it. She suspected Ren was quietly laughing at her, and tried to read the sly smile, but the moon glowed behind Ren's shoulder and cast her face in shadow.

"You're so beautiful," Ren said. She traced Isabelle's cheek.

"No, I'm not." Isabelle pulled away. "I don't understand what's going on, Ren. How are we connected? This doesn't feel real to me. I have so many questions and you won't answer me straight."

"I'll answer when you're well enough. I promise to. But you've had a serious accident, Isabelle. You were lucky I found you. Everything else is just…complicated." Ren gently pushed her back onto the pillows.

"And what makes you think I can't deal with complicated?" She knew instinctively that she could. Complicated was no stranger, Isabelle was definite about that.

"And where are you going? You can't just tuck me up in bed like a child whenever I get in the way." She wasn't so definite about that. She felt more childlike than ever at being abandoned. She wanted Ren's company.

Where Ren was concerned, she knew very little but felt a lot. She'd awoken into a world that confused and scared her as much as any nightmare. The only answers she had were those she scraped together from errant memories and Ren's cryptograms. She was in the middle of nowhere and she disliked the sight of herself in the mirror. What else did she know? Nothing. She was a vacuum. It was all a mess, and the one person who could help was walking away. At that moment the only certain thing was she wanted Ren to stay, to curl up beside her and hold her and keep the nightmares at bay. To stay and simply talk to her and help her make sense of it all.

"Hush. You need rest." Ren soothed her, even as she made to leave.

"Don't hush me. I'm your lover, aren't I?" Isabelle's anxiety put her on the offense. She watched Ren's eyes narrow. "Are we having an affair? Running around behind someone's back? Tell me the truth. Something isn't right." She pushed herself up to sit in the center of the bed. "Tell me. I can feel the truth writhing inside me, trying to get out, and it's not a nice feeling."

Ren bent over her until their faces were inches apart, her brow dark and frowning. Her eyes caught the moonlight in a weird amber glow.

"All you need to know is that you're mine," she snarled. "*Everything* about this is right." She straightened and glared at Isabelle. "So start feeling it."

A distant howl wavered from the woods, loaded with troubled melancholy. Ren stiffened, then abruptly strode from the room leaving Isabelle in bed, bewildered.

"Don't you tell me what to feel," she shouted with hollow bravado at the empty room. But she did feel it, in her own way. Ren was hers.

Now she was determined not to go to sleep. Despite feeling heavy-limbed and wooly-headed, she padded along the hallway on bare feet looking for the kitchen. A fresh pot of tea and a seat by the fire would help. She could sit and think and try and sift through the events of the past few days. Ren disturbed her. She drew out such a tangle of emotions in Isabelle. The liberty Ren had taken with that kiss, for example. Isabelle knew beyond all doubt they were lovers. She could feel it the moment they had touched; yet another part of her was uneasy with this insight.

"I'm a lesbian after all," she told the planked floor in the hallway, watching her bare toes move along the warm pine. It didn't feel wrong. In fact, it felt exhilarating and dangerous. "And I think I've fallen for the lesbian version of Heathcliff. 'My love for Heathcliff resembles the eternal rocks beneath, a source of little visible delight, but necessary,'" she quoted and froze mid-step.

"I can quote from Emily Brontë's *Wuthering Heights*? Wow." It thrilled her she knew the classic well enough to quote from it, and that it was a favorite book. Another piece of the jigsaw fell into place. She loved books. First *Frankenstein* and now *Wuthering Heights*. She knew the classics, she adored the Brontës...oh, oh, and Austen and Browning, and what about Eliot and Dickinson? Their names rattled through her head along with a dozen others. How strange: she could remember authors and book titles, and even prose and plot, but not her own address? It cheered her up, though. Her memories were returning. She was finally forming into something solid.

She tried to dredge up some other quote to build on the first, to underpin her discovery. Her mind went blank. *Okay, so I can't force it*. She thought again of the book Ren had been reading. *Frankenstein*. How fantastic that they seemed to like the same books.

"I felt emotions of gentleness and pleasure, that had long appeared dead, revive within me," she quoted from Shelley, much to her delight. The classics were a linchpin to her identity. Somehow she had turned a corner.

The kitchen fascinated her. Ren obviously spent time in here. It had a lived-in homely feel like the living room. Although the cupboards were battered and the paint chipped and scratched, like the rest of the cabin it was a well-loved, well-used space. Pestles and mortars, measuring cups, and stirring spoons littered the work surface. Dried herbs hung from hooks fixed in the low ceiling beams. Enormous, dented copper pans sat washed and ready on the huge, cream enameled stove that looked like a relic from the fifties. Rows and rows of jar-lined shelves filled the far wall over a scoured work counter. Most were filled with herbs and oils, and all were labeled in a scrawling, uninhibited handwriting she assumed was Ren's.

A thick, dog-eared volume on medicinal herbalism lay open on the countertop. Isabelle hovered over it, compelled by the beautiful plant illustrations to leaf through it and examine the pages in detail. It was an old almanac, a mixture of First Nation medicines, moon cycles, botany, and horticulture. Its spine gave the year as 1961, an exclusive, limited edition judging by the fine quality of the paper and the richness of the binding and illustrations. The flyleaf showed an inscription from the author: "To my darling niece, Dalia, with much love…" The name was heavily scored out with a sharp instrument, like a knife, but Isabelle could just make out enough letters to guess at "Sylvie." The book had been written by a Sylvie Garoul. Isabelle wondered if it was a gift from the author. It was a first edition collectable if only for the illustrations alone. They were quite superb, the work of one George Brookman, a name that rang a bell with her, but she couldn't remember any details. The book was too precious to be lying around a messy kitchen. Already it had stains all over it.

Isabelle reluctantly set the book aside as the kettle whistled. She picked a lemon and ginger tea from a home-blend mixture she assumed Ren had made, and cup in hand, set off to explore the rest of the cabin. If she wanted answers she'd damned well have to provide them for herself.

The living room was cozy, and she whiled away a pleasant half hour sipping tea and examining the books in the wobbly bookcase. Most were secondhand and were much read. But their covers had a creased softness and the subtle smell of a million fingerprints and a hundred shelves. The old bureau was crammed with invoices and paperwork for Ren's veterinary practice and what looked like a farming venture she ran nearby. A door to the left of the chimneybreast drew Isabelle's attention. She drifted over to it, cup in hand, and gave it a gentle push.

Ren's bedroom was tucked away off the main living room. Isabelle stood inside the doorway drinking in the detail. It was a total mess. What clothes weren't hanging out of the chest of drawers lay in a tangled ball on the unmade bed. The armoire door hung open, its full-length mirror catching the light from the hallway behind her. A jumble of shoes and shirts spilled from it onto the floor. Only the dressing table gave a clue as to the usual order of the room and reflected the general tidiness of the rest of the cabin. Though the drawers hung open, the surface was uniform and neat. Combs and brushes lay beside handcrafted wooden bowls filled with loose change and stray buttons. An antique leather manicure set and a few colored glass bottles took up the rest of the space. The only closed drawer in the dresser was locked. This was curious in itself, given the general upheaval of the other drawers. Isabelle shook the handle several times and looked for the key in the small bowls on the countertop, but to no avail. She gave up and turned her attention to an empty suitcase wide open on the bedside chair.

Had Ren been hurriedly packing to go somewhere? The thought made Isabelle anxious. A road map lay unfolded inside the case. Pushed on by her unease, Isabelle lifted it. A red marker pen traced a journey from Lonesome Lake, over to Bella Coola, and down across the U.S./Canada border straight to Portland, Oregon. She set it back and frowned. The journey meant something to her. She'd traveled that way before. But Lonesome Lake? That was miles east of Bella Coola in the middle of Tweedsmuir National Park. Ren had said they were in the Coast Mountains, but given the sheer size of the mountain range, they could be anywhere.

Isabelle dropped the map back in the suitcase. It wasn't that much of a clue after all. She turned her attention to the bottles on the dressing table. All held homemade lotions and looked medicinal rather than cosmetic. There was a heavy, languorous scent in the bedroom and she tried to identify it. She unscrewed a bottle top and sniffed the contents. It reminded her of the ointment on her shoulder, but it wasn't the smell she was now fixed upon. That scent was stronger on the hairbrush, and she realized it belonged to Ren. It was her scent.

Isabelle drifted over to the wide unmade bed. She lifted a shirtsleeve and pressed it against her nose to confirm the scent was definitely Ren's. The cloth was crisp and clean and held a thousand stories. Like fine wine against her palate, the flavors exploded onto her senses and her imagination galloped.

Ren's hot, peppery scent was subtlety layered with cherry and cool notes of vanilla. It drifted through her like opium smoke. She closed her eyes and saw sweat-slick skin, tight and tan, stretching in the sun, then contracting and twisting into swaths of ink-black fur that rippled like waves of prairie grass. She felt dense muscle weigh down her bones and heard the snap of twigs as her feet sank in heavy loam. Wind rattled the leaves and hissed through fir needles, and ran through her coat like a million stroking fingers. Fine rain misted her face and she flicked her ears against the damp. Her lungs expanded as she drew in more and more of Ren's scent and the heady visions that came with it.

Her heart hitched into a tight knot of want, and suddenly she needed Ren. Why had she left her? Why hadn't she told her where she was going and when she'd be back? Isabelle frowned, and a discontented growl rumbled in the back of her throat. She pulled her face away from the cotton shirt and scowled at it. She didn't want to sleep alone; she wanted the heat of Ren's body. She wanted to drift into dreams with this scent wrapped all around her. She took a corner of the cuff into her mouth and sucked, her teeth worrying the fabric.

Wire grass crackled with summer heat. The drooping heads of lady's slipper and clumps of purple violet shivered in a lazy breeze. Insects droned in a crown around her head—Isabelle spat out the fabric and stared at it in disbelief. She had been chewing on the sleeve like a pup on a slipper. What the hell was happening to her? Had she lost her mind?

Her tongue smacked against the roof of her mouth, wanting more. She recalled the images that had flashed through her head, as exciting and vivid as if she had really been sprawled out in a hazy summer meadow. It was addictive. She raised the shirt to her nose and breathed in. She felt sunshine dancing against her eyelids and heard the high-pitched trill of waxwings circling above.

A flicker of movement from the window startled her. The flicker was followed by a rustle as something dropped out of sight under the windowsill. Isabelle crept cautiously toward the window, her bare feet silent on the floor. Something or someone was outside. She heard the crunch of footsteps on fresh snow and held her breath. Pressed against the wall, she angled her head to peek out, but the glass tricked her and reflected back the light shining from the hallway. She could see nothing but the shadowy bedroom mirrored back at her…and then, she saw it. Distorted by the weak interior light, two eyes, elongated and slanted, glowed like burning embers as they glared through the glass. They darted from side to side searching the room for her. Isabelle began to make out other details—a pointed ear and a curved canine tooth, and a wet snout. She was alarmed that a wild animal would come so close to the cabin, but she felt safe enough inside the stout walls.

The animal's ears flattened, and with a sharp hiss, the face was gone from the window. Isabelle started, but saw what had spooked it. Across the room, she stood reflected in the armoire mirror, clearly visible from the window. Pressed against the wall, wide-eyed and fearful, she looked like some sort of half-crazed animal herself.

She glanced out the window and stared into the night. She could see nothing. Isabelle shivered. She was about to give up and turn away when a blur on the edge of the tree line caught her eye. Something crouched in the murk. As she watched, it lifted its head toward the cabin as if sampling the air. It hesitated for a moment, then slunk into the underbrush and melted away. From what she could make out it looked like a small wolf or a wildcat. Whatever it was, it moved like a predator and was bold enough to come right up to a human dwelling.

A wavering, reedy howl echoed close by in the darkness and was answered by a distant chorus from the hills beyond. A chill ran through her. It was wilderness out there, and she was miles from civilization. She had best remember that and hope the thaw came soon. She had to get out of here and find the missing pieces of her life. The questions were mounting and the answers were few…and selective.

CHAPTER SIX

Isabelle was curled up on the sofa when Ren came back. *Frankenstein* lay open on her lap and Ren's shirt was pillowed under her head. The quiet click of the door jerked her out of her fire-gazing stupor. She sat upright, groggy and disheveled. Ren appeared at her side and reached out to touch her shoulder. The night air clung to her clothes.

"Hey. Why are you sleeping out here? Is the bedroom too cold? I can put a heater—"

"There was an animal at the window," Isabelle said. Ren's hand stilled.

"An animal?"

"Yes. It ran off when it saw me." Isabelle felt awkward. What if Ren asked more questions and she had to admit she was snooping in her room...sucking on her clothes and acting weird.

"Just nosy, I suppose."

"Huh?" Isabelle started with guilt.

"The animal. Just being nosy. Lots of deer and elk come close. They're curious by nature, probably hoping to sniff out dinner in my garden," Ren said. "Under all that snow I've got some very tasty rosebushes."

"It had teeth. Big pointy ones. Elk and deer don't have pointy teeth."

"Oh?" Ren hesitated, as if unsure what to say to that.

"It ran away when it saw me."

"Ah. Okay." She seemed satisfied with this. "I'll check for tracks in the morning."

Isabelle shuffled upright, and Ren perched on the edge of the couch beside her and began to unlace her boots.

"Why won't you answer my questions?" Isabelle jumped right into the subject that had been burning her up all evening. She had to know.

"What makes you think I know all the answers?"

"Stop playing with me. You said you didn't want me to go home. You said it wasn't safe." *You said I had to stay here with you.*

"I'm not playing with you. Look at your face. Some of those injuries go way back. Beyond the car crash."

Isabelle touched her bruised face. It was true. She had seen her broken nose and the scar on her lip and knew they were old wounds. She'd even recalled the whining voice begging for forgiveness.

"Your arm's been broken before, too," Ren said, then shifted uncomfortably. "Isabelle. Your husband beat you and you started a divorce," she stated bluntly. "You came to Canada to get away from it all."

"I came here from Portland, didn't I?" Isabelle remembered the map lying open on Ren's suitcase. Ren looked surprised but nodded in reluctant agreement.

"So I'm married? How long was I married?"

"A year maybe. Not long. You knew you'd made a mistake pretty quick." The answer was brusque, and Isabelle surveyed Ren carefully. Ren was uncomfortable with the conversation. She pulled hard on her laces and kicked off her boots.

"How do *we* know each other?" Isabelle tried another approach. "Where did we meet? Here or in Portland?"

This was the most information she'd gotten out of Ren and she was anxious for the flow to continue, but already she could see the defensive shutters coming down. Ren was building another wall of shadows between them. Her gaze shifted around the room, she seemed unable to look at Isabelle. She stood and moved to the fire, unease pouring off her. Isabelle watched her and surmised that while Ren was not lying to her, she was being selective in what she chose to reveal.

Ren knelt by the hearth and stared at the dying embers, She made as if to reach in for something, but with a quick sideways glance at Isabelle turned her back on the fire and began to talk.

"We met in the Bella Coola Valley. There's not much to say, and you'll remember it all soon enough. Your aunt has a holiday lodge in Hagensborg. You were staying with her and we met when I called over with Atwell's medication."

"My aunt?" This was exciting news.

"Mary Palmer."

Isabelle frowned. *Mary Palmer*. The name wasn't familiar and that disappointed her. "Who's Atwell?"

"Her Pomeranian. He's got diabetes."

"Oh." Isabelle blinked. Aunt Mary had a sick dog. "Poor Atwell. Maybe we can go visit when the roads are passable?" The thought of nearby family cheered her up, but already Ren was shaking her head.

"Mary left already. She was only here to lock up for the winter."

"Oh." Isabelle felt gutted. "Have I any other family in Bella Coola?"

"No."

Her face must have shown her disappointment, for Ren became agitated and moved toward the kitchen. "Would you like tea?" she asked.

"No more drinks, thank you. Every time you give me something to eat or drink I conk out." Isabelle tried to shake off her gloomy mood with a weak joke. So her aunt had already left. Isabelle had to remember she was lucky. She'd had a nasty accident and was being looked after by a family friend. It could have been so much worse.

Ren's eyebrows rose. "You conk out, do you? I leave you all tucked up in bed and return to find you reading on the couch with a glass of my good port."

Isabelle squirmed. Ren didn't know the half of it. Her snooping had kept her tirelessly occupied for most of the evening. She'd investigated every square inch of this place. She knew more about its nooks and crannies than the mice.

"It seemed like a nice place to sit and watch the flames," she said.

Ren shrugged. "Okay, no tea."

She tugged off her padded shirt and pulled her T-shirt over her head and tossed them on the nearby chair. Her jeans soon followed. Ren's naked torso was athletic and tan, and puckered with dozens of small cuts and scars across her belly and breasts. The air around Isabelle condensed into a thick brume of heady scent. An image flashed before her of dappled sunlight on bronzed skin, before it tensed and folded into thick bunched muscle and black fur. It frightened her. Ren reached for the waistband of her black briefs.

"Keep your clothes on," Isabelle said, almost panicked. "Please."

Ren hesitated and looked at her questioningly. Isabelle felt heat scorch her face as an unreadable mask dropped over Ren's features, but not before she read disappointment there. Ren grabbed her T-shirt and pulled it back on.

How can she do that? Isabelle was stunned at the casual way Ren had displayed herself. She was unself-conscious in a way Isabelle knew she could never be with her own body. She wanted to ask about the marks on Ren's chest and belly but didn't know how. Ren's nudity upset her. It triggered thoughts and flashbacks to things that confused and frightened her. Yet, another part of her looked at Ren with deep interest. She wanted to ask questions about her scars, to talk about her wounds, but instead Isabelle had rejected her. She felt like the worst prude in the world.

Unhappy with her illiberal behavior, she decided to go back to her own bed and fret. She was about to go when Ren vaulted over her prone body onto the couch and settled in behind her as naturally as if they did this every evening. Isabelle started in surprise. Ren did not seem to notice her reaction and dragged the Indian weave blanket off the back of the couch over both of them. Isabelle lay there in mild shock as strong arms gathered her close. She liked the sensation of being held.

"You're cold," she muttered, trying to sound cordial, though her heart thumped like an express train.

"Not for long," Ren said. Already warmth was radiating off Ren's thighs and belly into Isabelle's body. She crept a little closer, leaching off the heat, bemused at the contentment and comfort she found in Ren's arms despite her finicky objections. Ren's hand gently smoothed the fabric of her robe, stroking her arm, down over her hip where she pinched the flesh.

"You're too thin. I need to fatten you up."

"You make me sound like a Christmas goose." Isabelle slapped her hand away, but not unkindly.

"I want to look after you. Make you big and strong." Ren snuggled into her, and despite herself Isabelle felt a rush of pleasure at the closer contact and caring words. "No one's ever going to hurt you again."

Isabelle objected to Ren's words. "I can take care of myself."

"I'll be the one doing that from now on."

The propriety in Ren's voice made her uneasy. She changed the subject.

"Where did you go?" she asked. "I thought the roads were impassable."

She was pleased that they had moved beyond their earlier awkwardness. Here they were, lying before the fire in the warmest room in the cabin, chatting away. Perhaps if she changed tack Ren would open up again. Isabelle could not allow herself to get so comfortable she forgot her number one priority, to remember as much as she could and as soon as she could.

"I managed to get where I needed to go." Ren's face was in her hair, and Isabelle could feel her breath puff against her neck whenever she spoke. Ren's hand continued to stroke her upper arm, soft and reassuring through the thin cotton. "I was checking on a sick animal. Go to sleep. You must be exhausted. We can sleep in here by the fire."

Isabelle was tired. She'd been fighting sleep since suppertime, but lying with Ren gave her stomach butterflies, and the last thing she wanted to do was close her eyes. She wanted to savor this moment of security. Her dreams still scared her. Though she didn't dare admit it, she was much happier now that Ren had returned to curl up beside her.

"You're healing well." Ren's fingertips slid under her collar and trailed over the welts on her bruised shoulder.

"It hardly hurts at all." She settled into a more comfortable position and the curve of her bottom nestled into Ren's groin. She froze, and then relaxed, surprised, yet at ease with her new audacity. "You smell nice," she said shyly.

"Oh?" She could feel Ren smile, her face pressed into her hair. "What do I smell like?"

Isabelle was unprepared for the unusual question.

"Trees and grass. Stuff like that." She felt stupid. What a stupid thing to say.

"Good. I'm glad that's what you scent," Ren said, though she sounded slightly disappointed.

"What I scent?"

"Yeah, scent. What you smell off me. Scent can tell us lots of things."

Isabelle considered this. It was a weird thing to say. Then she remembered the strange imagery triggered by sniffing Ren's clothes. Perhaps it was more than the medication playing with her head?

"Do I have a scent?" she asked, then cringed inwardly. *What a stupid question. I'm full of them tonight.*

"Yes, you do." Ren continued to stroke her shoulder, gently running over the ridge of knotted stitches. She buried her face in Isabelle's hair and inhaled deeply, holding the breath in. Isabelle's flesh goose-bumped delightfully and her spine tingled its entire length. She, too, was holding her breath. Ren exhaled and tightened her arms around Isabelle. "Your scent is forever."

CHAPTER SEVEN

Isabelle sat up and shivered. The fire had burned out and she was alone on the couch. A cold dawn illuminated the room with flat, gray light. She looked over at the empty hearth. Ren had raked out the ashes, and kindling and a fresh supply of logs were set nearby, ready for a new fire to be built. She wondered that there was no other form of heating in the cabin. It was a very basic home, more like a vacation rental that hadn't been upgraded for year-round living. The threadbare furniture and fittings, the basic build of the kitchen, told her money was tight in this home.

Wrapping the blanket around her shoulders, she wandered to the kitchen hoping Ren might be there, but in her heart she knew she was alone. Her insecurities rose and she had to wrestle them down, losing herself in the routine chore of making breakfast to ignore her misery.

In a corner of the kitchen an antiquated kerosene heater belted out heat, and Isabelle blessed the small luxury. Ren had left sooty fingerprints all over the countertop from her earlier hearth tending, and Isabelle tutted loudly as she wrung out a dishcloth and quickly wiped the surfaces clean. Job done, she started foraging for breakfast.

Herbs, plant roots, and stems seemed to be all Ren's kitchen had to offer. It was not well stocked with food. Isabelle peered into the barren depths of the fridge and begrudgingly settled for a meal of leftover bread and cheese. A strong pot of coffee took the edge off her meager meal. If the roads were impassible there was a good chance they would starve to death, unless Ren had a secret larder somewhere else.

Isabelle sat at the table and planned her day. She needed to sort out clothing. She couldn't bear to slob around in this robe any longer. She felt cooped up and wanted to go outside into the fresh air and explore her surroundings.

She took her breakfast dishes over to the sink, and noticed her teacup from last night on the drainer. She had forgotten she had left it on Ren's bedroom table after the beastie had peeped through the window. Her cheeks heated. She'd been caught out snooping. Returning to the scene of her crime, she found the room pristine. The clothes were tidied away, the bed made, and the suitcase stowed on top of the armoire. All the shoes were lined up in regimental rows. The room had been restored to its natural order, but she was embarrassed Ren knew she had intruded.

She showered and carefully inspected her wounds. Her shoulder hurt less and had a bigger range of motion than yesterday. She shrugged and rotated it, flexing and stretching under the stream of hot water. It was improving day by day. When she shampooed the gash on her hairline, the newly formed blood crusts washed away, leaving a thin pink line. She examined it in the mirror and was pleased at her rate of recovery.

The bruising around her face and body looked fainter. Her older scars drew her attention. She touched the cut on her lip and the bump on the bridge of her nose. Ren had told her she'd been battered. Isabelle traced these old wounds, expecting some emotion to resonate within her—anger, upset, maybe even sorrow. All she felt was shut down and cold. She remembered the bloody dish towel pressed to her mouth and the man's voice pleading for forgiveness. Was he her phantom husband?

She stood straighter and looked herself in the eye, hoping for an answer. She could believe she'd come all the way from Portland to avoid an abusive man. Her heart was hard. She could feel it, flinty and sharp-edged in her chest. She'd come to Canada to visit family and be rid of him. Isabelle shook her head at her reflection. She had no idea where she belonged—Bella Coola, Canada, or Portland, America? For the moment, the answers could wait. Today, she felt healthy and invigorated. Her body was vibrant and alive, totally reenergized, as if she were emerging from a cloud of heavy pollution into fresh, open fields. All she needed was for her mind to follow.

Back in her own room she was pleased to find clothes set out on her bed. They were Ren's and far too big for her, but they would have to do. The shirt hung off her shoulders, and the jeans fit with the help of a belt strapped tight around her waist. The pant legs were long and she had to roll them up like a seaside paddler. There were thick woolen socks, but no shoes.

In a flash of inspiration, she ran into the living room and knelt to peer under the couch. Her luck was in. Ren's discarded snow boots lay under there from last night. She hauled them out. They were far too big, but she stuffed the toes with extra socks until she could stomp around quite happily.

The day had opened up, filled with excitement and purpose. She had explored the inside of the cabin, now she would explore the outside and see where she had ended up on this strange journey. She would have loved Ren to be her guide and was a little disgruntled at being abandoned yet again. Tamping down her anxiety at Ren's mysterious comings and goings, she stopped to steal one of Ren's coats from the hanger behind the front door, a waxed jacket that swallowed her. As an afterthought, she snatched a wool hat and crammed it on her head, then she stepped outside.

She took a deep breath that made her convalescing lungs tingle. She felt giddy with the clean mountain air. Isabelle looked around. The cabin backed up under a wall of mountain before the ground rolled away to a steep meadow. A swath of fir and spruce flanked its exposed east side and kept the worst of the weather at bay. This was where her visitor had disappeared to last night, stealing into these trees. New snow had covered any tracks that might have been left, but Isabelle didn't care. This morning the world had opened up to her, and what a beautiful world it was.

There was no furniture on the porch, no chair or table. No one sat here and looked out at the stunning views on a snow-sharp morning such as this, and Isabelle thought it a shame. Frosted treetops pointed up from the valley floor, twinkling like candied minarets. They shivered in the swirling wind that blew from the surrounding mountains, throwing ice in the air in a million crystalline points of sunlight. It was a small, deep valley, no more than two miles across surrounded by steep walls of forest and the snow-capped peaks beyond.

The ground below the porch steps was churned and muddy from multiple comings and goings. A well-used path led straight to the meadow. Below, she could see the sharp pitch of a shingled roof.

Isabelle followed the trail to find a small barn and two long, low outbuildings that looked like old stable blocks or storage rooms. They huddled around a large, open-ended gravel yard. The snow was cut up by several sets of tires. It was used as a parking area but this morning it was empty. She glanced around. No one was about. Uncertain of where to go next, she noticed the barn door stood ajar. The gleam of a tractor grill winked out from the shadowy interior. Isabelle slid through the opening into the dry and cozy gloom.

The barn smelled of clean straw and engine oil. Hand tools hung on hooks, and canisters and storage bins lined the walls. The tractor was an old Case 400. Isabelle walked around it, her hand skimming the burnt orange paintwork. She knew the tractor make, it was a showpiece dating back to the fifties. She liked that something this big and solid meant something to her.

A battered motorcycle was propped against a workbench. Was it Ren's? Did she rebuild these old vehicles? Isabelle wished she knew. She wanted to build up an image of Ren as much as she wanted to understand herself. They were both mysteries to her.

Toward the back of the barn, straw bales were stacked six feet high. Some had toppled over and the straw had burst into a large, disordered mound. The center of the mound was indented, and several old blankets were scattered in the depression. Isabelle stood and examined the large nest-like shape. What slept there? Maybe dogs?

"Ren?" a sleepy voice asked from the straw. Isabelle watched in amazement as the far edge of the nest rustled, then erupted, and a face peeped out at her. A young girl sat bolt upright in a straw-strewn flurry, confounded at seeing Isabelle standing before her.

"No. Not Ren," Isabelle said and smiled. The child was perhaps eleven or twelve, not quite in her teens. Her straggly, long brown hair had stalks of straw poking out at all angles, and her face was smudged with dirt. Her clothes, what Isabelle could make of them half buried in the straw, were grimy with dried mud.

"I'm Isabelle," she said. "I'm staying at the cabin up the hill." The girl blinked in surprise and examined Isabelle's borrowed waxed jacket and ridiculous rolled-up jeans with deep suspicion.

"Where's Joey?" she asked suddenly, seemingly satisfied with the introduction.

"I don't know who Joey is. Who are you?"

"Mouse. Joey's getting me breakfast."

"Mouse?" Isabelle smiled at the nickname. Small, brown with dirt, and ferreted away in the straw bales, the moniker fitted her perfectly. "Lucky you, getting breakfast in bed. Do you usually sleep here, Mouse?"

"I don't like the bunkhouse. Noah and Patrick snore."

More new names. Isabelle had already met the unwelcoming Patrick, but she didn't know anything about a Joey or Noah. How many others were living at Ren's place? Did they work here? Where were Mouse's parents? Did they live here, too?

"Hey. Is there a Mouse in the house?" The barn door creaked as someone shuffled in to join them. Isabelle turned toward the smell of cooked food, her stomach growling as if it hadn't been fed in years. A young man on a crutch hopped precariously across the barn floor, balancing a tray with his free hand. He had dark blond hair cut in a shaggy surfer style and looked like he pumped iron all day long. He was big, looked to be in his mid to late teens, and seemed extremely cheerful despite his awkwardness with the crutch.

"It's you should be getting me breakfast in bed, Mouse," he said, all attention on the tray. "I got the bad leg. Have you any idea how hard it is not to tip this dang thing over—" He broke off when he saw Isabelle. "Oh." His guileless blue eyes blinked and his jaw slackened. Her appearance seemed to throw him.

"Let me help." She went over and took the tray from him, and brought it back to Mouse. She had crept over to the edge of her nest and now hung over watching them both, refusing to leave its confines but anxious for her breakfast to arrive. Isabelle set the tray down before her. A plate was piled high with bacon, steak, and eggs and swimming in a sea of spilled orange juice. It was more than enough food for a grown man, never mind the diminutive girl before her, but Mouse fell on it with a gusto that made Isabelle jealous.

"Thanks." Joey's uncertainty passed, and he hopped over beside her and eased himself down on a bale. Beside him, Mouse guzzled as if she'd never seen food before, though she still managed to keep a wary eye on both of them.

Joey shuffled and shifted. It was clear his hip and leg caused him pain. Finally, he propped his crutch on the bale beside him and straightened out his bad leg.

"Hey." He turned his attention back to Isabelle, his cheerful smile back in place. "You're Ren's—" Mouse made a strange little spitting sound and Joey shut up with a confused look.

"You're Ren's houseguest, yeah?" he said, this time with a sheepish grin. He rubbed his hip and thigh. She wondered what he had been about to say before Mouse had shushed him. She had a good idea, and it made her uncomfortable. What were the preconceptions about her and Ren?

"Sort of. I'm staying at her cabin for a while. I'm Isabelle, and you're Joey, right?" Isabelle was just as canny back. She was unsure what she was to Ren, but if she was careful, these two might provide her with some concrete answers. "What happened to your leg, Joey?" She might as well ask since he was constantly drawing attention to it.

He gave a mirthless barked laugh and received another warning look from Mouse.

"Hunting accident," he muttered and looked everywhere but at Isabelle.

"Oh no," Isabelle said. "What happened?"

Joey warmed to her interest. She decided he wasn't used to getting much attention and gloried in it when he did.

"I split my spleen and crushed this hip, and the thigh bone broke in two places, see? And I cut a nick out of my kidney. All down this side, it was." He wobbled to his feet and lifted his shirt. His left side was a rash of livid yellow and purple bruises, and freakish Frankenstein stitches. She winced, suitably impressed. Her shoulder wound was trite compared to his mangling.

"Oh, Joey. That looks so sore." She paid due respect to his wounds. "When did this happen?" Lord knew how many operations the poor guy had to undergo.

"Last week. Tuesday I think it was," he said. Mouse gave a frustrated hiss and he glared at her. Isabelle managed to bite back her smile. It was nonsense; his wounds were healing well, so they had to be months old at the very least. Nevertheless, she decided she liked Joey, with his open expression and childlike exuberance. It was obvious he wasn't the brightest match in the box. And he was certainly emotionally immature compared to his sharp-eyed little friend, who at nearly half his age was so censorious of him. She watched the interplay between the two, how Joey accepted Mouse's directions with a minimal amount of grumping.

"Well, it was." He glared back at Mouse, then dropped his head and fell into a massive sulk. Isabelle ignored the little contretemps and filled her voice with sympathy and understanding.

"I'm very glad to see you're on the mend, Joey. You're one tough guy." She tried to soothe him. This was greeted with silence. Joey was still huffing, but he did turn in her direction, head still down and his back to Mouse.

Mouse watched it all with a shrewd intelligence well beyond her years as she continued to stuff her mouth with her fingers. Isabelle frowned. The child's behavior was positively feral. Why was she here? Who looked after her?

"Do you stay out here often, Mouse?" she asked.

"She's a barn rat," Joey butted in good-naturedly and sat up straight, his bad mood evaporating in an instant. Mouse stopped eating and watched intently, as if trying to figure out Isabelle's next line of approach.

"She'd stay out here all the time if she could," Joey said. "I have to smuggle her food out of the cookhouse, and that ain't easy because Jenna's got eyes in the back of her head and I'm already in her bad books because of the mess in the floor which wasn't my fault." Joey was determined to share the minutiae of his daily struggles. "Jenna's very house proud, and it was only a little spill."

"Ah." Isabelle nodded wisely, noting the new name, Jenna. "And I thought Mouse stayed out here because Patrick and Noah snored," she joked with him. Mouse's eyes widened and Joey fell into hoots of laughter.

"They do! They do! They're great big honkers!" His shoulders shook with laughter, and huge smile lit up his face. "But that's not why. She says that, but she wants to sleep out here anyway. All the time. Most of us sleep here when we can. It's way more cool to wake up in the nest after a night out on the furry. I—"

"Shut up," Mouse said, her voice a high, worried squeak.

"It's true. It is. You don't like the bunkhouse. You only sleep there when Ren makes you."

Mouse reached over and poked him hard on his bruised side. He yelped.

"Hey, fish lips, quit flapping and shut up." The snipped words came from directly behind Isabelle. She spun around, startled, to face Patrick. She hadn't even heard him enter the barn.

"I don't have fish lips," Joey muttered but didn't look at Patrick. He rubbed his poked side and gave Mouse a woeful stare. She had the grace to look contrite and threw a quick downcast glance in Patrick's direction. As Isabelle watched, a slight smile twitched the corners of Joey's mouth. Mouse might have hurt him, but they shared a secret communication about Patrick. She had saved him from a lot worse than a sore side, judging by the glower on Patrick's face.

Patrick turned on Mouse next. "I told you, you eat with the rest of us."

She shrank back into the straw and gazed at him in childlike innocence. A total contrast to the beady-eyed suspicion she'd cast Isabelle's way earlier. It didn't fool Patrick for one minute.

"You don't eat with us, you don't eat at all." He snatched up the tray with her partly eaten breakfast and pushed it into Joey's chest. "Take that back to the kitchen, dumbass. Jenna's been bitching in my ear all morning about you and your messes."

Isabelle bristled at his rudeness. It was bullying behavior and there was no need for it.

"And *you* shouldn't have left the cabin. Ren won't like it." His tone to Isabelle was reined in but still cold and curt. He did not like her at all. She already knew this from his snub at their initial introduction, and it would become a mutual dislike if he didn't mind his manners. She could feel Joey's empathy flow toward her in big, sloppy waves. He was familiar with this tone, too.

"Ren told me nothing of the sort. In fact, she even left out clothes so I could explore." She was just as curt back. There was no denying she wore Ren's clothes. She was acutely aware of her scent clinging to everything. She had no idea what Ren's intentions were when she left out the clothes, and as she hadn't the decency to hang around and explain, then Isabelle would do whatever she damned well pleased in them. And no cocksure boy, barely out of his teens, was going to tell her what to do either.

"What exactly is the problem?" She pressed at his supposed authority over her. His face darkened and his right hand twitched as if he ached to slap her. Mouse scurried deeper into her hidey-hole and Joey sat wide-eyed holding his breath. There was a sourness in the air. Isabelle was very aware of it and knew it came from Patrick. Curdled and bitter, like milk on the verge of going off, and it matched the expression on his face.

So Patrick was not used to people standing up to him. Well, he'd better understand right from the start that she didn't think much of him and his self-styled authority. She had seen him scuttling off to do Ren's bidding, and though she didn't fully understand it, she knew she held sway with Ren and it would not do to let this young man try to boss her around.

She nodded at the tray in Joey's hands. "There's a cookhouse? I'll take that and drop it off to Jenna. See what's on the menu." She threw Jenna's name out casually to see how Patrick would react.

Patrick spun on his heel. "The cookhouse is closed. Jenna will bring food up to the cabin so you can cook for yourself." He strode off, his back rigid with anger.

"Joey, follow me. You got chores. Mouse, go wash. You stink," he yelled over his shoulder, not slowing his pace. His barked orders were a stand-down, a compromise until he discovered where he stood with her, how far he could push—and they both knew it. As far as Isabelle was concerned, Patrick would not be pushing her at all. He had just met an immovable object.

"See ya." Joey hobbled past, trying hard to catch up with Patrick. Mouse slithered back into the depths of the straw and left Isabelle standing alone.

Isabelle's stomach growled louder than ever. She thought about Ren's kitchen with its little heater and roomy old stove and the pleasant odor of drying herbs. A second breakfast sounded like a fine idea, and she would be happy to cook it if there was food in the cupboards. The tray was already in her hands. It was the perfect opportunity to visit Jenna and the cookhouse and to finish her exploration of the rest of the outbuildings.

"Mouse?" There wasn't so much as a twitch from the straw nest. "Mouse, I know you're in there. Come show me the rest of the place," she said. "Where do you wash?" The straw heaved, but only because Mouse was burrowing deeper. She was obviously a law unto herself around here.

"All right, young lady. Get out here right now. Time to clean you up," Isabelle ordered, and wondered where such a commanding tone came from. It worked. Mouse stuck out her nose, then her head, and gave Isabelle a look of consternation.

"Right now, missy. Patrick's right about one thing, you are a disgracefully dirty little girl." Isabelle's inner mom was on a roll. She pointed to a spot on the floor beside her where Mouse was to report immediately.

Reluctantly, Mouse disentangled herself from the straw and hoary old horse blankets and crept out to stand before Isabelle. She was even smaller than Isabelle had first thought, and she revised Mouse's age down to maybe nine or ten. One look at those world-weary eyes made it impossible to guess. Mouse was a scruffy little preteen who channeled the Wisdom of Solomon through a pink sweater with appliquéd ponies.

"Where are your folks, Mouse?" Isabelle asked in a gentler tone.

Mouse shrugged. "Ren looks after me," she said.

Ren was her caretaker? The news intrigued Isabelle. She looked at Mouse's tatty clothes, filthy sneakers, and mud-encrusted hair. She needed more than a good scrub; she needed care and attention and someone to make sure she didn't spend the night under a straw bale. Isabelle clucked her tongue disapprovingly and held out her hand. Ren needed to do better.

"Come on. Show me where we go."

Mouse looked at the offered hand suspiciously. Her nose twitched with a surreptitious sniff before she took Isabelle's hand in her own small, cold one. Isabelle allowed herself to be led from the barn out into a bright and bitter morning.

Chapter Eight

They trudged across the yard toward what looked like an old, wood-clad storehouse. Smoke billowed from a tin chimney. Isabelle was certain it hadn't been smoking before. She would have noticed the acrid smell of burning greenwood as she came down the track.

"Bathwater," Mouse muttered darkly. She let go of Isabelle's hand to bounce up the porch steps and bang the plank door back on its hinges.

"Jenna," Mouse bellowed. "I got the girl stayin' at Ren's." It was more a warning than an introduction.

Isabelle followed and found herself in the bunkhouse. Rows of narrow cots lined the wall, head to toe, all tucked up with thick woolen blankets. Ten cots in all, five on either side of a narrow walkway that led to a straggle of hard-backed chairs around an ancient wood stove. She could see why Mouse preferred her nest. This was a stern, comfortless barracks of a room.

A young black woman bent over the monstrosity of a stove and pushed a log through the top plate. She straightened and stared over at Isabelle. It wasn't a friendly or even curious look, nor was it hostile. Jenna's gaze was steady and assessing, as if she had been waiting for Isabelle to turn up. Isabelle guessed her recuperation at Ren's cabin was of high interest to this little community, if she could call it that. She wasn't sure what this collection of young people in the middle of nowhere was all about.

Though she didn't feel threatened by Jenna's stare, she didn't relax under it either. Isabelle guessed Jenna to be in her late teens, about the same age as Joey. She was shorter than Isabelle, about five foot six, and was comfortably plump, though there was a definite steely strength in her eyes and attitude. Isabelle decided Jenna was likely generous by nature, but once a line was crossed then all hell would break loose. She wondered if she lived up to Jenna's expectations. She hoped so.

They cannily took each other's measure.

"She's called Isabelle and she tugged Patrick's ear hairs real hard." Mouse was unaware of the adult weighing-up going on over her head. Pleasure bubbled under her words.

"I bet he appreciated that," Jenna said with a wry grin, more for Mouse than Isabelle. Her gaze leveled on Isabelle, and her grin deepened until her cheeks creased into a smile of genuine welcome. She came forward and took the tray from Isabelle, then held out her hand. "Hi, Isabelle. I'm Jenna, but I guess you heard that already." Her words were followed by a little cough she concealed behind her cuff.

Isabelle shook hands. Jenna's grip was firm and she held on a little longer than was necessary, and Isabelle realized this initial touch was important to her. She was being delicately and deliberately scrutinized, and she wanted to pass muster.

"Joey and Mouse have been praising your cooking," she said, and cast an eye over to the wood stove. Its top plates were bare, and her disappointment grew that Patrick was right and breakfast was indeed over.

"I'm heating the water for Mouse's bath. Look at you; you're a dirty little troglodyte." Jenna scolded Mouse, ignoring the face pulled back at her. She turned her attention to Isabelle. "The cookhouse is across the way. Once I get this one in the tub, I'll take you over."

"I only need a loan of some groceries," Isabelle said. She didn't want Jenna thinking she had to make her breakfast. She was more than capable of doing that herself, if she could restock Ren's larder. "There's no food at the cabin."

Jenna snorted. "I'll bet." She set the tray aside and began ushering Mouse toward a door by the stove. "Come on, you. I've already started running your bath. Hop in, and I'll top it up with more hot water."

Isabelle followed them to a large bathroom covered from floor to ceiling in thick white industrial tiles. It looked clinical and cold despite the billowing clouds of steam that hung from the ceiling. To one side she saw a long shower stall that held four showerheads and no partitions in between for privacy. Beside that was a single toilet stall and then a double basin. Mouse was heading straight to a large tub on the other side of the room, under high, steamed-up windows. She shed her soiled clothing as she went, dropping it at her feet, with no show of modesty or tidiness whatsoever. Her skinny little body was as filthy as her jeans and sweater. Jenna followed, clucking and fussing over the discarded clothes. Once she'd seen Mouse safely into her bath, she dumped the lot into a washing machine tucked into the farthest corner and started a wash cycle.

The bathroom was charmless but practical, and together with the rows of cots in the other room gave an austere, institutional feel to the bunkhouse. Isabelle longed to ask Ren about this place and its young inhabitants, but she had no idea when she would next see her. Ren's constant comings and goings were beginning to irk her. Which was another strange thing. She wanted to know where Ren was every minute of the day and became anxious when she didn't. What was all that about?

The steam encouraged Jenna into a fit of coughing. She struggled to catch her breath, but finally pointed at Mouse.

"Scrub hard and I'll come back and do your hair. And don't forget behind your ears and under your nails." Jenna left Mouse splashing contentedly in the bath. Despite her earlier complaints, she was happy to play in the big, suds-filled tub.

"Come on with me." Jenna brushed past Isabelle, collected her tray, and led them out of the bunkhouse and back into the yard. The wind had dropped away and the midmorning sun had warmed the air by a few degrees.

Wind chill had to be a major factor in the valley, Isabelle thought. She looked up at the peaks that surrounded them. In the summer it must boil in its own little microclimate. She remembered the tractor in the barn and wondered what crops they managed to grow on these steep slopes and how long their season ran. Her brow knit. Once again, she was surprised such questions dropped into her head from nowhere. It confirmed once more that she somehow knew this region, or a place much like it. That she was in some way connected to the land to consider crops and growing seasons, or even the topographical lay of the valley for farming.

As Jenna led her across the yard, their boots scraped through the mud-streaked snow to the loose gravel beneath. The tire tracks were melting away.

"How many vehicles do you have here?" Isabelle asked. She was still on a mission to find out all she could for herself.

Jenna shrugged. "Three or four bikes and a few quads. Ren and Patrick have trucks."

Isabelle kept fishing."Oh, I saw a bike in the barn, but it was in bits."

"Joey and Noah are fixing it up between them. It's an old bike Ren found for them to work on."

"Was the tractor a project, too?"

"We've always had it. I think Ren fixed that up herself. It was here before I arrived."

It was the opening she'd been waiting for. "Where do you come from, Jenna? What do you all do around here? Apart from fix machinery."

Jenna gave her a sideways look. "I came in from Ontario. And we fix fish around here."

"Fish?"

"There's a natal stream for sockeye running through this valley. We farm the eggs for the big hatcheries in Bella Coola, and keep a pink channel."

"A pink channel?" Isabelle had no idea what that was.

"It's a man-made river with flow control. We use it to raise salmon fry. Ask Ren, she'll maybe take you down and show you. It's more conservation than commercial."

"It sounds fantastic. Baby salmon." Isabelle wanted to go and see the pink channel now, but her stomach groaned again and food took precedence. It had to be the fresh mountain air giving her the appetite of a bear.

The cookhouse sat opposite the bunkhouse. Isabelle noticed there was no woodsmoke hanging over its shingled roof; the stove must be stone cold with breakfast over for the morning. Still, she would soon have Ren's old burner lit up for cooking. The thought cheered her up. She needed routine in her life. She needed function and structure.

Jenna stepped up onto a wide porch that ran the entire length of the building. It was furnished with an assortment of chairs and bench tables. Isabelle guessed this was the gathering place on balmy summer evenings when cool breezes wafted down the mountainside. It offered a fantastic view of the valley and its perpetual crown of snowcaps. It had to be a wonderful place to sit and eat outdoors, no matter what time of year.

She noticed Jenna was a little breathless after the walk. She pushed open the door to the cookhouse without a glance at the majesty around them, too busy concentrating on her breathing. Isabelle followed, entering a huge, modern kitchen. It was not at all what she expected. No primitive wood stoves burned here. This room was fitted out to a very high standard with professional kitchen equipment.

Well-scrubbed wooden countertops wrapped around two walls of the room. Two large refrigerators stood shoulder to shoulder near the entrance, and a huge propane range in gleaming stainless steel sat against the far wall. A double drainer sink stacked with drying dishes was tucked in under a large picture window opposite the door. Whoever did the cleaning could dream the chore away looking out at the distant mountains.

The windowsill was lined with more of the hand-painted pots and plants Isabelle had seen in Ren's bathroom window. Sunshine poured through the glass and bounced off the shiny surfaces, bathing the room with warmth. The range pulsed out heat, along with the mouth-watering smell of baking bread.

The center of the room was dominated by a long pine table with bench seats. Paperbacks and magazines on all manner of interests lay scattered over it. Some were for a younger age group, and Isabelle imagined these were for Mouse. It was obvious this was the real home hub, not the barren bunkhouse. The butter yellow walls resonated with goodwill and homeliness, and Isabelle could see by the way Jenna bustled around the kitchen that she was its heartbeat. This was her space, her domain.

"What a beautiful kitchen," Isabelle said in genuine admiration. Her words won a look of approval from Jenna.

"Do you cook?" she asked Isabelle. A little uncertainty crept into her voice. "Will you be taking over?"

Isabelle was surprised. Taking it over? She shook her head.

"Why would I do that? This is a wonderful kitchen and I bet you're the one who made it like this." She couldn't see Ren or any of the others managing to organize it. If Ren's kitchen was anything to go by, this place would be filled with bunches of dried herbs, bubbling unguents, and Lord knew what else. This was a cook's kitchen, not an apothecary's.

"I used to work in catering." Jenna looked around her. "When I first came here it was full of cobwebs, with a wonky table and that old wood stove you saw over in the bunkhouse." Jenna ran her hand over the countertop with pride. "I got Ren and the boys to build me these cupboards and a new table with seats to match. And I was adamant about getting a proper stove and the biggest fridge Ren could find. In the end, she got me two." There was no mistaking the pride in Jenna's voice.

"How long did that take to build?" Isabelle grabbed at Jenna's enthusiasm. "It looks gorgeous, all the wood tones. Did you plan it all on your own?" It was shameless the way she exploited them all for an extra snippet of information, but it was justified, especially as Ren was being so recalcitrant.

"About three weeks. They went full at it. I planned it all out, and Ren told me what wood was available. It's my dream kitchen for my big family." Jenna abruptly turned away, a sudden discomfort in the conversation showing, as if she were embarrassed she had revealed too much.

"I love these." Desperate to keep Jenna with her, Isabelle reached for one of the brightly painted pots on the windowsill. "I saw some in Ren's bathroom."

"I buy the plain clay pots and Mouse paints them and plants them up." She seemed happier that she wasn't the subject of conversation any longer. "She can't sit still. It's hard to keep her focused on anything for long, but tell her it's for Ren and she tries harder. Given her own way, she'd be out running these woods ragged night and day."

"Doesn't she go to school?" Isabelle asked. Another question popped into her head, one she'd asked Mouse earlier. "Where are her parents?"

"She lost her parents. Ren looks after her now and she gets schooled here." A defensive edge had crept into Jenna's voice. She was protective of Mouse.

"Then she's a lucky girl," Isabelle said. "What a fantastic place to grow up. How long have you all been here?"

"I'll get you some food. What do you need? Milk, eggs, steak?"

Jenna moved to the fridge ignoring the question. The conversation about the farm and the people living on it was over. "I baked bread earlier." Jenna choked back another cough.

"Are you okay? That's a nasty cough."

"I'm fine." The reply was curt, and Isabelle understood Jenna did not want to talk about her health either.

"The bread smells fantastic." Isabelle changed the subject back to food. She moved around the kitchen noting the little details, she paused to look at Mouse's artwork tacked to the walls and on the door of the fridge.

"Got any greens?" she asked hopefully. She was coming to realize just how clever the kitchen layout was. Jenna had planned the entire space to function effortlessly for the cook. Isabelle was pleased she recognized the fact. It seemed she was a homebody, and she itched to cook in this kitchen. It would be a pleasure.

"Greens?" Jenna looked over.

"Yes. Whatever vegetables you have in. Can you spare any?"

Jenna gave a short bark of laughter. "It's clear you're new." She went back to her foraging. "There might be some carrots. Joey likes to crunch on them from time to time, like a big rabbit. But then he's hopping about like a big rabbit anyways."

Isabelle was surprised. It didn't seem an unreasonable request. Fruit and vegetables were an important part of a healthy diet. How could Jenna have worked in catering and not keep greens? She came to a side door next to the big stove. It was the equivalent of the bathroom in the bunkhouse. The door stood ajar and frigid air wafted through. Expecting another bathroom or maybe a larder, Isabelle gave the door a gentle push; it swung open to reveal the room beyond. She froze.

It was indeed a larder of sorts. A meat locker. Tiled throughout, like the washroom, in basic white tiles from floor to ceiling, and with similar drainage holes in the floor. But instead of baths and basins, this room was empty, barring several huge hooks driven into the ceiling. From each hook hung the headless carcass of an adult deer. The freshest still dripped blood onto the floor where it pooled in huge coagulating puddles around the drain holes. Her stomach heaved and she swallowed a surge of bile.

"Fresh game." Jenna's voice came from behind her. "Needs to hang." She reached over and closed the door with a firm click.

"Why are bits missing from the carcass?"

"Huh?"

"The legs. They have their forelegs missing."

"No meat worth having on the foreleg. Here's your stuff," Jenna said gruffly. She pressed a cotton shopping bag into Isabelle's hands. It was clear the visit was over and it was time for Isabelle to head home. Jenna clearly had a day of chores on her mind, and entertaining Ren's guest was not one of them.

"Thank you." Isabelle hefted the heavy bag in her hands. "I promise to replace everything as soon as I can get to a store. Where's the nearest one, by the way?"

Jenna looked at her peculiarly before turning away and heading for the door.

"Get Ren to take you there." She side-stepped the question. "I better go and untangle Mouse's hair." She sighed. "Get ready for some squealing."

Isabelle followed her out. She didn't want to go back to Ren's cold cabin just yet. She wanted to stay and help bathe Mouse and chat with Jenna. She liked her company and knew that under all that brusqueness beat a heart of gold.

These young people were interesting and fun and just what she needed to pull her out of her own maudlin melodramas. It also helped her form a picture of Ren's home life. Jenna and Joey were in their late teens, Patrick in his early twenties. How long had they been here, and how had they arrived? What did they do? Did they all work for Ren and the fisheries?

"You come along for dinner tonight. The boys are going down to the station this afternoon and I'm planning dinner for about six thirty. That okay with you?" Jenna asked just before they parted.

"I'd love to," Isabelle said. Her heart gave a happy little flip. This was a welcome gesture and she greatly appreciated Jenna's overture.

She watched Jenna head back to the bunkhouse, her stride full of strength and purpose. Although she had been politely welcomed and generously provided for, Isabelle knew she had also been kept at arm's length. Trust was a big thing here. She had seen it in Mouse's corralling of Joey's loose tongue, and Jenna's wariness, and even, to some extent, in Patrick's bossiness. They were all careful around her.

Full of thought, she trudged up the track to the crescent of trees that hid the cabin from the buildings below. She had just entered the canopy of fir when she heard Ren. Her voice was low and held barely contained anger. Isabelle stopped dead in her tracks.

"We don't even need this meat." Ren's voice was hard. "It's a stupid, needless kill."

Isabelle dipped her head and slunk to a crouch. From under the lowermost branches, she could just make out a small group of people standing several yards away. She could see Joey balancing on his crutch, looking very shamefaced. Beside him Patrick slouched, red-faced and sullen. A tall young man Isabelle had not seen before stood next to him. He was slight and dark skinned, and looked younger than Patrick but older than Joey. He stood square to Ren, taking the force of her anger unflinchingly. He held a red fox by its tail, and Isabelle's heart constricted with compassion for the dead animal. Flame-furred and full-bodied in its winter coat, it dripped blood on the snow from a large tear in its throat.

"I'm sorry, Ren," the new boy said, his voice passionate with apology. "It was such an easy kill, and I never thought—"

"It's lactating," Ren interrupted him, waving a dismissive hand. "So you've killed its kits, too," she said with disgust, then walked away leaving the three young men standing.

There was a moment of silence before Joey wobbled over and gave the boy a pat on the back.

"Don't worry, Noah. She's been cranky since the fuckup last week," he said.

So this was Noah, Isabelle thought. Now all Ren's group was accounted for.

"Guess I better get it skinned for Jenna," Noah mumbled.

"Way to go. She'll be so impressed with a fox fur. Maybe next time you can kill a mink," Patrick said.

"Oh, shut up, prick," Noah snapped. Joey gave a sharp snort of laughter that was quickly quelled. They began to move away.

"You're the prick for getting Ren mad," Patrick bit back.

"If Ren's mad at anyone it's you. *You* destroyed the books," Noah said.

"I told you. It was an accident." Patrick said. He was huffing. "I got confused."

"You always fuck up." Then Noah relented and took the sting out of the brewing argument. "It doesn't matter anyway. Ren's moody all the time since that woman arrived."

"I met her. She's nice," Joey said. "I showed her my scars."

Noah's and Patrick's guffaws drifted back up the slope. They were out of sight now but their voices carried clear.

"Did she admire her handiwork?" Patrick said before they moved out of hearing range.

Isabelle emerged from the trees and stared after them in shock. By her boot a sad trail of scarlet drips showed the path the boys had taken. *Blood on snow*. And Joey's mashed-up injuries. *Blood on snow.*

It came back in a flurry, her fear and panic. The thump of her car hitting flesh and bone. The jerk of the seat belt across her chest, the engine almost stalling. She remembered an agonized roar as a ball of fur and fury slammed against her windshield cracking the glass. What the hell had she done?

She'd hit an animal with her car. She'd crashed and injured herself. But what did Noah and Patrick mean about her handiwork? She had not hit Joey; he'd had a hunting accident. Hadn't he told her so himself?

Was this the secret of why she couldn't go home? Why she felt like a bad person when she looked in the mirror? Because she'd driven into the boy?

Isabelle felt sick to her guts. She walked back up the slope and thought through this most recent flashback. It was bloody and nauseous. She was certain that it was an animal she'd crashed into—some huge, unrecognizable, bearlike creature. Not Joey. She realized with relief she had not run Joey down, but she had certainly hit some sort of animal.

Chapter Nine

R en checked the nest hole. No Mouse.
"Don't tell me she did what she was told for once."

She strode over to the bunkhouse. With each step her temper cooled and she felt ashamed for shouting at Noah. She had to stop these knee-jerk reactions every time something went shit side up. He'd been hunting; it's what she'd taught him to do. Now she would have to teach him about seasonal selection. In fact, she'd better teach them all that. And not just about killing, but the gestation cycle of every goddamned mammal in the forest.

Mouse's singing greeted her as she entered the bunkhouse and she couldn't help smiling. Her trilling echoed in the bathhouse acoustics.

"I thought you hated bath time?" She stuck her head around the door just as Jenna applied the final rinse to Mouse's hair.

"I do. I hate smelling clean." Mouse surged out of the tub, ignoring Jenna's scolding. Water sloshed everywhere.

"Come here, water rat. Let's mop you up." Ren grabbed a big white towel and wrapped it around Mouse, then scooped up her squealing bundle and took her back to her bunk, where Jenna had already left out clean clothes.

"Stop wriggling, you little varmint." She began to dry Mouse with a flurry of brisk rubs and tickles. Jenna leaned against the bathroom doorjamb and watched as the bath water gurgled away.

"Isabelle called down and collected some groceries. I think you'll be eating at your own place for a while," she said, watching Ren with inquisitive eyes. Ren hesitated, and Mouse took the opportunity to wriggle out from the towel and pull on clean clothes.

"She did?" Ren was surprised Isabelle was out and about so soon and anxious that she was meeting the pack without Ren to make introductions. "Good." She was unsure how to react.

"I saw her, too," Mouse piped up, not to be outdone.

"Do you like her?" Ren asked, sliding home the zipper on Mouse's top.

"Yes. She told Patrick off for shouting at me and Joey."

"Did she, now? And what did you and Joey do for Patrick to be shouting at you?"

"I saw her smelling your stuff," Mouse said, slyly changing the subject. "She held up your socks and went pooooooo."

"She what!" Ren cried in mock anger. She grabbed Mouse and swung her upside down holding her by her heels.

"She did. She did." Mouse placed her hands on top of Ren's feet and they walked around the room like that, Ren taking giant steps with Mouse doing a handstand on her boots.

"I'm gonna bite your knees." Mouse laughed uncontrollably.

"And I'm gonna bite your butt." Ren smacked her on it instead. "Were you snooping around my cabin last night, young lady?"

"A little."

"A little?"

"I saw her pawing at your clothes." Mouse was adroit at turning attention away from her own misdoings. "She was chewing on them. Don't you feed her?"

Ren righted Mouse and set her on the ground. "Enough, your hair is too long for this. I'll end up stepping on it. Mouse, keep clear of my cabin, all right? I want Isabelle to take her time settling in. No surprises, okay?"

"Okay." Mouse straightened her clothes. "I like her," she announced, as if that was all there was to it.

Ren growled. "Haven't you got a math assignment to hand in today? Better get to it."

Jenna shooed Mouse to the door. "On you go. Your books are on the kitchen table. I'll be over in a minute and we'll bake cookies after you finish, okay?"

When Mouse had scooted off she turned to Ren. "Isabelle looked a little lost this morning. Asked lots of questions and needs even more answers."

"The answers are the hard part, Jenna."

"Her memory will come back when the shock starts leaving her system. It's best she hears it from you than figures it out for herself. That would be mean." Jenna's voice was soft, but her eyes held worry and a little admonition.

Ren bristled at the subtle warning. They both knew how mean it could be. "I won't hurt her."

"The hurting's already been done, Ren. Your job is to make it better."

"How's the cough?" Ren asked her.

"That last tincture seemed to help more."

"Any blood?"

"A little. Not much. I'll be okay. You better concentrate on that new girl." Jenna gave Ren a cryptic look before leaving to catch up with Mouse.

"You're both invited to dinner tonight, by the way. I happen to like her, too," she called over her shoulder.

Ren sank down on the edge of a bed and rested her elbows on her knees. Jenna's cough had her worried. She was running out of ideas, and the bleeding hadn't stopped. She'd look through the almanac again tonight and see if anything else caught her eye, but her choice of herbs was limited in winter.

She was pleased Mouse and Jenna approved of Isabelle. It was important they all got along. Her little group was too small for confrontation. That could pull it apart. She thought of Patrick and his prickly behavior with the others. There would be a run-in soon if she didn't act now to pull his claws in.

She felt weary and a little lost herself. Running a young pack was exhausting. She looked around the narrow room with its rows of cots, bare walls, and meager personal possessions. It was not a home, and she hadn't a clue how to make it one. Jenna had worked wonders with the kitchen but seldom moved out of it. She was content in her domain and in sharing the comfort she'd created with others. Before Jenna arrived, the cookhouse was a wreck of a building. Not that Ren or any of the boys had cared.

"I have no idea what I'm doing," she murmured. "Why is this is so damn hard?"

Was she wrong to even try? What choice did she have? She

dreaded to think where Mouse or Jenna, or any of the others, would be without this place. Most likely dead.

Not many ferals survived on their own. They just didn't have the skills. With their humanity in meltdown and their wolven side spasming out of control, they were a danger to themselves and everything that crossed their path, if they even got as far as full transmutation. Like a robust cancer, the wolven contagion reproduced quickly at a cellular level throughout the host body. The human genome was supplanted by wolven DNA flushing through the cells, reprogramming them. Lycanthropy was a fragmentation of the human self at its cellular core, not some wild call of the moon. The body either re-oriented to the invading DNA or became totally apoptotic. If victims did survive this dismantling of their physiology, the psychological stresses of that first change usually tipped them over. It was survival of the fittest, both physically and mentally, and what made you the fittest was a strong pack. An Alpha with any gumption should be able to nurture her initiates through this torment. The old Garoul almanac sitting in her kitchen had been a lifeline for more than one of Ren's strays.

Ren glumly thought of her little pack and the various sad ways they had come to her. Isabelle, however, was a different matter altogether… She remembered the colors of the picnic blanket. The sweet smell of wine on Isabelle's breath as she leaned in to her for that first kiss. Isabelle's eyes widening as she realized Ren's intention. And that slight lift of her chin as she accepted. Ren's skin still goose-bumped as she recalled the thrill that had run through her on that first kiss. She had at last found her mate, but that was no excuse. No amount of isolation and loneliness could absolve what had happened.

Ren left the bunkhouse and its glum interior and made her way home. Explanations were due, and soon she would have to provide them—no matter what the consequences.

❖

Ren was greeted by the smell of home cooking. She found Isabelle at the kitchen table, gazing off into the distance.

"Hungry?" Ren nodded at the half-eaten steak in a pool of bloody gravy.

Isabelle snapped out of her reverie. "I didn't hear you come in. You move like a cat."

"You were daydreaming." Ren took the seat opposite. Isabelle looked over at her puzzled.

"I just realized something." She looked mournfully at her bloody plate. "I'm a vegetarian. I even asked Jenna for greens."

"Oh?" Ren was unsure how to tackle this. It was an opportune segue, but she hesitated to grab it.

"Yes," Isabelle said. "And suddenly I love meat? Rare meat? Really, really rare meat. The taste is…is fantastic." She cut another mouthful. "I don't know what's come over me."

"Maybe your body needs the protein." It did, lots of it. Ren was pleased with Isabelle's robust physiology. She was coping well.

"I cooked you one."

"Thank you." Ren grinned, pleased at the cozy domesticity and thoughtfulness.

"This is it." Isabelle pointed at her plate and its oozing contents. "I was so hungry I ate them both." Isabelle stared at her dolefully. "I don't understand it."

"Your body's expending a lot of energy to heal. It needs a ton of calories and proper nourishment." Ren shrugged, making light of it. "It's nature's way. You're an animal after all."

"Jenna said you work for the fisheries here." Isabelle's conversation changed direction. Ren smiled. Isabelle never missed an opportunity to ferret out some new information.

"Yeah. We're a satellite station for the Creeker hatchery. They have dozens of sites all over this area."

"A satellite station?"

"Yup. I'm heading down there now with the boys. Come along and I'll show you."

"Is that why you all live here in the middle of nowhere? You work for the hatchery?"

"The hatchery contract is only part-time. It brings in some extra money, but my main income is from my veterinary practice. I keep a summer surgery in the valley."

"And the young people working for you, Ren? Where do they come from?"

"They just drift in, mostly from Vancouver and a hundred other places in between. If there's enough work, then I offer them a bunk and a wage." She could tell by Isabelle's frown her story was not as easily swallowed as the last of the steak.

"What about Mouse? What happened to her parents?"

"I was a friend of her mother's. I never knew her father. He was long gone before Mouse was born. Mouse stayed with me when her mother became...became ill. We...lost her, and Mouse lives with me now. I'm her legal guardian." The words were curt and pain-filled, though she tried to hide it.

"Isn't she lonely way out here? What about school, or friends of her own age?"

"She gets home schooling and she has plenty of company."

"But she's so young—"

"Enough." Ren rose to her feet. "It's the way it is. This is the best place for her. It's her home." She realized she sounded sharp and tried to soften her words. "Are you ready to head down to the river?"

She was relieved when, after a moment's thought, Isabelle nodded and gracefully accepted.

❖

Ren's truck bounced over a mud track that was barely wider than the cab. They were hard on the tail of Patrick and Noah's truck. A steep incline of tight hairpin curves drove them deeper into the forest. Isabelle imagined they were being swallowed, sliding down an intestinal tract into the murky belly of the valley.

"What's the name of this valley?" she asked.

"The Singing Valley. And the river's called the Tearfell. It's a salmon race, and it's in the center of a conservation bioregion."

"The names sound so beautiful...and sad. I've often wondered how places got their names. There must be a sad story behind this place."

Ren looked sideways at her. "Local legend has it the ghosts of wolves gather here, and at night the valley is filled with their singing."

"That's spooky. What about the Tearfell?"

"Someone must have thought it was salty." Ren shrugged, disinterested.

"Filled with tears," Isabelle mused. The deeper they descended, the gloomier the surrounding forest became. It was a woebegone, claustrophobic place. The weak winter sun barely penetrated the tree canopy. The light that did manage to creep through was marbled gray, consumed by the shadows before it reached the forest floor.

They swerved around another wild bend and the track began to level out. Over the rattle of the engine Isabelle thought she could make out the splash of the nearby river.

"We're nearly there," Ren said. "The valley's about three miles wide and the Tearfell cuts from the northeast down to the coast. The water runs slower in this particular spot, so it's easier to collect the fish eggs and milk. Today it's running faster because of the thaw."

"Milk is the fish sperm, isn't it? I'm not going to ask how you collect that."

"Later, after the eggs hatch, they're brought back up here and we nurse the fry. That's what the channel is for. We rear pink salmon fry until they're big enough to head downstream."

"Does it hurt them? Collecting the eggs and milk?"

"The fish come here to breed, then die. We leave most to do it the natural way and collect from a few, just to be sure. They all die in the end. It's their destiny. Breed and die. But we can use their life cycle to monitor the coastal ecosystem. They are a fantastic species indicator for the health of the river and coastline."

"Poor fish. So more survive because of the harvesting?" Isabelle asked. The truck hit the level of the valley floor, and Isabelle saw they were headed for a clearing by the riverbank.

"They'll mature at sea and come back in a few years to this exact river to breed. We collect the brood stock annually. The pinks are mostly a sporting fish and we get a remit for how many we raise. The conservation side is for sockeye and coho. They're more susceptible to disease so we have to tag and monitor their populations carefully. There's a little less money in that, but to be honest, I'd do it for free anyway." Her love for the valley and its nature was apparent in the warmth and energy of her voice.

"So you collect the eggs and they're taken down to the hatchery and then the hatched fry are sent back so they can mature in the river they came out of?"

"Exactly."

Isabelle looked around her. "I feel like I know this area. At least some of the names sound familiar, like Singing Valley and Lonesome Lake."

Ren stiffened. "We're nowhere near Lonesome Lake. What put that in your head?" Her voice was flat and careful now, the previous energy muted with caution.

Isabelle shrugged and acted casual.

"Can't remember." She could hardly say she'd been ransacking the contents of Ren's suitcase and found a marked map.

"The Tearfell's a smaller tributary of the Old Ironshoe River. I guess when you stayed with your aunt Mary you visited some of these places. Parts of the Old Ironshoe are very touristy. You can water raft, and fish, and stuff."

Ren was trying hard to look nonchalant, but it was obvious Lonesome Lake was an off-topic subject for her. Maybe she was right, Isabelle pondered. Maybe she had visited these places and that was why the names were vaguely familiar. It made perfect sense. But the map proved that Lonesome Lake was important to Ren in a way that wasn't connected to hatchery work.

"Here we are. There's not much to see. It's a fairly basic setup."

The trucks pulled into parking spaces before a small lodge built onto the waterside. Patrick opened the lodge doors.

"What's in there?" Isabelle asked.

"Nets, temperature-controlled cold boxes, waders, all sorts of fishing gear." Ren and Isabelle followed the boys into the cabin. It was a work hut. Reams of nets hung across the roof beams. Plastic cold boxes were piled everywhere. It smelled of fish and disinfectant. Hosepipes, hooks, life jackets sat in rows. It was an orderly and efficient storage space.

"The different fish have different breeding seasons, so it's mostly year-round work. But there's not much to do in the winter." Ren made a quick inspection. "Looks good, boys," she said.

Noah and Patrick puffed up with the praise. Isabelle remembered the scolding they'd gotten earlier for the fox. This must be the make-up, she decided. At least Ren tried to keep a semblance of balance in managing them, but it was a strange setup. They seemed to worship her.

Again, Isabelle wondered how this little group had congregated here in the first place, especially if the work was only seasonal. Did they all go their separate ways later in the year, or stay and farm the upper slopes? When would her growing list of questions ever stop?

"How do you get the fish eggs down to the hatchery?" She had no idea how the system operated. Did they float them down the very river the brooding fish struggled to swim up? How ironic would that be?

"The hatchery plane comes for them," Noah said. He stood beside her pairing off a pile of mismatched rubber boots.

This was news. "Planes? I thought we were isolated."

"Nah. We have a courier service every couple of weeks or so, for provisions or to ferry people down the valley." He gave an easy smile at her confusion. "Jenna would bite my hand off if she didn't get her regular supply of Tootsie Rolls."

Isabelle was dumbfounded. Tootsie Rolls? Wasn't her car crash enough to merit a flight down to Bella Coola General? She'd lain for days in a hallucinogenic fever suffering brutal nightmares, to awaken with partial amnesia and a face like a prizefighter. Isabelle felt her temper begin to fray. Ren's whole attitude to her accident was far too cavalier.

"Where do the planes land?" she asked, keeping her voice calm. She needed to find out all she could from Noah. It was obvious Ren was not going to surrender the information.

"Over the ridge. There's a lake there." Noah had stopped work and edged a hip onto a stack on boxes. He seemed content to take a break and sit with her.

"What lake is that?" If the answer was Lonesome Lake, she was going to explode right then and there.

"The Black Knife. Jenna and me will take you swimming there in the summer. There are some great rocks to dive from." He gave her a huge, enthusiastic smile. "Jenna makes a killer picnic."

He assumes I'll be here in the summer? Isabelle dismissed the thought. She could mull over that little tidbit later. She was on to something more substantial here.

"Tell me about the plane. You mean it flies in and lands on the water? Like a float plane?" That sounded exciting.

"Yeah. Float planes. We got supplies coming in the next few days. Mostly medical stuff, right, Ren?"

Ren was poking about the cold boxes checking out the thermo

gauges, Patrick shadowing her every move. She grunted at Noah, not really listening.

Isabelle took advantage of her distraction. "Why do you need extra medical supplies?" she asked quietly. "Because Ren's a vet?"

"Sort of. Joey's accident used up masses of stuff. Ren went through almost all our stitching silk and saline pulling him back together. He looked like a rag doll by the time she'd done."

Isabelle felt a renewed twinge of anxiety. Joey hadn't been bragging when he said his wounds were from last week.

"What happened to him?" she asked, determined to lay at least one of her fears to rest. Had he been mauled? Accidentally shot? Fallen from a tree? What the hell had happened to him? It couldn't possibly have anything to do with her.

Noah gave a graceless laugh. "He forgot to look left and right before crossing the road," he said cryptically.

"Noah!" Ren called sharply. "I need you over here. Go over the inventory with Patrick. We need to replace several cold boxes. The thermostats are clouded."

She took Isabelle by the arm and guided her out of the lodge. "Come see the channel. Then we have to go. Jenna's invited us for dinner."

It was midafternoon and already the sun was dipping over the valley lip. The gloom deepened and the woodland around them became even more oppressive. What little light there was had almost disappeared. The valley floor would never see much sun, not even at the height of summer; it was too overgrown and crowded. The area they were standing in would be a mosquito pit on hotter days.

Ren led them toward her truck.

"We need to drive about half a mile along the riverbank to get to the channel." She raised her head and sniffed the air. Her skin glowed and her eyes narrowed. She seemed content; a new kind of vibrancy entered her step with the lowering light. It was almost imperceptible, but Isabelle was aware of the subtle changes and looked around for the source of Ren's excitement. Whatever it was, it eluded her.

"You never told me there was a plane."

"I didn't think to mention it," Ren answered. "Are you always this dogged?"

"Yes, I am. Especially when it's clear I could have gone to a hospital at any time."

"You had a fever, that was all. I took care of your stitches. You didn't need to go to a hospital. You were safe here."

"Ren, I whacked my head. I lost my memory. Jesus, doesn't that worry you?"

"It doesn't matter where you are, here or in a hospital ward, your memories will come back. It's best you're with me when they do."

"And why's that?"

Ren's fingers tightened on her arm. "Because I'm the one with all your answers."

"Oh, for God's sake. Then tell me."

"I can't. You don't know the questions yet."

The channel was a disappointing concrete trough, about thirty feet long and covered with a metal mesh to keep the birds out. Fresh river water constantly flushed through a series of end valves while the fry swam against the man-made current becoming bigger and stronger. Isabelle pressed against the wall and squinted at the brown fry squirming in their concrete prison. Her mind was on other things. She pushed away her annoyance at Ren and her riddles. It would get her nowhere. If she wanted answers she had to deduce them for herself. But it was interesting that a plane was arriving in the next couple of days. When it left she hoped to be on it.

A flash of blue caught her eye as a belted kingfisher dive-bombed into the river. An instant later it splashed free with a wriggling brown blob in its beak.

"Someone's caught his dinner," Ren murmured. "Maybe it's time we did the same."

"There goes a good reason all fish aren't reared in channels like this. Some have to be fodder for other species to survive." Isabelle pulled away from the channel wall. "I suppose that's easy for me to say, being on top of the food chain."

"Yes, I suppose you are now." Ren gave a wolfish grin and started back to the truck. "Come on. Let's go back."

Twilight cast a spectacular gloom over everything as they walked back to the truck. Unnerving, organic shadows crept out of the undergrowth. The headlights on Ren's truck were the only pinpoints of safety in the entire valley, and Isabelle was grateful for them as she clambered into the front cab. Singing Valley was a spooky place at night. She could see why there were ghost stories about it.

"Aren't the boys coming with us?" Isabelle asked.

"Later. They have other things to do."

"But it's getting dark," she said, looking around uneasily.

"Nighttime's the best time." Ren gunned the engine and began the steep drive back up the valley side.

Chapter Ten

E at your greens."

"I don't wanna," Mouse whined. "I hate greens. Why do I have to eat them? We never had greens before."

"Eat them," Ren roared across the table.

"Ren," Isabelle said. "Stop shouting at the child."

A quick glance around the dinner table told her everyone was uncomfortable. Jenna sat ramrod stiff, and Joey shifted uneasily in his chair. Mouse hung her head and sulked at her plate. Isabelle realized the discomfort was not at Ren's barked reprimand but rather her challenge to it. Her gaze swung full circle back to Ren, who stared at her in startled surprise.

"Well, you shouldn't," she said sternly. "She's just a child."

"She'll eat whatever Jenna gives her," Ren said in a quieter tone, but still a little disgruntled. An uneasy silence followed that Isabelle felt obliged to fill.

"Thank you for a lovely meal, Jenna." It had been a splendid meal and the third steak dinner Isabelle had eaten that day, much to her stomach's delight and her own surprise. She had wondered at the greens Jenna had managed to serve with the rich venison. All, except Mouse, had stoically munched their way through a bitter winter herb salad. Jenna must have gone foraging for her ingredients, and Isabelle more than appreciated the gesture. She warmed to Jenna's generous nature and was eager to show it.

Mouse pushed the last of her food around her plate until Ren lost patience with her again.

"You. Bed. Now." She pointed at the door. Mouse flung down her fork, and with a loud, tearful sniff, stomped out of the room.

GILL McKNIGHT

"She is one little alpha brat." Ren sighed as soon as the door slammed shut.

"Tell me." Jenna began to gather up the empty plates. "I'm the one teaching her math."

Joey rose from the table.

"Where are you going?" Ren asked. Joey flushed a violent red.

"It's my turn to babysit tonight," he mumbled. "I swapped so Jenna could hang with Noah."

"Who said you could swap the schedule?" Ren frowned. Now Jenna turned beet red.

"It's just until Joey's more mobile," she stammered. "I'll pay back the babysitting hours later, when he's better and wants to run—" Her sentence jerked to a stop at Ren's frown. Jenna threw a guilty glance toward Isabelle.

Isabelle felt sorry for the girl. She'd already suspected Jenna and Noah were an item. Her impatience with Ren grew. Why shouldn't the girl go meet her beau, though Lord knew what there was for them to do around here. Ren must have read her thoughts, for she grudgingly complied.

"Okay, you can swap tonight. But no more schedule switches without clearing it with me first. I need to know who's where, doing what."

Joey and Jenna exhaled in relief. Joey left to follow Mouse, and Jenna continued to clear the table.

"Let me help." Isabelle collected the dirty dishes. "Please let me wash up." She was trying desperately to smooth over Jenna's embarrassment.

"I'll get coffee." Ren stood. "With a shot of brandy. Jenna, you get going, we'll finish up." With a grateful smile Jenna untied her apron and headed for the door.

"What on earth is there for them to do around here?" Isabelle asked as she piled the sink full of dishes and ran the water.

"Plenty. Here, let me help." Ren took up a dish towel and began to dry as Isabelle washed.

Later they sat on the cookhouse porch and sipped brandy-laced coffee.

"The valley is magical at night." Ren sounded content.

A plaintive howl echoed from the forest below, and Isabelle

shivered under her thick jacket. "The valley sounds dangerous. It's the mountains that are magical." She gazed at the circle of snowy peaks; they glowed against the velvet night sky.

Another howl rent the night air.

"God, listen to that. Will they be all right out there?" Isabelle asked nervously.

"That wolf is miles away. The acoustics of the valley make it sound closer." A chorus of howls answered the first cry, and for a moment the whole valley resonated with the eerie melody. "Sounds like a party."

"I can see why it's called the Singing Valley." Isabelle settled back in her seat and watched the tip of the waxing moon balance delicately on a distant mountain ridge. The sky was cloudless and the night air crisp and sharp. A million stars swathed the heavens above them in expansive swirls of design.

"It's beautiful here." Isabelle's breath escaped in little misty puffs. "I wish I knew the constellations."

"See that W shape?" Ren pointed overhead. "That's Cassiopeia. And right up there, Ursa Major, or the Big Dipper." She continued to point while Isabelle struggled to see what she was actually pointing at.

"Wait. What W shape?"

A cry from the bunkhouse brought Ren to her feet before Mouse's scream had even registered with Isabelle. By the time Isabelle stood, Ren was already halfway across the yard, running for the other building. Isabelle chased after her. She arrived at the bunkhouse in time to see Ren bend over a tearful Mouse. She was sitting in her bunk crying and had obviously woken from a nightmare. Isabelle was full of sympathy. She'd suffered enough nightmares to last a lifetime.

"What is it?" Joey hobbled in bare-chested from the washroom. Toothpaste rimmed his mouth.

"Just a bad dream." Ren lay Mouse back down and tucked the blankets up under her chin. "It's okay, Mouse."

"It's under the bed." Mouse kicked the blankets off again and sat up.

"What is?" Ren asked.

"The vampire." Mouse was very determined to exit a bed that had a vampire under it. "I was sleeping and it touched my arm and I screamed and it vanished."

"Vampire?" Ren glared over at Joey. He went chalk white. "Have you been showing her those stupid comics again?"

"No, Ren. Honest." He backed up a little.

"Ren. No more shouting, please." Isabelle went over and gathered Mouse in her arms. She perched on the edge of the bed and cuddled her on her lap. Mouse burrowed into her. Although her tears had stopped, she was still upset.

"There's nothing under the bed, honey," Isabelle said.

"There is. I saw it."

"You saw it? Under the bed? Goodness." Isabelle sounded suitably surprised.

"Uh-huh."

"Nonsense. There's no such thing as vampires. I told you before." Ren said.

"Ren." Isabelle looked over Mouse's head. "Check under the bed, please."

"What?"

"Check under the bed. Mouse says she saw a vampire, and I want you to check."

"You want me to look under the bed?" Ren was astounded.

"Yes, please," Isabelle said calmly. "If a vampire is stupid enough to come into this bunkhouse and hide under Mouse's bed, I want you to find it and give it a pounding it never forgets. Better still, it tells all its friends that Singing Valley is off-limits to vampires unless they want a pounding, too."

With a puff of exasperation, Ren bent on one knee and dipped her head to look under the bed.

"There's nothing there."

She stood and looked at Mouse curled up on Isabelle's lap. Her face held a strange expression that Isabelle found impossible to read.

"See, honey. There's no monsters under there," Isabelle murmured into Mouse's sweaty hair. "Vampires are afraid of Ren. They know she'd chase them away."

"Yes, she would. She'd bite them bad." Mouse mulled over this new logic. It seemed to calm her. She still clung to Isabelle's neck. Isabelle rubbed her thin little back with big, soothing circles. She liked comforting Mouse. Mouse needed hugs.

"Of course she would. And then there's Joey, and Jenna, and

Noah, and Patrick, too. Think about it. A vampire would never come here. They'd bash him good. You're safe here, Mouse. This is the safest place in the whole world."

"There are no such thing as vampires," Ren stated again, frustration in her voice.

"And even if there were, you've got bigger teeth." Mouse sounded cheerful. "You'd bite them to pieces."

"But there are no such things," Ren grated out.

"I swear I never showed her no comics, Ren," Joey said, fretfully. "It's just a silly dream you're having, Mouse."

"Of course there are no such things as monsters, but it doesn't stop us from having bad dreams about them," Isabelle said. She remembered the vague, black blurs with slick yellow eyes of her own nightmares. "Let's get you all tucked up." She deposited Mouse back in bed and pulled the blankets over her.

"Can I go out and play tonight?" Mouse pleaded, her eyes big brown pools over the rim of the blanket. Isabelle was stunned. One moment the little girl was terrified of monsters under her bed, the next she wanted to go play in the forest at nighttime?

"No, you cannot." Ren and Isabelle answered simultaneously, word for word. They glanced at each other in surprise.

"But I'm scared. I want to go running," Mouse began to whine. "Joey can come with me."

"Joey will be in the bed right next to yours." Ren pointed at the bed and Joey shuffled into it double quick.

"Now get to sleep, the both of you," Ren ordered. "Mouse, it's way too late for you to be up, and Joey, take your meds and get an early night. I'll need you to be a hundred percent soon."

"Sure thing, Ren." He radiated a new confidence under Ren's attention.

"Good man." Ren nodded.

Mouse's complaints trailed away and were replaced with yawns as Isabelle tucked her in and settled her for the night.

"Sweet dreams, guys," she called softly before closing the bunkhouse door behind them.

"Does Mouse have many nightmares?" she asked once they were outside.

"She sneaks peeks at the boys' horror comics and it frightens the bejesus out of her," Ren muttered. "I've told them not to leave that stuff lying around, but no one listens."

"Oh, somehow I think they do."

Rather than go back to the cookhouse, Ren took the path to her cabin. Isabelle fell into step beside her.

"No, they don't, unless I get mad. Then everybody runs round like a hangdog for weeks."

"It's what kids do," Isabelle said.

"Is it?"

"Yes. They push to see how far they can go. Test the boundaries." It seemed obvious to Isabelle that the kids adored Ren.

"Why do you collect them, Ren?" she asked.

"What do you mean?"

"I mean it's more than just giving a few drifter kids seasonal work. You've got some sort of project going on here. What's going on? These kids seem…vulnerable. Damaged even."

"Damaged?" Ren halted. She stood stock-still, waiting for Isabelle to clarify.

"Yes. Emotionally damaged." Isabelle was not going to be shy with her answer. "They all crave love and attention. And they all adore you. I mean, look at Noah, or Patrick even. They're both so insecure in themselves and struggle so hard not to show it. And Jenna, she tries her hardest to please. Joey would do anything for anyone who had a kind word for him. And as for Mouse, she's just begging for love and cuddles."

Ren's shoulders sagged and she continued her uphill path.

"What's wrong?" Isabelle followed, concerned at Ren's dejection. "I didn't mean to be hurtful. Ren?" But Ren was striding ahead.

"Ren?" Isabelle grabbed her by the arm to slow her down. "Stop speeding away and talk to me. What did I say that upset you?"

"Nothing."

"It's hardly nothing."

Ren turned to face her. "It's just that I can't do those things."

"What things?"

"The things that make it all right. That take away the insecurities and give reassurance and…cuddles."

"Anybody can cuddle."

"I can't tell them it will be all right because I don't know that myself."

"Know what will be all right?"

Ren shrugged impatiently and moved away again "I don't know. Life. The future. Everything."

"Nobody knows those things."

"I should. I should be able to help them more." She strode off, leaving Isabelle to chase after her.

"I think you're beating yourself up here. This valley, this home you've made." Isabelle waved at the outbuildings on the slope below them. "Even the seasonal work you supply, these are the *beginnings* of security, the start of a future. I don't know where these kids have come from, or the stories each one carries. But I do know this is a safe place for them, and you made it that way."

Ren hesitated and looked at the buildings and the valley beyond. Another howl wavered out from the far side of valley, an empty, forlorn cry.

"Maybe," she said, but her words sounded flat, as if she had no faith in them. "But it's not enough. It's never enough."

"Never enough what?"

"Everything. Money, hope, work…everything. We're running out of time. The kids are ill. I can't help them all—It doesn't matter. I shouldn't be dumping all this on you. You have enough to contend with." Ren swung away, seemingly determined to put distance between herself and the conversation.

"Well, they have some work lined up for the hatchery. *And* a roof over their heads, *and* food in their bellies. That's a good start. In fact, it's a great start." Isabelle was damned if she'd let Ren wallow in misguided self-pity, no matter how good moodiness looked on her. As an outsider she had fresh eyes and could see this setup for what it was. It upset her that Ren should be so negative about all she had accomplished.

"And starting is always the hardest part, so what comes next should be easy." She continued her encouragement.

"What? What comes next?" Ren stopped dead, sounding alarmed.

"This comes next." Isabelle stepped in and wrapped her arms around Ren's waist and hugged her.

Ren's long body froze ramrod stiff in her arms, but Isabelle refused to be fazed and tightened her hold. Her ear was pressed against a rapid heartbeat and her head swam with the heat pounding off Ren's body in time with her heart's rhythm.

Isabelle closed her eyes and was lost in the hot scent of Ren's hair, skin, clothes. She squeezed tight and was rewarded by a low growl reverberating in the chest beneath her ear. It ran on and on like an engine purring, until the long muscles of Ren's back at last relaxed and their bodies melted together. Isabelle felt giddy, greedy for the connection. Ren's arms wrapped loosely around her in an awkward return hug. It added a million times to Isabelle's bliss. She could have stood there forever, simply holding Ren, listening to that deep rumble from somewhere close by her heart.

"See. You do know how to cuddle," she whispered.

Reluctantly, she pried herself away and gave Ren's arm a half-hearted, platonic pat. Isabelle stepped back on slightly wobbly legs and tried to regain some composure.

"You're lying to yourself about those kids, Ren," she said, taking the lead on the cabin track. "They're happy here. They've found a home. And you're one good human being."

Chapter Eleven

Isabelle scuffed along the hallway in the oversized sweats and socks Ren had left out for her as sleepwear. She didn't care that she could wrap the top around herself twice, it was cuddly and warm, and the cabin was chilly.

Isabelle wondered how long Ren would stay with her this evening, if she would head out to tend to her mysterious veterinary patients. No matter what Ren chose to do, Isabelle was going to light the fire and curl up on the couch with a good book and a glass of wine. It would have been nice to have Ren's company, but she didn't expect it. Ren was elusive. They'd have to talk about Isabelle leaving the valley, and soon. She hoped to be on the next plane out.

She headed for the bathroom and pushed open the unlocked door before registering the splash of running water. Ren stood under the shower, water cascading down her lean, tan body. Isabelle stopped, unable to either enter or withdraw.

In her mind, she played out the logical, social conclusion to the scenario before her. She'd say, "Oh, pardon me. I didn't know you were in here," and would turn around and leave. Or perhaps Ren would turn off the faucet and pull a towel around her, and say, "It's okay. I'm done anyway," and she would leave, with a cheery smile. Isabelle's barging in on her would be a silly, embarrassing moment…nothing they couldn't deal with.

Instead, Isabelle was rooted to the spot watching soapy water run down Ren's long legs. Her body was powerful and muscular. Her hair was plastered to her back and shoulders, and several jagged scars showed through the wet tendrils. Proprietary lust shot through Isabelle, increasing her heart rate. It knotted her stomach and made her tongue tingle and her jaw tighten.

Ren turned and smiled, totally at ease.

"Are you joining me?" she said with a teasing glint in her eye.

"Uh…" Isabelle's cheeks burned. Her feet were cemented to the bathroom floor, while her brain struggled for words of apology for her intrusion.

Ren turned off the faucet and stepped from the stall. Dripping water, she walked naked across the bathroom floor and slid past Isabelle, making sure their shoulders bumped.

"It's okay. I'm done anyway," she said, and with a sly, crooked smile, she left.

"Uh…" Isabelle mumbled at the steamed-filled room.

Her body was still buzzing when she returned to the living room to light the fire. She cursed her stupidity in the bathroom, and then cursed Ren for teasing her. She hated the emotional vulnerability she felt around Ren. It seemed to permeate every layer of her existence… well, as much as she knew of it.

Ren had rescued her, nursed her through a serious injury. Alluded to a caring relationship that Isabelle could not remember but sort of felt. And how could she deny the sexual tension that had coiled in her gut from that possessive first kiss to her practically slavering over the woman while she showered? Isabelle's face flamed.

She knelt by the fireplace, glad of a chore to take her mind off her salacious and highly inappropriate thoughts. It would take a little while, but she would soon have the cabin snug and cozy and make it a perfect little haven for her to while away another lonely evening.

She raked out the dead fire embers. Ren had done a very poor job of cleaning the hearth.

"I'm surprised she ever gets a fire to light if this is her idea of clearing out the ash," she muttered.

She hesitated. Wedged behind a charred log, in the far corner of the grate, lay the book Patrick had burned last night. Isabelle could just make out the word "Toyota" on the melted plastic cover. These were car papers. She reached for the booklet. Its innards fell away from the twisted plastic. They were badly scorched and unreadable. A few pages came away and clung to her fingertips like filmy cobwebs, the ink a spider's scrawl. *Her* car papers! It had to be. Burned last night before her very eyes. What the hell was going on?

Her hands came away blackened with ash and she remembered Ren's sooty fingerprints all over the kitchen this morning. Ren hadn't been cleaning the fireplace; she'd been rummaging among these burned remains. What had she been up to? Checking that the book was properly destroyed? Isabelle seethed at the deceit. *How dare she destroy my stuff?*

The door opened and Ren walked in, dressed in old sweats, her damp hair clinging to her shoulders. The pages in Isabelle's hand exploded to dust in the draft of air that followed her. Isabelle looked at the ashy fragments in disbelief. She couldn't believe it; all the evidence was gone before she'd had a chance to examine it.

"Hey. I was going to light the fire for us." Ren squatted on her heels beside her. She began to gather up kindling. "Look at your hands. They're black with soot. Go wash and let me finish this."

Isabelle stared at her.

"Why was Patrick burning my car papers?" she said.

"What?" Ren's whole posture stiffened, though she still bundled kindling into the fire grate as if nothing untoward was happening.

"He burned my car documents last night. Right before my eyes, like I was some kind of idiot. And you told him to. I heard you just before I came into the room. You told him to burn them, and he did." She could feel fury frothing up inside her. She had been trying so hard to piece together what little she knew. Running all over the place like a fool looking for clues, when all along they had been burning them right in front of her. How they must have laughed.

Ren looked from Isabelle's soot-black hands to the ashes in the hearth. She continued assembling the fire, her actions automatic, her face a mask.

"Your car papers?" She tossed a match into the grate. The paper and kindling caught with a whoosh, the fire glow bathed her features and blazed across her eyes.

"*My* documents. Mine!" Isabelle gave Ren a mighty shove and sent her rolling off her haunches and onto her backside on the floor.

Ren growled and twisted back up, but Isabelle launched herself at her, throwing them both back onto the floor.

"You bastard, you burned them." She boiled over with rage, even as part of her looked on from afar, aghast at this loss of control. Ren's arms wrapped round her, easily pinning her to her chest. "You played me for a fool."

"I don't know what you're talking about," Ren said, unperturbed.

"You said burn it and he did." Isabelle tried to work herself free. She regretted her outburst now and wanted distance. Ren's closeness made her even more agitated.

"I don't know what you're talking about," Ren said again. "I didn't tell him to burn your papers." Her attempts at reasoning only made Isabelle more determined to get away. "Stay still. Isabelle, stop fighting me."

It was too much for Isabelle. She couldn't corral or control this violent emotion. It shrieked through her like a banshee, rattling every bone in her body. Ren's scent swamped her, seductive and dangerous. The heat of her body pulsed through their clothes, more urgent than when they had curled in bed together naked. Isabelle hissed in frustration at being thwarted yet again. How was she to ever know who she was if they kept hiding things, and burning things, and not answering her questions?

The neck of Ren's shirt pulled open, revealing her strong column of throat and the muscular sweep from her collarbone to her breastbone. Her skin was tanned, the rise of her chest lacerated with small raised scars.

Isabelle struggled futilely against the arms around her. Her nose burrowed in the scented heat of Ren's chest. Her mouth brushed the mesh of scars and her lips tingled. Saliva flooded her mouth. She bared her teeth and grazed along Ren's skin. The chest muscles twitched and bunched at her touch. Ren smelled of forest ferns after rainfall, earthy and rich. She smelled of sunlight on warm fur, and spring glades carpeted with salmonberry and Indian plum.

Isabelle buried her face deeper, soaking up the scent. She licked the skin stretched tight across Ren's sternum. And then she bit. She bit down hard, lathering the captured skin with her tongue and growling deep in her throat like an animal.

Ren bucked beneath her, then lay still, her hold slackening.

Isabelle worried at the skin and sucked hard, her initial growl becoming a contented rumble. She was fully focused in marking the flesh, in claiming these old scars and all that history for herself. Ren's skin was plump and hot with a salty sheen. The taste exploded in her mouth.

Ren eased her hold and ran her hands down the curve of Isabelle's back.

"Do you know what you're doing?" she asked quietly. Her hands rested on Isabelle's hips, as if undecided whether to hold on to her or toss her aside at any moment.

Isabelle reluctantly surrendered her mouthful of flesh. She didn't know what she was doing. She kept her head lowered, her eyes fixed on the redness spreading across Ren's chest. Her spittle covered the indents of her teeth marks. A bruise was already beginning to form. She panted lightly with a mixture of shame and delirious excitement. Her face reddened until it burned painfully. She had bitten Ren...actually *bitten* her. *God, I must have rabies or something.* She was a sad, sick woman.

Ren rolled Isabelle onto her back on the floor and rose over her on all fours, bringing her face close until they were nose-to-nose. She was breathing heavily. Her eyes sparked sharply, like shards of crystal. Tendrils of damp hair as cold as mermaid's fingers brushed Isabelle's face. Isabelle could see the tremors running through Ren's shoulders and down along her arms. Her mouth felt empty, her tongue and teeth useless—all of her was hollow. This was more than a need to bite Ren. She wanted to taste and take, to break the skin, to find a way inside and stay there.

"Do you know what you're doing?" Ren asked her again, quietly.

Isabelle didn't know what she was doing or what was happening to her. She was acting on an innate directive that drove her from within. In answer, she reached up and bunched her hands in Ren's long, wet mane, and taking great fistfuls, pulled Ren that last inch closer and kissed her.

Isabelle wasn't exactly sure why she felt compelled to start the kiss, but a microsecond later she was sure of one thing. She had no idea what to do. *Maybe I'm not a lesbian after all?* Yet here she was, glued to the face of a woman she had grabbed by the hair, bitten, and forced to kiss her. It didn't get much more Neanderthal than that.

And now, with the texture of Ren's lips on hers, all her earlier exasperation and anger drained away. There was only this exquisite pressure and heat.

How come their mouths fit so well together, yet apart looked so different? Hers with its thin upper lip and little scar, and Ren's, so full and heavy, like lazy, overripe summer berries. The soft flesh of her plump lower lip was silky smooth. Isabelle darted the tip of her tongue along the velvety inner surface. Ren groaned, and Isabelle's confidence surged, so she deepened the kiss until she drowned in it. She felt dizzy, and swamped and swirled in all directions; spun out like fine thread until she snapped. Her only hope was to find something solid and hang on to it. So she clung to Ren.

Realizing Ren was letting her lead the kiss, she became braver, sucking on that luscious lower lip and trailing her hands across Ren's shoulders and down her back. Her fingers twitched, fighting the urge to dig her nails in and mark. Her kiss deepened, she became hungrier, more demanding. She wanted it all, more, and more again—

"Enough," she said, breaking the kiss. Isabelle lay staring into the flushed face above her. Ren stared back, her gaze brooding and unfathomable.

"It will never be enough," Ren said.

Isabelle shivered at the finality in the words. They were devastating in their truth. She began to wriggle out from under Ren, acutely aware of the chill once their bodies parted. She wasn't sure how to respond to those words, so she threw herself into denial.

"I don't know why I grabbed you like that. I'm sorry." Her gaze dropped to the red mark on Ren's chest, just over her heart, and her shame and confusion deepened. "I'm…I'm so sorry I bit you. I…" She had no excuse. She had no idea why she'd done it.

Ren cupped her face and drew their gaze level.

"Never be ashamed of that," she said. "It's what makes us."

Her lips grazed the fluttering pulse of Isabelle's throat. Isabelle's hands came up to mesh in her hair as Ren's mouth moved over her.

"I know something about you." Isabelle lifted her chin to be nuzzled. Ren's lips rested over her thumping pulse.

"Oh?" she murmured into the flesh. "And what's that?"

Isabelle's kiss had sucked the very life out of her. Now Ren hovered over her, a quivering wreck, barely holding her weight on her elbows.

Her body grazed the length of Isabelle's and heat pulsed between them. Ren's mouth flooded with so much need it burned her tongue.

Isabelle gave an incoherent moan as Ren's lips found another sweet spot. Ren's jaw muscles bunched and tightened as she struggled to keep her muzzle down. The tightness in her face warned her how close she was to changing. Her feet were boiling hot—cramped and aching in her shoes—another sign her wolfside wanted to rise.

"You know something?" she asked again, her lips moved over Isabelle's silky throat. She darted the tip of her tongue out to taste. Isabelle tasted fresh and clean, like juniper, or new-mown hay. A delicious scent, but Ren was anxious now. What did Isabelle know?

"Uh-huh." Isabelle nodded. Ren waited. The time would soon come when the werefever would pass and Isabelle's mind would clear of its protective fog. This brought a new kind of misery for the unprepared.

"What do you know?" Her voice tightened as the beast inside struggled to take control.

"I know you can't lie. At least not to me. You can evade my questions, and you do, wonderfully well. You can even get angry and bang out of the room to avoid answering, but you never lie."

"I can't lie to you," Ren said, wary of where this was leading. Isabelle had already surprised her with her resourcefulness. She was a sneaky little thing, determinedly digging away for information. A true tracker. Ren was well aware the whole cabin had been tastefully ransacked the minute she'd walked out the door.

Her lips trailed to a spot under Isabelle's ear where her pulse fluttered delicately. Isabelle squirmed delightfully under her. A low growl rumbled in Ren's chest. She was enthralled by Isabelle's scent, stupefied by it, and happily uncaring because she knew Isabelle was becoming sensitive to her scent, too. Soon their scents would trigger each other. Soon they would bond so tight there would be nothing else.

"You know all my best places." Isabelle sighed. Ren nipped gently along Isabelle's jaw and buried her nose in her hair to breathe in more of her.

"All your places are best," she said. She could lie with her face in Isabelle's hair all day.

"Why did you tell Patrick to burn my papers?"

Ah, back to that then. "I didn't."

"I heard you tell him to."

"You did *not* hear me tell him to burn your documents."

Isabelle stared at her for a long time, her blue eyes glinting through the bruising. Ren smiled inwardly at the scouring gaze, almost afraid to blink in case she somehow endorsed her supposed criminality. She held the stare, amused and proud at Isabelle's audacity and perseverance. She was a determined problem solver, which could either bode well or ill for her, depending on the strength of Isabelle's patience. If she took her time and trusted Ren, then she would make the jump to her new life easily. But that was the problem. Ren knew that deep down. Isabelle didn't trust her. Oh, she wanted to. Ren could feel her trying hard. But in the end, Ren had to earn her trust all over again, and she willingly accepted that.

"What happened to Joey?" The next question came fast.

"Joey had a hunting accident."

"How? What happened?"

"I wasn't there at the time."

This was dangerous ground. Ren took a calming breath, but inside she struggled for clarity. She began to untangle herself and move away. Isabelle had a way of clouding her senses, and she had to stay alert while being bombarded with these types of questions.

"Oh no you don't." Isabelle grabbed at her and spun them over so she now lay on top. A pleasurable growl rumbled in Ren's chest. Isabelle's bite still stung and Ren was lusty from it. In other circumstances they'd be crashing around the floor, sending furniture spinning. But not yet. Isabelle was still too weak and Ren had to be careful with her.

"Don't run away from me, Ren," Isabelle said, her fingers fluttering against Ren's cheek. Behind the cuts and bruises Ren saw uncertainty in her eyes, and her heart constricted. It should never have been like this.

"I won't." She gazed up into eyes as sharp as a spring sky. *We should have had a proper courtship.* The thought flew into her head and crushed her. Ren would have loved to woo Isabelle, to steadily and surely win her, instead of living this…this mockery. "It's you who'll leave me," she said.

The words came out before Ren could censor them. Inwardly, she squirmed at such a maudlin premonition. It had been her growing fear every day since Isabelle arrived.

Isabelle's eyes darkened. She opened her mouth to speak, but no words came. Instead, she held Ren's gaze and lowered her head until their lips touched. Then she whispered against them, her breath exhaling into Ren's mouth, "I have to."

Chapter Twelve

Her appalling truth hung between them. Nothing she could do would diminish the sting of her words. Her mouth cupped Ren's in a deepening kiss. As if she could shield them from their sadness. Ren's arms wrapped around her, her grip tight, almost panicked, and Isabelle knew her blow had landed hard. She could never take back those words, so she closed her eyes and poured her regret into the kiss.

When she opened her eyes again, Ren was staring back. Her eyes shone like wet obsidian, every emotion flickered across their surface. Isabelle's heart caught. She had never been looked at that way, with such yearning, yet challenge. The intensity froze her. These were hunter's eyes, impossible to break away from. Ren reached up and cupped her face.

"When you leave I will follow you. I *will* find you. Every breeze will carry your scent. Every bent blade of grass, every rustling leaf will betray you. I will hunt you, and I will find you, and I will keep you. You are mine."

Ren's kiss was not hesitant or proper. She held Isabelle's head in her hands and ravished her mouth. A growl resonated deep in her throat, making Isabelle tingle through to her backbone. Ren crouched over her. Her curtain of hair delicately flowed over Isabelle's face and throat. Isabelle buried her fingers in its damp silkiness and twisted great fistfuls. Their eyes locked, bold and daring. Isabelle gave an extra tug, pulling hard. She bared her teeth in a sly smile. Ren was hers, too.

Ren's growl rumbled with pleasure at the display. Her eyes glittered and her white teeth flashed from behind blood-red lips. With a throaty growl she covered Isabelle. Her fingers traced the nape of neck and throat. She followed the trail of her fingertips with a burning tongue. Her fingers hooked in Isabelle's shirt collar and she tore it apart and licked the revealed flesh. Isabelle's small breasts quivered; her nipples hardened. She released her hold on Ren's hair and clawed the shirt off her back with grunting satisfaction.

Bare-chested, they rubbed against each other. Isabelle ran her hands over Ren's scars.

"These are beautiful," she murmured and run her tongue across the ridges on Ren's chest, across her own mark. She practically purred with content. And then, she froze as a sudden anger flashed through her. She glared at Ren.

"These marks. Did other lovers make them?" Her voice was acid.

Ren laughed. "No. These are a collection of scars from all the beasts I've helped. I do dangerous work." Her smile showed her amusement at Isabelle's irrational jealousy.

Isabelle tensed. She was not jealous by nature, but the thought of Ren with other lovers enraged her. It seemed her placid nature was changing.

Ren lowered her mouth and captured a nipple, rolling it between her teeth, and all Isabelle's jealousy evaporated. Ren worshipped Isabelle's breasts with her tongue and teeth until they were swollen and glistened with her saliva and the areolas puckered hard. Isabelle murmured in disappointment when her mouth moved away, and then Ren was kissing the soft skin of her stomach, all the way down to her navel where her tongue dipped in ticklish curiosity. Isabelle kicked off her shoes and pants and helped drag off Ren's clothes. Their legs and arms entwined as they locked against each other.

Ren pushed her thigh between Isabelle's and kissed a track from Isabelle's jumping pulse down to the valley between her breasts. Isabelle bore down, rolling her hips until Ren's thigh was wet with her excitement. Ren slid down her body to tease her navel, dipping her tongue in the salty indentation until Isabelle's belly quivered with each touch. Her hands knotted in Ren's hair, guiding her lower, demanding attention where she needed it most.

Isabelle took command and raised her hips, offering herself up. She gasped when Ren's dark head plunged onto her sex. Ren dove on the tender folds and ground her lips onto them, plundering with a thick, hungry tongue. She nuzzled and sucked on the plump clitoris as Isabelle rose to meet her. She laved her in long, firm strokes, driving Isabelle relentlessly toward orgasm. Her hair was pulled, her shoulders scratched as Isabelle cried out. Every molecule of her body centered on her—and then exploded in a tidal wave of pure, white heat. Her core melted and blew off a dozen pyrotechnics.

Isabelle lay dazed, panting at the ceiling as Ren crawled up her body. An enormous smile played across Ren's lips, and Isabelle could smell her own scent on Ren's face and hair. She gathered her into her arms and held her. Isabelle struggled for words but failed to find any. She was incapable of speech. Ren nuzzled her neck and across to her injured shoulder. Carefully, she pulled away the bandage. Isabelle twisted her head to see the curved row of scabby stitches. She was pleased they were healing well. Ren put her mouth to the wound and kissed it. Isabelle relaxed, a satisfied smile on her lips. The kiss became a deep, burning bite. Isabelle screamed as molten lead poured through muscle, then bone. Darkness enfolded her and nausea rolled through her in lurching waves. Then Ren let go of the bite and pulled her close, just as Isabelle thought she might pass out.

Seconds later, she felt a wet kiss on her ear and smelled her blood and sex on Ren's breath.

"You bit me," Isabelle managed to gasp. Was it revenge for her earlier bite?

"I love you," Ren murmured in Isabelle's ear. "Now we're bonded. You are mine."

"You bit me," Isabelle said again, still disbelieving.

"And you bit me. Ask yourself why."

"I don't know why."

"Soon you'll understand. And then you'll stay forever."

Ren gathered Isabelle in her arms and carried her to bed.

"Beep beep," Mouse called, and ruthlessly revved the throttle of her junior quad bike.

"What have you got there?" Isabelle emerged from the cabin. She stood on the top porch step and looked suitably impressed at Mouse astride her DayGlo pink quad.

"This is mine," Mouse said. "Ren got me it for Christmas. But the horn's broke. Joey's gonna fix it for me now."

"It's fantastic."

"Come on. There's one for you, too. Joey says you can borrow his so I can show you around. Follow me." Mouse did a nifty U-turn and scooted back down to the barn. Intrigued, Isabelle followed on foot. This was a welcome turn of events in what could have been a boring day. The morning air was chill but promised a brighter afternoon. She had awoken energized, her shoulder bruised but otherwise painless from Ren's bite. A quick shower and a glance in the bathroom mirror showed her face was a healthy color and her eyes were brighter. She buzzed. She was alive. Ren loved her, and she was reeling from it.

Joey was waiting for her beside a much larger beast. His quad was the adult version, and looked bulkier and more threatening with its black paintwork and glowing wolf eyes on the front fenders. Isabelle approached, unsure if this was a good idea after all.

"It's easy," he said as soon as she was settled on the seat. "Look. Clutch. Brake. And this little lever here lets you change gears, and if you need to reverse use this lever here."

"Okay."

"Oh, and the lights don't work, but you won't need them."

It seemed simple enough. She circled the yard a few times, becoming more and more confident while Joey worked on the wiring for Mouse's horn.

"Are we ready to go now?" Mouse had been champing at the bit to get under way. Now that Isabelle looked semi-competent, she was anxious for their adventure to begin.

"It depends where you're taking me, Mouse," Isabelle answered. "Nowhere dangerous...or too steep." Considering they were perched on the slope of a valley, maybe that was a silly request. "Or where we reverse a lot."

"I'm gonna show you the biggest tree in the whole world!"

"Wow. That I'd love to see."

"It is *not* the biggest tree in the whole world," Joey said. Isabelle dropped him a wink and he brightened that they shared a joke.

"It's only about a mile and a half away. It's not like an expedition," he said.

"It is so," Mouse piped up, outraged at being contradicted. "It's an expedition to the biggest tree in the whole forest, so there."

"If it's half as big as your butt, then it ain't far off." Joey gurgled with laughter at his joke. Mouse stuck her tongue out at him and turned her attention on Isabelle.

"You ready? Follow me." And she took off with a long, loud beep, not waiting to see if Isabelle was ready or not.

"Hey! Wait up." Jenna came out of the cookhouse waving frantically. Isabelle waited as she approached with a small satchel. "I made you a picnic of sorts, considering it's far from picnicking weather. I packed a few cans of soda, some beef sandwiches, and a flask of hot soup."

"What a great idea. Thank you, Jenna." Isabelle shrugged the straps over her shoulders.

"Make sure she eats something. She gets too excited and forgets." Jenna nodded in the direction Mouse had taken. A loud series of beeps said Mouse had realized Isabelle was not right behind her as ordered.

"I'll do my best." With a huge smile, Isabelle released the brake and took off slowly after Mouse. Her smile remained for a long time. These little instances of kindness and inclusion made her feel more and more welcome.

Mouse was waiting for her around the next bend. She sat revving her quad at a branch in the trail. When she saw Isabelle catching up, she took off again along a different track from the one Isabelle and Ren had taken to the river. This track went east and kept high, while the other went down to the river and the hatchery lodge.

On the higher track the views were spectacular, and Isabelle would have dearly loved to find a place to dismount and enjoy them. Mouse was unconcerned with the panorama and pressed on at a daredevil pace Isabelle found hard to keep up with.

After about a mile a clearing appeared. It was big enough for a large vehicle to swing around in, and from the look of the cut-up ground, it was in frequent use. Isabelle scrambled to locate her horn and beeped a few times to catch Mouse's attention before tucking her quad in off the track. She dismounted and stretched, taking in the wonderful view down into the heart of the valley.

"What's wrong?" Mouse pulled up beside her.

"I'm old, and the trail's bumpy."

"You got numb bum." Mouse glared at the offending body part.

"Let's have a soda break." Isabelle reached into the knapsack. Perhaps a cold drink would cool Mouse's heels. "It's not like we're having a race."

Mouse's eyes lit up. "Can we? Later? Joey always races me and I always win. And it's not because he lets me or anything, it's because he sucks."

"As long as you give me a head start."

"Deal." Mouse leapt from her bike and popped the soda can.

"It's beautiful up here." Isabelle sighed. Mouse responded with loud slurping and a small burp.

"'Scuse me."

Isabelle wandered over to the edge of the clearing to peep into the surrounding woods and found the start of a well-trodden trail. It was narrow enough for one person to move along it and dipped steeply until it disappeared from view altogether.

"Where does that go?" she asked Mouse.

"To the skinning hole."

Isabelle pulled a face at the ugly name. Mouse obliged her with an explanation.

"It's where Ren wants the carcasses skinned. No smellies are allowed near the farm. It brings in other animals."

"Ah." It made sense to Isabelle. The clearing must have been created so deer carcasses could be carted in, skinned and prepped off-site, and then transported back to Jenna's cold room for storage. That surprised her. From the coagulated blood on the cold store floor, Isabelle assumed the meat had been prepared there.

"Can we take a look?" she asked. Mouse shook her head.

"Ren won't like it. I'm not allowed to go there. Someone has to be with me."

"I'm with you."

"Pffh. Not you. One of the others." Mouse guffawed. "Well… maybe you later. But not now," she added more seriously.

"Is it scary? Is that why you can't go there?"

"Nah. It's because I can't skin yet. Noah's gonna show me when I'm older. He's our best skinner. Next to Ren. Ren showed Noah how to do it first. She showed Joey and Patrick, too, but they suck. Especially Patrick. He sucks at everything. His hands shake all the time."

"Okay." Isabelle was dubious. The explanation was a little garbled and hard to follow. Mouse stood back and gave her a look of great consideration. Finally coming to a decision, she smiled slyly.

"I'll show you if you want, but you can't tell Ren. I been before, but I swore to Joey I'd tell no one."

"I'm not a snitcher." Isabelle acted offended. She did want to see the skinning hole; she wanted to see all of Ren's valley, whether it was fry channels, big trees, or hunting places like this.

"Okay, but you gotta do what I say." Mouse bristled with importance.

Aha, the truth comes out, Little Miss Bossy Boots. Isabelle hid a smile and fell in behind Mouse as she trudged through the undergrowth down the steep embankment. The smell caught her first, and she realized that was what had first intrigued her in the clearing. Without being fully aware of it, she had been lured in by the gamey odor. Thank goodness it was winter and the outdoors was like a walk-in freezer. In spring and summer this place must stink to high heaven.

"Told you it was boring. No meat left."

Mouse was right. It was a disappointment. The trail stopped at the edge of a large, cleared hollow in the forest floor. The soil was uneven and heaped all around, giving the impression of a small crater surrounded by shallow graves. Bones lay scattered across the center. Isabelle poked at one with her boot. It was covered in large gnaw marks. Other bones lay splintered nearby. *Some huge animals come here to scavenge.*

Isabelle shifted uneasily. Her skin crawled, and she glanced around. "It's spooky here. Like we're being watched."

"There's always eyes in the forest. I feel it all the time." Mouse looked around unconcerned, so Isabelle dismissed the notion. She kicked a bone at her foot. It was the foreleg of a deer; the hoof was still attached. Isabelle frowned. The deer hanging in Jenna's locker had their forelegs missing. This must be where they dismembered them. Why not butcher the carcass in the comfort and convenience of that wonderful kitchen? It could hardly be less hygienic than doing it here in the woods.

"Yawn. Boring. Let's go." Mouse handed over her empty pop can and headed back. Isabelle gave up. What did she expect from a nine-year-old souped up on sugary drinks? She stashed their soda cans in her backpack and took one more look around. The feeling of being watched returned. She felt cold and vulnerable all at the same time, as if the surrounding trees oozed malice like sap. It coated the pores of her skin and left her feeling choked and poisoned. Unable to shake the feeling of unease, she slung the bag over her shoulder and hurried after Mouse.

"The Big Tree is this way. Race you." Mouse took off at top speed again, leaving Isabelle in her dust. She swung her leg over her quad when something caught her eye in the weeds on the far edge of the clearing. She couldn't quite make it out, but the sheen and texture looked so out of place that she dismounted to take a closer look.

The brushwood had been flattened. Tree branches were snapped at odd angles and the earth was heavily scored, as if a huge object had been dragged or pushed toward the edge of the clearing. The path of destruction ceased where the edge gave way to a sudden drop. Something big had been moved here recently. Something very big, that squashed everything before it.

Isabelle stooped to pull on the piece of silver plastic that had caught her eye. It poked out from under a flattened bush, covered with melting snow. The plastic was brittle and broke apart as she wedged it free. Isabelle stood stunned with part of a car fender in her hand. *What an odd thing to find.* She doubted Ren would use the valley as a dump for old vehicles. How had this trashed piece of fender got here?

Her stomach coiled into a sick knot. She'd had an accident, and she hadn't found out exactly where yet. Ren had alluded to a branch road off Highway 20. Not by any stretch of the imagination could this be called a branch road. It was too great a leap of logic to conclude it was her car. She couldn't afford to be fanciful. She needed hard facts, and the best way to do that was go down the slope and examine the area.

A distant beeping told her Mouse had realized she was in a solo race. She was such a forceful, demanding little madam. So like Ren in many ways.

Isabelle set the piece of plastic back where she'd found it. It was as a marker for her mystery. Something was not sitting well with her. She would come back at the first opportunity and investigate.

Another long beep made her scurry for her quad. She had a race to lose. A last look over her shoulder helped her to memorize the exact spot with its telltale marker. Isabelle stepped on the gas and chased after Mouse, determined to see this big, big tree.

Chapter Thirteen

The Big Tree was a sight to behold. Mouse made Isabelle march around it with her two times just to be sure how big it really was. Then they paced around it again, measuring it with their steps, thirty-nine of Isabelle's and fifty-two of Mouse's, though she admitted cheating a little and taking extra-long ones. Then they sat on a large rock under the lower branches and ate the picnic Jenna had made them, thankful for the warm soup.

"This is the biggest tree in the whole valley," Mouse informed her between bites. "Ren says the Nuxalk used to worship it hundreds of years ago. They hung their wolf skins from it so the wolf ghosts would guard the valley, and that's why they come back at night and howl."

"Does the howling scare you?"

"Nope."

Isabelle was amused at this daylight bravado from a girl who'd sworn there were monsters under her bed last night. The howling unnerved Isabelle more than a little. Mouse took a massive bite out of her sandwich, her cheeks bulging. Her lustiness and high energy kept calling Isabelle's mind back to Ren. Was she like this as a child? Isabelle would have loved to have seen photos of the young Ren.

"The Nuxalk are the indigenous community, right?" She brought her mind back to the present.

"Yeah. But Ren says the wolves have been here longer," Mouse said with her mouth full.

They were high up, near the lip of the valley. There was more wildlife on display than in the denser woodland farther down the slopes.

Red-winged blackbirds squabbled in the mighty branches above them, and several feet away a nervous shrew scurried back to its nest.

"The thaw's waking 'em up early." Mouse nodded sagely at the disappearing tail. "They'll grab what they can from their food stores before the next big snow."

"You know a lot about the wildli—What's that!" A distant rumble startled Isabelle. Mouse looked over her shoulder.

"It's the logging trucks. They come along the top road whenever they can."

"Logging trucks? Where are they going?" Between float planes and logging trucks, Isabelle felt they might as well be on a traffic intersection. So much for the rural isolation Ren purported they were living in.

"They don't come often. Only if the Black Knife camp is open for cedar. And this time of year they hardly move at all." Mouse shrugged.

"Where do they go?"

"Dunno. The log harbor at Bella Coola, maybe?"

The rumble of the giant truck engine died away and Isabelle became aware of the silence and gloom around them. The birds had taken their noisy fight elsewhere, and even in the early hours of afternoon the light was already becoming muddy. She shivered.

"Time to pack up and head back, I think."

"Race you." Mouse was on her feet in a flash, brimful of energy. Isabelle was about to refuse when a thought struck her. When would she be out this way again, or get the loan of a quad to explore the valley for herself? Not anytime soon, she reckoned. She was growing more and more uneasy at the vagueness of Ren's plans to help her leave. Even Noah assumed she'd be around for summer picnics.

"But it's not a fair race. You know the trail," she said.

Mouse screwed her face up. "So?"

"So you have the advantage. Instead, you should take the long way home and let me go back the way we came. You're quicker anyway, so it's more even."

"Okay, then." Mouse brightened at the challenge. "I'll go along the river road. That's miles longer, but I'll still be first. Ready, steady, go!" And she was off, leaving Isabelle with all the picnic packing to do.

Isabelle shook her head ruefully at such a competitive streak and continued packing. When she was ready, she revved her quad and went back the route they'd come. She easily found the clearing and the plastic fender. She had to find out what had been pushed over the edge. She had to prove her hunch either right or wrong, though in her heart she already knew.

She lay on the edge on her belly and inched forward until she could clearly see the bottom of the fifty-foot drop. The area below was in heavy shade; the thaw had barely touched it and it was deep with snow. Even so, she could clearly make out the blackened metal of a burned-out vehicle protruding from a snowdrift. Against the soft, white snow and the frost-jeweled pine needles it looked hideous and twisted.

Isabelle lay and looked at the car until the damp seeped through her jacket. Her stomach cramped and her fingers curled so tightly to the ledge they lost all feeling. She was barely aware of the numbing discomfort. Her head was ringing with the order she had heard Ren give Patrick on the night she had finally clambered out of her sick bed. Round and round the words spun. "Burn it. Burn it. Burn it."

Ren had not lied to her. She had not told Patrick to burn her car documents. She had ordered him to burn her car.

❖

"I win. I win. I'm the winner!" Mouse crowed as Isabelle finally drew up before the barn. Joey set aside his broom and came to claim his quad.

"How'd she go?"

"Oh. Great, Joey. Great. Thanks for the loan."

"I won!" Mouse crowded her for attention. Isabelle was still upset and distracted by her find, and she had to focus hard to present an amiable front to Mouse and Joey.

"Yes, you did. I'll think twice before I challenge you to a race." Isabelle wrapped an arm around Mouse's shoulders and gave her a hug. "You're a speed demon. Now, let's take this bag back to Jenna and thank her for our picnic."

She had to act calm, even though her heart pounded and her hands tremored. No one must know about her discovery. Not yet. Not until she had processed what it meant. She caught herself watching Mouse and Joey as they locked up their quads, and decided they knew nothing. They were so guileless, so happily innocent. She couldn't bear it if they knew about her car.

Mouse led the way to the cookhouse, and Isabelle took a deep breath before mounting the porch steps. What about Jenna? Was she in on it?

Patrick was idling at the kitchen table while Jenna worked. Isabelle could tell by Jenna's sharp, constricted movements she was annoyed at having him there. Patrick didn't gel with this group at all, Isabelle noted, despite his supposed authority.

"We're back," Mouse shouted as they entered. "We went to Big Tree and had a race back and I won."

Isabelle placed the backpack on the kitchen bench, tactfully avoiding eye contact with Patrick. She was angry, but careful not to show it. It was important not to tip her hand too soon, and especially not to him. He didn't seem pleased to see her either. He picked up a magazine and pretended to read. The pages tremored in his hands and Isabelle remembered Mouse's earlier comment about Patrick having the shakes. He did. His entire body trembled ever so slightly, his hands in particular.

"Thank you for the picnic, Jenna," she said. "It was very much appreciated. Mouse? What do you say?"

"Thank you, Jenna. The sandwiches were nice and I liked the soda best."

"Wow. That's a first." Jenna stopped to look at Mouse. "Mouse, are you learning some manners at last?"

"'Bout time," Patrick said. "She needs to learn respect for her elders."

"You're not an elder," Mouse retorted. "You're just old." She slid onto the seat and dragged one of her play magazines over and began to color in a picture.

Isabelle and Jenna both smiled, and even Patrick let it go. He sat sprawled with his magazine, his feet up on another chair watching Jenna. Isabelle noted how he gauged Jenna's reaction to Mouse's behavior and followed her lead.

So he's sweet on Jenna. That will cause problems later. I can't see Noah letting it go. And between the two, my money's on Noah. Isabelle was surprised she was picking up these little nuances so easily. And that she was becoming concerned about the internal workings of this small group.

The door opened and Ren walked in. She hesitated on seeing Isabelle there, then smiled and came farther into the room.

"Any coffee on the go?" she asked. Patrick scooted upright in his chair and Jenna went to pour a generous cup.

"Busy day?" Jenna asked.

"Manic," Ren answered. "Hi there," she said to Isabelle, and came over to stand close, making sure their arms touched. "I hear Mouse took you on a guided tour."

"Yes." Isabelle side-stepped and went to stand behind Mouse, resting her hands on her shoulders. She was too upset to have Ren touch her. "We went all the way to Big Tree and had a picnic." Her face muscles ached from trying to keep a bland look. If her hands weren't sitting on Mouse's shoulders they'd be two balled fists.

"Then we had a race back and I—" Mouse piped up.

"Won," Ren finished for her. "You win all the time. Like your mom used to."

"Because she cheats," Patrick said. He seemed to begrudge Mouse getting any of Ren's attention.

"I do not!"

"No, you don't, honey. You're just the best, that's all." Isabelle reassured her with a shoulder squeeze. "Don't let him tease you. I know you won fair and square."

This seemed to appease Mouse, and a temper tantrum was avoided.

"I told Isabelle all about Big Tree and the ghosts," Mouse told Ren.

"Did you now?" Ren took a seat opposite, and Isabelle slid in beside Mouse, glad of the tabletop between them. Even looking at Ren hurt her. She surveyed her sitting nonchalantly at the table, as if butter wouldn't melt in her mouth, or cars burn in her valley. The afternoon light pooled behind and haloed her, and Isabelle felt the siren's pull. Her fingers tightened on the table. She wanted to give up and give in. She wanted it all to be untrue. She wanted never to have found the damn car. She wanted Ren.

What did a beautiful woman like Ren want with her?

Isabelle tried some self-scrutiny. She was a bedraggled specimen of womanhood, far too thin, sallow and haggard with illness. She had memory blackouts, and night terrors so fierce she was afraid to go to sleep. Why would Ren cheat her into staying in the valley?

Perhaps I'm rich? She pondered the possibility for a microsecond, then dismissed it. Ren's property was run-down and threadbare, and in no way did Isabelle believe she had the funds to change that. Look at her. Her hair and complexion had never had money thrown at them. She was no missing heiress. Ren pulled her attention back to the conversation.

"Did Mouse tell you the whole legend?" Ren was asking her.

She shook her head. "Only that the Nuxalk hung wolf skins from the tree. Sounded pretty icky to me. What's the whole legend?" She tried to sound casual, normal even.

Patrick muttered something about work, then stomped out the door.

"He's a scaredy cat," Mouse whispered to Isabelle.

In Isabelle's opinion, he was annoyed his time with Jenna had been interrupted. Jenna looked relieved he had gone.

"Oh? Maybe I'm a scaredy cat, too. Is it a scary story?" Isabelle said.

"Hold my hand if you're frightened." Mouse held out a grimy hand and Isabelle slipped hers in it. Across the table Ren watched them with a curious expression. Her face softened and her shoulders eased into a less tense posture. Isabelle hadn't been aware she was so keyed up until these little changes occurred. She realized Ren was as awkward around her as she was back.

At first she worried she had given herself away and somehow shown the discomfort and suspicion she'd tried so hard to conceal. She chanced a quick glance to see if Ren's face revealed any clues. The inky surface of Ren's eyes spilled out words that Isabelle could read as easily as print. They shone with adoration and with pride, and showed gratitude for her presence in this home. Ren looked at her with love. Isabelle broke away and fussed over a tangle in Mouse's hair. She was overwhelmed. Ren loved her, and she was afraid of the intensity in that look, and all it meant.

What if Ren could read her as easily? She was not ready for her secrets to spill out. Isabelle was jealous and guarded of her heart and what it held. She was falling in love, too. But she was fighting it. She was fighting it hard.

"The stories are old and the words worn," Ren began in a soft voice. Jenna settled in beside her. This seemed to be a well-loved story. "They actually belong to the people who were here before the Nuxalk, but no one knows who they were, or how long ago they passed through this valley.

"They tell of a Wolf-demon who came to these mountains. She found the valley beautiful, and settled here. Soon the hunters noticed the wildlife behaving differently. The animals were skittish. They stopped having young and began moving away. The shamans asked the bear why the forest was out of balance, and the bear told them a Wolf-demon had come who devoured souls, and so the animals were leaving.

"On hearing this, the elders sent their best warriors to hunt the Wolf-demon, for if the animals left, the tribe would starve. One by one the warriors set out. The bravest and best went first, and the less experienced last. One by one they disappeared until the tribe had no hunters left.

"Then one day a bedraggled, half-dead youth stumbled out of the forest. He had been the last hunter to leave, and he spoke wildly about an ancient tree and bad magic, but he was half mad with terror and no one could make sense of his words. So the elders traveled to the ancient tree, Big Tree as we call it today, and found it draped with the skins of their warriors. They had been flayed and left to hang in the wind like so many drying hides. And late that night as the elders made their sad way home, the valley began to ring with the howl of multitudes of wolves, and the elders knew these were the souls of their lost warriors the Wolf-demon had trapped in wolf bodies.

"And so the elders killed as many wolves as they could find, and hung the pelts from Big Tree to release the souls of their brothers and sisters up to the mountains. Then the tribe, like the animals, packed up and moved away."

"What happened to the Wolf-demon?" Mouse asked.

"The Wolf-demon ran out of souls to eat, so she moved on, too," Ren said. "The howls you hear at night are supposed to be wolf souls still trapped."

A lot of things get trapped in this valley, Isabelle thought.

"They wander the valley singing for release," Jenna said.

"And that's why it's called Singing Valley," Mouse added with great aplomb.

"Well, that was creepy…and sad, too. I'll think differently when I hear the wolves crying," Isabelle said.

"Do. They might be your ancient sisters and brothers." Ren rinsed her cup in the sink. "I've got to go to Williams's horse ranch, would you like to come?" she asked Isabelle.

"Me. Me. Can I come?" Mouse bounced in her seat.

Part of Isabelle would have loved the excursion, but her secretive, cunning side knew this was the ideal opportunity to explore Ren's cabin again while she was away for a few hours. There had to be some information about the float plane delivery schedule somewhere. All she had to do was check out the farm accounts in Ren's bureau.

"Thanks, but I've got a headache. I think I should lie down for an hour or two."

"A headache? Do you want a poultice for your forehead?" Ren was immediately concerned. "I have homemade remedies for headaches."

"No, honest. I'll be all right. I just need to rest." Isabelle held her breath at her blatant lie, relieved Ren couldn't read her well at all. Quickly she said good-bye and excused herself, and headed straight back to the cabin.

❖

Isabelle ignored the bureau and walked through the living room to Ren's kitchen. Straight to the bread bin where she had cleaned up Ren's sooty fingerprints only yesterday morning. Her car lay burned out at the bottom of a gully. Her car documents had been tossed in the fire. So why was Ren rummaging about in the cold ashes? What had she been looking for? What else had been burned?

Isabelle was certain she had not crashed in this valley, but most likely somewhere close by. The marks in the clearing suggested her car had been towed in, dragged to the ledge, and pushed over. When Ren said "Burn it" she had meant the car, not the car documents. Ren had not ordered that, so she hadn't lied to Isabelle about it. For some unfathomable reason, she could not lie to Isabelle, but she could omit the truth. Isabelle was bitter, and she worried Ren had no intentions of letting her leave the valley at all. She had covered Isabelle's tracks so no one would know she was even here. And that left the question of why?

Isabelle opened the bread bin. It was empty. She checked the tin containers on either side. Empty. The cups on the shelf. Empty. The spice jars. Empty. Everywhere she looked she drew a blank. There was something she was not seeing. It was frustrating. Ren's sooty fingerprints had left clues, and all Isabelle had done was wipe them clean.

She stepped back, drew a breath, and glared at the kitchen cabinets. What had Ren found in the ashes? Patrick had dumped a book in the flames. What if it was not just her car documents, what if there was something else?

Then she saw it—a thumb smudge on a soup ladle. It hung from a hook with other utensils. Isabelle tipped out a small brass key into the palm of her hand. A key! But to open what?

She ran into Ren's bedroom and went straight to the dresser. The key fit in the locked drawer and turned with a perfect, oiled click. She opened the drawer.

"Oh God." Her fingers touched the battered cover of a Canadian passport. She knew it was hers even before she checked the ID page. Her driver's license was there, too, and a wallet with American and Canadian dollars. The credit cards were all in her name, and there was a set of house keys—for where? What was her address? Her driver's license gave a characterless apartment building on a boring Portland street. Everything about her was nondescript. She was the perfect person to grab and hide away. What were Ren's plans for her?

At the back of the drawer she found a battered digital camera and another burned book. It was the remains of a handmade journal. An expensive one, and that was what had saved it from total annihilation. The thick covers had protected some of the pages, but most were lost to the flames. The inner cover showed it was a Christmas gift from her aunt Mary, but the last section of the book was the more intact; a few pages were just about legible. Isabelle recognized her own handwriting. The journal entries were chronologically consistent, and ended at a date sometime in the last week or so.

This was her journal, and Ren had salvaged it from the ashes. She had wanted to preserve it after Patrick had carelessly tossed it away. Why was it so important? What did it hold?

Isabelle perched on the edge of the bed and opened the soot-caked covers. It smelled acrid, but she could still make out ash-smudged words on the cracked pages.

13th

It's Friday the 13th today. Do I feel particularly unlucky? Well, I signed the last of the divorce papers and mailed them off to Jaggart, Swartz, and Tresco this morning, and that felt very, very good, if not a little lucky.

Aunt Mary says Paul Jaggart is a "damned good divorce lawyer," and she should know, she's used him three times already. She's being so sweet and support—

15th

I am so looking forward to seeing the Old Ironshoe falls. I've even packed a picnic. I love spending time with her—so much fun and easygoing. She's exactly what I need right now. A new friend and such a beautiful person—

Aunt Mary adores her, too, because of Atwell— poorly—

16th

—arrived this morning on a massive quad! Fantastic day, we went miles and—Came home and downloaded my photos immediately to show Aunt Mary.

18th

—kissed—can't believe I did that.—as gay!! But it feels so right. As if I have been waiting for this moment all my life. And she is so wonderful. I think I must be—

23rd

—acting so strange—we argued because I did not want to visit this lake she insists on going to. I became very upset. I hate it when—cold and distant. Lonesome la—Unpleasant—

too intense, and—I feel awful, but she's acting like she owns me, or something. I told her I was leaving in a few days and said good-by—

27th

—glad of the break. Drove Aunt Mary down to the Port Hardy ferry for a sad farewell. I will miss her, but promised to lock up tight and call her when I arrive back in Portland.

I must admit it is nice to have the house to myself for this last night. The full moon is beautiful this evening—

—all packed and ready to go at seven a.m. sharp—the weather looks good for the—

28th

—she really lost it, and scared the hell out of me. Glad to get away. What an intense woman, and she was so lovely at the start—

Isabelle closed the journal. There was no more to read, and what little she could make out told a bizarre tale. Was Ren hiding the journal because it showed their troubled past? Why not let the book burn? Eventually, Isabelle's memories would return, and journal or not, she would remember this suffocating friendship. Except it wasn't a friendship any longer. Last night she had allowed it to become something else. Isabelle sank her head in her hands. What had she done? It was all such a mess, when only last night it had felt so right. Her *coup de foudre* had collapsed into dust. Last night she had unwittingly flung herself from a point of safety into Ren's arms. Today, secrets had been laid bare, and she realized she had fallen—heart, head, and soul—into a trap.

She slipped the journal and her passport and papers into her jacket pocket. As an afterthought, she grabbed the camera, too. Her mind was made up. She had to get away. If she stayed, she might well recover all her memories as Ren had promised. And then what? Find she was a captive in the valley? It sounded implausible, but the odds were stacking up against Ren. She had been devious without lying, manipulative under a mask of caring, and if the journal was anything to go by, predatory from the start. Isabelle patted the documents in her pocket, drawing comfort from their presence. They told her she was Isabelle Monk of Billinghurst Drive, Portland, Oregon, USA, and she was twenty-nine years old. It was all she needed. She now knew where home was. She was getting out. Somehow, between float planes, logging trucks, quads, and her own two feet, she was going home.

Chapter Fourteen

I've got to go out tonight." Ren's arms enfolded her from behind; she buried her nose in Isabelle's hair and breathed her scent. Standing before the kitchen sink with soapy water splashing up her forearms, Isabelle tensed. Mundane household chores had helped her through the rest of the day while she mulled over her limited options and tried not to fret. Now Ren had returned and she wanted to turn her anger on her and demand to know why she had stolen her journal, and torched her car, and stalked her, and hidden her away in this valley like Sleeping Fucking Beauty. But she also knew if she turned in Ren's arms not only would she scream at her, she would also be staring into eyes that would melt her like molasses. She wasn't used to being loved. She could sense it in herself, her awkwardness and reserve, her neediness. If she challenged Ren now she would be easily manipulated because she wanted to believe her. She wanted everything to be okay, she wanted to stay in love, and that was dangerous. A big part of her wanted to believe Ren's half-truths. It would be so easy to just accept and take the easy way out. She'd come to Canada to end an abusive relationship, and she'd be damned if she was going to sink back into another one. If she blurted out her discovery she would concede an important advantage.

Ren's scent was knocking her senseless. She had to stand firm and not start the fight she so dearly wanted. Not because she was any less angry. If anything, her anger fueled a need to pound on Ren and bring them both to the floor in a writhing mass of teeth and nails and ripped clothing.

Powerful emotions rippled through her. Ren was hers. How dared she act like this? How dared she try to lock her up, to hide her away like a dirty secret? She gripped the edge of the sink with soapy hands. Ren nuzzled her nape, as if sensing Isabelle's heightened state.

"I promise I'll be back by dawn." Her voice rumbled in Isabelle's ear, causing the fine hairs on her neck to rise. She shivered.

"Why so late?" she asked. "Do none of the animals around here get sick during the day?"

"It's a mare. She's begun to foal and I need the work." Ren abruptly moved away. Isabelle turned into the space she'd left.

She was fine-tuned to Ren's elusiveness, and little escaped her now she knew what to look for. The knotted muscles of Ren's jaw, even the slightest quirk of her lips betrayed her. Her thoughts paraded across her eyes with fanfare. Isabelle read the clues as Ren tightened and twitched before her—a shoulder shrug, a hip slouch, restless hands. Every movement screamed a million messages until Isabelle's head banged, until it felt she was living inside Ren's skin. She wondered why she'd never noticed this acute sensitivity before. Now she thrummed with it.

Did sleeping with a person make your nerve endings mesh with hers, your heartbeats synchronize, your skin tingle as if magnetically charged, just because she stood beside you? No, of course not. So why was it that way with Ren?

"Stay with me." The words were out before she'd barely thought them. She was embarrassed by the plea. What she wanted to say was, "Don't go. Tonight is important. Curl up in bed with me and make love and tell me about our history. Give me all the missing pieces of our time together, the good and the bad, and I'll forgive. I promise I will. I know I will."

"I have to do this, Isabelle." Ren was awkward and unhappy. "I'll come back as soon as I can. And tomorrow will be different. Tomorrow will be special."

"Tomorrow, then." Isabelle turned back to the sink. She felt Ren hesitate behind her, swore the air moved as her hand reached out to touch. Instead, Ren turned for the door.

Isabelle stood in the empty kitchen for some time looking at her refection in the windowpane. Straggly, dirty blond hair framed a thin, angular face. The swelling had gone down and her bruises were less vivid. She was healing quickly. She concentrated on her eyes, as if scrying secrets from their surface.

I'm no longer numb. The thought unfurled, and she realized she had been coiled up and frozen in the lead-up to her divorce. Ren had somehow dissolved all that. She wished her journal had been more complete. There had been happiness in those lines, as well as anger and regret. Ren had wooed her out of her numbness. Then it had all gone wrong. Isabelle ached to know what had happened between them. There was such connectivity and yet so much deceit.

"Tell me something new," she asked her reflection. She ticked off what she did know. She'd come up to Canada to divorce her American husband, visit her aunt, and return to Portland, where she lived and presumably worked. She knew a lot about classic literature. No—she *loved* classic literature, and suspected she either taught or studied it. At least she had money now. A few hundred dollars was tucked away in her wallet along with her credit cards. A dollar for every mile she had to run. All she had to do was take a quad up to the logging road and hitch a lift with one of the trucks heading for Bella Coola. It all sounded suspiciously easy.

And suspiciously not what she wanted to do.

What she really wanted was for Ren to come clean. Running away was her last resort. She had run up here to end her marriage. She could feel it, the relief, the absolute rightness of that decision, but running from Ren—the very thought of it made her feel nauseous. Weak. Out of place in the world.

Had emerging from her amnesia made her form an unnatural bond with her rescuer? Was Ren really her rescuer, or was this another face of the woman in the journal? If so, then Isabelle was in some weird, stalkerish wonderland.

She cleared her head of her clamorous thoughts and breathed deep and slow several times, trying to not think, just feel. She liked it here. She liked the little group Ren had rescued with an offer of bed and board, and occasional work. There it was again, that word, "rescued." Perhaps they were *all* trapped here in some shape or form by Ren.

And as for herself, her bait had been the same as everyone else's. She wanted to be loved and cared for. Her journal told her she had deliberately embarked on a lesbian affair after her marriage breakdown, and for once she had done the right thing. She had never felt so alive, so strong and purposeful. Sleeping with Ren was akin to drinking rocket fuel and swallowing a lit match. She glowed inside, burning up with a ferocity that was outside her normal sphere of feeling. She had no emotional reference for these feelings and did not need a restored memory to know this was new.

Isabelle slumped against the counter. She wanted Ren to validate her right to these emotions, to make them solid and dependable. To make them a gateway to their potential future together. What she did *not* want was Ren to be a mad stalker, and all this newfound feeling to be fool's gold. She did *not* want her time with Ren to be the only thing she wanted to forget.

Night had drawn in, and a fat-bellied moon hung over the eastern peaks. Wind-tossed pewter clouds scudded across its surface. Tomorrow night it would be plump and full, a pregnant goddess with a thousand starry ladies-in-waiting, all twinkling fussily around her. Isabelle laughed at her fantasies. She was restless. The wind made the cabin rattle and bang, as if shooing her outside. Usually a glass of wine, a blazing fire, and a good book would keep her snuggled down on a night like this. But not tonight. Tonight she wanted to taste the air. To feel the wind whip her hair, its cold sting ruddying her cheeks and ripping the breath from her lips.

Perhaps she should take a walk down to the farm and return the bag Jenna had lent her to carry groceries. Isabelle grabbed the bag, shrugged on the large coat she had more or less permanently borrowed from Ren, and stepped out into the night. The air assaulted her, slamming into her lungs, spinning through her cells until they snapped and popped. Everything around her was loaded with the tang of damp earth and pine needle. Far away came the musty scent of woodsmoke. The world smelled sharp, and satisfying, and clean.

Isabelle inhaled deeply through her nose. Clean, she could smell clean. Clean air, clean earth, trees, everything smelled natural and clean. She had never been in a place so wholesome, so connected, so right for her. And yet she had to leave it. She became bitter at the thought, and angry at Ren all over again for making her decisions so impossibly painful.

In a burst of giddy energy, she pushed it all away, and living in the pure, undiluted mountain-fueled moment, leapt from the top porch step. Instead of the satisfying crunch of new snow, her boots squished on slush. The thaw was a deep one. Mouse had assured her one more freeze was on the way and then it would be springtime proper. Isabelle smiled at the rustic wisdoms Mouse recited by rote. According to her, only the southern wind was keeping the temperature up. Soon it would die away and the snow would return for one last flourish.

Isabelle moved through the cedar windbreak. It hummed with fretful nocturnal life. Small creatures were making the most of the break in their hibernation to forage and stock up their body fat. For them the thaw was a boon. Predators were also making the most of this unseasonable abundance, picking off this sudden rash of fresh prey. Overhead, wings fluttered and folded. A squeak told her a snowy owl had found fresh meat. The winter thaw offered amnesty, not mercy.

Isabelle exited the windbreak and took the steep track down to the cluster of farm buildings. She noticed the yard was full of vehicles. All the trucks and quads had returned and were now parked up for the night. She slowed her step. This was what she had promised herself. A free ride out. But now? Tonight? With a bright moon and a crazy wind? She flexed her fingers against her pocket, touching her wallet through the waxed cotton.

Lights from the cookhouse windows paved the yard with oblongs of waxy yellow. Everyone was home for the evening. There would be witnesses. She noticed Ren's truck parked beside Mouse's lurid pink quad. It was craziness to bolt now. Isabelle's anxiety rose. Maybe she should talk to Ren after all. Maybe she should try to understand what the hell was going on.

It looked like Ren hadn't left yet. Perhaps she could ask to tag along with her. Isabelle wondered how far away the horse ranch was. They could talk in the truck and be honest with each other. They both had fears. Ren had secrets, and most of Isabelle's life was currently a secret to her.

But what would she ask?

"Why have you behaved in such a manipulative and controlling way? Why have you hidden me in this valley and seduced me when I was at my most vulnerable?"

It amazed her. These vehicles were her ticket home, and yet here she was hesitating, wanting to talk, wanting to see Ren again and not just disappear without a word. She was borderline insane to hesitate even a second. She needed to get out. If she still felt like this when she got home then they could talk—long distance! First step was to find a set of car keys.

Only the cookhouse lights were on, and after a quick rap on the door Isabelle entered to find the huge kitchen empty. *Good.* A furtive check of every cupboard and drawer produced no keys. She went back to the porch and frowned at the curious quiet. All the vehicles were accounted for, but no one was home? She checked the bunkhouse; it was empty, too. Not even Mouse was there, and it was well past her bedtime. Isabelle's hope for a set of car keys left on a bedside table soon evaporated. Wherever they were, their keys were in their pockets. But where were they?

The barn door still lay ajar. One step into its murky interior and she knew it was deserted. The entire complex was deserted. Uncertain, she went back to the yard and contemplated the row of vehicles, unsure what to do next. *I wish I knew how to hotwire a truck.*

The howling started on the far side of the valley and shook her out of her indecision. An answering chorus tore across the Tearfell, carried by the wind. Her skin tingled with excitement. The smell of smoke brushed her nostrils. It was not cookhouse or bunkhouse smoke. This came from farther down the valley. She could see it rising, dancing on gusts of wind like a pale specter. Smoke was an ominous sign in the forest during summer, but what did it mean in the depths of winter?

Joey's huge black quad sat before her. Would Joey carry his keys with him all day long? He couldn't even ride his quad with his bad leg. What had he done with them after she had returned his bike that afternoon? *Think, Isabelle, think.* She strode over and unclipped the seat. Joey had stashed his keys underneath. She blessed his predictability and started the engine. It burst into life, loud and unforgiving. The roar was whisked away by the wind, its horsepower an ineffectual whisper against the raw power of nature. She twisted hard on the throttle to prevent the engine from stalling. Maybe it was the colder night air, but the engine seemed temperamental and sluggish.

She took the dirt track for Big Tree and kept an eye out for where it forked off to meet with the logging road near the north end of the valley. She knew she could find her way to Big Tree easily enough in the moonlight, but Joey still hadn't fixed the headlights, so finding the exit track would be tricky.

Under the forest canopy her engine noise was muted. Solid walls of bark and the density of the snow that covered everything blanketed the sound. The thaw had not yet made its way here to the shadowy interior. Even the wind was beggarly under the low-slung boughs.

She scooted up to the skinning hole clearing where she'd found the burned-out car, and eased up on the throttle. Was it worth another look? What did she hope to find? Confirmation it was not her car after all? Was she willing to twist every fact to make Ren the good guy? To give her one last chance? No. She wasn't. They could talk when she was safely in Portland, in her own home and settled in her old life.

The smell of smoke grew stronger. Even in the darkness she could see thick gray wisps weaving through the trees. It was not a forest fire—the smoke was too thin and wispy; the wind shredded it and sent it swirling in all directions.

Eventually, she saw the actual flames through a maze of tree trunks. A huge bonfire crackled before Big Tree. Orange flames swirled and danced, casting livid sparks up into the night sky. It was primitive and magical on this dark winter's night.

Isabelle braked and sat watching, her breath huffing in the cool air, a stark contrast to the blazing heat up ahead. Mesmerized, she fixed on the fiery flash and roils of the flames. Shadows danced around and across them, like the wings of huge black birds fluttering and swooping through the blaze. She was uneasy now, as if she had gate-crashed a private event and was somewhere she shouldn't be. There was something about the fire that was so personal, almost intimate.

As much as it unsettled her, she could not turn and ride away, either. Instead, she dismounted and carefully approached on foot through the woods. She hid in the shadows, lurking behind trees. Her apprehension prompted quiet steps and cautious movements, but an insatiable curiosity drove her on. Why were birds fluttering around the bonfire? Who had built it, and why was it unattended, roaring away, spitting and crackling like a coven pyre?

She crept closer, until only a few yards lay between the sheltering trees and the bonfire. The howling came again, this time closer. The wolves had crossed the river. They were on her side of the valley now. Isabelle was no longer excited by the eerie, singsong cries. Fear began to creep through her. Here, under the Big Tree, before this monstrous blaze, she was all too aware of the legends of Singing Valley and its ghost wolves. Now the old stories seemed far from fanciful. They crept across her skin like spiders.

Just one more step, one more tree to crouch behind and spy, and then she would go, she promised herself. She took the step…and caught her breath.

There were no shadow birds swooping on the bonfire. Only rags. Hundreds and hundreds of tattered rags hung from the lower branches of Big Tree. They billowed in the wind and in the updraft from the fire, their long shadows swooning and swirling among the flames. From deep in the forest they looked like a flock of elongated, black-winged birds, circling the blaze like demonic phoenixes.

Isabelle stepped out of the shadows and into the circle of orange firelight. She gazed in awe at the strange sight. Cottons and linens and wool in all colors danced from the branches. A rag of pale blue chambray caught her eye. She fixated on it, watching it droop exhaustedly only to twitch and leap back into the dance at the slightest breeze.

"That's my shirt sleeve." Her gaze darted from branch to branch. Each scrap of fabric was hers! Every piece of clothing she'd had in her suitcase now hung from this tree in a thousand rags. Flapping and dancing and ripped into shreds.

Isabelle turned and ran. She bolted for the quad and viciously kicked the engine into life, swinging it around in too tight a turn. It spluttered and shuddered as it hit a bank of mud. She bullied it on through and shot off along the track at full throttle.

Now the smoky tendrils crossing her path were menacing fingers that tried to catch at her face and clothing. She gunned the engine. *Slow down, you'll crash*, her common sense screamed. But she couldn't slow down. She flew on recklessly.

Her shredded clothes hung from Big Tree like the skins of ancient ghost wolves. It was ceremonial magic of some sort, shaman and black, and it freaked her out to be at the core of it. She cannoned back toward the skinning hole as if the hounds of hell were after her.

Up ahead, headlights bounced off tree trunks. A truck was coming from the direction of the farm. Soon it would round the bend and pick her out in its lights. Isabelle yanked on the twist grip and swerved into the skinning hole clearing. She drove into the scrub for camouflage, thankful for Joey's black paintwork and her lack of headlights.

The quad coughed angrily, spluttered, and cut out. Isabelle ducked behind it and peeped out from behind a wheel. The other driver was upon her now, but drove by unaware she was crouched only yards away. She could make out Ren's profile at the wheel. It was a fleeting glimpse, but enough to set Isabelle's heart racing for all the wrong reasons. It was Ren driving. She remembered seeing Ren's cold beauty for the first time at the cabin. Classic features cut out of flawless marble, and her initial dismay and disbelief that she should be the object of Ren's affections. Ren. Someone who could have anyone, yet chose her?

Isabelle watched that classic profile pass. Ren looked relaxed, pleased. Even from several hundred paces and from an oblique angle Isabelle could read that face. Ren was happy and charged. Was she heading for the logging road and the horse ranch, Isabelle wondered. Or was she going to Big Tree and the bonfire to get naked and dance around it?

Isabelle slumped behind the quad wheel and rested her head in her hands, her mind full of grim thoughts. The forest was eerily silent now. Even the wind had died away. She glanced over her shoulder. There was no further movement on the home track. It was time to go. She had to back up the quad and find another way out, and hope she managed to before Ren or one of the others found out she was missing. She tried to start the quad. No amount of bouncing on the kick-start, twisting the key viciously, or cursing would make it roar into life. It was done for.

Tears pricked the back of her eyelids, tears of humiliation and anger. She wanted to howl with rage. A flicker of movement in the shadows freaked her out. She threw herself off the quad and skittered into the brush, not caring if it was a loose leaf, a nocturnal scavenger, or worse. The stench from the skinning hole was strong, but she slithered toward it. The smell would disguise her scent. Her instincts told her this, but she had no time to think about these newfound survival skills. She part slid, part ran down the steep path to the hollow below. At least from here she could orient herself. The farm lay to the northeast, toward the top of the valley. She knew where the home track ran, but she dared not walk along it. They could be out looking for her.

Isabelle would follow a parallel path. Somehow, she'd scrabble through the woods back to the farmyard. From there she could find her way to the Tearfell and with luck find the back road to Black Knife

Lake, and maybe another route out. There was no soul-searching this time, and no wrestling with the facts or skewing the truth to how she would like it to be. She had to save herself, not wallow in self-pity over another twisted relationship.

Chapter Fifteen

It took her hours to make her way back to the farm. With every stumbling step she worried she was doing the wrong thing. But where else could she go? She wasn't going back to Big Tree now that it was being used for ceremonial witchcraft.

The Black Knife track that forked from the hatchery station was the only other option she knew of. What she needed was a vehicle to take her down to the hatchery station and then on to Black Knife Lake. She had gone in circles and was right back to the car key dilemma. *One problem at a time. Get back to the farm first, and then worry about keys.*

Her approach brought her in by the far side of the barn. The yard and outbuildings lay quiet in the gray predawn. Isabelle stood motionless in the shadow of the barn wall, her legs shaking from the long hike. She watched and listened for several minutes. Everything was still. Not even the morning birds had begun to sing. She had just screwed up enough courage to dart across the yard when she heard a truck approach from the river.

Panicked, she darted into the barn and stepped back into the warm, dry darkness. The truck came to a standstill outside, and its door slammed shut with a bang.

"Hey, Ren. How'd it go?" she heard Patrick call and then the crunch of footsteps as the two met to talk. She hadn't noticed Patrick lurking—he must have been out there all along. Isabelle shuddered to think what would have happened if she'd taken another step toward the parked vehicles.

"A fine filly." Ren sounded upbeat. "Old Man Williams was so pleased he paid on the spot."

"Good job. I made some coffee, want some?"

"No, thanks. I'm going up to the cabin and check on Isabelle. How are the others?"

"All tucked up snoozing. It was a great night. Pity you had to go on to Williams's place in the middle of it."

"Tonight will be even better. Isabelle will be there..." Their footsteps receded as they moved out of earshot.

Isabelle stood in the barn, completely indecisive. What she had overheard had not terrified her. She had detected no horrifying consequences for her in Ren's voice. And she was attuned to that voice. She could make it do things, like roar and purr. Ren's tone with Patrick had been so casual, so matter-of-fact, so...so un-sinister? She was dithering again and it annoyed her. A part of her just didn't want to go. Leaving the valley was like pulling off skin.

Footsteps warned her of Patrick's return. He was making straight for the barn. She slid farther along the wall into the deepest shadows. This was awful. If he came in here, she could end up trapped. Why couldn't he go back to the cookhouse and his coffee? Isabelle looked around her in a panic. She contemplated her chances of bashing Patrick on the head and making a run for it. She even lifted a shovel and hefted its weight in her hands. Could she do that to him? How would she know what was a good debilitating thump compared to a whack that might kill him? She didn't want to hurt him.

Patrick's footsteps stopped by the barn door and her dilemma was forgotten. She waited with bated breath. What was he doing? She could hear the rustle of clothing. Was he undressing? Then he began to groan in pain. Deep, guttural growls and keening that unnerved Isabelle until she dropped her shovel and pressed against the rough-planked walls. What the hell was happening? Did he have an animal out there with him?

She sidled farther into the barn looking for somewhere better to hide. The old Case 400 sat between her and the door. She slipped under it. No. It wouldn't do. She was too exposed. She slithered out. Above her head was a storage ledge about a yard deep. It ran along the barn length nearly eight feet off the ground. It had probably been used to store excess bales but now lay empty and neglected.

Outside, the grunts had stopped and the ensuing silence gave her no clue to Patrick's intentions. Perhaps he had gone? Perhaps she should sneak out now while the coast was clear and—

The barn door creaked on its hinges and opened a crack wider. Pale morning light spilled across the floor. Without hesitation Isabelle placed a foot on the rim of the tractor tire and the other on the hood, grabbed for the ledge, and hoisted herself up out of sight.

Flat on her belly she peeped over the ledge and watched in dismay as a huge beast slipped into the barn. It was taller than a bear, and it had a broader chest and shoulders than a bear. The creature walked upright with an awkward slouching gait and was covered in a thick brown pelt. Its face was thankfully turned away from her, but she could still make out a short, stubby muzzle and long, nasty teeth. It passed by her ledge unaware of her presence and moved toward the back of the barn.

Isabelle craned her neck and watched its progress, fascinated and at the same time repelled. It went to the straw bales, to the exact spot where she had found Mouse. Mouse's hidey-hole was occupied. Several more of these creatures lay tangled in a tight ball, all fast asleep. Dust motes danced over their coarse fur. Soft snores and heavy breathing broke the quiet at the back of the barn.

As she watched, the newcomer stepped carefully into the nest and sank down into the huddle. The others twitched and growled sleepily, making room for the addition to their litter, for that's what they were— Ren's litter. Isabelle looked down on the sleeping forms from her perch and could make out each individual. The black pelt of Noah curled around the smaller form of Jenna. Joey, huge and golden red. Great gashes covered his furry underbelly where he lay spread-eagled, flat on his back. And Mouse, little dun brown Mouse, lay sprawled across them all, snuffling in her sleep. Her ears twitched as she dreamed, and Isabelle remembered that same small, squashed face spying on her through Ren's bedroom window.

Patrick had settled and was asleep already. She knew him now, from before. From her nightmare. Just as she remembered the red-gold flash of Joey rolling over her car hood, howling in agony. Patrick had been the sly face at her driver window. He had started the attack that threw her into such a terrified panic she had crashed her car. She had interrupted a deer hunt; it was as simple as that. And had somehow ended up back here, at Ren's farm. Ren, who had apparently known

Isabelle from before. Ren, who nurtured these creatures. Isabelle had been brought here, her car destroyed, her clothes shredded, and her papers either burned or hidden.

Isabelle slid from the ledge and sneaked from the barn. She stumbled out into the early light in a daze of disbelief. She could not grasp the enormity of what she had just witnessed. What she was forced to conclude—

"Isabelle!"

The call came from Ren's cabin. She had been discovered missing. The call was not an alarm, it was merely inquisitive. Perhaps Ren thought she was taking a walk. That she was outside enjoying the dawn forest and the morning light on the mountaintops—impervious to the monsters she was living among.

Ren? What was she? Isabelle remembered the heat of Ren's skin as they rolled in glorious, sticky union across the bed. The muted growls of pleasure, the graze of teeth across Isabelle's sweaty flesh. And the bite.

The gash on her shoulder itched. Isabelle's blood ran cold, and for one dizzying moment she thought her legs would fail her. She ran for the nearest truck. It was Ren's and the keys dangled from the ignition. She jumped in and took off toward Big Tree and the logging road at full speed, raising dust and spitting grit behind her.

CHAPTER SIXTEEN

"Domestic or European?" Hope stood before the cooler cabinet.

"Domestic, of course. Always domestic." Godfrey looked over her shoulder at the rows of glistening wine bottles. "Why are you even asking?"

"Because it's not really champagne unless it comes from Champagne." Hope tutted at the vast range of sparkling wines before her. It was a hard choice.

"Is this extravagance for you and Jolie only, or will others be invited to partake?" he asked, lifting a Pinot Noir to examine the label. "Because if I'm having some, then get the Louis Roederer Cristal 2002. Top left-hand shelf, third along."

"That's nearly three hundred dollars! And this is just for Jolie and me."

"Oh, please. As long as you're on the end of the glass Jolie won't give a damn if it's champagne or Seven-Up."

"It's not the expense, it's the occasion."

"What occasion? You mean 'Happy homecoming, darling. Let's lick this off me'?"

"No, Mister Too Much Information. I don't need to know how you greet Andre after an absence."

"Well, it's hardly a business trip. I still think we could have gone with them. They're just handshaking a lot of Greek werewolves."

"Shush." Hope glanced around the wine boutique, making sure no one had overheard.

"Oh, please. Who would eavesdrop on an attractive, witty couple like us." Godfrey set his wine down and joined Hope by the cooler.

"The champagne is for something else." Her decision made, Hope snatched up a bottle of Taittinger Comtes de Champagne 1998. It was going to be the real McCoy for her special news.

Godfrey gasped. "You're pregnant!"

"Idiot boy. Of course not." Hope gave a loud guffaw that did attract unwanted attention. A woman with straggly blond hair, wearing a padded jacket much too heavy for the mild weather outside, glared at them through the shop shelving.

"Whew. I'm not ready to be the favorite uncle just yet. What then? What are you celebrating?"

"Do you know that woman?" Hope murmured, moving slightly to afford Godfrey a view. "She keeps staring at us."

"Where?"

"Don't gawk. Over there."

"Nope. Don't know her. She's staring because we're witty and attractive, as I pointed out earlier. So tell me, what are you celebrating?"

Hope remained mysteriously silent as she paid for her purchase and waited for Godfrey to have his wine wrapped.

"Thanks, Sam." With a flirty grin for the sales assistant, he followed her outside, where her cryptic moment evaporated.

"Tell me," he said. "Tell me right now or I'll sulk all the way home."

"Okay, but you're the first to know, so please, please, keep it to yourself. Don't go blurting it out to Andre. He's useless with secrets. He'll only crumble in front of Jolie, and I want to tell her myself when she gets back."

"Tell her what, for God's sake?"

"Cross your heart and promise."

"I can do better than that." He raised three fingers solemnly. "On my honor, I will try to help old people all the time and live by the Girl Scout law."

"The Girl Scout oath? Where did you learn that?"

"I Wikied it."

"Well, you Wikied it wrong."

"Oh, shut up and tell me."

They reached Hope's car and put their shopping on the backseat. Hope looked over the car roof. "I've got the all-clear," she said.

"What! When was this?"

"I went for the MRI the day after Jolie and Andre flew out. I didn't tell her because I knew she wouldn't go, and I wanted to do this by myself. Just in case it was bad news. I called my doctor this morning and he said my blood tests were clear. I'm cancer free, Godfrey. I'm in remission." She could hardly believe it.

"Oh, my God." He ran around the car to hug her. "I should have gone with you. I'm your BFF, after all. You should have called me. You should have." He hugged her tighter. "Oh, Hope, I'm so happy. I'm so...so..."

"Are you crying, you big Girl Scout?"

"These are manly tears of joy." He snuffled into a fresh linen handkerchief that had materialized from his pants pocket. "To celebrate, I'm taking you to lunch, missy. Better loosen that belt." A final eye dab and he was done.

As they pulled away from the parking lot Godfrey said, "There she is again. Our little friend."

Hope glanced over and this time met full-on the haunted stare of the gaunt woman from the wine shop. Her hair hung in lank strands around thin shoulders. Her face was sharp and angular, and her hollow cheeks held deep shadows that matched those around her eyes. Whoever she was, she looked exhausted and miserable.

Now there's one tormented soul. The thought popped into Hope's head as they swung out onto Woodstock and headed over to Milwaukee Avenue for lunch.

❖

"Sam?" Isabelle approached the salesman.

"Yes?" He looked up, giving her a cagey look. She made a mental note to go home and clean up. It was bad if people were mistaking her for a bag lady, though she was as good as one. She'd found it impossible to stay in last night. The walls of her apartment had closed in around her. Her skin itched unbearably until she wanted to tear it off her bones. She had ended up in Oakes Bottoms again, roaming aimlessly until she'd fallen asleep under a birch tree, to be awakened at dawn by scornful and scolding squirrels.

"That guy that's just left. The blond one?" She pointed vaguely at the parking lot and set a key chain on the countertop. "I think he dropped his keys."

They were her keys. Her old keys, for the house she used to share with Barry. It had a For Sale sign on it now, and all her worldly goods had been removed one difficult afternoon.

"Oh, gosh." Sam came alive with the possibility of a mini drama. "I know him. He owns a florist shop on Milwaukee. I'll call in case he's going straight there." He reached for the phone.

Isabelle turned away. She had no need to strain to hear the conversation on the other side of the line. Her hearing had improved immensely these past few days.

"Hello, Enchanted Florist. Mel speaking."

"Hi, this is Sam from the Naked Vintner over on Woodstock. Godfrey was just here and may have dropped his house keys. Tell him they're behind the cash register if he wants to come by and collect."

Isabelle moved for the door. She had all she needed.

"Thank you, ma'am. That was kind of you," Sam called over to her. She exited with a friendly wave, her good deed of the day over.

The Enchanted Florist. She knew it. It was local to Sellwood, a small, rather quaint florist shop near the park. She used to love walking past it and smelling the blossoms. How weird that it should now be part of her tenuous link.

She had sat for weeks becoming sicker and sicker until she could deny it no longer. She'd been infected by…it. Her shoulder itched like crazy, she was ravenous, and always for meat. She could eat until she threw up, and then she wanted to eat again until the sweat ran down her face and meat grease dripped from her chin. She needed help. She needed medicine. And that's when she thought of the potions in Ren's kitchen and understood their purpose. They had stopped the aching, stifled the crushing need to devour everything in sight, and prevented these mad urges to run all night that she was succumbing to. The recipes had come from a Garoul almanac. A beautiful book. Isabelle would never forget it. She had diligently researched these almanacs. She could find out anything about books. Literary research was her profession and her all-consuming passion. At least in her old life it had been. Now there was something else all-consuming in her life, and it lived inside her.

The Garoul almanacs were rare and collectible, but hardly ever on the market. The family firm that produced them was reclusive. But they had a connection right here in Portland. A software firm called Ambereye.

Isabelle had slunk over to the Ambereye offices and picked up the glorious scent of wolven. She could not track successfully in a city this size, but she stealthily noted the license plates of cars that came and went.

The small, dark-haired woman in the wine shop worked at Ambereye. She had a special parking space, she was important, and Isabelle had followed her and found she lived close by to where she rented. The woman bloomed a rich Were scent with every move she made. Isabelle was fascinated by her.

The blond man she was shopping with, the one the wine merchant had called Godfrey. His scent lured Isabelle, too. Though the couple were not themselves wolven, they knew something of it.

Isabelle headed over to the Enchanted Florist to see if she could pick up further clues. It was a circuitous route home, but the flower displays would be lovely on a sunny spring day. Maybe she would even pick up some more of the intriguing scent that had zoned her in on the couple. It was the first sense of comfort she had had since returning to Portland. The subtle scent had bathed her like a balm, soothing her nipped nerves and the never-ending, itchy unrest she had felt since her return.

Godfrey. Now she had the name of one of them, and where he worked. She did not know the name of the woman, but she did know where she lived. She was closing in on them. Now her hunt could begin in earnest.

❖

"What are you in the mood for?" Godfrey asked over the top of his menu.

"I like the Caesar salad here. I'll go for that."

"I'll have the shrimp linguine. What wine?"

"Rosé. Something light and fruity to match this marvelous spring day. And the company."

"Très drôle—" Godfrey's cell phone rang. "Hello...No, not yet. I'm with Hope at Daguerre...Yes, just down the block...No. They're in my pocket." He plunged a hand into his pocket. "Call him back and tell him they're not mine. Okay. Bye." He put his phone away. "Well, that was odd."

"What was?"

"Apparently, I left my house keys at the Naked Vintner, but I have them here." He patted his pocket to a reassuring jingle. "I had to admit I was a mere several yards away stuffing my face with you, instead of dropping by work as promised. Now I'd better go show my face."

"If you were my boss I'd keep you on your toes instead of gadding around town with your fancy woman."

"I'm not gadding around town. I'm taking the day off to celebrate my fancy woman's good health. And you already have a boss to keep on her toes. Poor Jolie." He sighed. "But she does seem to thrive under your special brand of authority."

"That's because I'm a den mother." Hope shook her head. "Don't ask. She's reformed my household into some sort of pack home. The other day I caught her putting Tadpole in charge while she was gone. I swear his tail has been bristlier and his strut cockier since she walked out the door." They both burst into giggles at the thought of Tadpole as a guard dog, and quickly stifled their laughter as the waiter approached for their order.

After lunch they window shopped along Milwaukee to the Enchanted Florist so Godfrey could see his staff for a few minutes.

"It's her again." He pointed surreptitiously across the street. "Over there, on the seat outside the bookstore."

Hope glanced over and noticed the woman from earlier. She sat in the sun, her face raised toward its weak rays. She hadn't seen them yet and it gave Hope a chance to examine her without having to fend off that morose, lost stare. The general untidiness and skinniness concerned her. This was a very unhappy person. But there was something more that Hope could not quite put her finger on. The scrawny, rangy body held an economy of movement, an understated confidence and strength that reminded her of something else—

"Hope! They've got the John White London collection. Let's go see." Godfrey ducked in the door of a shoe store, abandoning Hope on the sidewalk. She turned to follow, and threw one last look at the seat outside the bookstore. It was empty.

"Excuse me. Do you have these in a ten?" Godfrey's voice drifted out the open door. "And in tan? Hope, come see."

Hope looked up and down the sidewalk. There was no sign of the woman. She must have moved at lightning speed. With a mental shrug, she stepped into the shoe store to give Godfrey her full attention.

❖

"Don't you just love the smell of new shoes?" Godfrey held a John White brogue to Hope's nose.

"Ick." She ducked away. "Stop that, or we'll crash." She was driving him home after a pleasant afternoon of browsing in bookstores, boutiques, and shoe shops. Aside from wine and shoes they had a cache of paperback books on the backseat, along with some beautiful imported gerberas Godfrey had snatched from his shop for her "special" news.

"Godfrey," she said. "What did you make of that strange woman we saw at the wine shop and then later on Milwaukee?"

Godfrey shrugged. "I'm not sure. I mean, is it that odd to see someone twice in one day? She was just shopping."

"No way was she shopping. She was odd. Did you get any…vibe from her?"

"Vibe? No. She looked a bit tatty to me. Why? What's up?"

"Nothing. She just seemed a little lost, I suppose. I can't explain it."

"Lost gals are your forte," Godfrey said. "Look at Jolie. She was hopelessly lost until you scooped her up and rocked her hairy little world."

A soul in torment. That's what I thought when I first saw her. Hope frowned. Godfrey's inadvertent comparison made her uneasy, as if she had missed a vital clue. How could she compare that scrap of woebegone she'd seen in the wine shop to her Jolie? Jolie was strong and strapping, and though she looked like she might snap anyone who annoyed her in two, inside she bubbled over with love and kindness.

Yet Hope had seen that same haunted look in her eyes, too. Before she had told Jolie she loved her. Before they had made a commitment to each other, and a home together, and the promise of a happy future.

Her mind drifted to the bottle of champagne wedged on her backseat so it wouldn't topple. With her latest prognosis she felt more confident in that future than ever. The threatening cloud always hanging over them had passed. They had huffed and puffed and blown it away. Soon Jolie would be home and they would uncork the bottle for a private celebration.

Maybe they'd head up to Little Dip and take one of the smaller cabins farther back in the woods. There they would drink champagne and make love. And afterward Jolie would run, just as she always did when her heart grew so big and happy her human body could barely contain it.

And when the moon sank low, she would crawl back home to where Hope sat reading by the fire, waiting for her. Exhausted, Jolie would lie beside her and place her heavy head in Hope's lap. And while the fire crackled, Hope would stroke the soft fur of Jolie's throat. She could never keep her hands off Jolie in wolven form. She'd tickle her ear hairs until they twitched and run her fingers over the damp, leathery creases of her muzzle. She adored the texture of coarse fur and fine hide that covered Jolie's stubby features. She'd trace the long curve of her canines and press her fingertip against each sharp point. The beauty of Jolie as a beast astounded her. Hope could gaze for hours into amber eyes that burned back at her, full of devotion. She could spend the rest of her life wallowing in that gaze, simply loving her monster.

Chapter Seventeen

"What the fuck is going on in there!" Her neighbor thumped on the paper-thin dividing wall.

Isabelle awoke with a start and found she was shaking. She reached up to stroke her damp cheeks.

"Stupid fucking bitch!" He fell silent with one last bellow.

She'd been crying in her sleep again. Always the same, every time. Same dream, same desolate heartache. She was running through a sun-dappled wood. Her powerful leg muscles churned; her claws dug deep in the earth for purchase, breaking open the scent of the forest floor. Ren was at her shoulder. Together they raced through the forest, leaping over fallen branches and weaving through the trees. Exhilarated, she hurtled into a meadow of blowsy wildflowers, and found herself alone. Ren had been ripped from her side. Lost and alone, Isabelle squatted among the blue buttons and bittersweet and threw back her head and howled.

Isabelle touched her throat. It was raw, as if she'd been screaming all night long. She struggled out of bed on weak legs, embarrassed she had agitated her neighbor again. She'd be evicted soon if she couldn't control these dreams.

She went to the bathroom and ran the shower until the water was scalding hot, then stepped under it with a painful gasp. Isabelle didn't look in mirrors these days. Her soapy hands told her she was losing weight. They ran over flaccid muscle and the ridges of her rib cage. Her hair lay lank and lusterless around thin shoulders. She knew how unkempt and anorexic she must look.

The hot shower did not work. She was listless and only half present, even though her skin stung from the hot water.

Isabelle roamed about the apartment naked until her skin dried. She moved to the kitchenette and poured a glass of water and gulped it down in one go, then she poured another and another. She itched, she moaned. She shuffled about, unable to settle. Outside, the streetlights glowed over wet streets, and rain rattled through the windblown shrubs before the building steps.

Isabelle pulled on some old sweats and sneakers and settled on the couch with her digital camera. She played with the buttons until she finally opened the slideshow of her Canadian vacation. Trees, mountains, and colorful birds slid by. Aunt Mary smiled up at her with Atwell cuddled in her arms. How she adored her aunt Mary. The woman had fostered her as a child and had offered only hope and happiness for the six years Isabelle had stayed with her. Mary was in Miami now. Isabelle had spoken to her once since her return to Portland, but had hesitated from telling her about her ill health or misadventures. What could Mary do besides worry herself sick? She was seventy-two and on the other side of the country. Isabelle would talk to her when she eventually knew what to say about this episode in her life.

The next shots were a series on river toads; the photos made her nostalgic for a holiday she could still barely remember. Then came the photograph she was waiting for, the one that mesmerized her. Ren and the mysterious stranger. They sat side by side on a fallen log. They had to be sisters, both dark and brooding, and both incredibly handsome women. One looked at her; a ferocious passion danced across her hooded eyes. Her cheeks dimpled as her lips creased into a happy smile for the camera. This was Ren. Ren with an unconcealed look of love for her alone. Isabelle's stomach knotted at the loss of that day. She could not recall it, but here it was frozen and digitalized forever so she could look at it in wonder and longing again and again.

Beside Ren sat the other woman, and though a mirror image to look at she was her polar opposite in attitude. This woman was cold. Her eyes were black as pitch. They captured light and refused to release it. Her gaze was not happy or warm, but defiant and calculating. Her hair shone blue-black in the weak sunlight, and a scarlet smile curved her lips like a saber. She was as beautiful and venomous as a blue coral snake.

Who are you? Why do I dislike you so much? Isabelle snapped off the power and set the camera aside. She couldn't remember this other woman so like Ren, but Isabelle did not trust her. She worried that in her partial amnesia she had muddled the two in her mind. Was she right to trust the memories she had striven so hard to find? Her idea of Ren was blurred. Her feelings toward her did not harmonize with Ren's actions in Singing Valley.

Maybe she had no true memory of Ren after all. Everything was so polluted with the possibility of the sister. Like her journal, all her memories of Ren and their time together were burned around the edges. Vast chunks were missing, possibly lost forever.

Isabelle's throat scorched with an uncomfortable rash. Her eyes itched with tears of frustration. Everything was burning her up—her clothes, the apartment. She was allergic to normal these days. The dry, heated air in her lungs made her feel wizened from the inside out. Claustrophobia clawed at her. She felt panicked. Isabelle knew what she had to do.

The door clicked shut after her, and she stood in the hall drawing in cool mouthfuls of air. After a few minutes her heartbeat settled and her panic lessened. She strode along the hallway to the stairwell, avoiding the elevator with its confined space, and stale air, and mirrors. She stepped out into the night and walked briskly away from her block. Then she jogged for a few more streets. Then she broke into a full run, sprinting across Sellwood straight for Hope Glassy's house.

"What is it, Taddy?" Hope opened the kitchen door. Tadpole hovered on the doorstep and sniffed the breeze. "Hurry up, you silly dog. I can't stand here all day being your doorman."

Usually, he was tripping her up in his eagerness to get outside for his morning patrol. With a nervous nose twitch, he finally cleared the threshold, making straight for the locust tree that marked the boundary with the neighbor.

Hope poured herself a cup of coffee and, nursing the mug in both hands, followed Tadpole into the garden. Early-morning dew glistened on every blade of grass, the first rosebuds peeped shyly from glossy green foliage, and birdsong filled the air. Her spirits lifted. Spring was a favorite season.

Tadpole ran an excited circuit from the locust to her decking and back again, his nose buried in the grass. Hope's steps faltered. Large mud-spattered footprints covered her back deck. From the amount she could tell they belonged to one creature, and from the size and shape, Hope knew they were wolven.

❖

"Godfrey. Get over here now." Hope had her phone pressed to her ear and Tadpole wriggling under the other arm. She had grabbed him and locked them both inside the house. "I don't care what time it is. I don't care if it's a minute past midnight and you're a pumpkin. I've got a prowler, and it's the hairy kind. Get over here as fast as you can." She hung up and put Tadpole down. He ran straight to the kitchen door, begging to be let out to sniff some more.

"It's not a good time to be curious, Taddy. We've got an unwelcome visitor. You're staying indoors with me until we find out what's going on."

He ran back to the living room, jumped up on the couch, and pressed his nose to the window, clearly on sentry duty. Hope left him there, glaring up and down the street. Now that Jolie was out of town and he'd assumed the rank of protector, he had decided he was allowed on the furniture, especially at times of high alert. Hope hadn't the energy to chase him off her couch. Her stomach was churning with nerves.

She returned to the kitchen to sit and fret at the small kitchen table. She wished Jolie were home; she'd know what to do with trespassing werewolves. Zagoria was not the easiest place in Greece to catch a phone signal. It had been two days since she'd last heard from her, and Hope missed her badly.

She had to keep busy until Godfrey arrived, so she clanged about the kitchen, breaking eggs into a bowl for pancake batter. The snap and splinter of the shells became an anodyne for her shattered nerves. The sharp crack of the whisk on the ceramic bowl was strangely soothing. At least she was keeping her panic at bay. Godfrey would be here soon and they would both need a good breakfast and strong coffee before they started to investigate her midnight prowler.

❖

"Oh, my God." Godfrey examined the ground around Hope's backyard with dismay. Her flowerbeds were trampled and mud was tracked all over the path and back decking. "This thing's huge!"

"I can see that. It's hardly reassuring."

"Look at those scratches." He pointed out the long scores on the paintwork around the patio doors. "It was looking for a way in. I don't like this, Hope. You and the Tadpole are coming home with me. Jolie and Andre can deal with this when they get back."

"They won't be back until next week. And I don't want to leave my home. All my stuff is here."

"Stuff? Stuff! This is a feral werewolf, Hope. I hardly think it's after your fruit teas of the world collection, or your Doris Day forty-fives! It wants to *eat* you! There'll be nothing left except what forensics find in its poop."

"Does *American Theater Magazine* know you're missing?"

"This is not mere drama, Hope. This is factual. *You* are on a menu."

"I don't want to move out, Godfrey." Hope said, feeling defeated. "This is my home. My and Jolie's home. Our den. If I run away I'll feel like I let her down or something."

"Nonsense. It's the only sane thing to do. Jolie would never forgive me if I let you stay here. Besides, I've got your keys." He waggled a bunch of keys at her.

"You filched those off my kitchen counter." Hope made a grab for her keys, but Godfrey swung them out of reach. She tried a more adult approach. "Look, whatever it is, it must know the house is alarmed. It was just snooping. It smells Garoul all over the place and is checking out the scent."

"It's snooping around because it knows Jolie isn't here. No way would a feral come anywhere near a Garoul den," Godfrey said.

"Exactly. How does it know Jolie's gone, huh? I think it's just a stupid, nosy feral."

"And I think it's opportunist and extremely dangerous. You're coming home with me. I'm lonely. Get packed." Godfrey stood back and looked up at the building. "How did it get so close with these sensor lights? The glare should have sent it scooting."

"The bulbs burned out ages ago. With Jolie around I guess I didn't think it was that important," Hope said, a little shamefaced.

"Well, having a werewolf in the house does make one a little blasé about home security. Let's get these lights up and running. We'll replace the bulbs and redirect the sensors onto the patio. Might as well give Mr. Snoopy a little razzle-dazzle next time he comes around. Not that you'll be here to watch him run."

Godfrey was right. It was silly to stay here when something big, ugly, and carnivorous was sniffing around outside her house. Besides, Jolie arrived from Athens next Wednesday; a long stay at Andre and Godfrey's luxury penthouse might be fun.

"Okay, Home Depot it is for the spare bulbs. I'll leave Tadpole here. He's fast asleep under the couch. Seems a whole hour on guard duty has pooped him out."

"See? Look at us holding the fort. Wouldn't Andre and Jolie be proud at how clever we are? So grab your purse and let's go."

❖

She'd started with the blond guy. Godfrey. She watched as he went about his work, and skulked around the bookstores and coffee shops close to his flower shop. His scent was good, a tart lemon verbena that promised summer and smelled of sunlight and fizzy sorbet. But it was only a top note. His underscent was dark and very sexual. His mate was strong, not an Alpha like Ren, but important enough to saturate his lover in a wolven musk that signaled his ownership for miles.

Isabelle had no interest in him. It was the woman who accompanied him that snared her. A small, dark-haired, compact woman, who had been wounded somehow, but was not weak. *Her* scent was something else. Complex and powerful…and safe. Isabelle couldn't break it down into component parts. She didn't fully understand it, and that intrigued her.

In a matter of days, she had discovered the woman's name. Hope Glassy. And where she lived. At first, Isabelle's wanderings had brought her by Hope's small house. Drawn by scent and a vague, unfocused notion that some sort of solace could be found by simply being close by.

Now she actively sought it out. By day she would casually walk past unseen on the other side of the street, confident in the knowledge

Hope had gone out to work. She knew because she watched Hope bustle out the door with her bag and umbrella at six forty-five a.m. on the dot. At night, after Hope returned and walked her dog, Isabelle would lurk in any handy shadow and watch the darkened windows.

Sometimes the little ginger dog would bark from inside the house. He knew she was there, but he didn't threaten; he wanted her to know he was aware.

Isabelle was fascinated. This was a pack home, a small one, and the woman was central to it. A big wolf lived here. A mean one. But the woman kept it tame and cared for it. She wondered what it was like to be on the inside. What comfort and answers lay behind the happy yellow door? But she could sense warning, too. This woman was mated, she was a mainstay in a wolven world Isabelle knew nothing about. The house, its walls, roof, yard, windows, even the path leading up to that yellow door pulsed with warning, as if a protective spell had been wrapped around the entire building. Isabelle felt it right through to her bones, and coveted it.

She'd been out all night and was starving. Her appetite was enormous these days, despite the fact she was losing weight at a steady pace. She was exhausted now. Her feet hurt from walking, but she didn't want to go back to her apartment until her neighbor had left for work. She didn't want to meet him in the hall. She prickled around him; she wanted to snap her teeth and growl out a warning for him to leave her alone. To step back and keep out of her head space, it was too crowded in there already.

Barry made her feel like that, too, with his whining self-pity and passive threats. Thinking of him always made her upset and uneasy. She didn't trust him. He'd been trying too hard to find out where she'd moved to. He wanted her to go back to him. He begged and cried and pestered her until she felt choked.

Isabelle circled Eastmoreland with a graceful, measured stride and slowly headed back to the only segment of city that made her feel secure: Sellwood and Hope Glassy's house. If she kept too far away it made her anxious. Hope's home was the nucleus to her ever-contracting world.

The neighborhood was waking up to a sun-filled Friday morning. People were beginning their commute. Traffic was increasing. Cars and school buses passed by her. She had stopped running once she hit the busier streets. Now she wrapped her coat tighter around her body and trudged on, trying to blend in.

Two blocks away from Sellwood Park a dark luxury car cruised past. Isabelle glanced up and locked eyes with the woman in the passenger seat. Hope Glassy stared back; it took a split second before recognition flashed across her face. Isabelle turned away to stare blindly at a shop window.

The car rolled on, and in the window's reflection Isabelle could see Hope twist in her seat to look back. Isabelle ducked her head and scuttled away. It was a bad thing to be seen this close to Hope's house. Part of her was panicked, and part thrilled that Hope remembered her. Perhaps she had some sort of an affinity, too? No. More likely Isabelle had been careless and Hope was aware of her. Her rashness had sabotaged even the simple luxury of walking past Hope's house. If she wanted to continue her quiet visits, then no one had to know. If she couldn't go to this house and soak up the scents and the calming ambience that pulsed out of it, she would die. As simple as that. She was withering away as it was, becoming more and more lost and incapable. For some unfathomable reason, this little house gave her hope and promised all manner of possibilities. It was her oxygen. The most basic component of her current existence.

She stumbled on. The streets were quieter now that the initial commuter rush had tailed off. She turned the corner of Hope's block. The yellow door winked invitingly at her. Hope's Ford was parked out front, but she knew she had gone away in the big black car. It was safe.

Isabelle began her vigil by slowly walking by, her eyes glued on the house, always looking for clues as to the pack that lived there. She basked in the fleeting calm that filled her, and wondered at the lure that kept bringing her back. A fuzzy ginger head popped up at the window and the little dog began to bark. The glass muted his shrill yapping. Isabelle hesitated. He was barking out some sort of welcome rather than the warning she'd half expected.

Now he was playing a game. He'd duck down from the window and run along the couch, only to pop up at the other end and bark at her again. Isabelle crossed the road and stood before Hope's front lawn watching. Back and forth he ran for a good five minutes or more, popping up at one end of the window, then the other until a smile creased Isabelle's face and a chuckle bubbled in her chest. She could not remember the last time she'd smiled; her face was etched into a blank mask these days. People didn't register her, or if they did, they ignored her. The dehumanizing suited her—she was a no one, a derelict, an invisible. Now this little dog and his antics had her standing in the street giggling.

The laugh lifted her spirits and made her feel giddy. She forgot herself for a moment and came right up to the living room window. His barks became louder and more excited. Her reflection caught her eye and wiped the smile from her face. She looked awful. Her hair was a mess and she had dark smudges under her eyes and scratches on her cheek and neck. That did not surprise her. Her skin had become unbearably itchy these last few days no matter how much she bathed or smothered herself in creams. She focused beyond her reflection and into the room itself. She had never been this close to Hope's house before, and her eyes devoured every little detail. She saw a cozy living room, airy and bright, and styled in neutral shades and warm cherry wood. Bold artwork adorned the walls, and occasional mementos and photographs were scattered on various surfaces.

Isabelle zoned in on one of these now. On a small table beside the couch she could make out a framed photo. Hope Glassy stood before a tall, dark-haired woman. They'd been skiing, and they glowed against a backdrop of white slopes and blue sky. The taller woman had her chin resting on Hope's shoulder and her arms wrapped around her. They were laughing for the camera. Isabelle's stomach did somersaults. She felt physically sick to the point of staggering. Hope Glassy smiled up at her from the circle of Ren's arms.

In a fit of foolhardiness, fueled by stupidity and pure jealously, she slunk around the side of the building. The backyard was secluded from the neighbors but she was still uneasy. She wrinkled her nose. A musky scent lingered in the air, faint and spiced with anger and a slow, simmering malice kept on a short leash. A shiver ran through her. She was on another wolf's territory, skulking around its mate. Her fingers brushed across the rough scratches on the doorjamb. Deliberate marking, a warning of some kind, but she couldn't read or understand the scores.

A tinny bark rang out. The dog had followed her around to the kitchen door. Isabelle reached out and touched the handle, and with the gentlest of pressure, she pushed down. It slowly swung open on well-oiled hinges.

CHAPTER EIGHTEEN

"We went to buy home security stuff and you left the door
wide open?"

"*You* left the door wide open. You stole my keys, remember? I
assumed *you'd* have the wit to lock up." Hope took a timorous step
into her kitchen. It had been ransacked. The fridge lay open, its shelves
stripped, the contents strewn on the floor and over the countertops. All
the kitchen cupboards hung open and cereal packets, cookies, raisins,
fruit, flour, rice—everything edible had been ripped apart. But Hope
had other, more pressing concerns.

"Taddy?" she called in a fear-filled, wobbly voice. He came tearing
down the hall to meet her. "Oh, thank God you're all right."

He jumped up on his hind legs to welcome her, smearing her
skirt with buttery paws. Before she could grab him, he snatched a raw
sausage from the floor and made for the living room, his tail wagging
all the way in triumph.

"Oh my God," Godfrey said. "Look at this place. How did he
manage it?"

"Tadpole didn't do this. He's grabbed at the heaven-sent
opportunity some other intruder left for him."

"Well, he seems happily unconcerned," Godfrey said. "We'd
better check the rest of the house, then call the police."

Tadpole's sticky paw prints were everywhere, evidence of his
delight at the ransacked kitchen. But Hope wasn't looking for his paw
prints. She was worried there might be other, far larger ones. There
were none that she could see, but they had to check the rest of the house
just in case.

"Do you think it was the feral?" Godfrey cautiously moved ahead of her to follow Tadpole.

"Maybe. It could still be in the house. Be careful, Godfrey."

"Nah. It must be long gone or Taddy wouldn't be so cheerful. Even he wouldn't dive on a free feast if there was a feral loose in the hou—" His words were cut short as they entered the living room. Tadpole sat shivering with excitement on the couch, his eyes glued on the woman in the chair opposite. His tail thumped up and down nervously, but it was obvious he liked the stranger.

Godfrey froze by the doorway, and Hope had to push past him to confront the stranger. This was the woman she'd seen lurking around the neighborhood in the past few weeks. Now she sat in Hope's house, in Jolie's favorite armchair, nursing a photograph taken on their winter vacation.

"Hello," Hope said with as much calm as she could muster. Quickly she assessed the situation, but felt no immediate danger. The floor around the woman's feet was littered with Tadpole treasure brought for her delectation. The snatched sausage lay there, along with some broken cookies, his bed blanket, and a favorite play ball. It was almost a shrine. Whoever she was, she had Taddy's seal of approval, and that made Hope relax ever so slightly. They were not in immediate danger.

"There was no need to break and enter. You only had to knock." She set out to take control with courteous authority. This was her home—den, whatever. She was the boss here.

"I didn't break in. Honestly. The door was open. I'm sorry about the kitchen. I can't stop eating. I get a little crazy around food these days."

"I think I understand," Hope said, examining the woman more closely. Who was she? Where had she come from? There was no mistaking the air of vulnerability around her. She was strung-out and plainly wretched.

"Well, I don't," Godfrey muttered behind her.

"I promise to clean it all up." The woman addressed Godfrey directly, picking up on his quiet words.

"I've seen you before," Hope said, and steered the conversation where she wanted it to go. She needed this woman to trust her enough to explain what was going on. "Over on Milwaukee, and again by the park."

The fact that she had been hanging around the neighborhood showed she wanted to establish contact of some sort, but was probably unsure how.

"Oh my God." Godfrey had picked up on who she was now.

"I live nearby. Close to Reed," the woman said.

Reed College was ten minutes away. Hope tried again, more direct this time. "I'm Hope Glassy and this is my friend Godfrey Meyers. What's your name?"

"Isabelle. Isabelle Monk. Are you going to call the police? I didn't mean to come in. But I did eat all your food. I'm sorry." Her voice sounded tight and panicked.

"It's okay, Isabelle," Hope reassured her. "I don't think the police would be useful in this situation. You're wolven, aren't you?"

Isabelle stiffened. "No. No, I'm not. At first I thought you were. But when I got closer, you both seemed different. You smelled…"

"Human."

"Not quite. Not like everyone else does."

Hope indicated the photo frame Isabelle nursed in her hands. "That's because our partners are wolven."

"I know." She looked down at the photo, her hands trembled. "Your partner is so like Ren," she said. "I saw this through the window and had to take a closer look. I thought it was her for a moment."

She seemed very crestfallen.

Hope perched on the edge of the couch and scratched Tadpole's ears before pushing him off onto the floor.

"That's my partner Jolie. I don't know anyone called Ren." This was interesting and confirmed Hope's suspicions as to why Isabelle had latched on to her and Godfrey's scent. There had to be a Garoul connection.

"She's so like Ren," Isabelle repeated, confounded by the likeness.

"Look closer. Do you see that little chip in the lower front tooth? Jolie also has a fleck of black outside the edge of her iris. Look at her left eye. The fleck is on the upper outside edge. See?"

Isabelle studied the photo, becoming more confused. "I can see the differences up close, but from a distance it's really spooky how alike they are."

"The Garouls are a big family. I suspect this Ren of yours is connected to them in some way."

"She's not my Ren."

"Tell me what happened, Isabelle," Hope said softly. Isabelle was squinting at the photo, turning it at different angles to the light. She was either still transfixed by the likeness or entranced by something that so reminded her of this Ren person. Finally, she set the photo frame back down.

"I really thought that was Ren with you." There was a little relief in her voice, but not enough to make her sound entirely happy. "Now I feel stupid."

"Don't. When you know them better it's easy to tell them apart. But at first glance all the Garouls bear a strong resemblance to each other," Godfrey said.

"Can we assume your Ren is probably a Garoul?" Hope asked.

"She's not my Ren and I don't know the Garouls." Isabelle's tone hardened. "Well, I did see one of their almanacs once. In Ren's kitchen…" She trailed off, embarrassed and distracted.

Hope could see she was becoming agitated. She needed Isabelle to remain calm, to tell them what had happened so they would know how to help.

"Can I talk to you for a moment," Godfrey said. It was a statement, not a question, and he indicated Hope follow him back out into the hall.

"Are we mad? There's a feral sitting in your living room. Shouldn't we be calling someone? Getting advice. I think we should call Marie," he whispered urgently once they were out of the room.

"Taddy seems to think she's harmless."

"Taddy also drinks from the toilet bowl, hardly harmless."

"He hasn't done that in ages. But you have a point. I'll keep talking to her and try to find out who this Ren is. She sounds like a Garoul, but none that I've met."

"Me neither. The name isn't familiar. I wonder who she is?"

"Look, you go to the kitchen and call Little Dip. Tell Marie what's going on and see what she says."

"Okay. But I'm still nervous. Don't turn your back on her for one second. It's too convenient that she should come calling the minute Jolie and Andre are out of town."

Hope returned to the living room. "Godfrey's going to clean up the kitchen and make us some tea."

"What's Little Dip and who's Marie?" Isabelle asked. "I could hear you talking."

So she had other heightened wolven senses besides smell. Her hearing was exceptional. Hope jotted this away for future reference. She decided to be straightforward with Isabelle. She needed her trust if she was to help her in any way.

"Little Dip is the Garoul home valley. And Marie is the Garoul Alpha. We're asking her for advice." She kept her answers honest and to a minimum. "For the moment, let's just concentrate on your story, Isabelle. Tell me what happened to you, from the beginning."

"What sort of advice?"

"I'm not sure yet. But Marie will know how to keep you safe."

"I don't feel safe. I feel like I'm going mad." Her voice and body trembled.

"Godfrey will bring us some tea. It will warm you up. Meantime, tell me how you got to be…unsafe."

"That's part of the whole mess. Some of my memories are missing. I had a car crash. Well, I know now that I probably strayed into the middle of a hunt. There was this deer…" Her voice faded away and her eyes took on a distant, troubled look.

"What about the deer?" Hope gently called her back to the present. Isabelle took a deep breath and continued.

"They were hunting deer. There seemed to be dozens of them everywhere, but I found out later there were only five or six." Again her voice took on an edge that worried Hope. How much control did Isabelle have? Godfrey was right. It was madness to stay in the house with her, but Isabelle was here now and ready to talk to them, to share her story. And they had to find out what the hell had happened to her in order to help her. A feral werewolf should *not* be prowling the streets of Portland. And no matter how much Isabelle might deny it, she was wolven. The Garouls had to be told, but Hope wanted the full story before the Garoul machine went into motion.

"I passed out." Isabelle spoke haltingly, as if reluctant to share, or maybe to recall her story at all. "When I came to I was at Ren's farm. I was in a bad way, my shoulder was dislocated and my face black and blue. Ren was...is a vet. She dressed my wounds, but I'd had a bang on the head and couldn't remember much. It all came back in dribs and drabs later...Well, most of it. I still have blanks. Every day a little more falls into place." Throughout her talking Isabelle's hands couldn't remain still. She plucked at her loose clothing, twisted and pulled on strands of hair. She poked at her fingernails and cuticles. She was a ball of nervous energy eating itself up. Hope watched, fascinated; her heart went out to the young woman. What was hurting her the most—the memories she struggled to relay, or those still to surface?

"Ren was good to me, at first. They all were. She had a group of young people staying with her. She told me they were drifters and runaways. She employed them to help with the farm work."

Hope frowned. "You mean she had a pack? Where was this, Isabelle?" she asked.

"I don't want to tell you. Not yet. It's in Canada, in the middle of nowhere. That's all you need to know right now."

"We're not going to go after them or harm them in any way. I'm just interested in your story," Hope said. Trust had to be earned. It was enough for now that Isabelle was telling her this much. It would be useful information for Marie later. Somewhere in the background of this story was a Garoul who ran with ferals. That had to be mightily important.

Her reassurance calmed Isabelle.

"It was a hard spring and the valley was under a lot of snow," Isabelle continued. "Ren told me we were snowed in, and that's why she couldn't get me to a hospital. But I found out later there were logging roads nearby and a float plane that could come in at any time with supplies. I was being held captive...in the nicest possible way, of course. She hid my passport and my money." Her eyes implored Hope to believe her. "I know it sounds weird. I even found my wrecked car burned out in a gully."

"I believe you." Hope meant every word. Amy Fortune had been hunted by a feral in Little Dip, under the very noses of the Garouls. She believed anything of these creatures with the guile of a wolf and malice of mankind. It was alarming if this Ren had Garoul connections yet behaved like a feral. Ferals were a maverick force.

"I found out what they really were. At first I thought I'd lost my mind, that the knock on my head had given me hallucinations. But I know what I saw, and I ran. And now I'm having the strangest dreams." She pulled at a loose fold of clothing. "Look. I'm fading away, getting thinner and thinner. I can't get warm, then suddenly I overheat. I can't stop eating, but I'm skeletal. It's as if I have a disease. A cancer that's eating me up, and I'm frightened. What if they changed me?" Her fingers fluttered to her shoulder. Her words poured out faster and faster, becoming garbled. "I don't want to be a…a werewolf…wolven, whatever you called it. But I think I am. Everything looks different and smells different. Everything is sharper, cleaner, clearer. I see colors I never knew existed. And smells tell me actual stories, and it freaks me out."

"Okay. Okay." Hope held out her hands to calm Isabelle down. She was becoming extremely upset, and Hope was shaken, too. She understood this panic, the struggle for control over one's body, the stress that something malevolent was eating you up from the inside out. She'd been prisoner to that feeling herself, only to gain a reprieve a few days ago. She'd do anything to give Isabelle hope, to reassure her there was light at the end of the tunnel.

"I've cleaned up the kitchen and made us all a nice pot of tea." Godfrey breezed into the room with a tray and lifted the whole atmosphere. "The mess was driving me mad."

He gave Hope an intense look as he poured.

"I know you were calling your friend," Isabelle said. She was tired and her words were listless. "Marie and Little Dip. I could hear you both talking in the hall. What did she say? Can she help?"

Godfrey threw Hope a shocked look.

She shrugged. "Wolfie ears. What did Marie say?"

"Well, she's fascinated by this Ren person, and Claude is on his way even as we speak. Claude is Andre and Jolie's father," he explained to Isabelle. "He sort of counsels the younger ones and looks after any of the partners who choose to change. He's a sort of…educator, I guess."

"Partners who choose to change? You mean become werewolves?"

"It's always an option. Werewolves mate for life. Once you enter the Garoul clan you have the choice to remain human or change, if you wish," he said.

"But changing can be dangerous, so it's a big decision," Hope said.

"I had no choice. If…if that's what's happening to me."

Godfrey and Hope both shifted uncomfortably.

"What's happened to you is unforgivable, Isabelle. There's a term we use called 'feral.' It's for people who have been attacked and… forced into transmutation," Godfrey said. Hope was thankful for his diplomatic choice of words. It was rare to survive a werewolf attack, never mind become one through a mauling. "But because they are outside of a wolven pack and its protection and rules, the odds of surviving as a werewolf are much harder. That's why *some* ferals band together to form packs of their own. But it's kind of anarchic compared to established wolven society."

"And the Garouls will help me?" Isabelle asked. Her voice was weak and tired.

"We can't think of anyone better. They have been around for hundreds of years and will know what to do. You'll be safe in Little Dip, and Claude is coming to collect you. He's the best. Honest," he said.

"Isabelle," Hope spoke gently. All the talk of Garouls and their partners had made her thoughtful. "Forgive me for asking this, but you and Ren…were you close?"

Isabelle stiffened and Hope had her answer. She swapped a telling look with Godfrey. This young woman was the partner of the Were who'd bitten her. That was probably not a good thing. She was not the product of an erroneous attack, or a hunt gone wrong as she claimed. She had been deliberately chosen. Hope widened her eyes and nodded at the door, giving Godfrey the "clear off" message. He shook his head, obviously uneasy at leaving her alone in the house. Hope glared at him hard. She had to get Isabelle to trust her enough to tell her about this relationship, and that would not happen if Godfrey stood guard. There was a risk, but Hope felt safe enough to take it.

"Ladies." Godfrey tactfully broke the silence. "This little fella looks like he needs some tinkle-time. I'll take him over to the shop with me for an hour. Call me if you need me." He looked pointedly at Hope. "Come on, Taddy, let's go to the park and leave the gals to gossip."

Tadpole was glued to his heels in seconds. Hope waited until the front door closed before turning her full attention on Isabelle.

"I'm asking because Ren's behavior, in a wolf sort of way, could be seen as a sort of, well, courtship?" she said.

Isabelle held her gaze with an unfathomable look that unnerved Hope completely, but she pressed on anyway, hoping her instincts were correct and she had not got it appallingly wrong.

"What I mean is, this marking you and hiding you away, it's very wolven. Marking can take the form of a bite, or layering on of scent, for instance." Still, Isabelle held her gaze unblinkingly. Her eyes were overly bright and focused entirely on Hope. Hope perched on the edge of her seat, her discomfort growing. Why had she let Godfrey go?

"I mean, when Jolie decided she…liked me, like that, she bit me. Okay, so it was in her sleep, but she's…well…odd like that. But it was a mark nevertheless, and though I didn't realize it at the time, it was a sign of ownership among her clan. Perhaps your Ren and her pack have something similar? Do you think that may be the case?"

This was met with a wall of silence.

"She's not my Ren," Isabelle muttered but broke her gaze from Hope's. She sat staring at the back of her hands. It was a subconscious submissive gesture and Hope took the initiative it afforded her.

"I think she is."

A minute of silence ticked by before Isabelle said, "I miss her. She made me feel…I don't know. Something. Something that was good for me. But I don't know if it was because she bit me or because we knew each other from before."

"You knew each other before?" This threw Hope. "Where? How?"

"I don't know. That's the part of my memory that's still missing." Isabelle's frustration flooded out. She thumped her knees. "If only I could remember, then I'd know if she was good or bad for me. It's awful when you have strong feelings but can't remember the root cause of them. I can't just follow my heart like other people do. I need to understand why I feel like this. Where it came from, how I changed and came to love—" She broke off and blushed scarlet. She trembled all over.

"Oh, sweetie." Hope moved to sit beside her and put her arms around her. "I understand. Really I do."

When she fell in love with Jolie Garoul her world had blown apart. A small world, but one she had guarded jealously because of her ill health. Wolven lovers catapulted all order, reason, sense of self out the window. They bounded into your life, pounced on everything, and took over, offering nothing in return bar unconditional love, devotion, protection, adoration—the list went on and on. She hugged the shivering body closer, alarmed at how paper thin and fragile Isabelle felt in her arms. Her neck grew damp with Isabelle's tears.

"I'm so scared and exhausted. I don't want to be a werewolf. I just want my memory back and to read my books. I miss my books," Isabelle mumbled into Hope's shoulder.

"Your books?"

"I teach part-time at Reed and PCC." Isabelle sniffed and drew away, wiping her eyes and damp cheeks with the back of her hands. "Gothic romance. How bizarre is that? Gothic romance, and I'm bitten by a werewolf. I thought I'd dreamed it, it's so freaking fantastical. But every morning I wake up to it, and it's real, and my life's a mess. I can't even concentrate enough to read anymore. Books were my only escape, but now even that's lost. I had to take the whole term off, said I was ill. I know I'll lose my job but I can't go back looking like this. I'm a mess. I feel raw and exposed. There's nowhere safe."

"You can't make such dire predictions until you know all the facts, Isabelle. You said some of your memories are missing. Those pieces hold information to help you process what's happened and where you go from here. For the moment let's just concentrate on you, and what you need, and what you can remember. I promise to do all I can to look after you and make you comfortable. Godfrey and I will both help. We'll keep you as safe as we can until we get you to the Garouls."

Hope glanced at the clock. Godfrey had been gone for some time. It would have been nice to have his support here. He generally knew the best thing to say in situations like this.

❖

"Oh, my God."

Godfrey stood with the small crowd at Sellwood Park south gate.

Tadpole flopped by Godfrey's feet on his leash, bored with the delay. Police tape crisscrossed the way in, and two police officers politely kept people at bay. Behind him on the street sat several assorted police vehicles with flashing lights.

"What's going on?" he asked the bystander on his right.

"Some guy was murdered."

"Oh, my God. In Sellwood Park?"

"Down in Oakes Bottom. A jogger found him. He was all beat up."

"He was mauled," the bystander on Godfrey's left said.

"Mauled?"

"Shredded," the new guy said. "Like jerky. Guts all over the place."

"Oh my God."

"Hanging from the trees, they were."

"Wow." The first bystander was fascinated. Their attention was dragged away from the gory details by a sudden flash. Bright lights lit up the police cruisers. A TV report was being broadcast live from the roadside using the dramatic flashing blues as a backdrop.

"What's he saying?" bystander number two asked. "I can't hear him."

"He's saying the dead guy jogged here frequently. First reports say he's Barry Monk, and he teaches at Marylhurst University," bystander number one answered.

Godfrey frowned. The name rang a bell. Barry Monk. Barry Monk. Monk. It was an uncommon surname, and he'd heard it recently. Monk. His blood pressure dropped into his shoes. Monk. Barry Monk with his guts hanging from the trees. And Isabelle Monk, the werewolf, sitting at home with Hope.

"Oh, my God." He had left Hope alone with a stone-cold killer! Godfrey sidled from the crowd as quickly as he could, dragging Tadpole behind him.

Once free of the crowd, he took off as fast as he could to Hope's house, uncaring that Tadpole's stubby little legs could hardly keep up.

CHAPTER NINETEEN

I didn't kill him." Isabelle was white as a sheet. "I didn't. Please don't say I did." Anxiety pulsed off her. Tadpole had managed to wriggle onto her lap, and now she sat stroking his soft fur unthinkingly.

"I'm not saying you did it. I'm just saying you're a werewolf and your ex-husband is in shreds in Oakes Bottom," Godfrey said. "Not a good look."

"He's not my ex-husband. We're not divorced yet."

"He's an ex-something. How about breather."

"Godfrey. That is not helpful. Can't you see she's upset?" Hope said.

"I'm upset, too. I'm the one who left you here with a possible killer."

"I didn't do it. I'm not a killer!"

"Let's all calm down." Hope glared at Godfrey, and he did manage to look a little contrite. She could see his nerves were stretched to the breaking point.

"I didn't do it. I didn't," Isabelle repeated like a mantra.

"What say I make us more tea? Hope, can you help me with it?" He nodded toward the door. Hope gave Isabelle an apologetic smile and followed him to the kitchen.

"Well, that was subtle." Hope took a seat at the table. "She might be able to hear us all the way down here, anyway. Her hearing is exceptional."

In answer Godfrey flicked on the electric kettle and started talking over its bubble. "This is crazy. She has to have done it unless a Bengal tiger is on the loose."

"Tadpole seems to be okay with her. That makes me hesitate to—"

"He's a ho for anyone who looks like they have a biscuit in their pocket!"

"Nevertheless, he's always right."

"Great, the dog wags his tail and we can all relax, assured she won't rip us asunder."

"Look, Taddy was okay when he met Jolie, and he knew she was wolven before I did."

"He nearly had a heart attack when you took him to Little Dip!"

"Please don't fight." Isabelle stood at the kitchen door, Tadpole in her arms. "I've brought you nothing but stress. I'm so sorry I burst in on your lives like this. I'm leaving right now." She set Tadpole down. "I've nothing to hide from the police. I'm going back to my apartment to wait for them."

"Honey, it's not the police we're worried about. If you didn't kill Barry, then something else did. I'm not sure you're safe."

"When you change into a Were, can you remember what you do?" Godfrey asked bluntly.

"I don't change. That's just it," Isabelle said. She sank into a kitchen chair. It was obvious she was still in shock.

Hope was annoyed at Godfrey for his blunt questioning but realized they needed answers, and fast. "You don't change?"

"What? Never?"

Hope and Godfrey spoke over each other in their surprise.

"I dream of it. All the time. And Ren is always there, running with me. Guiding me through a forest. But I've never physically changed." She looked down and plucked at the sweater hanging from her shoulders. "Maybe I'm too weak? Maybe I'm one of those ferals that won't survive a change, so my body somehow suppresses it? Can that happen?"

Hope and Godfrey didn't know, but they doubted it.

"Then what was outside your house last night, if it wasn't her?" Godfrey said.

Hope looked at him blankly. "I never thought of that. I just assumed it was…" She looked across to Isabelle.

Isabelle looked at them suspiciously. "What?" she asked uneasily. "What about last night?"

"Come with me." Hope rose and had them follow her to the back deck.

"This." She pointed to the muddy wolven prints. "Were you here last night?"

"I was. I'm here most nights. But not this close. Never this close. It took all my courage to come this far, and that was only because the dog told me to."

"Tadpole told you to?" Godfrey's eyebrows rose.

"Well, sort of. I'm not sure how, but I knew he was making me welcome and wanted me to come closer. And then when I saw the photograph and I was…compelled, I suppose. But I swear I've never come around the back of your house." She looked at the dried-out mud prints. "They're enormous. Is this your partner?" she asked Hope.

"Hell, no. Though it could easily be Jolie's feet," Godfrey blurted. "Shit. We need to think this through." He turned to Hope.

"I thought I could scent a Were earlier, and just assumed it was your partner. But the inside of the house smells different. Sort of nicer," Isabelle said. "Much nicer."

"Can you smell something here?" Hope pointed at the patio.

"Yes. The same scent as at the kitchen door. It's faint, but I can still pick it out, and it's not the scent that's inside your house. I guess that's your partner's. This scent is something else." They looked at the prints circling the deck. "You thought this was me, right?"

Hope nodded. "Seems we have a second visitor. I'm getting really spooked about this."

This was less simple than before. Before, they had only to rescue Isabelle by handing her over to Claude. Now there was another feral, plus a murdered man in the local park who happened to be Isabelle's ex-husband. The link was unmistakable, and the police would be involved. How would that affect their original plan? Thankfully, Claude was on his way. He might have some ideas of his own.

"I wish Claude was here." Hope finally broke the heavy silence. "We need to get you ready to go, and right now would be a good time."

"I need to go home. I'm going nowhere without my passport and papers," Isabelle stated emphatically.

"We can't go back there. The police will be looking for you." Godfrey was alarmed at this idea.

"I'm not worried about the police. I've been estranged from Barry for almost a year. I didn't do this. In fact, I'm happy to go see the police right now if I have to. But I'm not going anywhere without my passport. I'm a Canadian and I need my passport."

"What? It's Canada, for God's sake. It's on the goddamn doorstep. You can reapply for a passport. Just report it lost or stolen or something—"

"No. I need my passport. And my papers. *All* my papers." Isabelle dug her heels in. Her chin trembled into a stubborn set.

"The police could easily delay your getting to Little Dip," Hope said. "You need to get there soon, Isabelle. It's obvious something's happening with you. Your body is in meltdown." It was a sobering thought and Hope felt a little mean badgering her like this, but they had to get under way. Lord knew how much time they had left.

Isabelle looked troubled, but refused to budge. "I want my passport."

"Okay, okay. We'll go get your Canadian passport." Godfrey held up his hands. "And maybe we can stop for maple syrup and Joni Mitchell records on the way."

"Stop being facetious," Hope scolded him. "Let her get her passport. It will only take a minute."

Hope was worried. Was it illegal to help Isabelle leave the city when her ex was in pieces at Oakes Bottom? If she had her passport she could give them the slip at any time and run off. How much could they afford to trust her? But worse still, what would happen if Isabelle was taken into police custody in the state she was in? Hope felt a headache coming on. The thought was unimaginable. It was all such a mess, and she and Godfrey were up to their necks in it.

"Okay, let's go and do this. But *I'm* locking up this time." Hope held out her hand for her house keys, which he surrendered without a word. "Come on, Taddy. More den guarding for you."

❖

Isabelle rented a small apartment in a boring gray brick building on Colt Drive. They parked in a visitor's space and walked around to the front. Isabelle was twitchy as she led them through the corridors to her door.

"The neighbor always complains when he sees me," she said, her face burning. "I make too much noise." She didn't go into detail.

One step inside and they stood stock-still, viewing the vandalism in shocked silence. The living room had been smashed to a pulp.

"No wonder the neighbor complains." Godfrey looked around him in disbelief.

"I...I didn't do this." Isabelle jerked out of her dismay. "It had to be Barry. He found out recently where I live." She began to move through the mess stepping over broken furniture. "I didn't want him to know. He'd become a pest since our house went on the market."

She stood forlorn in a sea of slashed upholstery and shattered crockery and glass. Her secondhand stereo was upended. CDs lay in snapped bits on the floor. Books were torn apart, the pages scattered like confetti. Everything had been destroyed in a fit of rage. The carpet was wet and sticky with wine and Coke, mixed with bleach from the bathroom. Every liquid available had been poured over the floor and soft furnishings. The smell was overpowering.

"Barry did this?" Godfrey sounded dubious.

"He has issues," Isabelle muttered. "Had issues," she said numbly.

"Yeah. With Ikea." Godfrey moved into the room and tried to straighten a table only to find a leg missing. "This stuff is trashed."

Hope looked around her, unsure what to do. "You do realize you're leaving fingerprints everywhere," she told Godfrey.

"So? We're hardly going to report a burglary. And we're her friends. Why shouldn't we be in her apartment touching her stuff?"

"Oh." They looked over to see Isabelle rub at her face. She had started to cry.

"What is it?" Hope tried to make an avenue toward her through the mess.

"I've only just met you, and you're both so kind." She scrubbed at her damp cheeks with her cuff. "I've been nothing but trouble, and you've done everything to try and help me. I can't tell you...how much..." Embarrassed, she looked away.

Hope looked at her then, really looked at her. And saw a thin, anxious woman, living on her nerves, standing in a small, bleak apartment, surrounded by crappy secondhand furniture that had been smashed into matchsticks. What little that was actually hers, her personal things, had been particularly vandalized. Isabelle picked up a cover torn off a book. A flash of deep hurt crossed her face. It was an achingly raw emotion and Hope felt she had trespassed in witnessing it. Isabelle's life was as tattered as the paper in her hands. She had lost so much more than the meager contents of this apartment. Hope couldn't begin to imagine what that must feel like. To lose everything, even your humanity.

"It's going to be okay. Let's pack a few things while we're here. Where's the bedroom?" she asked, rubbing Isabelle's back with a comforting hand.

Godfrey found the phone and plugged it back into the wall. He lifted the handset to his ear.

"Eureka! It works. He must have forgot to kick it to death along with everything else," he said. "Hey. You got voicemail."

He pressed the button and a stream of messages poured out into the room.

"Darling, I've been trying to reach you for days. I've been worried sick. I wanted to tell you how sorry I am for everything. It was all my fault. I was such a jerk, but I love you, and I want us to try again. Please, Issy. Please come back. I miss you so much."

"Please, Issy. It will never happen again. I mean it, I really do. I'll do anything. I've even put myself into therapy. I want to understand all this anger that's eating me up. It's not you, Issy, it's me. We're exploring my intermittent explosive disorder. I'm stuck, Issy. I'm stuck in an ego-dystonic pattern."

"My therapist says you're my target for vengeance. It's because when things surpass my level of control I strike out at the first—"

"My therapist says—"

"I want you to meet with my therapist so we can talk about my irrational belief system and you can help us with some cognitive

exercises. See how hard I'm trying, Issy. Call me back, Issy. Please? At least tell me where you are."

"Issy? Some more mail came for you. Please don't just sneak in and collect it behind my back. We need to talk, darling."

"Issy? Where the fuck are you? It's been weeks—"

Godfrey slammed the Stop button. "Oh, my God. I'm exhausted just listening to all that ego-dystonia."

Isabelle gave a sour laugh. "It's a borrowed phone. I didn't realize there were messages. No wonder he sounds pissed. I've been inadvertently ignoring his calls for weeks."

"Bet that didn't help his intermittent explosive disorder."

"Guys? The man is lying in the city morgue right now," Hope said. "Probably on several different slabs. Isabelle, do you really think he would do something like this?" Her hand swept the room.

Isabelle sighed and looked around her. "No. To be honest, I don't. He was angry, but only when the house went on the market and the divorce papers arrived. Before that, he was just…well, whiny and irritating." She nodded at the phone in Godfrey's hands.

"He got angry when it started to hit his pocket, you mean." Hope tried to hide her sarcasm but failed.

Godfrey tsked. "It's so not right to speak ill of the dead."

"Oh, shut up, Meyers." Hope turned to Isabelle. She needed there to be openness between them. It was too dangerous to be otherwise. "What I mean is, he's talking about therapy for domestic abuse. Was that why your marriage ended, Isabelle?"

"There were several reasons, as in most marriage breakdowns. I found he was cheating on me and was relieved. I realized I was disaffected and wanted out, and he'd given me the ideal opportunity. He wanted reconciliation. We fought over making up more than we'd ever fought about anything else, and one night he lost it and hit me." She touched the small scar by her mouth. "He fainted at the blood, and when he came around he never stopped crying and apologizing. I knew I had to get out. I started divorce proceedings and went up to Canada to see my aunt and take a break." She looked around her. "I don't think he'd be this spiteful. He would have tried to hurt me over money. That's what mattered to him."

Her hand drifted back to the scar. Ren had warned her it was not safe to go back home. All along, Isabelle had assumed she was referring to Barry, but as her memories returned it was clear he was no threat. Now, looking at the devastation around her, she wondered who, or what, Ren had really been referring to.

She went to check out the bedroom. It too had been vandalized, but the viciousness here was tenfold. All her clothes lay shredded, but it was the bed that confused and shocked her the most. The bed lay crooked, its lower legs smashed and the mattress gutted. Long slashes tore through it down to the bed frame. A sour odor permeated the room. No longer masked by the smell of bleach, it assaulted her senses as crudely as the destruction of her home assaulted her eyes. Stronger than the residue in Hope's yard, this scent was purer, its message crystal clear. The heat that rolled off it was amazing, volcanic even. It scorched her to even think, or try and understand it. The anger and rage was palpable. The room sizzled with it. She recoiled back out the door.

"Isabelle?" Hope's voice came right behind her. "What is it?"

"The scent. It's the same as your yard. Only…worse. Much worse. It's so angry, all I can sense is cold, black-hearted…malice." And it was all directed at her. The scent was suffocating in its viciousness.

Godfrey took command. "Okay, ladies, we're out of here. Isabelle, grab your passport."

Isabelle steeled herself and reentered the room. She went straight to the far corner where a dresser lay overturned and peeled back the carpet, pulling out a plastic folder. She held it up for the others to see. "Passport, driver's license, U.S. work permit, medical papers, bank book. I've taken to tucking these away safely. You've no idea how helpless you are without them." Among the papers was a badly burned book, but she didn't mention that.

"Yeah. I'd feel naked. Now come on!" Godfrey shooed them out the door and locked it behind them with a satisfying click.

"What about my landlord? He'll go mad. I'll never be able to rent again."

"Marie will deal with it." Godfrey led them along the hallway toward the wide glass doors that led to the street. With relief, they walked out into the daylight, a welcome respite from the malevolence and gloom of the trashed apartment.

"Thank God to be out of there," Hope muttered.

"Oh. That's her right there, Officer," a voice said off to the left.

Isabelle slipped her plastic wallet into Hope's hands.

"Excuse me. Are you Isabelle Monk?" A police officer approached.

Isabelle stepped forward. "Yes?"

"I'll need you to accompany me to the station, Mrs. Monk," he said politely.

"Is it to do with Barry?"

"You know about that." He watched her every move with shrewd eyes.

Isabelle nodded at Godfrey and Hope standing behind her, totally helpless.

"It's the talk of the neighborhood." She moved toward him. This was inevitable, she acknowledged. It had to be dealt with. It was crazy to think she could just cut and run. Nothing would ever be that easy again. Those days were gone forever. The real issue here was to keep the police out of her apartment if possible.

She glanced over her shoulder at Godfrey and Hope. "Thanks for your help. I'll call as soon as I can."

And with that she slid into the police car, leaving them both speechless on the sidewalk.

CHAPTER TWENTY

I can't believe we lost her." Godfrey was aghast.

"She's a feral. If she freaks at a police station it will be national news. It will be the end of the world…" Hope watched the police car pull away.

"Now who works for *American Theater Magazine*?"

"Do we know any wolven lawyers? What are we going to tell Claude? What are we going to tell Marie?"

"The truth. There are two ferals running loose in Portland. One is a gut-spilling murderer, and the other you invited for tea. Of course, we don't know which is which, but for the moment we're backing Tadpole's hunch."

"Don't you blame this on me. If you hadn't left the goddamn door open in the first—" Hope bit her tongue, realizing she was rising to the bait. "At least my fingerprints aren't all over her apartment."

"Oh my God! Can we go back and wipe them?"

"She's back," Hope said.

"Huh?"

"She's back."

They'd been so busy bickering they hadn't noticed the squad car stop down the street, then quickly reverse back to the apartment steps.

"They're coming for me." Godfrey's fingers bit into Hope's arm.

Isabelle sat in the back talking earnestly to the two police officers before one of them got out and helped her exit the vehicle. She slowly mounted the steps toward them at the officer's side. He seemed intent on handing her over safely.

"Your friend seems a little faint," he said.

Hope stepped forward and took Isabelle's arm. "Isabelle?"

"Do you want us to go down to the station with her?" Godfrey asked, audibly swallowing a lump in his throat.

The officer shook his head.

"We're looking for a wild animal. Big cat or something. Probably from a private zoo."

"Oh, dear." Godfrey tried to look shocked.

"Barry's family have identified his bod—him. The police don't need me for the moment," Isabelle said. "Can we go now? I don't want to stand out here." A small crowd had gathered near the steps.

"Of course." Hope steered her toward their car, leaving Godfrey to give the officer the new contact details. "We'll go back to my house."

"I thought we'd lost you for an awful moment. What did they ask?" Godfrey put the Lexus in gear and pulled out onto Colt. Isabelle sat huddled in a corner of the backseat. She looked sickly. "Are you all right? You look very pale."

She nodded and stared out the window.

"They wanted to know where I was last night. I said I was at home and a neighbor could probably verify it. And then they started to ask about my relationship with Barry. But they already knew all that. I guess his parents filled them in. Then the call came over the radio that it was an animal attack. People have been calling in sightings all over the city. It's mass hysteria out there. They couldn't wait to dump me and go shoot a lion." She sank back into her seat exhausted. Sweat shone on her brow.

"We can't sit and wait for Claude, not with this other feral on the loose. It's dangerous and seems to be homing in on Isabelle," Hope said. She had some ideas of her own, but Isabelle didn't look capable of sustaining a hard conversation at the moment. Hope decided to quiz her later.

"We need to grab Taddy and get the hell out of here. Perhaps we can arrange to meet Claude along the way?" she asked Godfrey. "Isabelle can go on to Little Dip with him, and I'll come back and stay with you until Jolie comes home. She'll know what to do."

"Now, that's a good plan. In fact, it sounds a lot like *my* plan." He pulled up in front of Hope's house. "Go get Taddy. I'm going to call

Claude on his cell and organize the exchange. Where will we meet? That service station about halfway?"

"Perfect." Hope quickly collected Tadpole. He scrabbled into the back and made a big fuss of seeing Isabelle again.

"Okay, lover boy." Hope slid in beside Godfrey. "Settle down. We're off on a big adventure."

"You talking to me or the dog?" Godfrey asked.

"Like you even have to ask. What did Claude say?"

"Don't take the interstate. If a feral is this brazen, it's not alone, and it may be watching the interstate service stations. He suggested 26 to Prineville. He'll come down 395 and meet us somewhere near Mitchell."

"That will take hours!" Hope said.

"Five hours, thereabouts. Eight in total, if we were going all the way to Little Dip. But we'll turn around once we meet up with Claude."

"Okay. Claude knows his ferals better than we do. Long way around it is." Hope nodded, content with the plan of action.

❖

Traffic was light and they exited Portland heading south through Sandy and Rhododendron into the Mt. Hood corridor road. The lull between the winter holiday period and spring break meant the park was empty of the usual tourist hordes, and often they had entire stretches of road all to themselves. They drove for four hours solid in an attempt to gain distance from the horrifying events in Oakes Bottom.

"Is she all right?" Godfrey whispered, nodding to where Isabelle sat quietly in the backseat, her face flushed and eyes overbright.

"I don't know. She's had a terrible shock."

"She's shaking. I can see her in the mirror. We need to stop soon. Get some food? Stretch our legs."

Hope twisted in her seat. Isabelle was shivering all over. Two bright spots colored her cheeks, a thin sheen of sweat beaded her upper lip. Tadpole lay across her lap, his head resting on her forearm. He flicked Hope a morose look.

"Honey," Hope said, "are you cold? Can I get you a blanket?"

Isabelle shook her head. "I think I've got motion sickness."

"I think it's a little more than that. Godfrey's going to find somewhere to stop and grab a bite to eat. Maybe you just need some food?"

Isabelle nodded. "I'm famished."

The light was leaving the afternoon sky. Winter wasn't ready to surrender the season, and twilight still came early. The weak light filtered through a jumble of darkening storm clouds and treetops whipped in the heightening wind.

"It's getting stormy." Godfrey squinted at the sky. "Rain's coming."

Up ahead the red and blue lights of a service station winked in the lowering gloom.

"Tack-a-rama, but it'll do," Godfrey said, pulling up before the Lucky Seven diner as heavy raindrops started to splatter the windshield. "Considering we haven't eaten since breakfast, it looks like the Ritz."

The Lucky Seven was just as garish on the inside, but its bare strip lights and loud music provided security. Hope hadn't realized how tense she'd been until they took a seat near the door. She cricked her neck and stretched her back before reaching for the menu. Their booth was retro fifties with plastic ketchup bottles and a paper tablecloth dotted with the standard western motifs of horses, cowboys, and teepees. It was all so tackily familiar, a million miles away from werewolves and gory mutilations. Would wolven even frequent a bright place like this? If she hadn't taken a werewolf lover, Hope would never have believed in the supernatural beasties. Her thoughts returned to Isabelle, sitting opposite. She had been attacked and survived, but barely, from the ghastly look of her. Isabelle had not taken a wolven lover; she had simply been taken. Stolen away like a shiny trinket. They had to have a talk about Ren. Was she the murderous feral? Was she tracking down her runaway mate? Knowing what fierce possessiveness Jolie was capable of, Hope would bet money Ren was hot on Isabelle's trail, itching for retribution. The thought chilled her.

"If this place did martinis, I'd have a bucketload," she murmured scanning the menu. "Tuna for me. Godfrey?"

He didn't even look over, intent on three young men who'd just entered. They were dressed in work shirts and jeans, and rainwater dripped from them.

"Same as you," he muttered.

"And I know what you need." Hope turned to Isabelle. "The same thing Jolie and Andre order when we're on the road. A big blue steak. Don't worry. I'll eat the fries."

The waitress arrived and Hope fussed over their order.

"What are you looking at?" she asked Godfrey once the server had gone.

"Those guys over there. They're staring at us."

"Perhaps because you stared first?"

Godfrey shook his head. "I've been looking at them indirectly through the whiskey mirror on the back wall. They followed us in, and they've not ordered anything to eat or drink. In fact, the waitress is getting pissed with them."

"What do you think?"

"They smell like wolf," Isabelle spoke up. "But new. Newish. There's no strong scent, so I'm guessing they're not long changed. Two of them smell sickly."

"I was worried they were feral." Godfrey slid lower in his seat, a gloomy look on his face. "How do we work this?"

"Call Claude. Tell him where we are. We'll sit here and wait it out until he arrives. They'll hardly start something before all these witnesses," Hope said. She glanced around and was relieved to see a small security camera above the bar. It was some measure of protection.

The waitress appeared and deposited their order.

"The weird thing is, though I can identify them by smell, you two know more about wolven behavior than I do," Isabelle said, cutting open her steak.

"Only the snuggly sort," Godfrey said. "When they creep into bed beside you and curl around you. Then you wake up an hour later dripping sweat like you sleep in a sauna." He looked mournfully out the rain-lashed windows. "It's been cold these last nights. I miss him. By the time he gets back I'll probably be as dead as this dolphin-friendly bluefin. Which tastes surprisingly good, by the way."

"Stop being so maudlin and call Claude. Let them see we have resources at hand," Hope said. "Let's relax and eat and show we're not intimidated. It's all in the psychology."

"Ah yes. Psychology will save us. We can Jung-fu our way out,"

Godfrey said, his cell phone pressed to his ear. "It's cutting out while it's ringing. He must be somewhere with bad reception."

"Eat and we'll try again later."

"What's it like? Having a wolven partner, I mean," Isabelle asked, and then blushed furiously.

It was the opportunity Hope had been waiting for. "It's intense. It's a honeymoon period that never ends, but that doesn't mean real life stops. We still have our arguments. We still go to work, earn money, eat, drink, rest, play…but the heightened emotional element, the time in our relationship when we first fell in love, that intensity never seems to fade."

"Would either of you become wolven like Andre and Jolie? Would that double the emotion, make it stronger, almost unbearable, even?"

"I don't know about both partners being wolven making the emotion stronger. What I feel is enough for me," Godfrey said. "The reason I didn't want to change is that I have a wonderful life already. I've found my soul mate, even if he is a werewolf. I love my job. I live in a fantastic city and have the best of friends around me." He reached over and squeezed Hope's hand. "All of my time and energy is used up with this life I've made. Weird as it seems, I don't think I could fit a call-of-the-wild thing in. I'd be afraid it might take me over, and it took me a long enough to find myself as it is. I feel so lucky in my life. I'm satisfied. I'd be worried something as big as lycanthropy would fuck it all up. Andre has never pressed me, and I really, truly feel no inclination. Does that make sense?"

"Yes. Perfectly." Hope nodded. "You are happy with life as it is. You don't need another bolt on. I think that's a sensible and mature approach."

"What about you?" Isabelle asked her.

Hope pointed at her glass eye. "I had intraocular melanoma—eye cancer—and had to have my eye removed. My big issue is my ongoing health. No one has any idea how cancer cells react to lycanthropic mutation. I've had some good news recently, but I'd never risk my health doing something so potentially dangerous with so many unknowns. Jolie would never ask it of me. Plus, I don't think a one-eyed wolf would be any more capable than a one-eyed human, so I'll just stick with what I got." She finished with a smile.

Hope and Godfrey finished their meal, but Isabelle still poked her steak around her plate in a pool of bloody gravy.

"Is the steak not good?" Godfrey asked, picking up the cell phone for the umpteenth time.

"I'm hungry but my stomach's in knots." Isabelle pushed her plate away.

"Your turn now. Tell us about Ren. Is she your partner?" Hope asked, finally getting the conversation to where she needed it to be.

Isabelle's face closed over.

"You can trust us," Hope said. "Are those her guys over there?" She nodded at the three young men hunched in a booth in the far corner. "Is she chasing you, Isabelle? Did she kill Barry?"

"No!" Isabelle jerked in her seat. "Ren is kind. She would never do that."

"Kind? She burned your car, took your passport and money. Hid you away in some valley of the damned," Hope said. "That's not kind. That's a dog with a bone."

"She is kind. She has all these kids that belong nowhere—"

"They had to come from somewhere, Isabelle. How do you know she didn't 'make' them, just like she made you?"

Isabelle was floundering. "I know she didn't. She's looking after them. She's trying hard, but sometimes it gets to be too much. I've seen her worry about real things, like money, the kids, about work and the future… Look, I just know, okay? I just know." She bit her lip and looked away. "You don't fret about next season's workload if you're making werewolves for the fun of it."

"So she has a pack of what? Runaways? Feral kids from the city? Where does she find them?" Godfrey asked.

"I think they find her. I'm not sure. I couldn't…didn't ask. When I found out what they were I ran, remember?" There was bitterness in her voice. "I wish I'd known you then. I wish I'd someone to talk to."

This was not what Hope expected.

"But I do know this," Isabelle said quietly. "Those kids adore her. Whatever they are, and wherever they came from, they are lucky to have found her and they know it. They're nice kids. I don't know how any of them could have survived without her."

Isabelle stood. She was obviously upset. "I need the washroom."

She slid out of the booth. The young men watched her every move, then relaxed as the ladies' room door swung shut behind her.

"Do you need to go with her?" Godfrey asked anxiously. "What if she makes a run for it?"

"I don't think she will. Where's there to go around here?"

Hope threw a look over to the three guys. They shivered over their glasses of tap water under the scathing eyes of the waitress. Two of them looked very poorly, their faces waxen under the harsh light. Hope had seen that look before, in lines outside homeless shelters. A great sorrow filled her. She thought of Ren's pack. Isabelle was so certain they were the lucky ones. Yet she'd run away as—

Godfrey's phone rang.

"It's Claude," Godfrey whispered excitedly. He passed on their information and listened carefully to Claude's instructions. The three guys fixed on him, making Hope suspicious. They hadn't minded while they sat and ate their meal, but now that Godfrey had received a call they were getting edgy. It dawned on her that they were waiting on instructions, too. Their job was to keep them under surveillance and in one place until reinforcements arrived. They became agitated when it looked like Hope and Godfrey might be making tracks with Isabelle in tow.

One of the youths caught her eye and bared his stained teeth; the other two tried to scowl menacingly but only managed to look more bilious.

"We need to get going." Godfrey ended the call. "Claude says to get out of here and keep to the original plan. We're a harder target if we're moving. So much for brazening it out here and waiting for help. Go get Isabelle."

Hope entered the ladies' room. It was small, just a waiting area with a sink and a lockable door to the toilet cubicle.

"Isabelle." Hope rapped on the locked door. "Claude called. We need to get going." Her knock was greeted with silence. She grew uneasy that Godfrey had been right, and Isabelle had run for it. She knocked again, more vigorously. "Isabelle!"

This time she was answered with shuffles and some wet sniffs. It sounded as if Isabelle was crying.

"Let me in. Let me help," Hope said softly. The lock snipped and she gently pushed the door open and froze.

Isabelle stood in the middle of the small room, her face wet with tears, her thin body trembling. Her fingers were stained dark with blood and a sour smell assaulted Hope's nose. The floor was littered with the contents of the sanitary bin.

"Oh, honey," Hope whispered, shocked.

"I couldn't help it." Isabelle choked on a small sob. "I just had to tear it apart. I'm insane. I'm crazy for the smell of blood, yet I can't eat the steak I'm craving. This morning I emptied your fridge, this afternoon my guts are on fire. I'm changing and it's going to kill me. I know it will, and I don't know what to do, Hope."

"I know you're going through hell. I've seen it with the young Garouls. The first time is hard, but once we get you to Little Dip, Marie will have potions and stuff to help." What else could she say to make this any better?

Hope wrapped her hands in toilet tissue and scooped the contents back into the bin. She dragged Isabelle to the sink and briskly scrubbed her face and hands with cold water and ran wet fingers through her disheveled hair.

"Okay?" Hope rested her hands on Isabelle's skinny shoulders and gave her a small shake of encouragement. "We need to get going. Godfrey will be freaking out."

They left the washroom arm in arm and strolled back to their booth and Godfrey's fretful face.

"Those guys were snarling at me. They need some serious dental work," he said as they sat down beside him. "What the hell kept you?"

"What happens in the ladies' room stays in the ladies' room." Hope patted his arm comfortingly. "What's the scoop?"

"We run for it. That's the scoop."

"It might be difficult shaking these guys on the way to the car," Hope said.

"We need a distraction. Oh! Maybe we could set fire to the tablecloth? It deserves it," he said.

"That would bring everyone's attention on to us. Hardly ideal for sneaking out." Hope shook her head in disbelief.

"Order them some food," Isabelle said quietly.

"What?" Hope turned to her.

"They're broke and famished. Look at the way they're watching everyone else's orders pass their table. They're practically salivating.

Have some burgers sent over. If their hunger is anything like mine, they'll be distracted all right."

"But you didn't eat your steak," Godfrey pointed out.

"I don't feel good. I'm starving, but I can't eat." Under the garish lighting Isabelle was paler than ever.

"Why's that?" he asked.

"I don't know. Maybe it's shock," she said.

"Okay. Let's do this." Godfrey waved for the waitress. "Excuse me, miss."

"When we make a run for it, will you hold my hand?" Hope asked Isabelle. "My depth perception is out of whack. When I move too fast, I get disoriented and fall over my own feet."

"Deal." Isabelle reached over and gave Hope's hand a reassuring squeeze.

Fifteen minutes later the young men were staring in confused longing at the food set before them. While the waitress unloaded her tray and explained the people at table two had already paid, Hope, Godfrey, and Isabelle slid outside as quickly as possible.

They were halfway across the parking lot when the diner door crashed open behind them. Godfrey reached the car first, jumped in, and revved the engine savagely into life. Hope and Isabelle, running hand in hand behind him, piled into the backseat, squashing Tadpole.

Godfrey shot out of their parking space before the rear door was shut, narrowly missing their closest pursuer. Hope looked out the back window, puffing with exertion and relief. All three guys had backtracked and were piling into a beat-up Ford Escort.

"I think we're okay," Hope said. "They'll never catch us in that old bonerattler."

A huge, hulking shadow dashed across the road before them, just out of range of the headlights. It was a meaningful charge, more for show than an attempt to halt the car.

"What the hell was that?" Hope asked, her heart sinking. She clambered in beside Godfrey. "Reinforcements?"

Godfrey tightened his grip on the wheel. "I don't know. But I don't think they'll be coming after us in a bonerattler, somehow."

CHAPTER TWENTY-ONE

R en stood on the roadside opposite the trim, well-ordered house with its happy yellow door and neat flowerbeds. She could tell by its quiet demeanor, from its blank windows and general stillness, that no one was home. The air around it, though, that was a riot. Wolven musk, den markings, warnings, mate claiming, there was a lot of werewolf activity at this house.

She glanced up and down the street. It was empty of people and traffic. Lunch was long over, and the schools had not closed for the day. The early afternoon lull in neighborhoods such as this would continue for at least another forty minutes. Taking advantage of the quiet, Ren crossed over and disappeared around the back of the house.

In the secluded yard she took her time and soaked up the multilayered smells. It was a wolf den, calm and well-ordered, and Isabelle had been here. Had this den taken her in? Ren growled, but it came out sad and lowly. Not the aggressive claiming growl that had rumbled from her chest at the strangest, most inappropriate moments. The one that had alarmed fellow passengers on the plane, or the line at the car rental kiosk, and the ATM. Even the staff at her motel were avoiding her.

Ren hung her head. This home shamed her. It was happy, full of love and positivity. It shone with all she had failed to bring to her own den. This house had become a cornerstone of the Portland circuit she constantly trawled looking for Isabelle.

She had started by skulking around Reed College and the surrounding area. She hung out around Isabelle's old address in

Billinghurst. But the For Sale sign, and the weaselly little man who stormed in and out, became another dead end. In desperation she had taken to following Barry Monk. To his work, his parents' house, the gym, his therapist…anywhere. But he never went near Isabelle.

She had done this for weeks. Going over the same old ground, ever hopeful of a new clue. One whiff was all she needed. Around and around she went in her self-styled circuit. At night she'd change and do it all again, only better. And she'd found her. A trace of her in Sellwood Park. Sweat and stress poured out off her. She'd been running, and Ren knew what she was running from and that it would eventually catch her. She had to find Isabelle first. She had to be there for that first change. It was dangerous for Isabelle to be alone.

Ren looked at the scratches on the patio door. The only discordant note about this den, and this time her growl came out sounding right. A snarl of pure white rage. The scents were old, they were weak and sour, but she recognized them and the story they told. This was bad. This was dangerous.

Isabelle was on the run again, and rightly so. This den was helping her, and Ren was jealous and morbidly downcast. She wanted to be the one Isabelle turned to. Ren knew this pack scent. It told her who lived here, and who came and went. And it told her where to look next.

"How fast can these things run?" Godfrey glanced warily out his side window. The Lexus zoomed along night roads. Rain beat on the windows, the tires threw up water, and the wipers slammed back and forth at high speed. Every so often a shadow would detach from the surrounding gloom and race toward the car. Godfrey hauled on the wheel and swerved to avoid it.

"They're playing with us," Isabelle murmured, an oasis of calm in the tense atmosphere inside the car. Her mind was relaxed where her companions were on the verge of panic. The attack plan seemed crystal clear to her. She wondered how she could see it while Godfrey and Hope couldn't.

"Why don't they just jump and try to stop the car?" Hope asked.

"I don't think that's the plan. They can chase alongside for short bursts, but we'll always outrun them." Isabelle watched as another beast came crashing out of the trees. Rainwater flew off its coat; its eyes gleamed in the approaching headlights.

"Shit, here comes another one." Godfrey gripped the steering wheel tighter.

"Don't swerve this time," Isabelle said. "They want us to swerve away from them. These lunges are just distractions." She glanced off to the opposite side of the road but could see nothing through the rain-beaded glass. "Remember, they have better night vision. You don't know what you're driving toward every time you swerve."

"I can't just drive over it." Godfrey was panicked.

Stressing out the driver was probably part of the plan. It all clicked into place in Isabelle's mind. She saw the logic in it. It made sense. She must be acquiring some sort of inherited hunt instinct.

"Believe me, it can see you. It will move." She gripped the back of Godfrey's seat and watched over his shoulder as he hit the gas and kept a steady line. The beast roared and ran toward them. With a grating thud it bounced off the passenger side front fender. They all winced.

"So much for that theory," Hope said. "They're obviously on a suicide mission."

"I think it expected me to swerve." Godfrey kept on going. "Can you hear that noise? I think the fender is rubbing on the tire or something. Shit."

Isabelle stared out the back window into the night. She'd had countless nightmares reliving the moment her car hit Joey. His tawny, blood-soaked fur crushed against her windshield was an image etched on her mind now and forever. The hunt and her terrified efforts to escape it had returned to her full force soon after she'd arrived in Portland. She had nearly all her memory now, except for a frustratingly small segment...meeting Ren. Their first meeting and the start of their friendship still eluded her. Often she had thumbed through the charred pages of her journal hoping that some word, some daydream, or idle thought would bring it all flooding back. But always she drew a blank, while the images of Joey howling in pain and the rest of the pack closing in on her were as vivid as if it had happened only yesterday.

Her guts roiled as parts of her nightmare were re-enacted before her. This was a standard hunt procedure, to unnerve a moving prey by continuous charging, making it swerve and skew until it became disoriented and exhausted.

She looked back to see if the creature had risen or was still lying wherever it had been thrown, but couldn't see in the red glow of their taillights. The darkness had swallowed it. She should feel sorry for it, perhaps lying by the side of the road badly hurt, but all she could think was, *One down, God knows how many to go.* In a fight for survival, she could be as cold-blooded as the rest of them.

Her hands were shaking with adrenaline, and her heart thumped until it felt pinched and sore. She wanted to get out of the car and run, run and never stop. Run through the rain into the wet world of the forest, where the earth would dig between her toes and raise a myriad of scents. She wanted the rain to stick to her pelt like jeweled buttons, and the wind to fill her head with forest sounds until her ears twitched with pleasure. Her tongue clicked on the roof of her mouth. She licked her lips and flicked the edges of her teeth. She wanted to live her dreams. It was almost time.

"Do you really think if we swerve around them we could be driving into something worse? Like a trap?" Hope asked her anxiously.

"I'm certain of it." Isabelle spanned her fingers as far as they would stretch until every bone in her hand popped. Her feet were hot. Too hot for her shoes. She kicked them off.

As if to prove her words, up ahead another creature slid from the woods. This time they looked for a trap and could plainly see two others waiting on the opposite side of the road.

"Why didn't they trick us the first few times?" Hope said.

"Timing? Luck? Maybe you didn't swerve far enough. Maybe they weren't all in place. It's not meticulously planned, it's just opportunism. There aren't that many of them, and they have to run through the woods to the next turn in the road to catch up with us. They'll be getting exhausted and desperate by now," Isabelle said with satisfaction.

"You know a lot about it," Godfrey said.

"I do."

"So we're stuck with them because this road is twisty?" Hope asked. "How soon till we hit a straight stretch and get the hell out of here?"

Godfrey shrugged. "I'm not sure. This road is for tourists to enjoy the scenery, you're not meant to drive through it like Casey at the throttle."

The Were began its run toward them and Godfrey stepped on

the gas, steadied the steering, and aimed straight for it. It stumbled uncertainly, then leapt aside at the last minute. It avoided the car by inches but slammed hard into a tree.

"Aha! Take that, you bastard," Godfrey crowed. "How's that for a taste of your own medicine."

"Another one bites the dust." Hope high-fived him. "Take your mama bowling tonight—" The roof above their heads dented in with an almighty bang. "What was that!"

Isabelle peered out the back window as a huge branch bounced off the roof onto the road behind them. "They're in the trees throwing things."

They all peered overhead in disbelief.

"In the trees?" Hope was flabbergasted. "I've never seen Jolie in a tree in her life."

"Duck!" Isabelle yelled. A huge branch shattered the sunroof, showering them in glass and rainwater. At the same time, they rammed into a pile of rocks scattered across the road. The Lexus tore over the top of them with an excruciating screech. Metal ripped and grated. Part of the exhaust jettisoned across the asphalt.

"Holy shit!" Godfrey struggled with the wheel. "We keep veering to the right. The steering's damaged."

Hope and Isabelle pushed the branch back out of the sunroof.

"It's an ambush." They were closing in. Isabelle could sense it. The car was damaged. Godfrey was freaked. The hunt was winning. The Lexus and its passengers were becoming more helpless by the minute. In the red glow of the taillights, Isabelle could see a stream of oil in the wake of the car.

"Andre will kill me. He loves his car," Godfrey said.

"Shut up and keep driving," Hope shouted at him over the clatter of a trailing exhaust.

"I've got to get out," Isabelle said. She was burning. She pulled at her clothes; they stuck to her sweat-slicked body, uncomfortable and claustrophobic.

"What?" Hope turned to her. "Oh God. Not now."

"What? What is it?" Godfrey asked, his eyes glued to the road.

"She's changing." Hope bit out.

"Jesus. Talk about timing. Oh, my God. Oh, my God," Godfrey shrieked. "What will we do? What will we do?"

"You drive. I'm going in the back with her." Hope grabbed a bottle of water and clambered awkwardly in beside Isabelle. She cupped her hand and poured some water in it.

"Here, honey. This will cool you down a little." She bathed Isabelle's burning face and cupped her cool hand around the nape of her neck.

"I want out." Isabelle raised her face to the rain and cold air racing in through the broken sunroof. She was ablaze. "The car's had it. Let me out. They'll follow me and you two can get away."

"No." Hope shook her head. "Won't work. You know I can't move fast, and Godfrey runs like a pregnant teenager. We'd get ten paces and it would be over. We need to stick together, Isabelle, or we all lose."

"I'll need to pull over soon," Godfrey shouted from the front. "This car's going nowhere…well, nowhere I point it at. The oil light's on and I smell smoke. It's kaput. What will we do? What will we do—Oh my God! It's the Lucky Seven."

They rolled into the parking lot, into the same space they'd vacated just half an hour ago. Several inquisitive faces peered at them through the plate glass windows.

"You mean we drove in a circle all this time?" Hope was outraged. "No wonder they kept bombarding us. All they had to do was stand still and wait for our next circuit!"

"Well, how was I to know with all that swerving?" Godfrey yelled back.

Isabelle kicked open the door and staggered out into the night air.

"Isabelle," Hope called after her.

"I just need air. Lots and lots of air." Isabelle sucked great gulps of it.

"You guys okay?" The waitress stood on the top steps under the awning, out of the rain.

"That's what a big tip gets you," Godfrey muttered, pleased. "We had a run-in with a rock. Can I get a tow truck out here?" he called over.

"Sure, hon. Come in and use the phone."

"I'm staying here with her." Hope nodded at Isabelle.

"I'll be two minutes." Godfrey ran over to the diner steps.

Isabelle urged Hope to follow him. "Go and get warm. I'll come in a moment."

"No. I want to make sure you're okay."

"I am. Leave me. I'm fine."

Hope shook her head. "No way."

The bushes nearby rustled and Isabelle whipped her head around and snarled out a warning. Hope blinked.

"That's a very impressive snarl," she said. "Is there something out there?"

Isabelle shook her head. "I was spooked." Nevertheless, she headed toward the bushes to make sure. "Wait here."

She slid through a gap into a thicket and stood still, her face raised to the breeze. Fox musk. That was the rustling. They came here to scavenge around the diner bins. Her nostrils flared delicately. Mice in abundance, and squirrel, too. New shoots, old wood. Spring. It made her want to grin, and stretch, and scratch her back on fresh, new grass. Tadpole's tinny bark turned her toward the parking lot. She pricked her ears, the wind snatched at another, weaker bark, and tore it away from her.

"Hey!" Godfrey's call came from close by.

"You guys," he called again. "Come in here and get some coffee. The tow truck's on its way."

Hope didn't answer. Isabelle pushed through the bushes back to the parking lot.

"There's pie." Godfrey was even closer now. "Hope? I said there's pie—Jeez, you scared me." He jumped when Isabelle appeared beside him.

He looked past her. "Where's Hope?"

Isabelle frowned. "In the car."

"No, she's not."

They looked over at the Lexus. Rain drummed on its bent and scratched paintwork. The fender was crushed, grill dented, and left headlight busted. The back doors lay wide open. Not that it mattered. Rain poured through the broken sunroof staining the luxury cream leather to a lurid butter yellow.

"Where is she?" Godfrey asked again, his voice scratchy with panic. "Hope?" he called out to the half-empty lot. A soft whimper came from the far side of the car. They ran toward it.

"Oh, Taddy." He knelt down beside the rain-soaked dog. Tadpole lay on the grass, his side swelling and falling as he fought for breath.

He gave a wheezing whine as they approached. He lay there, unable to move, even when Godfrey reached out with trembling hands to touch him. "I think his ribs are broken." Godfrey's voice shook.

The wind shifted in a sharp, leaf-rattling swirl. Isabelle's nostrils filled with a familiar and unwelcome scent.

"Patrick!" she spat out. She lurched to her feet, and in a crouched run took off across the parking lot, leaving Godfrey kneeling in the mud calling her name.

CHAPTER TWENTY-TWO

Ren's tires squealed on the wet asphalt. She screeched to a halt before the stricken man. He hunkered on his knees, water running from his clothing, a scrap of a dog in his lap. She pushed open the passenger door.

"Get in," she growled over the downpour. "Now. There's more on the way."

He shivered all over from shock and the cold, and stared at her unmoving. Across the lot bushes rattled. Dark shapes slunk through the shadows, leery of the light from the diner windows and the neon glow reflecting off every wet surface.

"Now!" she roared. He lurched to his feet and staggered into the passenger seat. He cradled the injured dog in his arms; rainwater dripped off both of them onto the floor. She had to stretch across to slam his door shut. He stank of fear and despair and wet dog…and Garoul. She stepped on the gas.

"My friends are back there. I have to help them," he babbled, shivering violently.

"We will."

He squinted at her through the gloom. She could hear his heart pounding, the faint chatter of his teeth, the short, snatched puffs of his breath.

"Who are you?" he asked. The quiver in his voice gave him away. He knew who she was. She turned her head and stared him directly in the eye.

"Ren."

"You're a Garoul." He wasn't asking a question.

"Yes."

"I've never seen you before."

"No."

They sped on in silence while he digested this. The drum of rain on the roof and the swish of tires on the wet road were the only sounds.

"You must be the talkative one," he finally said.

She ignored him and smoothly drove her car at top speed around the broken tree boughs and huge rocks strewn across the road. The crude ambush had been the giveaway. Ren knew this trick well. Isabelle and her companions had to be nearby, hopefully still unharmed. The oil spill and telltale drag of their exhaust along the road had led her to the Lucky Seven parking lot.

"I'm Godfrey. Andre's partner," he said.

She grunted. The little dog whimpered weakly.

"It's going to be okay, Taddy. Ren will help us. She's family," the man whispered, his fingers gently stroked a bloody paw.

She looked at him sideways and made up her mind.

"Yes," she said, and kept driving.

❖

He dragged Hope from the car trunk by her hair. She tried to swing out at him but his fist connected with her temple. Hope saw stars, her stomach lurched, and she felt her temporal bones creak. She sagged and went along quietly. She didn't need a shattered eye socket. Not on her good side.

The shack he was hauling her toward was shabby and weather-worn, and perversely enough, she recognized it. She had passed by here with Amy Fortune last fall, looking for *Castilleja levisecta.* The shack was about five miles outside of Lost Creek, and several more from Little Dip. She had tried to guess how much time she had spent in the suffocating car trunk while empty beer bottles bumped against her head and the smell of oily rags choked her. Little had she known their breakneck speed was taking her in the direction she'd been headed in all along.

Whoever he was, he had chosen his bolt-hole poorly, unless the proximity to the Garoul home valley was deliberate. It was dangerous for a feral to come this close to Garoul territory. The fact she was still alive told her she was a pawn in someone's game. Already she could feel the side of her face swell from his punch. Her current ill treatment did not bode well. Whatever their plans, there was a good chance her general well-being was of no importance.

He kicked open the door and tossed her on to the floor. Without a word, the door slammed closed and the lock rattled. She was plunged into darkness. Hope sat up and brushed dirt off her gashed knees. Her head throbbed, and her temple was bruised to the touch. Her fingers gently probed the tender patches on her scalp where her hair had been torn out in clumps. She struggled not to cry, but every time she thought of Tadpole the tears welled up and rolled silently down her cheeks. He had tried so hard to protect her. She prayed Godfrey was caring for him.

And where was Godfrey? Had he managed to get Isabelle to Claude? A metallic clink snapped her from her desperate thoughts and into pure panic. Her throat closed over with fear. It came again, the quiet clink of a chain scraping against the wooden floor. She was not alone. Something was in here with her.

"You smell nice," a child's voice whispered in the darkness. It sounded lost yet hopeful all at the same time. "Who are you?"

Hope scanned the room. As her sight adjusted to the dark, she could just about make out a small, shadowy figure sitting on the floor diagonally across from her.

"I'm Hope. Who are you?"

"Mouse. And that's Patrick who pushed you in here. He's mean. He made you cry."

"Just a little."

"Did he hurt you?"

"Not much. He pulled my hair."

"He pulled mine, too. I hate him."

"He's not my favorite person either. How'd you get here, Mouse?"

"I was sleeping and he grabbed me."

"From your bed?" Hope was horrified. What did they want with a child? Then it occurred to her the child was in chains and she, the adult, was not. Her stomach felt leaden.

"Mouse? Why did he chain you up?"

"Because I'd bite him and he's scared."

"Ah, I see." Hope nodded. "You're wolven."

"Yeah. And after I bite him, Ren's gonna bite him more and she's got big teeth. He's gonna be one sorry pup."

Ren. Hope was confused. So it was not Ren's pack that had chased them out of Portland and terrorized them on the road.

"Where is Ren, Mouse?" she asked.

"Dunno." The voice sounded small again. "She left to find Isabelle and we were to mind the farm. Then Patrick grabbed me. He pulled my hair. Ren will be mad at him because he did that *and* disobeyed orders."

"Okay." This was interesting. So Mouse was one of Ren's pack… and Patrick, too, from the sound of it. Why had he grabbed her and Mouse? It was serious stuff to disobey your pack leader. Had Mouse got her facts straight?

Hope was surprised at the age range in Ren's pack. Isabelle had said they were young, but Mouse's age put them more in the category of a family den than a gang of feral scavengers. "Does Patrick not want to be in Ren's pack anymore?"

"I don't know." Mouse was troubled by this idea. "He's sneaky. Me and Joey never liked him."

"Joey?" How many were there running around out there?

Mouse sighed, tired with the questions. "Joey's in Ren's pack with me. He's my best friend. And there's Jenna and Noah. Jenna's kind. She's Noah girlfriend. And Noah's the best hunter, after Ren. He's gonna teach me how to skin as soon as Ren says I can have a knife," she explained patiently.

Mouse's adoration of Ren was obvious. This corroborated what Isabelle had said earlier. Ren was sounding less and less like the murderous monster she had expected. Hope needed to dig a bit more. Too many pieces of this puzzle were missing.

"I'm sorry for all the stupid questions. Isabelle only told me a few things about the farm." Hope chose her words carefully.

"Isabelle?" Mouse exploded with excitement. "You know her? She's my friend. She had to go away because of an emergency and Ren said she had to go help her."

"She's my friend, too," Hope said, wondering why Ren had covered up Isabelle's escape, and what that meant.

"I miss her."

"She misses you all as well." Hope realized it was true. When Isabelle talked about these kids, which was often, there was genuine warmth in her voice. She wondered how much Isabelle realized this. It was all very odd. Like a little family torn apart.

The chains rattled as Mouse moved her legs. Patrick had shackled her by the ankles. The chain looped through a steel ring attached to the floor and looked tight and uncomfortable.

"How long have you been here?" Hope asked.

"Two days. He goes away lots. Sometimes others come back with him. Three more. He bosses them about like he tried to boss us. The new guys don't like him much."

"Three guys were chasing me and my friends. Two of them looked sick. Could they be the same guys?" Hope tried to ascertain just how many there were.

"Yeah. The other two have bad guts. They're always moaning about it." Mouse sounded disgusted at such weakness. "They'll never be Weres."

"What'll happen to them?"

"They'll die. They always die once their guts start to rot," Mouse said, matter-of-fact.

Hope looked away remembering Isabelle's pain. She was in trouble. *Please let her be in Little Dip by now.* Marie could help her, perhaps save her. Hope guessed she'd been in the car trunk for about two hours, though it had felt like a lifetime. That was more than enough time for Godfrey to have found Claude and handed Isabelle over.

"Will your friends come for us?" Mouse asked hopefully.

Hope smiled at the "us." "I'm not sure. I have a rough idea where we are, though. It's not far away from some other friends I know."

The chains rattled violently, displaying Mouse's enthusiasm for this news. "Will they come?"

"They don't know we're here."

"Ren will find us," Mouse stated with certainty. "Patrick stinks. Ren will sniff him out and pound him for stealing me. She'll pound him for hurting you, too. Especially if you're a friend of Isabelle's."

Hope wasn't sure she wanted to meet this Ren at all, with her big teeth and pounding. But Isabelle clearly loved her, and Mouse adored her…and Patrick had betrayed her? Hope was confused. If Ren wasn't behind this double kidnap, who was? Someone—or something—much more frightening.

❖

Isabelle wasn't sure when she'd stopped being the prey and became the hunter. Best of all, her pursuers knew nothing about it. As far as they were concerned, they were hounding an exhausted woman up a sodden, muddy hillside.

She had lost Patrick's scent quickly, and with it all chance of finding Hope. The incessant rain had washed everything into one big gloop of earth scent.

It was strange, the connection she felt for Hope. Hope had a big heart and had offered nothing but unstinting support. Hope was a den mother. Isabelle realized that had been the magnet drawing her to Hope's house all along. And now she had lost Hope's scent and failed her as a friend.

Panicked, at first she had tried to stay close to the tree line, but as her predators flushed her into higher ground the trees had thinned, and her cover with them. It surprised her how fast she had adapted. It seemed second nature to lurk in shadow and move in short, sharp bursts of speed. She intersected these with longer, crouched runs, drawing her hunters farther onto the steeper slopes after her. They were unwell and tiring quickly. They thought they were chasing her, but she knew different. Somewhere, while clawing through rock and thorny scrubland, the roles had reversed. She always moved with a target already mapped out in her mind, be it a boulder or a lone, twisted tree. It gave her the advantage and exposed her pursuers.

On the way to her next waypoint, she realized she could pick up their scents even though they were far away. Higher up, and free of the forest, the air swirled the entire world of the hills toward her. She now knew exactly where her pursuers were, and how to execute her next move. That's when she decided her next move was to circle around behind them.

Her mind was as sharp and hard as a flint edge. Thoughts sparked off her, yet she moved on instinct alone. This wasn't learned logic; this was an innate wisdom. Somehow it had seeped through her pores into her organs, through every fiber of her body. Her chills and sweats had gone. She didn't shiver anymore. Her skin felt crisp and cool; only her feet and hands were hot. Her scalp prickled with excitement. Her chest rumbled in quiet pleasure with a purr for her own cleverness.

She lay on her belly on an escarpment, ignoring the mud creeping through her clothes and onto her skin, and watched her hunters flail about in the gorge below. Her tracks had long gone cold. The beasts circled and snarled and nipped at each other, the healthiest one bullying the weaker two, until all three were on the edge of frenzy.

She rolled away, pleased, and lay with her back in a cold puddle, looking up at the night. The rainstorm was passing. High winds were breaking up the tumbling clouds. Patches of starry sky peeked through, promising a bigger, brighter night. The stars burned holes in her, they riddled her with pinpoints of light and energy. The moon, when it came, would blow her apart.

Her clothes were sopping wet. With little thought, she pulled them off and gloried in the cold night pressing against her nakedness. She stretched her arms and arched her back until her spine popped and her shoulders and elbows crunched. Her ears rang with the splinter and creak of her facial bones shifting. Mandible, maxilla, zygoma all cracked and crunched. She had a moment's sharp, unpleasant pressure, and then it was past her. Her sinuses flooded with deeper, richer scents and flushed away the pain. These smells were headier than anything she'd experienced before. She felt faint from it, drunk on it.

Lifting her face to a strong gust of wind, she sniffed and snuffled, her wet nose twitching in its squat, leathery muzzle. So many scents— she wanted to explore each one. She wanted all the smells in the world to fill her head, she wanted to suck it all in until her lungs burst. She panted with delight and flipped over onto her hands and knees, then hunched into a sprinter's start. She licked her lips, flicked her teeth—so smooth, and long, and sharp. Very, very sharp. A bead of blood bubbled on her tongue, and the coarse hairs along the ridge of her spine rose in pleasure. She wriggled her toes in delight. She felt like running. Her thigh muscles were pumped and hard, bursting with energy. Her bare feet tingled and she dug her toes into the grass and dirt. She wanted to run for a million miles. She wanted to run around the widest part of the world, over and over again.

Her fingernails sank into the mud, curved and sharp, like claws.

They *were* claws! Massive claws, on massive paws. *I'm brown. My coat is brown.* Her last human thought hummed in her head as she shot out of her sprinter's crouch and bounded forward, leaping, howling, pushing her huge, bunched muscles to their glorious limit.

The wind caressed her fur, her ears twitching as it rushed past. She pulled her muzzle back and bared her canines, and snarled. These Weres had taken her friend. She couldn't recall much else. She had a friend, and now she was gone, and these three were somehow responsible.

The three wolven in the gorge below froze. They were ignorant, stupid, useless in their newness. Isabelle was new, too. But she knew what to do. She powered into them, bowling them over like ninepins. She flashed her wonderful claws. Throwing a loose roundhouse to the chest of one, she hooked several ribs and tore them from his sternum. His left lung popped like a balloon. She kicked out at the other. A tight, hard stab. Her clawed foot plunged into his unprotected underbelly, ripping his abdomen open like paper.

The healthy one ran, but she didn't care. She would find him later, and he would tell her whatever she wanted to know. But these two, the dying ones…she was doing them a favor.

Chapter Twenty-three

I t's not a punctured lung."

"Thank God." Godfrey breathed a sigh of relief.

Ren secured the bandage wrapped around Tadpole's torso. "His breathing is labored because of shock. His ribs are badly bruised from the kick and he'll need an X-ray, but I don't think anything's broken. At worst, a cracked rib or two."

"Bastards."

"I've given him a shot of Metacam, and he'll sleep now out of pure exhaustion." She dropped her stethoscope into her bag and snapped it shut. "That's all I can do for now. We're lucky I even thought to bring this with me." She tapped the leather. The truth was the bag and its contents had been packed with Isabelle in mind.

Godfrey looked around the dingy motel room he'd rented only half an hour ago.

"What do we do now?" he asked. "I can't leave him here alone, but I have to somehow find Claude and tell him Hope and Isabelle are missing."

"And what can Claude do about that?" Ren had speculated on what Wonder Boy's plans were, but he had been so distressed and useless about the dog that she had decided first things first. She would help his pet, and in return, he would help her.

"We were to meet up with Claude along the route, and he would take Isabelle back to Little Dip. Marie was going to help her with her medicines."

"Isabelle is sick?" Ren tried not to snap the question. Her guts lurched. Isabelle had been robust when she'd last seen her. How far had she declined in the last few weeks? She wanted no other wolven near Isabelle. Only her.

"She wasn't looking too good," he said.

"How? What do you mean, not looking good?" This time she did snap.

"Ill. Couldn't eat. She was in shock when we heard about Barry. But to be honest, she looked off before that. She said she'd been losing weight, not sleeping, stuff like that." He leaned away from her, unnerved at her tone. She'd better watch that. She didn't want to turn him off completely; unfortunately, she needed him right now.

Ren nodded. She wasn't happy.

"You mean Marie Garoul, don't you?" Her leather bag of tricks seemed lame compared to the famous author of the Garoul almanac's cure-alls. She pushed down her jealousy.

"Yes. Marie. The Alpha," Godfrey said uneasily.

Ren realized how cold she sounded speaking of the Garoul matriarch. She turned away and dragged an empty drawer out of the dresser. She had no time for his concerns. He'd find out soon enough she was not what he thought.

"Give me one of those pillows." She pointed at the bed. She placed it in the drawer and gently laid Tadpole on top. Her mind was racing. The plan had been to take Isabelle to Little Dip. In the circumstances, it was a good plan, except Isabelle hadn't made it. She was lost out there, sick, and pursued by feral Weres.

"Here." She handed the makeshift bed over to Godfrey. "Put this in the foot well at the back of the car. It's more secure and will keep the drafts off him."

"We're leaving?"

"We're going to find your Claude," she said. She needed reinforcements, no matter how distasteful the idea was.

"I don't think we can," Godfrey said. "I'd love to, but I've no idea where he is, and we're hours behind schedule. My cell phone is in the Lexus, and I don't know his number to call from a pay phone."

Ren stiffened. "Then we go back to the diner."

Every bone in her body wanted to snap open with frustration. Her marrow boiled with impatience. Isabelle had slipped from her fingers at every turn, and continued to do so. She needed to find her, to hold her, smell her…

"I have another idea," Godfrey said.

"What?"

"They took Hope for a reason. It can't be to negotiate with me. They must want to talk to Marie."

Ren grunted. She didn't get it. She didn't care about this Hope person. Or Claude and Marie Garoul, either, for that matter.

"Explain." She led him out to the car.

"Well, if the ferals chasing us weren't yours, then someone else took Hope. Isabelle seemed to recognize a scent or something. She yelled 'patchwork,' and ran off after Hope." He tucked Tadpole's box safely behind the passenger seat.

"Patchwork?" She glared at him. *Stupid man.*

He slid in the front seat beside her and shrugged. "It didn't make sense to me, either. But my point is, nobody kidnaps a Garoul's mate unless they want to deal with the Garouls."

He had barely time to click home his seat belt before Ren shot out of the parking space. His head banged against the headrest.

"Ouch. Where are we going?" he asked anxiously.

She slammed on the brakes at the motel exit, and he ricocheted forward in his seat belt with a sharp grunt.

"You tell me," she said. "Left or right?" She watched him puff for breath. "Which way is Little Dip?"

❖

"Hey. Psst! Hey." The urgent whisper crept through the shutters just as dawn began to turn the sky a steely gray. Hope jerked out of an uneasy doze. Her head hurt too much for her to sleep well. Mouse snored gently on the floor opposite, curled into a tight ball, the hard floorboards no problem for her young bones.

Hope scrabbled onto her stiff knees, feeling every minute of her thirty-one years.

"Mouse." She gently shook the girl's shoulder. Mouse grunted awake.

"Shush." Hope held a finger to her lips. "There's someone out there. At the window." She pointed at the closed rear window, just above Mouse's head.

Mouse was immediately alert. Unfortunately, her slightest movement was accompanied by the loud clank of chains.

"Mouse? Is that you?" The whisper came again.

"Joey," Mouse cried delightedly and scrambled as close to the window as she was able, scraping her chains across the floor.

"Shush, Mouse. Patrick will hear," Hope hissed and put her finger to her lips. "Joey? Your Joey? From Canada?" she asked. She could barely believe it. How had he gotten all the way down here? According to Mouse, Ren's pack was under orders to mind the farm back in B.C.

"Go tell him it's me. I can't move." Mouse tugged at the chain in a huff.

Hope moved over to the window. "Joey?"

There was silence for a moment. "Who's that?"

"I'm Hope. Mouse is in here with me. She can't come to the window. Patrick has chained her up."

Joey gave an angry hiss at this news. It tailed off into a forlorn silence. Hope waited, would he talk to her?

"Hey. How do I know she's even in there with you?" he suddenly asked, as if the idea had just occurred to him. "It could be a trap."

"It's not a trap."

"But it could be?"

Hope sighed. "If it was, you'd be caught by now," she said.

More silence as he thought this over. "Okay. Prove it."

"Prove what?" This was the worst rescue attempt Hope had ever heard of.

"Prove it's not a trap."

"Well…do you feel trapped?"

More silence followed this.

"No. But it wasn't a good test," he said finally. "Hey. I know. Prove Mouse is in there with you."

"How? She can't yell. That would wake everyone up."

"Get her to tell you something only she and me know." He sounded very satisfied with this plan.

"Okay. Wait a minute."

"Wait! How do I know you're not going to warn the others I'm he—"

"Oh, shut up. I'll be back in a minute."

Hope was back in seconds. "Mouse says you're stupid and you smell."

Joey giggled, and Hope took it she had passed the test.

"Okay, Joey. What's the plan? Can you get us out of here?"

"Um. I can pull the shutters off?" he said.

"Mouse is chained to the floor," she reminded him. "And Patrick has the key. We don't know how many there are of them out there."

"I'll go look."

"Please be careful."

Joey slid back a few minutes later. "There's only Patrick." He sounded excited. "I can take him any time."

"Mouse says you can't because your guts are busted and Patrick will whup you good," Hope relayed.

"I can jump him easy." Joey sounded petulant. This was dangerous. Hope didn't want him to try something rash. He was their only chance of escape, and that stacked the odds against them heavily.

"You'll need to surprise him, Joey. Be clever. Get him from behind somehow."

She could hear Joey sucking his teeth as he mulled this over.

"Mouse?" Hope turned back into the room. "We do get fed, don't we?"

Mouse nodded. "Breakfast is chicken bones. He'll bring that soon."

"I can hardly wait." She went back to Joey. "Joey. Lie low until you see Patrick bringing us breakfast. When he opens the door I'm going to distract him, and you sneak up on him. Okay?"

"What are you gonna do?" he asked eagerly.

"Never mind. You just sneak up on him and sucker punch him good." She thought that might appeal to Joey.

"He's coming," Mouse whispered.

"He's on his way, Joey. Leave the distraction to me. You get ready to pounce."

"You bet." And Joey was gone.

"What *are* you going to do?" Mouse asked. She sounded worried. "Patrick's sneaky. He'll open the door a crack and push the food in."

Hope could hear his footsteps now, long minutes after Mouse's keen hearing had picked up on them.

"Don't worry. I have ideas." She'd better. There was very little thinking time left.

The lock rattled, and the door screeched open about one foot. The dim light of a downcast day crept in around Patrick's shadow. He set a tin tray with a plate of chicken bones down on the floor.

"Better make it last, ladies. I'll be heading out…" His words trailed away as a small round object trundled out of the darkest corner toward him. It rolled slowly across the floorboards. He frowned. The ball bumped into the rim of the tin tray with a soft clunk. He reached for it, full of cautious curiosity. It was barely in his fingers when he let out a surprised yelp and dropped Hope's prosthetic eye back to the floor. At the same instance, Joey, in his wolven glory, gave a mighty roar from behind and dropped a huge rock on Patrick's head, sending him sprawling.

Joey threw back his head and howled in delight. The morning sun broke through the clouds, and for a hallucinogenic moment burnished his fur in a triumphant red-gold blaze, like some pagan god.

"Good boy, Joey." Hope scrabbled the key out of the lock, delicately side-stepping the pool of blood around Patrick's head. Joey sat on his hunkers panting with pleasure at the praise. Hope fumbled with the lock to Mouse's chains.

"Yes!" Mouse leapt to her feet and stamped them on the floor in a brave little dance. Hope couldn't begin to image how cramped she must feel after days in leg irons. She was one tough kid.

"Is he dead? I want to bite him." Mouse snapped her teeth. Her eyes gleamed with a wicked amber glow. Hope knew the telltale signs. There was no time for more wolven antics.

"Not quite dead. But don't bite him. Let's chain him up here and let him eat chicken bones."

Mouse's face lit up with glee. "And then I can bite him."

"What's the point? He's out cold. Help me drag him in here and lock him up. We need to get out of here before any of the others turn up," Hope said. Escape was paramount. Revenge, no matter how well deserved, could wait. "We'll let Ren have the first bite, okay? She'll like that."

It did the trick.

"Joey," Mouse said, and without a blink Joey lifted Patrick's dead weight and tossed him into the shack like a sack of cow fodder.

"Mouse, do me a favor. While I chain him up, could you look for my eye?" Hope bent to her chore. Mouse needed a distraction from the possibility of chomping on Patrick.

"Gross," Mouse said happily and began to scour the floor. "I wish I had a magic eye."

❖

"You go first," Ren said. "Someone will come out to challenge me. Keep going. Don't stop or turn around no matter what you hear."

Godfrey's frown deepened. She could tell he was nervous. He cradled the dog in his arms a little closer. They were standing by the car, on the western boundary of Little Dip valley.

"Challenge you?" he said uncertainly. "But you're a Garoul. I know that just by looking at you. Why—Oh."

He'd turned to her as she stripped off the last of her clothes. Now he was acting the gentleman and looked everywhere but at her. His cheeks flushed and she realized it was not because of her nudity, but her scarring. She bared her teeth. She was proud of her scars. She was a hunter, a fighter; she had a right to these scars. They were a badge of courage, a tattoo of her Alpha identity.

"Remember. Keep going," she said, annoyed at his stalling. He'd brought her all the way to the Garouls' golden valley, and now he was beginning to fret. But they had a deal, even if he didn't realize it, and he was carrying his part of the bargain in his arms. "Don't turn back, no matter what."

"Like Lot's wife," he muttered sulkily.

Her "Huh?" came out as a low rumble. A drop of her saliva dripped onto his shoulder. The dog drowsily stirred in his arms. At least it knew an Alpha order, even when half comatose. Godfrey peeped over his shoulder, checked out the bloody drool on his jacket, then gazed on up at her until his neck cricked and his eyes popped. She knew he had a wolven mate, but it gave her immense pleasure that he was nonetheless awed by her size and strength. She was a prime specimen. She was wild.

He paled and swallowed loudly. His temperature plunged. She could feel the heat drain off him as a chilling realization took hold. She was Garoul, but she was not family.

Another low growl, so soft the air around them bubbled with subtle menace. Her lips trembled delicately against her canines. He whipped his head around and fixed on the path before them. She snorted a satisfied puff past his left ear, lifting the hair at his temple. He had permission to step out and lead her all the way to the Garoul home compound.

How strange she had ended up here of all places. Her insides constricted in distaste, and she had to struggle not to leave belligerent claw marks on every rock and tree. She could not afford a fight. Her mate was in danger and she had come to parley, nothing more.

CHAPTER TWENTY-FOUR

Isabelle tracked the remaining Were for hours. He blundered, inept and frightened, around the shale slopes and scrubby flatlands. Just before dawn, he crouched behind some scraggly bushes. He grunted and moaned as she waited and wondered what he was up to. Finally, he emerged as a naked man and ran the last hundred yards before scrambling down a gully onto a deserted side road. She watched him hurriedly drag out a stash of clothes from his truck and pull them on any old way. He glanced about nervously, stinking of stale sweat and shaking with fright.

He knew she'd been following him; he just didn't know how close she'd got. She was right behind him, standing by a tumble of sandstone, deliberately so, because she blended beautifully with the colors in the murky dawn light. It was testimony to his incompetence that he didn't see her. He wasn't using his wolf side. Instead, he was letting his blunt human senses ride him.

She flew at him from out of the shrub and stones with the sudden burst of speed she had come to love, and slammed him against the side of his truck. He screamed, and she heard a satisfying crunch as she crushed several vertebrae. He slid to the dirt in a heap, shock and hopelessness draining the color from his face. She crouched over him, watching his dismay as his body instantly began sending messages to his brain—feet won't work, no legs, can't move, arms gone… She had broken his back. He could lift his head, barely. His chest rose and fell in panicked heaves; his mouth kept moving, but he had no words, no screams, just pathetic little grunts of effort as he defied his limbs to unfreeze and save him.

Now she was concerned. What if he couldn't speak? She hadn't meant to inflict this much damage. She must remember this. Human bodies took less punishment. She hunkered down beside him. His head had fallen back in the watery mud, and it swam up, filling his ears. She wanted information from him but was unsure how to get it. She supposed she should change into human form as he had done, and interrogate him before…doing what? Calling an ambulance? The police would come, and she didn't want that. What did you do after attacking a human? Was he even human anymore? She shook the thought from her head; she simply didn't know these sort of details. It was all a mystery to her.

She looked at him again. His chest still rose and fell too quickly. He was staring wide-eyed back at her. She could see right into his soul. His vulnerability, terror, and remorse were on display, all mushed up in one big ugly ball. If he could read her eyes, would he see doubt and perhaps a little remorse, too? She blinked and looked away. Her immediate problem was not remorsefulness; her problem was changing back to human form and questioning him…about something? What? What had she been hunting him for? He'd tried to harm her, him and his buddies. They were dead now, and so would he be, soon enough. But what did she need from him before he died? Perhaps if she were human she would remember better. Her human brain worked differently. In her wolfskin, human thoughts and recollections were nothing more than an irritating buzz in the back of her mind. A list of chores and boring details her wolven side wanted to ignore. All her wolfside wanted to do was sniff exciting things, and run, and hunt, and enjoy the world for what it really was.

She idly scratched her rump, then plucked at her damp ear hairs. How did she turn back to human form? She had no idea. He burbled something at her. She leaned in to him and paid attention. He was saying something about help please. No. None of that. She pulled away.

Then he said something about her friend. Isabelle bared her teeth. This was good talk. The buzz in her head increased significantly, so she leaned in closer and concentrated on his words. He said there was a shack to the northeast, near Lost Creek, in Wallowa County. He said Patrick had her friend there. Patrick! Her nostrils flared. Yes, she wanted Patrick. The hunt continued, and her heart swelled with joy. She knew there had to be more to it than these three sad specimens, these easy kills. He was talking again, trying to make a deal, trying to get her to help.

Disinterested now, Isabelle heaved onto her feet and padded away into the dawn.

❖

A grim, dull light crept over the hills and Isabelle became tired of moving onward. Though she was stronger than ever, her massive musculature demanded more fuel. Her earlier hunt had used up a lot of her reserves and she had not eaten since raiding Hope's fridge—Hope! Her tongue lolled and she tasted the crisp morning air with happiness. Hope was a friend. Hope was her target, not Patrick. She would kill Patrick because he had stolen Hope and hurt the little dog. The dog was a friend, too. They were den, yet not den? Her real den was far away, in the north, and she was parted from it.

The realization winded her. She squatted on the dirt and raised her muzzle to the gray skies and howled out her sadness and discontent. The mournful cry startled a nearby baby rabbit and it scuttled for home. Isabelle pounced, but its small frame slid through her claws. She snapped her jaws, and by pure luck, caught its hind leg, tossing it into the air. It landed stunned and she was on it in a second, ripping its head off with her teeth and sucking down fur and bone and blood and fuel. A warm kill, the sweetest of nectars, and an ensurance of survival.

Licking her muzzle, she rolled onto her back among the wet wiregrass and stared up at the slowly vanishing stars. The sky was cloudless and brightening by the minute, and the temperature dropping quickly. It would be a cold day. She could smell more rain on the wind. Her fur would keep her warm and waterproof, even though her breath puffed in the morning air. Her stomach felt happy. She could eat a dozen more baby rabbits. Perhaps if she found the warren hole she could dig it out and eat them all?

Satisfied, she curled onto her side and wriggled down into the grass, making a little nest. She would rest for a few hours. Then, before the sun burned too bright, she would head northeast in great galloping strides, eating up the countryside between here and her enemy, Patrick. No, she wanted Hope, not Patrick. Her friend Hope. She'd eat up the countryside between here and her friend Hope. Then she'd eat up Patrick.

❖

Her dreams were as thick and fuzzy as wool, but as comforting, too. Aunt Mary fussed about her living room. She wanted to lock up the house for winter, though the sunshine still shone through the opened windows. Shafts of light cut across the plump, chintz furnishings. Dust motes rose up in the air from their frantic cleaning. It was a fine day. Perhaps the last good day before the snows came for real.

Isabelle wore white. A white dress and a flowery apron. She had a yellow duster in her hand, and she was happy and laughing. Everything felt good.

The door rattled with a hard, jaunty rap, and Aunt Mary bustled toward it, excited. She had been waiting for this visitor. She adored this visitor. She opened the door, and the brightest of sunrays haloed Ren standing handsome and impressive on the doorstep. Her smile was radiant; her eyes gleamed as black and as wicked as Lucifer's heart, and fixed on Isabelle and nothing else.

Isabelle smiled nervously back. All the comfort of her dream world fell away. Her stomach turned stone cold under that stare.

"Why, hello, Luc," Aunt Mary said.

Isabelle awoke shivering. She was drenched in dew and stiff with the cold seeping through into her bones. She sat on a scrubby slope, in a patch of itchy wiregrass, buck-naked. Her stomach roiled with nausea, her mouth tasted foul—so revolting, in fact, she had to fight down biliousness. She crawled up onto her feet and fell right back down again on her backside on the prickly grass. Was this weakness the aftermath of her transition back to human form? She felt miserable, hungover, and self-loathing. She was aching and wretched, through and through.

Isabelle rolled onto her back and groaned at the sky. What had she become? She shrank from any thoughts on what she might have done, though images clamored at the edges of her mind, bloody and sickening.

"I change when I sleep?" She picked out the most pertinent piece of all the information ricocheting around her aching head. With shame she accepted the memory of the men she had attacked and killed. And the one she had left alive and paralyzed in the gully?

Isabelle lurched to her feet and this time managed to stay upright. With a shaking, swaying gait, she retraced her steps, her own wolven tracks quite obvious to her. She had to find the guy. She had to save him. It was a selfish action. By saving him she was really trying to save part of herself.

❖

She found him beside the truck where she'd left him. Approaching from the far side, she saw his feet first. One booted, the other bare. She hadn't given him time to dress before charging him down. Was he still alive? She came around the truck cautiously, afraid to face her carnage.

Remember, he's another werewolf from an enemy pack. They all were. They were hunting you down. They were going to hurt you. They've already hurt those you care for. It was a hunt, and you were the better hunter. She attempted to quantify her guilt. There was an instinct in her that told her she had to justify her wolven actions and rationalize them with her human side if she was to stay sane.

He was sprawled in the dirt, legs twisted, arms flailed to the sides where he had fallen. His head was still part buried in the mud, his horrified face staring bug-eyed at a slate gray sky. His chest had been stove in. Crushed flat. His unbuttoned shirt fluttered over an enormous, bruised hollow in his chest where before she had seen his lungs inflate with gulping breaths as he bargained for mercy.

Instead, she had abandoned him. She moved closer. She had not abandoned him like this, though. The ground around his body was churned with huge wolven footprints that were not her own. A clear trail showed their approach and retreat. And there, in the center of his caved-in chest, was one more muddy footprint. The beast had stood on his sternum and slowly crushed him to death.

Isabelle stood drinking in the callousness of the kill. This beast had not even bared a claw. There was nothing quick or merciful about this death. It was calculated for maximum cruelty with the least effort.

She sneezed. It brought her back to her own plight. She was naked and shivering and becoming ill because of it. She was in vulnerable human form at the scene of a vicious killing and didn't know how to mutate back to wolven at will. An enemy was out there. It had killed this man, and she sensed its ill will for her, too. She was not safe here.

The truck cab door still hung open and more clothes were piled on the bench seat. They must have belonged to his dead buddies. She jumbled through the mishmash for the best fit and threw on jeans, a shirt, and some boots. At least she had a sleeve to wipe her runny nose on.

Isabelle stared at the body beside the truck. She took a calculating look at the surrounding landscape and at the state of the track they were parked on. How often was it used? The truck keys were dangling from the ignition. Decision made, she pulled herself into the cab. She backed along the twisting gully track, away from the body, leaving the remains uncovered. Let it be a gift of ensured survival for the coyotes, wolves, and foxes, and anything else that might find him. He could feed his brothers.

The road she reversed onto was underused at that time of year. She headed northeast for Wallowa and somewhere called Lost Creek, following the man's directions from last night. With the cab heater on she soon warmed up and her body began to relax. Only then did she allow the remnants of her dream to resurface. She was careful with it. She did not trust the feelings it aroused.

Luc. Why had she disliked her so much? Luc's face swam out from the dream and also the photograph stored in her camera. Ren and Luc. They both sat on a log by the forest stream, smiling over at her. Isabelle knew instinctively she had never liked Luc.

When she thought of Ren, her heart ached like a sentimental song. She wanted to be with her. She thought she understood now—well, at least understood more than she had two days ago. Ren had been trying to protect her from the ferocious beast clawing at her from the inside out. Ren had wanted to help. She knew what awaited Isabelle. She knew there would come a moment when Isabelle would erupt in a spew of gore and blood, and run amok. Thank God her targets had been her wolven pursuers and not cattle, or tourists, or preschool picnickers.

"Get a grip," Isabelle scolded herself. She wasn't sure how it worked, but she knew it didn't work like that. Driving through the outskirts of a town, she felt panic well up in her chest and sweat prickle her scalp. She was shy around humans, cautious and careful not to draw attention. It was a good lesson. She would run a million miles away from a preschool picnic, and that was nice to know.

Ren. She sighed heavily. She wanted Ren, as much as she ever did back in the valley. Could she go home? She called it home now, and even thought of it as den. When had that shift happened?

And this Luc? What did she represent in her dream? She had to be related to Ren to look so alike. Sisters for sure, maybe even twins? Isabelle braked and pulled over, ignoring an angry honk from a passing car. She sat trembling at the wheel.

Her journal. Her burned journal was talking about Luc. *Luc and Ren.* The yin and yang of it came sharply into focus. She could not recall everything. She still was bleary about actually meeting Ren for the first time, possibly because the discomfort of meeting Luc had overclouded her memories. But Luc had frightened her. Luc had to be the scary woman in the journal, and Ren was her rescuer. Isabelle knew that as a fact. Ren must have tried to save the journal as some sort of evidence, an insurance against Isabelle's amnesia. An evil twin was such a cliché! No wonder she had been so upset when Patrick burned it.

Isabelle shook her head. It was a ridiculous assumption and only went to show how far she would go to make Ren the hero and lover she wanted her to be. Luc had not locked her up in a cabin, burned her car, or hidden her documents. Ren had. Just because someone glared at you in a photograph and scared you in dreams did not mean you could place the woes of your world on their shoulders. Isabelle had run away from Ren, not the mysterious Luc.

Her logic was gooed up with nonsensical wishes. Heartfelt longing was such a viscous thing. It clogged the arteries like cholesterol, starving the brain of oxygen-rich good, plain common sense.

Isabelle stared at her hands on the steering wheel. She was a stupid, shallow woman. Clogged to the gills with neediness and romantic twaddle. She read so much cheap romance she was swimming in it. She was even studying it in Classic form, for God's sake! Ren's face swam before her, darkened by thought, and then lit by laughter as she playfully tickled Mouse.

"I have been meditating on the very great pleasure which a pair of fine eyes in the face of a pretty woman can bestow." She quoted from Jane Austen to underscore her point. "See how ridiculous you are?"

Isabelle shook herself out of her reverie and reached for the gearshift. She had a friend to save, and an enemy to greet, at a shack near Lost Creek. She could not afford to wallow in what might-have-beens. Hope needed her, Patrick was out there hurting her friends, and something vicious was stomping on paralyzed people.

And Ren...Ren was nine hundred miles away, and even in the midst of all this chaos Isabelle was stupid enough to wonder if she was thinking of her, too.

CHAPTER TWENTY-FIVE

It's easy to hitch with crutches. Everyone wants to stop for you. They just pull over and say, 'Where' ya going, son?' and I say 'America, ma'am,' or 'sir,' if it's a man." Joey walked on ahead, talking nonstop over his shoulder. "And then I dumped the crutches under a bush because I could walk okay, all along." This was apparently a Joey joke, because he fell into hoots of laughter. "And then I came over the border as a Were. I just walked right into Washington one night. I had to, because I got no passport. I just stepped over into the U.S. of A." He took an extra-long step to demonstrate. Hope swapped glances with Mouse.

"He's all excited. He never shuts up when he gets excited," Mouse muttered. "Bet you wish your ears pulled off as easy as your eyes."

"It's just one eye, Mouse. I don't have two glass eyes." Hope's answer was buried in exhaustion. She was so tired. These kids kept a speedy pace, and she was finding it harder and harder to keep up. Her head thumped from lack of sleep, and she was hungry and felt very weak.

Joey had babbled on for an hour solid since they'd left the shack. Telling them about the morning he found out Patrick and Mouse had gone, and how Noah tried to call Ren and tell her, except Ren's cell phone always went to voicemail. And how Noah had ordered Joey to stay and help with the farm but Joey ran away to find Mouse all by himself. And how Noah would be mad, and maybe even Ren, too, but he had to find Mouse because she was his friend. And how he was glad he ran away even though he'd be in trouble, because he *had* found Mouse, and rescued her just like a hero.

Mouse puffed in frustration at the glory Joey heaped on himself.

Now that she was saved, she was much less gracious. "I was gonna get away soon enough. I just hung around to see if I could bite Patrick first."

"How did you find Mouse, Joey?" Hope asked.

"Easy! Ren had a tracer put on my mobile phone so she could find me if I ever got lost. I used to get lost lots of times," he said, a little shamefaced.

"He'd wander off for days and days," Mouse said, eager to highlight a weakness in her heroic rescuer. "At least with the cell phone tracker we could find his clothes, then track him down for ourselves."

"I wasn't *really* lost," Joey said. "It's just when I'm a Were I forget to change back. I keep on sniffing and exploring till I'm miles and miles away and forget where I put my clothes and have to come home naked."

"Ren was worried because he's so stupid," Mouse said. "She was worried he'd be smelling so much and not looking where he was going he'd walk out in front of a loggin' truck and get squished."

"So how does this tracer thing work?" Hope was intrigued.

"It's for parents to track their kids through their cell phones," Mouse said.

"And Mouse had your phone?" Hope asked Joey.

"Nope." Joey shook his head. "I left it sitting in Patrick's truck. So I traced him instead!" Joey sounded very proud. Then his shoulders slumped. "It was really Jenna's idea to use the phone tracer. I stole her phone so I could do it when I ran away." He looked ashamed.

"Jenna will skin your ears," Mouse said. Joey went quiet for a moment as he contemplated this threat. Then he dismissed it and bounced back with an in-depth, nonstop tale of how he used up the fifteen free trace calls to bring him closer to Patrick until he could sniff Mouse out for himself. His plan had traces of genius, Hope decided. It had brought him close enough to effectively save them, despite Mouse's thanklessness.

"Time out, guys." Hope sat down heavily on a fallen log. "I need a breather. You're moving too fast and I'm struggling." She had reached her limit.

Joey and Mouse stood over her, pondering her words. Then Joey slumped down on the log beside her, sitting much too close. His hip and side were glued to hers. Mouse attached herself to the other side, resting her head on Hope's shoulder. They sat there, sandwiching her until Hope was completely crushed and overheated, but she didn't push them away. They were dependent on her, and lost as to what to do next.

"We're moving too slow, not too fast." Mouse chewed her lip. "If we changed we could get to your friend's place in no time."

Their anxiety made them lean farther into Hope until she felt like a pressed flower. She tried to shrug her shoulders free, but it was impossible to move under their combined weight. She had let them down.

"I'm sorry, guys," she said. She felt inadequate and miserable. Her plan had been to try to direct them to Little Dip, the only place she knew that could offer shelter. She had no idea how soon Patrick's cronies would find him and come after them. Mouse had a point. Hope was slowing them down because she couldn't move at a werewolf gallop. She was endangering them all.

"I'm going to give you directions as best I can. You need to change and run on ahead without me. Look for a road north of Lost Creek—"

"We're not leaving you." Mouse was stern, and Joey nodded in aggressive agreement. They leaned in ever tighter in their mild panic, and Hope thought she would pop. "We're a pack. We don't leave a pack mate behind. We'll change, and Joey will carry you. Like a piggyback ride."

Mouse sounded incredibly pleased with her plan. She rose and began shucking off her tatty clothes.

"Now wait a minute," Hope said, alarmed.

Mouse paid no attention. Quickly, she stripped, dropping her clothes on the dirt around her feet. She knelt on all fours, and before Hope could blink, a small, dun-coated Werewolf squatted before her. Mouse stood and shook her coat vigorously. A sly wolfish grin creased her muzzle, and her eyes gleamed with amber mischief.

"That was the quickest change I've ever seen." Hope was amazed. It had to be a youth thing. Jolie and Andre were not half as fast, or quiet. In fact, they made quite a fuss about the whole thing.

Joey had the grace to slip off behind a tree to strip down. Now he emerged as a huge red-gold beast. He, too, sported a happy smile on his leathered face. He crouched down before her, his back turned toward her.

It was obvious what she was expected to do. In a move the likes of which she hadn't made since childhood, Hope hopped onto his broad back, and hooked her legs along his flanks. He rose, carrying her up to dizzying heights, and strode away with an easy rolling gait, her extra weight not affecting him in the slightest.

Hope clung to his shaggy neck and shoulders as Mouse trotted by his side. They picked up speed and were soon running through the forest at a very comfortable pace. Hope pointed over Joey's shoulder when they needed to move in a new direction.

It was a seamless and quick passage through the surrounding hills and woodland. Joey leapt over fallen obstacles, swerved around trees, slid down shale slopes, never once losing his stride. Mouse kept a steady pace beside him. Both were easy and confident in their Were bodies, moving ever onward to Hope's promised place of safety.

❖

They were a mile or more into the valley when Ren became aware of the first one. It hung back, scouting them. No doubt there were others not far away. Godfrey walked ahead of her, unaware of their silent escort. At least he was quiet for once; the sudden hush of the forest had unnerved him into a silence of his own. Ren was relieved. She had been worried his incessant chattering would drown out the telltale noises she so desperately needed to hear.

Another mile or so and there were three tailing them. One on each flank, and another at the rear to block any retreat. They knew what they were doing. These three would shadow her into the heart of their valley, toward their compound. As soon as she drew close enough they would reveal themselves, and more would come out to face her.

Except it didn't quite work that way. There was a vague noise to her right, a rustle or snap of a twig that distracted her momentarily. When she looked back, all of three seconds later, Godfrey was gone. She knew he wouldn't have run; he didn't fear her enough to run. They had spirited him away to a place of safety, out of her reach. That did not bode well. That suggested there could be confrontation. Her heartbeat increased. If they attacked without parley she could not possibly win. She was a strong fighter, but there were too many of them around her now.

For the first time she wondered at her plan. It had been quickly formulated, but she had no other options. Isabelle was ill and lost in the wilds of Oregon. She was being hunted, and if the transmutation did not kill her, there was a good chance her hunters would.

As if to underscore her concern, a quiet rumble came from behind her left shoulder, close to her ear. Oh, they were good. Very good.

They had distracted her enough to steal her companion, and while she fretted about that, they had sneaked up right behind her undetected. She felt a fool. All it took was her concentration to be fractured for a split second for them to move in on her silently.

The low growl came again, deep, and thoroughly menacing. It was a command for attention. Slowly, she turned her head to look over her shoulder, and found herself at eye level with a huge female. It was unusual for Ren to be at eye level with anything, especially a Were. This one was a senior. She was black with sliver streaks. Her golden eyes were narrowed, and she oozed confidence and authority. Ren held her gaze, then flicked her eyes away briefly in a mark of polite respect. This was not her valley, nor her den. She was on a mission. She did not want confrontation if she could avoid it. It could not hurt to be mannerly. She stood stock-still, her face turned toward the newcomer and her eyes averted. She gave a snarl to show she understood and complied.

Redirecting her gaze was luckily the correct thing to do. The beast's growl rumbled on, but the threat in it lessened. As the warning faded away, the Were carefully leaned over and clamped Ren's muzzle in her maw. Her sharp canines slid under Ren's upper lip, enamel scraped across enamel, until her teeth pressed against Ren's upper gum and the soft flesh of her inner cheek. Ren tensed. By acquiescing to this she had left herself open. One snap and jerk and she could lose half her face. Every muscle in her back and shoulders bunched and quivered. This was no den guard. Only the Alpha would have the right to do this, to demand this level of obedience. And as Ren was the interloper in her valley, she had to conform.

Ren gave a low, short rumble of compliance, hoping to communicate a nonaggressive, yet not wholly submissive position. She was an Alpha in her own right, and unless she was totally unwelcome in this valley, she should be greeted with a modicum of courtesy. If she proved unwelcome she would be torn to shreds. At the moment, her risk was fifty-fifty, but what were her options? She was doing this for Isabelle. If it didn't work she would lose her, and Ren would feel as if she were torn to shreds anyway. So she acquiesced to the Alpha and held back a yelp as the teeth on her muzzle tightened into a painful nip. It was a test, and she'd be damned if she'd yelp for a Garoul.

Her own growl deepened into a rattle of a warning. She would only take so much…and miraculously, just as she thought she'd lost the gamble, just as her temper and tolerance hung by a thread, the Alpha let go. She snapped loose Ren's lip and ran a huge, long tongue across the creases of Ren's muzzle, licking along her furry cheek and up into her eye, causing her to squint.

The Alpha panted and pressed her face close. Her snuffle of peace blew into Ren's twitching ear. She had been accepted. Ren blinked, confused and thankful. She had come so close to losing her last chance.

The forest around her shuddered and shook into life as about twenty Weres emerged onto the trail. They crowded around her pressing, and sniffing, and rumbling in muted, cautious growls. They herded her through the forest and around a sharp bend. Through the trees she could see the sparkle of the Silverthread, and then the compound opened up to her, an enormous pack home of maybe thirty cabins. They were scattered around a central area with a fire pit and dozens of bench tables. Farther back she could make out other cabins crouched quietly in the forest, away from the bustle of the camp. It was a small village and belonged to this one clan. Her clan. She had found her way back to the Garoul home den. A home she had once been cast out of.

❖

She was shown a small room. The clothes she had left at her rental car were neatly folded on a chair. Ren had noticed Godfrey and the little dog being shepherded into another building. They were the center of much concerned attention. She was pleased that the man and his dog were finally safe among friends. No harm would come to them here.

She was escorted, fully dressed and in human form, to a central lodge house. It was a larger, more permanent fixture than the vacation feel of some of the other cabins. Ren assumed some of the pack lived in the valley permanently, while others came and went in the outside world.

A tall, dark woman stood by the blazing fireplace. Her long black hair was streaked with silver, and Ren felt an unexpected gut wrench for her own mother. All she had was a black-and-white photograph, and the resemblance to the woman before her was uncanny. She also knew instinctively this was the Alpha who had caught her muzzle and tested her before allowing her to enter the valley. She was flanked by an immense bearded man who, in Were form, would be formidable and a small, intense woman who watched every move Ren made as if she could read her mind. She unnerved Ren, but she could feel the bond between the woman and the Alpha. They were mates, and the smaller woman was Were. Several other pack members filled the room. In human form their family resemblance was unmistakable, and Ren did not doubt for one moment that her own features blended right in. They all shared the same bloodline. They were Garoul.

"Welcome." The Alpha slowly approached. "I am Marie Garoul." She indicated the man and woman who still flanked her every move. "This is my brother, Claude, and my partner, Connie."

Neither welcomed Ren. They gazed at her impassively. The big man remained wary and on guard. The other woman watched her with clever, steely eyes.

Marie continued her introduction. "Little Dip is our home valley, and I am the Alpha here."

Ren nodded, unable to speak. Her heart thumped in her throat and she did not trust her voice at this important juncture. She needed this clan, but she was an outsider and unsure of their intentions. Isabelle was lost to her, out there somewhere in the wilds. This family had eyes and ears everywhere. If they would help, then it would more than halve her search time, and every hour brought Isabelle closer and closer to her first transmutation.

Marie's intelligent eyes watched her carefully. Finally, after a short silence, she spoke again. "How are your parents?"

"Dead."

Marie nodded at this. "I assumed that when I stopped hearing from Dalia."

Ren said nothing. She did not want to talk about her mother. She watched Marie carefully.

"How?" Marie asked bluntly.

"Cancer. Father had an aneurysm a few years later." Ren left it at that. Her jaw clenched and she knew her face had hardened into a stubborn mask.

"And which twin are you?" Marie asked next. "Luciana or Floriene?"

"Ren. I'm Ren."

"Floriene?"

"Ren."

"Ren Garoul it is." Marie nodded thoughtfully.

Silence fell again, and again it was Marie who broke it.

"So, Ren Garoul. What can your family do for you?"

"I've been tracking my ma—" She took a deep breath. "The woman I wish for my mate. She's in danger. Godfrey, the blond man who came with me. He and another friend were helping her. She's beginning transmutation and she's ill."

"Where is Godfrey?" Marie asked.

"He's with the dog," one of the others answered.

"Go get him," Marie said. She turned back to Ren. "Does your mate need medicine?"

Ren was uncertain how much she should reveal. Her trust did not run as deep as her relief. But she needed them to help her find Isabelle, and she had no idea what state she would be in when found.

She nodded.

The door opened and Godfrey came in. He looked fraught and tried.

"Are you all right, Godfrey?" Marie asked. He nodded.

"Ren saved me from some ferals, but they got Hope, and Isabelle ran after her to help and we lost her, too. Tadpole was hurt pretty bad, but Ren strapped him up until we got here." It came out in one big rush, as if he simply wanted to get it off his chest and hand over the hopelessness and responsibility of it to someone else. He looked exhausted with the effort, and worried sick. "We need to find Hope, Marie. Jolie will go insane when she finds out. And Isabelle is ill. I think she's about to change for the first time, and she's out there all alone."

Marie digested this. Her eyes narrowed and she bared her teeth. She stared at Ren, her look so sharp Ren felt pinned to the floorboards.

"I thank you for saving Godfrey and tending to Tadpole," she said curtly. "Who are these ferals? Why have they taken Hope? And give me more information about this Isabelle."

"Isabelle's my mate."

"You sired a mate and did not help her with her first transmutation?"

"Isabelle…left before I could help."

Marie's eyes narrowed to suspicious slits. "You sired a mate, and she ran."

"I did not sire her." Ren stiffened, as if ready for a fight. Her words were met with silence. "My sister did." Her tone was harsh. "And I stole her."

CHAPTER TWENTY-SIX

Isabelle followed the directions given by the guy with the crushed chest and headed for Lost Creek. She was maybe three miles out when her nose took over. Once she lifted wolven scents off the wind she abandoned the truck. The air was thick with scent and she became overexcited. Her mutation came almost thoughtlessly, almost painlessly. As soon as she stepped out of the truck the myriad of wolven scents slammed into her like an express train, and she found herself facedown in the dirt pulling at her clothes like they were on fire. She smacked her lips at the blood that filled her mouth while her flesh boiled and erupted. *I can't control this. It just happens. If there's a trigger, I need to find it fast.* Her rib cage cracked and popped as she took that first deep, unadulterated breath and the natural world flooded her senses. She was bombarded with information as if the forest had opened like the pages of a book. Growling softly with pure pleasure, she slid through the trees that rolled over hills and crept up the mountainsides. Dusk accentuated her senses even more. Smell became stronger, her sight keener. Before she realized it, she was crouched in the undergrowth, rubbing her flank against a tree trunk and growling contentedly as she scratched. The early evening scents were comforting. Night was drawing in, and she felt more alive than ever.

She moved fast, leaping over fallen logs and across creeks. She thundered through the forest, strong and powerful, much like in her dreams, only there was no Ren by her side. She was alone.

The springtime forest was filled with the sounds of songbird courtship and the musk of animals attracting mates. It filled her with a lust for life. It invigorated her. Her fur hummed and her teeth tingled.

She belonged in this body, and in this place. Maybe she would never go back. Maybe she would always hunt alone.

Hunger made her clumsy and careless in her hunting. She scattered four young deer on their way to the higher grazing grounds, chasing wildly after their zigzag runs. Soon, winded, she sank to her haunches and watched the taunting flash of their white tails disappear. She thrashed into a small lake and sent geese and ducks flapping from her greedy claws. Her growling stomach had to make do with frogs. She squatted in the reed water, all her earlier elation deflating along with her appetite. Mushy frogs tasted bitter. She chewed little and swallowed quickly. If she was to be alone then she had to learn to hunt more proteinaceous foods. Her ears flattened and she growled in dissatisfaction. She had no idea how to do that, how to learn any of the skills she needed. Last night's rabbit had been a lucky kill. She would be in trouble if she could not refuel soon.

Isabelle lurched to her feet and moved on. Her nose was good. She could pick up Patrick's scent around the lake edge. The dead boy with the crushed chest had told her of this lake and the small shack tucked back on its southern side. She moved away in a southerly direction and followed the telltale odors of Patrick's sweat and nervousness. When he changed, his wolven smell was cocky and swaggering, but there was always an underlying residue of insecurity that permeated everything he did.

She found the shack in less than an hour, and approached carefully. A truck and a few scattered tents were huddled in a makeshift camp before it. There were multiple Were scents crisscrossing. Some were older than others. She blinked and twitched her nose, intrigued. A small distressed whine vibrated in her throat. She smelled home. Far away home...to the north. And it reminded her of Ren, not that Ren was ever far away from her thoughts. Ren's shadow forever hovered over Isabelle's heart, keeping it dark and subdued.

She hunkered behind a tree and watched. The early evening was beginning to steal the light away, but her night vision helped her focus clearly. Nothing moved. It didn't feel like a trap. She sniffed the air faintly, picking up a memory of Mouse and Joey. Her longing for them grew so great she was unsure if she actually smelled them or imagined it out of longing.

She drew idle designs in the dirt with a long foreclaw as she thought this over. If longing made her imagine scents, then she would smell Ren everywhere. But she didn't, so that meant the scents were true. Mouse and Joey *had* been here, and recently.

She stood and circled the shack, to creep up from behind. The closer she got, the more scents and stories filled her head. Many wolven had used this place, but only one human. Her friend! Hope!

Isabelle's heart thrilled. She had found traces of Hope. Her ears crimped back on her skull, and her lips trembled with a low, vicious growl. The scent was faint. Hope was no longer there. Isabelle's frustration rose.

The shack was empty. She knew it as soon as she drew close. She stepped over large splashes of dried blood and pushed open the door. Broken chain links littered the floor. The place was rank with Patrick's fear. It overrode everything else. She stood patiently for many minutes trying to decipher the story of the last few hours in this barren hut.

Hope, Mouse, and Joey were here, but had been gone almost a day. They smelled energetic and healthy. Isabelle was pleased that they were well. Patrick's scent was shrill and panicked. And then came another scent. A sly, subtle smell that Isabelle recognized at once. It held a deep, dark undertone. A bittersweet bite. She had come across it before, in Hope's backyard and by the body of the crushed man. This was the predator who hunted them all.

Isabelle grabbed a plate of spindly chicken bones and reeled out of the shack, greedily gulping down the free meal. She licked her lips. Her eyes darted around as she thought through the overload of messages, and her task became clearer in her head. Follow Hope, Joey, and Mouse. Patrick, and maybe this other predator, would be following them, too, so she had to race and catch them first. She might not be a good hunter, but Isabelle had faith in her nose. She was a tracker, through and through. She would find them.

Her eyes picked out a large patch of blood-soaked soil in the clearing before the shack. She had not noticed it from her hiding place in the tree line, but standing elevated on the front step it was plain to see. It stained the earth near Patrick's abandoned truck and the few sagging tents that formed the crude camp.

Isabelle dumped her empty plate and slunk over to investigate. The dirt was black with blood, and the ground littered with fragments of human bone and tissue. The area smelled heavily of stomach bile, and feces. She peeked in the tents and checked out the truck, but found no body. With this much blood there had to be a body. Isabelle was worried—a human had died here—and her fears for Hope grew.

The raucous cry of crows in the treetops caught her attention. Up in the taller branches where the wood met the clearing, several crows fought over tatters, greedy for a free evening meal. More and more birds were descending, their clamor was deafening to her sensitive ears. Like a black blanket they fell on the treetops, screaming and flapping and clawing at each other and the human body parts that festooned the branches. Isabelle's heart hammered in her throat as her keen eyesight scoured the trees. It was not Hope. It was Patrick. Her shoulders sagged with relief. The scent story came together and made sense now. He had been torn apart where she stood, his limbs and innards tossed in all directions into the surrounding trees to feed the carrion.

Such casual cruelty scared her. Patrick and the young man with the crushed chest had been working for this unknown pursuer. Failure was obviously not an option in that pack. Failure equaled death. An unpleasant, painful death.

A small part of Isabelle felt sorry for Patrick. The air hung heavy with his failings and his ultimate terror. He had been no better or worse than any of the young runaways Ren had helped. Though now it seemed he had never been in her pack at all, but owned by some other Were. A much deadlier master.

Isabelle shook the sadness from herself. The setting sun still warmed her fur and her trail scents. The breeze was timid tonight. It would be a fine evening for tracking. She burrowed under the scent of Patrick and his short brutal life, and found Hope, Joey, and Mouse. Good smells, den smells. The sunset glowed brighter for her because of these scents. Her heart was filled with eagerness and she bounded into the trees to follow them, always aware of the darker, deadlier scent that fell between her and friends. Their predator had a head start and was following them, too.

❖

"There's more coming in from the south. From Lost Creek direction," Robért reported. "Amelie has been tracking them since noon."

"How many?" Marie barked.

"Three, so far."

Marie swung around to face Ren.

"More of yours?" Her tone was hard. It was clear her trust was wearing thin. Ren shook her head.

"I came with Godfrey. No one else." These had to be Luc's rogues. Maybe even Luc herself, except she'd be surprised if Luc entered this valley so openly. Her sister was stealthy. You didn't know Luc was there until she bit.

Ren kept quiet, even though she knew her silence was aggravating.

"This valley's like a thoroughfare today," Marie groused at Robért. "Help Amelie corral them toward the compound. Then we'll see what we've got."

"I'll send her some backup." Robért excused himself.

"You think it's your sister, don't you?" Marie said.

Ren shrugged. "I can't see her wanting to return here. Little Dip holds no good memories for us."

"It holds you. And *you* stole from her," Marie said. In the wolven world that was reason enough for a fight to the death.

"Tell me about Isabelle." Marie's demand was not to be ignored. Ren shifted uncomfortably. She did not want this. She did not need to be judged, especially by the Garouls.

"When she arrived in Bella Cool we both liked her." She held Marie's eye, Alpha to Alpha. "I met her through her aunt and was captivated quite quickly. It became clear that Isabelle liked me back. But Luc…Luc wanted her, too, I think because she knew Isabelle was special to me. Luc can be very competitive and she's used to getting what she wants. When it became clear Isabelle preferred me, then Luc decided it would be fun to give me a little gift…"

"So she sired a mate for you?" Connie, Marie's partner, spoke for the first time. Her tone was incredulous. Ren stiffened.

"I didn't ask for this. I tried to stop it, but I was too late. Isabelle had already been infected. Luc wasn't happy that I took her plaything away before she was finished."

"Finished? How bad was the attack?" Marie wanted to know.

"Luc clawed her and the infection started. But later…later I bit her, and reopened the wound. I pushed her deeper into it. I made her mine."

Ren's vice was flint hard. She dared them to challenge her claiming back her mate.

"I remember you both as cubs." Marie's voice was softer. "Luc was very strong-willed, very wild."

Ren's smile was so bitter she could almost taste it on her lips. "So was I."

"Luc was cruel," Marie said bluntly. "I don't sense cruelty in you. I smell strength and loyalty, and compassion, even. You're an Alpha, aren't you?"

"I have a small pack. They're very young."

"How young?" Now Claude spoke. His face darkened. "Why are you making a pack with young people? That's crazy."

"More gifts?" Marie asked.

Marie had seen through her. Ren stood rigid; anger pulsed from her.

"I was in veterinary college for years after our parents died. Luc stayed at home and ran the farm. It wasn't until I came back that I realized how feral she had become. She had moved out and taken permanently to the woods. I let her be, but over time she got it into her head that I was lonely. She began bringing me presents. Kids on the run she had found and…changed—"

"Attacked, you mean," Connie said. "Luc is feral. She's out of control."

Ren fell silent. Unease rolled off her. She hated exposing herself and her sister to their scrutiny. Luc *was* out of control, but she did not want her hunted down like an animal. She wanted Luc to have a chance. Ren believed her ferine behavior could change. She refused to believe Luc was lost to her forever.

"Don't judge her. You were the ones who sent us away. What did you think would happen to cubs without pack guidance?"

"My mother made the correct decision at the time." Marie's response was measured. "Your parents were to keep contact. There was a support network here for them. They knew that, and used it when you were younger."

"Our parents died and Luc followed her natural inclinations. She grew weary of fighting it."

"And her inclination is to attack humans? These young people," Marie said. "What happened to them?"

Claude bristled and Connie glared. It was not good. Ren reasoned there would be no help for her here. She had blown her chances by telling the truth about Luc and her own sorry life. She took a deep breath. She might as well leave and look for Isabelle on her own. She had wasted enough time on this futile quest.

"I don't need this—" Her answer was cut short by Robért's return.

"Marie! You need to come see this. Amelie has arrived with the intruders."

Ren moved to the front porch with the others. From the back of the small crowd she blinked in amazement at the scene before her. Godfrey joyfully swung a dark-haired woman into in his arms in a massive hug. Beside them Joey sat hunkered on the dirt, a huge shaggy pile of golden fur. He looked around with great interest, idly scratching a scab on his belly. Mouse sat curled up against him, a tight ball of nervous dissatisfaction. Her ears flattened, and her eyes darted left and right, looking for an escape.

A crowd of curious Garouls crowded around the arrivals, much to Mouse's hissed consternation. Joey, on the other hand, loved the attention. His tongue lolled out in a friendly leer for everyone.

"Amelie. Get them some water," Claude said.

A young woman approached with a jug of water. Mouse spat like a cat, while Joey happily gulped down the drink and burped his appreciation.

"Mouse! Joey!" Ren ran to them. They lurched to their feet, yelping in delight, and leaned into her. Mouse clung to her leg, and Joey squashed her in a joyous bear hug.

"It seems they're yours, after all?" Marie joined her, taking a closer look at the newcomers.

"I left them in Canada. I've no idea how they arrived here." Ren was mystified. She kept touching and stroking them. She ran her fingers through their fur, pressing her face into their necks and breathing them in with great big gulps of homesickness.

"Patrick's responsible." The woman who had arrived with them approached her. "Patrick kidnapped Mouse, and Joey came after her. He ended up rescuing us both." She held out her hand in welcome. "Hi, you must be Ren. I've heard so many good things about you. I'm Hope, and these are two of the best and bravest Weres I know."

Joey's chest puffed, and Mouse peeped out from behind Ren's leg to acknowledge the praise.

"Compliments indeed," Marie told Ren. "Take them to your cabin. We'll find them some clothes. It's been a long and eventful journey, and I expect to hear all about it over supper."

There was a warning in her voice. Ren caught her eye and realized the Garoul Alpha meant to have her answers. It was decision time. Her request for help would either be accepted or rejected this nightfall. Ren led her wards away, Joey loping at her side and Mouse still clinging to her waist. She could scarcely believe they were here but was thrilled to see them. She missed her pack and her home den, and wanted more than anything to hear Mouse and Joey's story.

❖

"And Hope wouldn't let me bite him. She said Ren got to have first bite and I said that was okay but I got to bite him next." Mouse stopped to draw breath and stuff more venison in her mouth.

"And I carried Hope all the way here on my back and ran real fast," Joey said.

"But it was my idea, so we could go quicker because Hope is so slow because she has only one eye." Mouse was not going to be outdone.

"And she threw her eye at Patrick and he screamed and I hit him with a rock."

"I told them that already!" Mouse barked at him.

"Okay, you two. Enough." Marie laughed. They were sitting outdoors by a blazing fire pit. A huge table was laid out before them, covered from one end to the other with food. Any Garoul who was not on guard duty had come by to share in the meal. It seemed everyone was mesmerized by the young guests. Their adventures were truly amazing.

"So this is your pack?" Marie turned to Ren, utterly charmed.

"About fifty percent of it." Ren looked across the table at Joey and Mouse, still barely believing they were safe and sound and sitting before her. A quick call to Jenna on Marie's phone had assured her all was under control at the farm. Jenna was delighted to hear Mouse had been found. It had been a tense week. Ren hung up content all was well in Singing Valley; she knew she could depend on Noah and Jenna. They were a more than capable couple.

"There are two more at the farm," she said to Marie. "Luc brings these kids to me when they grow ill. She doesn't know how to tend them through the werefever."

"But you did. You helped them survive," Marie said.

Ren nodded. "I have the almanac Grandma Sylvie gave my mother. I use the recipes in it, but it's outdated."

"Is it some sort of experimentation?" Connie asked quietly, so that Mouse and Joey did not overhear. "Why does Luc do it? She must realize the survival rate is low, if nonexistent."

"At first I thought it was because she wanted a pack of her own. But after a while it reminded me of a cat bringing home half-dead prey. Luc was proud of her presents; it took her a while to understand something was wrong. Too many weren't surviving."

"How many? Can you guess?" Marie asked.

Ren felt sad at her answer. "No. Most died before they reached me. Luc lives near Lonesome Lake. She has no pack with her, as far as I know. She lives alone."

"Why is she after Isabelle?" Hope asked. "She tracked her all around Portland, trailed her to my house, and then chased her all the way out here."

"I think because she knew I…" Ren cleared her throat. After all Hope had been through, she deserved the truth. "Because Isabelle is very special to me. I wanted to get to know her more, but she had to go back to Portland after her vacation was over. We agreed to keep in touch, but Luc laughed at the idea. She said I should just take what I wanted. I disagreed." She looked at Joey and Mouse eating their dinner and chatting happily with the younger Garouls. They were healthy and happy and proved that good things could come out of bad. "So she attacked Isabelle…for me. Because she knew I would never do it for myself. And she knew how much I loved her."

What else was there to say? The damage was done. Luc had taken the small pack hunting. Not an unusual thing to do. They had to learn. She had led them straight into the path of Isabelle's car, and then, with Patrick's help, it became another sort of hunt altogether. By the time Ren had arrived, Isabelle had been mauled and infection had set in. All she could do was help her fight the fever and hope that when Isabelle emerged as wolven she would accept Ren for a mate. It was a skewed and ill-conceived courtship, and Ren had moved too fast with her own needs. She had bitten Isabelle during their lovemaking to try to force their bond. She had been frightened Luc's poisonous touch would skew Isabelle's affections in some way. She had been insecure and greedy, and Isabelle had run from her. Now she had to find her before her wolfskin grew and she mutated. It would be a painful and terrifying ordeal for Isabelle to go through with help, never mind on her own.

And she definitely had to find her before Luc did. If she could save Isabelle, maybe she would be forgiven. Maybe they could start again. It was all Ren had to hope for.

"So Luc wants to find Isabelle and bring her back to you?" Hope asked.

Ren shook her head. "Luc wants to kill her."

CHAPTER TWENTY-SEVEN

The meal was over and Ren had ordered her cubs to go and rest. This was the time for strategy, to ask outright for help, and she didn't want the youngsters to overhear her plans. They moved to Marie's cabin to talk over the situation.

"Isabelle went after Hope, so there's a good chance she's still on Hope's trail. Perhaps she'll find her way to Little Dip, too?" Godfrey said.

"If she's following me then she'll walk straight into Patrick and his gang. I'm not sure how many there are of them. We counted three at the Lucky Seven," Hope said.

"Four," Godfrey corrected her. "Remember the big black one that ran across the road as we left the parking lot. It was humongous."

Ren stood. She was angry with herself on hearing this news. Why was she still here? Mouse and Joey were safe. She had a mission to find Isabelle, but the cubs' arrival with Hope had distracted her. Isabelle could be walking into danger while she sat and talked.

"Where is this shack?" she asked Hope. "It's time I had a word with Patrick. He didn't grab Mouse for a keepsake." She needed to know what on earth Luc was thinking to order a stunt like that.

"I'd like a word with him, too," Hope said darkly. She cast a glance across to the fireplace to where Tadpole lay in his dresser drawer, deep in a drugged sleep. "The shack is outside of Lost Creek. About five miles to the west along an old track that takes you down to the Silverthread." She stood, as if ready to go. "You'll need help if Patrick's buddies have arrived. You can't go alone, Ren. It might be dangerous."

Marie put a hand on Hope's shoulder and pressed her back down onto her seat.

"Ren will not be alone. Her family will be with her. Claude, gather the hunt. We'll head out together."

Ren shook her head. "I want do this alone now I know where to find her."

"You've no idea what your sister's intentions are," Marie pointed out. "She's infiltrated your pack, kidnapped a cub, and wants to kill your mate. This is a challenge. Is that why you want to face her alone?" She stood face-to-face with Ren. "Because understand this, if you fight and Luc wins, she will have to be destroyed. She's too volatile. I'll never allow her to have a pack of her own here, or in Canada. I will kill her." Her words were icy.

"I think Luc wants to talk to you, Marie." Godfrey cut through the silence. "I don't know why she got Patrick to steal Mouse. But grabbing Hope was a definite demand for your attention. She can't be far away."

"My number is in the phone book like everyone else's." Marie swung away and strode to the door, her pack hard on her heels. "She's got more than my attention."

"Are you going to head out with the Garouls after your sister?" Godfrey asked Ren.

Ren also headed for the door, the back door. "I need to find Isabelle first. Luc can wait."

"I knew you'd go off on your own." His words drifted after her. "I knew she'd do that." She heard him tell Hope. "She's the broody, loner type."

"Good luck, Ren," Hope called after her. "Bring Isabelle home safe."

❖

Night fell, the temperature fell, and her energy levels fell. Isabelle curled up, cupped in a massive tree root. She needed rest and food. She was ill for lack of it.

If I lie down for just ten minutes, I'll be refreshed enough to catch something to eat. What comes out at night that's tasty? Owls? Bats? She closed her eyes, and within what seemed like mere minutes was shivering herself awake. She had no idea how much time had passed, but it was longer than the ten minutes she promised herself. A new dawn streaked the skyline. She was naked and human. *It happens when I sleep. I change when I sleep.* This had happened to her before; sleep and scents were her triggers, there was no doubting it now. She lay blinking up at overhead branches, and curled up tighter to keep what little warmth she could.

A new awareness grabbed her. The carcasses of two freshly killed rabbits lay by her head. She sat up, startled, and looked at them in dismay.

"Aw. And I skinned them for you and everything." The voice came from her other side. She swung around to face a darker, leaner version of Ren. The face was angular, with a fox's cunning. The eyes were black and curiously flat, as if all light was sucked in and held. And they were cold, as cold as the blood-red smile on the beautiful and eminently wicked face before her.

"Luc," Isabelle said, and drew her knees up to cover her nudity.

"You remember me! How good is that." A dark gaze roamed over her body. "It's all flooding back. Werefever does that; it fucks up the head. Soon you'll remember what a lovely vacation you had in Bella Coola. How you flirted with the handsome twins, and even had a dalliance with one."

Isabelle inched away, unsure how to respond.

"It wasn't me, by the way. You preferred the wonderful Ren. I was too raw and edgy for you." Luc snapped her white teeth. "Too damn fine."

Again Isabelle could only gawk.

"You look lovely naked. You should do it more often." Luc raked her in idle curiosity, tinged with a little boredom. Isabelle knew this was not good. Boredom soon led to viciousness with people like Luc. "A tad too thin for my taste, but maybe Ren likes all those awkward angles."

"I knew you were here." Isabelle struggled to sound strong. "You killed Patrick and that other boy."

Luc shrugged. "Everything they touched turned to shit."

"That's all you can say? They suffered so much."

"Sums it up. They were dying anyway, if it makes you feel any better. All my changelings rot from the inside out. Talking of suffering, Patrick told me your old boyfriend ran straight into a tree. Now that was funny. I wished I'd seen that." Luc visibly cheered now that she had a wound to pick.

"Patrick killed Barry." Isabelle's chest tightened. Barry hadn't deserved to die like that. She would always carry guilt that she had brought these killers to his door.

"Patrick was stupid." Luc's tone hardened with dissatisfaction. "I already had your scent. I'd found all your favorite city haunts. It was fun following you around. By killing that man, Patrick made you run. Not good." She shook her head. "He spoiled the hunt. He had to go."

"So why are you chasing the others? Mouse and Joey and the human woman?" Isabelle fished for information. She kept Hope's name out of it. The Garoul connection was a card she was uncertain how to play. She needed to find out as much as she could. "You're out here hunting them, not me."

"You have a wonderful nose. I love your nose. I may keep it after I pull the rest of your face off." Luc gave the tip of Isabelle's nose a playful tap with her forefinger. Isabelle twisted her head away.

"I don't understand any of your actions," she said.

"That's because you're not wolfie enough."

"I'm wolfie enough to know you turned those kids Ren's trying to look after. Is that why they're becoming sick? Is it something you do when you attack them?"

"She's a saint, isn't she? And I don't *deliberately* infect them. It's a side effect of the werefever. Some pull through, some don't. Some relapse." Luc shrugged. Her skin had an oily, waxen sheen under her tan, and Isabelle wondered about Luc's health.

"Is that why you came out here after Mouse and Joey? Because they're ill, too? Were you going to kill them as well?"

Luc tensed. "Don't be ridiculous. They're not ill. They're the healthiest of the lot." There was almost pride in her voice. Her face flexed into a deeper, more menacing scowl as if daring Isabelle to dispute her.

"I know you're jealous of Ren and me." She changed tack. Luc would not reveal any more about infections, not if her own health was implicated. Isabelle was satisfied there was an illness running through Ren's pack and Luc was the root of it. "You've never liked me."

Luc barked out a laugh. "You wouldn't be my first choice for my sister's mate." Again, her eyes scoured Isabelle's face and body and found her wanting. "You were leaving and she was sad. I can't have my sister moping around the place." She placed her hand on her heart. "It's a twin thing."

"I know something else."

"You're so fucking erudite."

"I know why Patrick grabbed Mouse. I know why you're chasing those kids." A faint flaring of Luc's nostrils was the only clue Isabelle had hit her target. "Mouse is your daughter. Isn't she?"

"You fight sneaky. I say you're not good enough for my sister; and you come back at me and pull out my biggest secret. You're a nasty little thing, aren't you? I think I'll revise my opinion of you."

"It's hardly a deep, dark secret. Anyone can see she's yours."

"She could be Ren's."

Isabelle shook her head. "She has an…edge. That's all you." This brought a flicker of a smile, and Isabelle drove home her point. "So why are you kidnapping your own daughter? You know Ren looks after her well."

"Because she's older now and needs to know things not even Ren can teach her. Because all my other little darlings are dropping down dead, and I'll be damned if I'll let Mouse grow up in a diseased swamp hole. Ren needs to accept what's happening on that farm. Her pack is falling sick. They'll all die."

"You were bringing Mouse to Little Dip?" Isabelle was incredulous. "You hoped she'd find a home there. Were you going to be part of it, too?"

"Cleverness always goes with a great nose. It's the wolven way. The sniffers always were the thinkers." Luc avoided her last question. Her face held a curious, distant calm, as she was slowly detaching herself from all emotion. Isabelle knew time was running out.

"Why do you want to kill me?" she asked bluntly. She might as well get to the core of it.

"It's not all about you, you know." Luc looked grumpy at this direct approach. "It's about getting Mouse to Little Dip. You happened to be an interesting sideline. A mate is for life. *You* ran away. If you're not her mate then you're dead, simple as that. How else will Ren be free of you?"

"Isn't that for Ren and me to discuss? Why are you sticking your nose in the midd—Oh, I see." Isabelle's voice hardened. "You attacked me, didn't you? You're the one who started all this. Like you start everything, and then it turns to shit, right?"

"Ouch. You can nip when you want to. But yes, it was me who infected you. I feel so ashamed." Luc leaned into her, her eyes gleamed wickedly. "Was it the wrong thing to do? After all, you two did hit it off. Patrick told me you were getting along famously. Ren even adorned Big Tree for you." Luc had a roguish smile she used with great effect. "It's a metaphor," she whispered. "A sort of initiation thing." Her smile didn't work on Isabelle.

"If I was a Were I'd bite you right back," Isabelle said.

"You are delightful. I should have kept you for myself." Luc stood and kicked off her boots. "Bring it on. You've got thirty seconds by the time I strip and change." She pulled her shirt over her head. Before it was free of her body Isabelle had fled.

"I won't kill you, by the way. I think I like you better now that we've chatted," Luc called after her. "But I'll put another mark on that pretty face so you never forget me again."

Isabelle raced through the underbrush. It tore at her skin and hair. Branches whipped at her face, and stones and shale cut the soles of her bare feet. She had to get away, she had to put enough space between herself and Luc so that she could hunker down and change into a Were. But how? It had always just occurred before; she had never initiated the process as far as she knew. Sleep and scent were all she knew as triggers. Could she do it to order?

Luc was behind her in an instant. A sharp shove between her shoulder blades sent her reeling onto her knees. It had taken Luc less than thirty seconds to find her. The wind was knocked out of Isabelle. She'd never had a chance anyway. She lay sprawled naked on a bed of twigs and dirt, frightened and defeated. Where was her wolfskin now? Not that she could tackle an enormous beast like Luc, even as a Were, but it would have been less humiliating than scrabbling in the dirt like an earthworm. A huge part of her wanted to stand and fight, to swing her claws and roar out her anger. The fingers of her right hand twitched and her nails hardened and lengthened. Wide-eyed, she focused on her hand, willing it to make a claw, to begin her transition. *Please, please, let it happen.*

Behind her she could hear Luc pant as she decided on her next strike. Isabelle focused on her shaking hand. She trembled with effort, willing her wolfskin in to life—A massive clawed foot stepped into view, an inch from her face. A deep, menacing growl accompanied it. A second beast now loomed over her.

Isabelle peeped up at the enormous werewolf standing over her, facing off against Luc. It shimmered with a vibrant energy. Dew spangled its black fur like a thousand little diamonds. This Were had been roaming the forest all night. It was well settled in its wolfskin and filled with muted rage.

She sensed Luc draw back, surprised by the new arrival and the aggressive challenge. Isabelle twisted her head and found the beasts on either side of her, face-to-face, snarling at each other with increased ferocity. Their coats shone an oily blue-black in the weak morning sun. Both were of an equal height, though Luc had the leaner, wirier build. Her eyes were matte black; no golden light burned in them. The other beast shook with fury. Its eyes burned with an amber glow so fierce it could brand an opponent's heart. This was Ren. Isabelle knew it with every fiber of her body. Ren had found her just in time, like all heroes did.

Large dollops of saliva dripped onto her skin from their snapping maws. The ground below her trembled with their warlike rumbling. She dragged herself out of the center of what promised to be a vicious fight once the threats and posturing were over. Her feet were barely clear when Ren head-butted Luc squarely on the muzzle. Luc reeled back, caught unawares.

Ren drove her shoulder into Luc's solar plexus with a guttural roar and crashed her backward into a tree. Luc clawed at Ren's back and clung on as Ren spun her from tree to tree, bouncing her off the creaking trunks until the forest floor was littered with leaves and twigs. Debris rained down, and the ground shook as they spun in a roaring, thundering circle from tree to shuddering tree. Isabelle had never heard noise like it; it was prehistoric in its violence and barbarism. She crouched terrified, afraid to move.

Around her the forest began to vibrate with another ancient sound, the howl of wolves. Shrill and piercing, excited by the hunt, Isabelle easily picked up their intent. Wolven closed in on all sides until her head hurt with their cries. Luc, too, was affected. Her face creased into a grimace of panic. She clawed harder at Ren's back, her intention changed. She struggled for freedom, not to fight. Her bid for escape made her even more vicious.

Ren lifted Luc clear off the ground with one last victory howl and flung her across the clearing. Luc landed heavily, close to where Isabelle crouched. For one stunned moment she lay there, winded. Isabelle barely breathed. Their gaze locked for a split second, then, with a wicked wink, Luc was gone. Twigs and dust swirled behind her as she sprinted into the depths of the wood.

The howling clamor changed and began to spiral away, as if magically attached to Luc and her movements. The prey was on the move and messages were flying through the forest. Luc had fled, but the hunt continued hard on her heels.

Isabelle crawled back to lean against a tree. She did not trust her legs to hold her. She shook violently with shock. The growing coldness had marbled her limbs with blue blotches. She sucked in huge gulps of air and blinked back the tears that crowded her eyes now that the danger had passed.

In two steps Ren was beside her. Her damp muzzle sniffed Isabelle's tear-filled eyes, then her left ear, her neck, and armpit. Ren continued to investigate the valley of her breasts and her navel, her crotch, the back of her knee. Isabelle lay a weary hand on the hunched back of the huge beast nuzzling at her.

"I'm okay, Ren," she said wearily. "She didn't hurt me. You got here just in time. Oh God." Her hand came away slick with blood. Bright red and wet, it mapped out the lines of her palm. She shuffled onto her knees and began to comb apart Ren's fur with her fingers. Deep punctures and scores studded Ren's back.

"More scars. She hooked you good. I suppose all she could do was hang on. You gave her one hell of a pounding." She scratched the fur between Ren's ears and tweaked them with a gentle tug. "I guess you're the dominant twin. She's just the wicked one."

Ren responded to Isabelle's touches with a long, ticklish lick along her hand and arm, and then another across her belly that awoke a flock of butterflies inside her. Isabelle was suddenly awkward in her nakedness. She pulled back and rose to her feet. Several yards away Luc's abandoned clothes lay in a heap. She pulled on the shirt and screwed up her nose at the smell.

"It stinks of her, but it will have to do." She pulled on the pants, too. The clothes were much too large, but at least she was covered. Ren approached and sniffed at the garments, growling in dissatisfaction.

"I know. You don't like me smelling of her either. But once I get a shower I promise to burn them. A shower, a meal, and a big, big sleep." She was suddenly exhausted. Before she could draw another breath, Ren swung her up into her arms and began to make a path through the undergrowth.

"You know where we're going? I was trying to follow Mouse and Joey. You know that they're out here somewhere, right?" She got a big lick along her cheekbone right up into her eyebrow, and took it as an affirmative. Ren broke into a smooth run, moving through the forest like liquid. Cradled in her massive arms, all Isabelle could do was cuddle in and feel the safest and happiest she had ever been in her whole life.

"I burned them in the fire pit," Ren said with satisfaction as she raised the bedclothes and slid in alongside Isabelle.

"Couldn't wait, could you? I barely had them off me." Isabelle curled around Ren.

"I don't want her scent in the compound. The Garouls are not very happy with Luc. And I don't want Joey and Mouse to pick up on it. It's going to be hard enough explaining all this."

"We'll do it together."

"You're going home with me?" Ren asked hopefully.

Isabelle hesitated. "I think you should consider Marie's offer. They're so young, Ren, and they deserve all the help they can get. A summer in Little Dip sounds like a good deal to me. Plus Marie will send some of her pack up to tend the farm. They can cross-train each other. I think she likes the idea of a northern Garoul base. They're very acquisitive, this family of yours."

She could feel Ren tense as she considered the alien idea. Isabelle knew it was asking a lot of her, to bring her pack down to Little Dip while other Garouls ran the farm and hatchery station for her. She could stay on and work at her veterinary business, or take a sabbatical and visit Little Dip for the summer, too. The choice was hers.

"Luc was trying to bring Mouse back here, in her own perverse way," Ren said. "She must have thought it was a good idea. And for all her faults, Luc was never stupid."

"I think Luc saw the writing was on the wall for a small pack like yours. You did your best, but none of those kids had a healthy start and the future is very uncertain." Isabelle was kind but determined. "Claude has promised to train them along with the younger Garouls. It's a good offer. At least here they'd have a better chance."

"Where would we have the better chance, Isabelle? Our future is just as uncertain," Ren asked her. "Wolven mate for life, but I can't hold you to that. You were stolen, and I'd never stop you if you wanted to leave."

"Luc infected me, that's all. She's nothing more than bacteria. But you loved me and bit me and claimed me. I'm wolven, through and through, there's no escaping it, and I'm going to be a *great* wolven. I can track butterflies on a breeze." Isabelle smiled at her boast. "I'm happy in my wolfskin. If wolven mate for life, then I guess I'm in it for the long haul with you."

Ren snuggled into her. The heat under the bed clothes soared.

"I can't believe how easily you took to it," she said. "There's much to be said for a double infection. Maybe I should bite you again and make you über wolven." Isabelle slapped her arm playfully. They lay nose-to-nose, and Ren's gaze burned into Isabelle's. Little flecks of amber burst upon her iris like stray fireworks in a midnight sky.

"So blue," Ren murmured. "Your eyes remind me of summer."

"Aunt Mary always called them cornflower blue. I love my aunt Mary, and she adores you."

"She doesn't know I'm a werewolf. That might sway her opinion."

"She would adore you anyway. *My* pack accepts you, Ren Garoul."

Ren snorted back a laugh. "Mary adores me because of Atwell."

"And Hope adores you because of Tadpole. Hope's pack accepts you, Ren Garoul. See how it works? And if Hope and her den accept you, then the Garouls have to. It's a chain. Are these people going to be my in-laws?"

Ren rolled onto her back and pulled Isabelle on top of her.

"Maybe. It will take time for me to rest around them. But they came to my aid when I needed to find you, and I'll always be beholden to Marie for that." She growled and captured Isabelle's lips in a playful kiss. Isabelle broke the kiss. One more question hummed at the back of her mind.

"What about Luc? What will happen to her?"

Ren frowned. "That depends on Luc. Marie sent her best trapper after her. She wants her brought back here. After that, I'm not sure what the Garoul council will decide. But I won't let them kill her. Luc needs to be rehabilitated."

"She sent a trapper?"

"Yes. Not a tracker, like you will be, or an out-and-out hunter like me. A trapper is all those things, but with a subtle difference. Their job is to bring their quarry back alive. They're tricky and artful."

"Rehabilitation. You think that's possible for Luc?"

"I want it to be. Luc's been on the wrong side of feral for too long. She's ill. I want her back in the fold. I suspect she knew she was unwell and that's why she wanted to return to Little Dip and bring Mouse with her. I think she hoped for a fresh start. I hope Marie's trapper can catch her in time, and that maybe Marie can help her somehow."

"Time will tell. Our pack will come to Little Dip to learn and then we will return home to our own valley. We'll be another Garoul den."

"Then that's our way forward. I can do it with you by my side."

"I'll always be by your side. I'm your life bond, your mate." And with that Isabelle rolled into Ren's arms and kissed her Alpha.

Keep reading for a special preview of SILVER COLLAR, the fourth book in Gill McKnight's GAROUL Werewolf series.

L uc squatted beside the crab apple tree watching the lights go out one by one in the single-story farmhouse as the farmer and his wife made their way toward their bedroom. First the kitchen light extinguished, then the living room. The hall light went on and off in less than a minute. Luc waited patiently until only the back bedroom and what she thought might be the bathroom windows glowed yellow in the night.

She sighed and settled in for a little longer. She had to wait until the parents were sound asleep. Her stomach gurgled with hunger. Idly she inserted one curved claw into her wet, bubbling nostril and examined the mucus she withdrew. Clotted, green, and streaked with blood. Not good. Her head felt thick and her left ear buzzed annoyingly. She had some sort of fluid gathering on her eardrum.

Luc glumly poked at the gutted carcass beside her. She hated domestic cat meat; it was stringy and foul tasting. She had slit this one open out of boredom. Good thing she hadn't gorged on it despite her hunger. Its kidneys were rancid. Surprising, as it was a young cat, no more than a kitten really. She tinkled the little bell on its pink collar. A much-loved pet, in fact.

The last light in the farmhouse went out. Luc blinked in the darkness, her perfect night vision adjusting at once to the pitch dark. Heavy clouds blanked out the stars, and the night sky hung low and foreboding over the fields. This farm grew wheat, hay, and sunflowers. No animal husbandry at all. That was very disappointing.

She was on the run, hunted and famished, and she begrudged the farmer his lack of livestock. It would have been so much easier to pick off a calf or pig than go to all this trouble. Her ears flattened and she growled in discontent. She didn't have enough time to sit around all day, waiting for nightfall as her hunger and weakness and bitterness grew.

Carefully, she crept forward. Her keen hearing picked out the dogs prowling back and forth in their run. There were two of them, young and unsure, and they whimpered in agitation. While they were away with the farmer she had made sure to urinate on their bedding. Now they were locked in with a predator's scent that cowed them. They would do no more then whine in misery all night.

Luc trod through the family vegetable plot. Her huge paws flattened the leafy heads of beet, rhubarb, and potato. She knew which window she wanted. She had been watching it all evening. The pink curtains were pulled tight. A picture of a pony was stuck on the glass pane, and a butterfly spangle wind-chime hung limp inside the shut window. She needed that window to open just a crack. Enough to let her claws slide in under the sill and force it all the way up.

She lifted the pink collar she'd torn from the cat's body and tinkled the little bell. *Meow.* She mimicked the dead animal to perfection. *Meow.* She sank to her haunches by the window and waited.

A second later a light went on. The soft, five-watt glimmer of a child's night lamp. The whole window suffused in a gentle pink glow. Luc smacked her thin leathery lips in satisfaction.

"Tinky? Is that you?" a little girl's voice called sleepily. "Tinky?"

Luc slid into the shadows to the side of the window. The latch fumbled open.

"Tinky? You're a naughty kitty. You know you're not allowed out after dark."

The hinges squeaked as the window opened. Luc reached out, almost lazily. She knew what to do. A single foreclaw to pierce the throat and rip apart the vocal cords. The rest of her claws would hook her muted victim under the chin, up into her mouth cavity. Then Luc would drag the child out by her face.

The farmer should have kept livestock. He'd learn.

The air thrummed. It whistled and quivered. Luc fell to the ground. Instinct threw her onto her belly. *Thunk!* Wooden splinters fell on her, blasted out of the plank wall by the barbed shaft embedded in it.

Luc scrabbled onto all fours, then lurched forward, running hunched in a crooked path, past the vegetable plot and out into the cover of the orchard. She didn't have to look back to see a silver arrow glint evilly in the pink bedroom light. She knew it was there. She had heard it whistling toward her heart. All she had to know was run. Run from the hunter on the other end of the crossbow.

About the Author

Gill McKnight is Irish and moves between Ireland, England, and Greece in a nonstop circuit of work, rest, and play. She loves messing about in boats and has secret fantasies about lavender farming.

With a BA in Art and Design and a Master's in Art History, it says much about her artistic skill that she now works in IT.

Books Available From Bold Strokes Books

Dying to Live by Kim Baldwin & Xenia Alexiou. British socialite Zoe Anderson-Howe's pampered life is abruptly shattered when she's taken hostage by FARC guerrillas while on a business trip to Bogota, and Elite Operative Fletch must rescue her to complete her own harrowing mission. (978-1-60282-200-9)

Indigo Moon by Gill McKnight. Werewolves Hope Glassy and Godfrey Meyers are on a mercy mission to save their friend Isabelle after she is attacked by a rogue werewolf—but does Isabelle want to be saved from the sexy wolf who claimed her as a mate? (978-1-60282-201-6)

Parties in Congress by Colette Moody. Bijal Rao, Indian-American moderate Independent, gets the break of her career when she's hired to work on the congressional campaign of Janet Denton—until she meets her remarkably attractive and charismatic opponent, Colleen O'Bannon. (978-1-60282-202-3)

Black Fire: Gay African-American Erotica, edited by Shane Allison. *Black Fire* celebrates the heat and power of sex between black men: the rude B-boys and gorgeous thugs, the worshippers of heavenly ass, and the devoutly religious in their forays through the subterranean grottoes of the down-low world. (978-1-60282-206-1)

The Collectors by Leslie Gowan. Laura owns what might be the world's most extensive collection of BDSM lesbian erotica, but that's as close as she's gotten to the world of her fantasies. Until, that is, her friend Adele introduces her to Adele's mistress Jeanne—art collector, heiress, and experienced dominant. With Jeanne's first command, Laura's life changes forever. (978-1-60282-208-5)

Breathless, edited by Radclyffe and Stacia Seaman. Bold Strokes Books romance authors give readers a glimpse into the lives of favorite couples celebrating special moments "after the honeymoon ends." Enjoy a new look at lesbians in love or revisit favorite characters from some of BSB's best-selling romances. (978-1-60282-207-8)